DOCTOR DOLITTLE
OMNIBUS

" She peered into the badger's mouth "

Hugh Lofting

DOCTOR DOLITTLE OMNIBUS

DOCTOR DOLITTLE'S ZOO

DOCTOR DOLITTLE'S CIRCUS

LEOPARD

This edition published in 1995 by Leopard Books,
20 Vauxhall Bridge Road, London SW1V 2SA

Doctor Dolittle's Zoo first published in Great Britain in 1926
by Jonathan Cape
Copyright © 1926 by Hugh Lofting
This revised edition copyright © 1992 by Hugh Lofting

Doctor Dolittle's Circus first published in Great Britain in
1925 by Jonathan Cape
Copyright © 1924 by Hugh Lofting
This revised edition copyright © 1988 by Christopher Lofting

ISBN 0 7529 0133 8

Set in Century Schoolbook

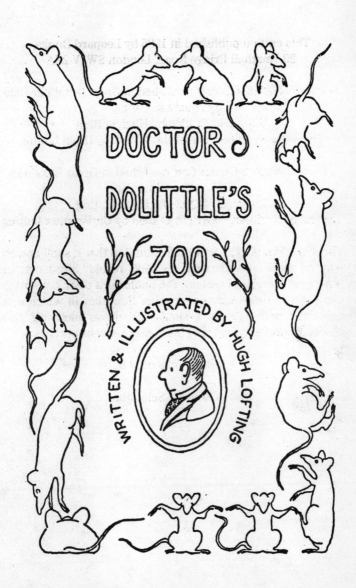

DOCTOR
DOLITTLE'S
ZOO

WRITTEN & ILLUSTRATED BY HUGH LOFTING

Contents

Illustrations

Doctor Dolittle's Zoo

'POLYNESIA,' I said, leaning back in my chair and chewing the end of a quill pen, 'what should you say would be the best way to begin another book of Doctor Dolittle's memoirs?'

The old parrot, who was using the glass inkpot on my desk as a mirror, stopped admiring her reflection and glanced at me sharply.

'Another!' she exclaimed. 'Is there going to be *another* Dolittle book?'

'Why – er – yes,' I said. 'After all, we are writing the Doctor's life and we haven't nearly finished yet.'

'Oh, yes, I quite see that,' said Polynesia. 'I was only wondering who decides how many books there shall be.'

'Well, I suppose – in the end – the public does,' said I. 'But tell me now: how would you begin?'

'Thomas Stubbins, Esquire,' said she, screwing up her eyes, 'that's a very difficult question to answer. There is so much of interest in the life of John Dolittle that the problem is what to leave out, rather than what to put in. Already I see grey hairs showing at your temples, Tommy. If

you try to write down everything the Doctor did,
you'll be nearly my age before you've finished. Of
course, you're not writing this book for the scien-
tists exactly, though I confess I often think, since
you are the only person so far – besides the
Doctor – to talk animal languages at all well, that
you ought to write something sort of – er –
highbrow in natural history. Usefully highbrow, I
mean, of course. But that can be done later
perhaps. As you said, we are still engaged on the
story of the great man's life. . . . How to begin? –
Humph! Well, why not go on from where we all got
back to Puddleby River inside the Giant Sea Snail,
you remember? – after our journey under the
ocean?'

'Yes,' I said, 'I thought of beginning there. But it
was more *how* than *where* – I mean, the things to
leave out and the things to put in; what parts to
choose as the most interesting.'

'Ah!' said she. 'Yes, that's the problem. How often
have I heard the Doctor himself say those very
words as he was packing his little black bag to go
on a voyage: "What to leave out and what to put in?
That's the problem." '

'Indeed,' said I. 'But you haven't answered my
question yet.'

Polynesia pondered a moment.

'What are you calling the book?' she asked
presently.

' *"Doctor Dolittle's Zoo"*, ' I said.

'Humph!' she murmured. 'Then I suppose you
ought to get on to the zoo part as soon as possible.
But first I think you had better put in a little about
your own homecoming and your parents and all

that. You *had* been away nearly three years, you know. Of course it's sort of sentimental. But some people like a little sentiment in their books. In fact, I knew an old lady once who simply loved books that made her weep. She used to –'

'Yes, yes,' I said hurriedly, seeing that the old parrot was drifting into another story, 'but let us keep to the point.'

'Well,' said she, 'I think this would be the best way: you read it all out aloud to me as you put it down; and if it starts to get tiresome you'll know, because you'll see me dropping off to sleep. You will have to keep it bright and lively though, for as I grow older I find it harder and harder to stay awake after lunch – and I've just had a big one. Have you got enough paper? Yes. And the inkpot is full? Yes. All right. Get along with it.'

So taking a new quill pen and sharpening the point very carefully, I began:

Chapter One
A MESSAGE FROM DAB-DAB

IT suddenly occurred to John Dolittle that in the excitement of getting back he had not said good-bye to the snail who had brought us through this long and perilous voyage and landed us safely on our home shores. He called to us to wait and ran down the beach again.

The farewell did not take long; and presently he left the great creature's side and rejoined us. Then for a few moments the whole party stood there watching, with our bundles in our hands, while the giant snail, half-hidden in the mists that writhed about his towering shell, got under way. Truly, he seemed to belong to this landscape – or seascape – for his long grey body looked like a part of the long grey sandbar on which he rested. With easy muscular motion, so fluid and smooth that you could not tell how he moved at all, his great hulk slid out into deeper water. And as he went forward he went down, and down, and down, till only the top of his shell's dome, a dim grey pink in the colourless sea, could be seen. Then, without sound or splash, he was gone.

We turned our faces towards the land, Puddleby and home.

'I wonder what supplies Dab-Dab has in the house,' said the Doctor, as we formed into single file and, following Jip, began to pick our way across the boggy marshland. 'I hope she has plenty to eat. I am thoroughly hungry.'

'So am I,' said Bumpo.

At that moment, out of the wet, misty air above our heads two handsome wild ducks curved fluttering down and came to a standstill at John Dolittle's feet.

'Dab-Dab asked us to tell you,' said they, 'that you're to hurry up and get home out of this rain. She's waiting for you.'

'Good gracious!' cried the Doctor. 'How did she know that we were coming?'

'We told her,' said the ducks. 'We were flying inland – there's a pretty bad storm over the Irish Sea, and it's headed this way – and we saw you landing out of the snail's shell. We dropped down at the house to let her know the news. We were awfully glad to see you back. And she asked would we return and bring you a message – she herself was busy airing the bed linen, it seems. She says you're to step in at the butcher's on the way home and bring along a pound of sausages. Also she's short of sugar, she says, and needs a few more candles, too.'

'Thank you,' said the Doctor. 'You are very kind. I will attend to these things. You didn't take long over getting there and back; it doesn't seem to me as though more than a minute had passed since we landed.'

' "Dab-Dab asked us to tell you that you're to hurry home" '

'No, we're pretty good flyers,' said the ducks; 'nothing fancy, but steady.'

'Well, now,' said the Doctor, 'let us be getting along. Jip, you lead the way, will you, please? You can pick out the firm ground so much better than the rest of us.'

'Look here, you fellows,' said Polynesia, as the ducks prepared to take wing, 'don't be spreading the news of the Doctor's arrival too fast, will you? He's only just back from a long and tiresome journey. You know what happens when it gets known that he's home: all the birds and beasts of the countryside come round to the back door with coughs and colds and what not. And those who haven't anything wrong with them invent some ailment just to have an excuse to call. He needs to rest a bit before he starts doctoring.'

'No, we won't tell anyone,' said the ducks; 'not tonight, anyway, though a tremendous lot of wild-fowl have been inquiring for him for ever so long wondering when he was going to get back. He has never been gone so long before, you see.'

'Humph!' muttered Polynesia, as the ducks, with a whir of feathers, disappeared again into the rainy mist above our heads. 'I suppose John Dolittle has to give an account of his actions now to every snipe and sandpiper that ever met him. Poor man! How dare he be away so long! Well, such is fame, I suppose. But I'm glad I'm not a doctor myself. Oh, bless this rain! Let me get under your coat, Tommy. It's trickling down between my wings and ruining my disposition.'

If it had not been for Jip's good guidance we would have had a hard job to make our way to the

HUGH LOFTING

'Jip was a guide worth having'

town across the marshes. The light of the late
afternoon was failing. And every once in a while
the fog would come billowing in from the sea and
blot out everything around us, so that you could
see no farther than a foot before your nose. The
chimes of the quarter-hours from Puddleby church
tower were the only sounds or signs of civilization
to reach us.

But Jip, with that wonderful nose of his, was a
guide worth having in a place like this. The marsh
was riddled and crossed in all directions by deep
dykes, now filling up like rivers with the incoming
tide. But in spite of continuous temptation to go off
on the scent of water rats, Jip, like a good pilot,
steered a safe course through all the dangers and
kept us on fairly solid ground the whole way.

Finally we found he had brought us round to the
long, high mound that bordered the Puddleby
River. This we knew would lead us to the bridge.
Presently we passed a hut or two, the outposts of
the town. And occasionally in the swiftly flowing
water on our left we would see through the lifting
mists the grey, ghostly sails of a fishing boat coming home, like us, from the sea.

Chapter Two
THE ADVENTURER'S RETURN

AS we came nearer to the town and the lights about Kingsbridge twinkled at us through the grey mist Polynesia said:

'It would be wiser, Doctor, if you sent Tommy in to get the sausages and went round the town yourself. You'll never get home if the children and dogs start recognizing you. You know that.'

'Yes, I think you're right, Polynesia,' said the Doctor. 'We can turn off here to the north and get around on to the Oxenthorpe Road by Baldwin's Pool and the Mill Fields.'

So the rest of the party went off with the Doctor, while I went on into the town alone. I was a little sorry not to have been present at John Dolittle's homecoming, I must admit. But I had another thrill which partly made up for it. Swaggering across Kingsbridge, alone, I returned to my native town a conquering adventurer from foreign parts. Oh, my! Christopher Columbus just back from his discovery of the New World could not have felt prouder than I, Tommy Stubbins, the cobbler's son, did that night.

One of the little things that added to the thrill of

it was that no one recognized me. I was like some
enchanted person in the *Arabian Nights* who
could see without being seen. I was three years
older than when I had left, at an age when a boy
shoots up and changes like a weed. As I swung
along beneath the dim street lamps towards the
butcher's in the High Street I knew the faces of
more than half the folk who passed me by. And I
chuckled to myself to think how surprised they'd
be if I told them who I was and all the great things
I had seen and done since last I trod these cobble-
stones.

In the Market Square, before a dimly lighted
shop, I saw a figure which I would have known
anywhere, seen from the back or the front. It was
Matthew Mugg, the cat's-meat-man. Just out of
mischief, to see if he, too, would be unable to
recognize me, I went up to the shop front and
stood, like him, looking in at the window.
Presently he turned and looked at me. No. He
didn't know me from Adam. Highly amused, I
went on to the butcher's.

I asked for the sausages. They were weighed out,
wrapped and handed to me. The butcher was an
old acquaintance of mine, but beyond glancing at
my old clothes (they were patched and mended and
sadly outgrown) he showed no sign of curiosity or
recognition. But when I came to pay for my
purchases I found to my dismay that the only
money I had in my pockets was two large Spanish
silver pieces, souvenirs of our stormy visit to the
Capa Blanca Islands. The butcher looked at them
and shook his head.

'We only take English money here,' he said.

'I knew the faces of more than half the folk who passed'

'I'm sorry,' I said apologetically, 'but that is all I have. Couldn't you exchange it for me? It is, as you see, good silver. One of these pieces should be worth a crown at least.'

'Maybe it is,' said the butcher. 'But I can't take it.'

He seemed sort of suspicious and rather annoyed. While I was wondering what I should do I became aware that there was a third party in the shop interested in what was going on. I turned to look. It was Matthew Mugg. He had followed me.

This time his eye (the one that didn't squint) fixed me with a curious look of half-recognition. Suddenly he rushed at me and grabbed me by the hand.

'It's Tommy!' he squeaked. 'As I live it's Tommy Stubbins, grown so tall and handsome his own mother wouldn't know him, and as brown as a berry.'

Matthew was, of course, well known to the tradesmen of the town – especially to the butcher, from whom he bought the bones and odd pieces of meat for the dogs. He turned to the shopkeeper.

'Why, Alfred,' he cried, 'this is Tommy Stubbins, Jacob Stubbins's lad, back from furrin parts. No need to be worried about *his* credit, Alfred. He's shopping for the Doctor, I'll be bound. You brought the Doctor back with you?' he asked, peering at me anxiously. 'Don't tell me you come back alone?'

'No,' I said. 'The Doctor's here, safe and sound.'

'You're just in, eh?' said he. 'Tonight – eh? John Dolittle couldn't be in this town long without my knowing it.'

'Yes,' I said. 'He's on his way up to the house

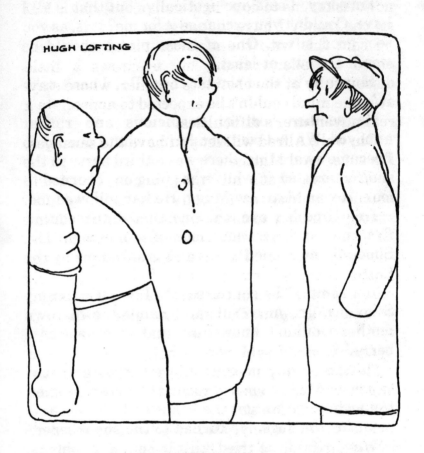

'It was Matthew Mugg'

now. Asked me to do a little shopping for him. But all the money I have is foreign.'

I said this with the superior air of an experienced traveller, raising my eyebrows a little disdainfully at the obstinate butcher, whose stay-at-home mind couldn't be expected to appreciate a real adventurer's difficulties.

'Oh, well, Alfred will let you have the sausages, I'm sure,' said Matthew.

'Why, yes, that's all right, Tommy,' said the butcher, smiling at my airs. 'Though we ain't exactly a money exchange, you know. But if you had said at first who you were, and who the sausages were for, I'd have charged them to the Doctor without a word – even though his credit hasn't always been of the best. Take the sausages – and tell John Dolittle I'm glad he's back safe.'

'Thank you,' I said, with dignity.

Then, with my package beneath one arm and Matthew Mugg firmly grasping the other, I stepped forth into the street.

'You know, Tommy,' said Matthew, as we set off in the direction of the Oxenthorpe Road, 'all the years that John Dolittle's been returning from voyages he ain't never got home once without me to welcome him the first night he got in. Not that he ever tells me he's coming, mind you. No, indeed. As often as not, I fancy, he'd rather no one knew. But somehow or other I always finds out before he's been in the town an hour, and right away I'm up there to welcome him. And once I'm inside the house, he seems to get used to me and be glad I'm there. I suppose you've seen an awful lot of adventures and strange sights and things since I saw you last?'

'Yes, Matthew,' I said. 'We saw even more than I had thought or hoped we would. We have brought back notebooks by the barrow-load and a collection of wonderful herbs which were gathered by an Indian naturalist – frightfully valuable and important. And – what do you think, Matthew? – we came back inside the shell of a giant sea snail who crawled along the bottom of the ocean with us all the way from the other side of the Atlantic!'

'Oh, well,' said Matthew, 'there be no end to the strange things Doctor John Dolittle's seen and gone through. I've given up talking about his voyagings and queer doings. Down in the taproom of the Red Lion I used to tell about his travels – of an evening like, when folk enjoy a tale. But never no more. It's like this business of his speaking animal languages: people don't believe you; so what's the use?'

We were now some half-mile along the Oxenthorpe Road and within a short distance of the Doctor's house. It was quite dark. But in the hedges and the trees all about us I could hear birds fluttering and chattering. In spite of Polynesia's request, the news had already spread, in that mysterious way it does in the Animal Kingdom. The season was still cold and few more than the winter birds could be found in England now. But round about the famous Little House with the Big Garden they were gathered in thousands – sparrows, robins, blackbirds, crows, and starlings – to welcome the great man back, prepared to sit up all night just to see him in the morning.

' "People don't believe you, so what's the use?" '

And it occurred to me, as I walked up the steps and opened the little gate at the top, that such was the great difference between this strange popularity and friendship that the Doctor enjoyed and that of ordinary human society: with some friends, if you were away three years, it would mean you'd find yourself forgotten when you returned. But with John Dolittle and his animal friends, the longer he was gone the greater the welcome and rejoicing when he came home again.

Chapter Three
THE SURPRISE PARTY

AS a matter of fact, I did not entirely miss witnessing the Doctor's homecoming. When Matthew and I entered at the kitchen door we found an air of mystery in the house. We had expected, of course, an enormous amount of noise – greetings, questions, and so forth. But there wasn't a soul even visible besides the Doctor himself – and Dab-Dab who promptly upbraided me for taking so long over getting the sausages.

'But where is Gub-Gub?' the Doctor was asking as we came in.

'How on earth should I know, Doctor?' said Dab-Dab. 'He'll turn up presently – and the rest of them, no doubt. Have you washed your hands for supper? Please don't leave it to the last moment. The food will be on the table in five minutes. I'll want you to help me, Tommy, with the sausages. By the way, Doctor, we're going to have supper in the dining-room.'

'In the dining-room!' cried John Dolittle. 'What on earth for? Why don't we use the kitchen as usual?'

'Not big enough,' grunted Dab-Dab.

I suspected from an odd look in the housekeeper's eye that there was some surprise in store.
And, sure enough, when the dining-room door was
opened, there it was. The whole crowd of them,
Gub-Gub, Too-Too, Swizzle, Toby, and the white
mouse, all dressed up. It was a surprise party
given in the Doctor's honour.

The dining-room was a funny old stately
chamber which the Doctor had closed up years and
years ago – in fact, it had not been used since his
sister Sarah had left him. But tonight it was gaily
decorated with coloured papers, ribbons, and
evergreens. The animals were all in their old pantomime costumes, even the white mouse was
wearing a tiny waistcoat and trousers in which he
used to appear in the famous Dolittle Circus of
bygone days.

Now, with the Doctor's appearance at the door,
the noise which we had missed began in earnest.
Barks, yelps and squeals of greeting broke forth.
But there was very little disorderly behaviour, for
apparently a regular programme of entertainment had been arranged. The meal was most
elaborate, the table piled high with fruits and
dainties of every kind. Between the courses each
one of the animals who had stayed at home had
some performance to give. Gub-Gub recited one of
his own food poems, entitled 'The Wilted Cauli-
flower'; and the white mouse showed us what he
called 'The Punchbowl Circus'. This took place in
a large glass bowl, and was the most thrilling
thing of its kind I have ever seen. The white mouse
was ringmaster, and he swaggered about on his
hind legs with a tiny top hat on his head made of

'Gub-Gub recited one of his food poems'

paper. In his troupe he had a lady bareback rider, a clown and a lion tamer. The rider was another mouse (using a cutlet frill for a ballet skirt), and she rode a squirrel for a horse — the fastest mount I ever saw. The lion tamer was still another mouse, and his lion was a large rat dressed up with strings on his head for a mane.

Taken all in all, the Punchbowl Circus was, I think, the greatest success of the evening. The white mouse had even, in a way, made himself up. With some heavy black grease paint, which Swizzle, the old clown dog of the circus, had lent him from his own private make-up box, he had waxed his whiskers together so that they looked exactly like the long, ferocious moustaches of a regular ringmaster. The lady bareback artiste leapt through paper hoops, the mouse clown (also made up with a red-and-white face) threw somersaults, and the rat lion roared savagely.

'I don't know how on earth you all managed to get the show ready in time,' said the Doctor, tears of laughter running down his cheeks at the antics of the mouse clown. 'It's better than anything I ever had in my circus. And you only knew I was coming half an hour before I got here. How did you do it?'

'You'll soon see how it was done if you go upstairs, Doctor,' said Dab-Dab severely. 'It was Gub-Gub's idea. They turned the house inside out to get the costumes and the ribbons, and they turned the garden upside down to get the evergreens. Tut! Such foolishness! And just when I needed every one of them to help me put the house in proper order for your coming.'

HUGH LOFTING

'The Ringmaster of the Punchbowl Circus'

'Oh, well, never mind, Dab-Dab,' said the Doctor, still laughing. 'It was worth it. I never enjoyed anything so much in all my life. We can soon get the house straightened out. You have Stubbins and Bumpo and me to help you now, you know.'

'Yes, and I don't know where I'm going to put Bumpo to sleep, either,' said Dab-Dab. 'None of the beds we have will fit him, he's so tall.'

'Well, we'll manage,' said the Doctor. 'We can always put two mattresses together on the floor.'

'And now, Doctor,' said Gub-Gub, 'your part of the performance begins. We want to hear all about your travels since you left here.'

'Yes, yes,' they all cried. 'Begin at the beginning.'

'But, good gracious!' cried John Dolittle. 'I couldn't tell you our complete diary for three years in one evening!'

'Well, tell us some of it,' squeaked the white mouse, 'and keep the rest for tomorrow night.'

So, lighting his pipe, which, with the tobacco jar Chee-Chee had brought down off the mantelpiece, the Doctor began at the beginning – the tale of his travels. It was a wonderful scene – the long dining-room table packed all around with listening faces, animal and human. The Doctor's household had never, to my knowledge, been so complete before: Bumpo, Matthew Mugg, myself, Dab-Dab, Gub-Gub, Chee-Chee, Polynesia, Jip, Too-Too, Toby, Swizzle, and the white mouse. And then, just as he was about to begin, there came a thud at the window, and a voice said:

'Let me in. I want to listen too.'

It was the old lame horse from the stable. He had

heard the noise, and, realizing that the Doctor had
arrived at last, had come across to join the party.

Greatly to Dab-Dab's annoyance the double
French windows which opened on to the garden
were unlatched and the old lame horse invited to
join the party. The good housekeeper did insist,
however, that I should brush his hoofs clean of
mud before he was allowed in on to the carpets. It
was surprising to see how naturally he took to
such unusual surroundings. He passed through
the room without upsetting anything and took up
a place between the Doctor's chair and the
sideboard. He said he wanted to be near the
speaker, because his hearing wasn't what it used
to be. John Dolittle was overjoyed to see him.

'I was on my way out to your stable to call on
you,' he said, 'when supper was announced. You
know how particular Dab-Dab is. Have you been
getting your oats and barley regularly since I've
been gone?'

'Yes, thank you,' said the old horse. 'Everything's been quite all right – lonely, of course,
somewhat, without you and Jip – but all right
otherwise.'

Once more the Doctor settled down to begin his
story and once more he was interrupted by a tapping at the window.

'Oh, goodness! Who is it now?' wailed Gub-Gub.
I opened the window and three birds fluttered in –
Cheapside, with his wife Becky, and the famous
Speedy-the-Skimmer.

'Bless my soul!' chirped the Cockney sparrow,
flying up on to the table. 'If anybody ever broke
into this 'ouse 'e'd deserve all 'e could pinch. That's

HUGH LOFTING

' "All right, Cross-eyes" '

what *I* say. Me and Becky 'as been pokin' round
the doors and windows for hours, looking' for a
way in. Might as well try to get into the Bank of
Hengland after closin' time. Well, Doc, 'ere we are!
The old firm! Glad to see you back. Me and the
missis was just turnin' in up at St Paul's when we
'eard the pigeons gossipin' below us. There was a
rumour, they said, that you'd got back. So I says to
Becky, I says, "Let's take a run down to Puddleby
and see." "Right you are," says she. And down we
come. Nobody can't never—'

'Oh, be quiet!' Too-Too broke in. 'The Doctor is
about to tell us of his voyage. We don't want to
listen to you all night.'

'All right, Cross-eyes, all right,' said Cheapside,
picking up a crumb from the table and talking
with his mouth full, 'keep your feathers on. 'Ow
long 'ave *you* owned this 'ouse, anyway? Hey,
Speedy, come over 'ere where it's warmer.'

The famous swallow, champion speed flyer of
Europe, Africa, and America, modestly came forward to a warmer place under the branching
candlesticks. He had returned to England a little
earlier this year than usual, but the warm
weather which had tempted him northward had
given way to a cold snap. And now in the brighter
light near the centre of the table we could plainly
see that he was shivering.

'Glad to see you, Doctor,' said he quietly. 'Excuse
us interrupting you like this. Please begin, won't
you?'

Chapter Four
THE NEW ZOO

SO, far into the night, John Dolittle told his household the story of his voyage. Gub-Gub kept falling asleep and then waking up very angry with himself because he was afraid he had missed the best parts.

Somewhere around two o'clock in the morning, although he was not more than half done, the Doctor insisted that everybody go to bed and the rest of the adventures be put off until tomorrow night.

The following day was, I think, the busiest day I have ever seen the Doctor put in. Everybody and everything demanded his attention at once. First of all, of course, there were patients waiting at the surgery door: a squirrel with a broken claw, a rabbit who was losing his fur, a fox with a sore eye.

Then there was the garden, the Doctor's well-beloved garden. What a mess it was in, to be sure! Three years of weeds, three years of overgrowth, three years of neglect! He almost wept as he stepped out of the kitchen door and saw the desolation of it fully revealed in the bright morning sunlight.

'Patients waiting at the surgery door'

Luckily the country birds who had been waiting
all night to greet him helped to take his mind off
it for a while. It reminded me of the pictures of St
Francis and the pigeons, as the starlings, crows,
robins and blackbirds swarmed down about him in
clouds as soon as he appeared.

Bumpo and I, realizing how deeply affected he
was by the sad state of his garden, decided to put
our shoulder to the wheel and see what we could
do towards cleaning it up. Chee-Chee also
volunteered to help, and so did a great number of
smaller animals such as field mice, rats, badgers,
and squirrels. And, despite their tiny size, it was
astonishing to see how much they could do.

Then, in the middle of the morning Too-Too, the
accountant, wanted to go into money matters with
the Doctor, so that Dab-Dab might see how much
she had to keep house with. Fortunately, the
Spanish silver we had brought back from the Capa
Blancas (largely out of Bumpo's bet, which the
Doctor didn't know anything about) looked, when
changed into English pounds, as though it should
keep us all comfortably for some months at least
without worry. This was a great relief to Dab-Dab,
though, as usual, she kept an anxious eye on any
new schemes of the Doctor's, remembering from
the past that the more money he had, the more
extravagant he was likely to be.

It was a funny sight to see those wiseacres, Too-
Too, Polynesia and Dab-Dab, putting their heads
together over the Doctor's money affairs while his
back was turned.

'But, look here,' Polynesia put in, 'the Doctor
ought to make a lot of money out of all these new

HUGH LOFTING

'Putting their heads together over the Doctor's money affairs'

and precious herbs of Long Arrow's which he brought back.'

'Oh, hardly,' said I. 'You'll probably find he'll refuse to profit by them at all. In his eyes they are medicines for humanity's benefit: not things to sell.'

And then, in addition to all the other departments of his strange establishment which claimed the Doctor's attention that morning, there was the zoo. Matthew Mugg was on hand very early to go over it with him. Not very many of the old inmates were there now. Quite a number had been sent away before the Doctor left, because he felt that in his absence their care would be too ticklish a job for Matthew to manage alone. But there were a few who had begged very hard to remain, some of the more northerly animals like the Canadian woodchucks and the minks.

'You know, Stubbins,' said the Doctor as we passed down the garden between the clean, empty houses (Matthew had in our absence really kept the place in wonderful condition), 'I have a notion to change the whole system of my zoo.'

'How do you mean?' I asked.

'Well,' said he, 'so far I have kept it mostly for foreign visitors – rather unusual animals – though, as you know, I always avoided the big hunting creatures. But now I think I'll give it over almost entirely to our native animals. There are a great many who want to live with me – many more than we can possibly manage in the house. You see, we have a big space left here, over an acre altogether. It used to be a sort of a bowling green hundreds of years ago, when an old castle stood

where the house is now. It is walled in – private
and secluded. Look at it. We could make this into
a regular ideal Animal Town. Something quite
new. You can help me with the planning of it. I
thought I would have several clubs in it. The Rat
and Mouse Club is one that I have been thinking
of for a long time. Several rats and mice have
asked me to start it. And, then, the Home for
Cross-Bred Dogs is another. A tremendous lot of
dogs – of no particular breed – call on me from
time to time and ask if they can live with me. Jip
will tell you all about it. I hate to turn them away,
because I know many of them have no place to live
– and people don't want them because they're not
what is called thoroughbred. Silly idea. Myself,
I've usually found that the mongrels had more
character and sense than the prize winners. But
there you are. What do you think of my idea?'

'I think it's just a marvellous idea, Doctor,' I
cried. 'And it will certainly relieve poor old Dab-
Dab of an awful lot of worry. She is always grumbling over the way the mice eat the pillow slips in
the linen closet and use the fringes off the bath
towels to make their nests with.'

'Yes,' said the Doctor, 'and we've never been able
to find out who the culprits are. Each one, when I
ask him or her, says he or she didn't do it. But the
linen goes on disappearing, just the same . . . Well,
now, Stubbins, supposing as soon as we get some
of these poor old fruit trees into shape you plan out
the new zoo for me. Get Polynesia to help you.
She's full of ideas, as you know. Unfortunately,
I've got my hands more than full already with the
surgery and the writing-up of the notebooks we

'I think it's just a marvellous idea!'

brought back (I'll want you to help me on that, too)
– to say nothing of Long Arrow's collection. Otherwise I could work with you on the first layout of
the zoo. But you and Polynesia can do it between
you. By the way, consult the white mouse about
the quarters for the Rat and Mouse Club, will
you?'

Well, that was the beginning of the new Dolittle
Zoo. It was, of course, a thing that interested me
tremendously, and I felt very proud that the
Doctor had entrusted such a large measure of the
responsibility to me. But I had very little idea, at
the outset, into what an enormous institution it
was to grow. 'Animal Town' or 'Animal Clubland'
is really what it should have been called, instead
of a zoo. But we had always called that part of the
garden the zoo, and that name persisted.

But if it wasn't a regular zoo to the ordinary
public's way of thinking, it was very certainly
Doctor Dolittle's idea of one. In his opinion, a zoo
should be an animals' home, not an animals'
prison. Every detail of our zoo (as with the first one
the Doctor had shown me long ago) was worked
out with this idea foremost in mind, that the
animals should be made comfortable and happy.
Many of the old things were kept the same. For
example, the latches to the houses were all on the
inside, so that the animals could come in and go
out when they chose. Latchkeys were given out (if
a tenant wanted one) when a house or room or hole
was let. There were certain rules, it is true,
although the Doctor was not fond of rules, but they
were all drawn up to protect the animals against
one another, rather than to enslave them or cut off

their liberty in any way. For instance, anyone wishing to give a party had to notify his next-door neighbour (they were very close, of course); and no tenant was allowed to sing comic songs after midnight.

Chapter Five
ANIMAL TOWN

ONE of the greatest difficulties the Doctor had in all his dealings with the Animal Kingdom was that of keeping anything secret. But then, I suppose, when we remember how hard it is for people to keep secrets, that need not be so surprising. Polynesia, as soon as I told her about the idea of the new zoo, immediately warned me.

'Keep this to yourself, now, Tommy, as long as you can. If you don't, neither you nor the Doctor will get any peace.'

I certainly kept it to myself. But nevertheless the news leaked out somehow that John Dolittle was reorganizing and enlarging his zoo in order that a lot of new animals might live with him. And then, exactly as Polynesia had prophesied, we were pestered to death morning, noon and night with applications. You would think that all the animals in the world had been waiting the whole of their lives for a chance to get into the Doctor's household.

He at once had it announced that as I was to be the assistant manager of the new zoo all applications must be made through me. But even so, of

course, while that did relieve him of a good deal of
annoyance, a great many animals who had known
him a long time applied to him direct for a home
in the new establishment.

Not only were there many applications from
single animals and families of animals for accom-
modations in our zoo, but as soon as it got abroad
that John Dolittle was going to set up his long-
promised Rat and Mouse Club every other species
of animal on earth, it seemed to me, sent commit-
tees to him to ask couldn't they have a club, too.

'I told you what it would be like,' said Polynesia,
as she and I were pondering one day over a map of
the new zoo which I had laid out. 'If the space you
had were ten times as big you couldn't accom-
modate them all.'

'But look here,' said the white mouse (it was
most amusing to see how important he had
become now that he was being consulted in the
Doctor's schemes), 'suppose we set out on your
drawing here all the different establishments,
private houses, flats, hotels, clubs and what not,
then we can see better how much room there is left
and how many clubs we can have.'

'Yes,' I said, 'that's a good idea, because once we
get the zoo running it will be very hard to dig
things out and change them around afterwards.
The animals would very naturally object to that.'

'And then I think we ought to have some shops,'
said the white mouse. 'Don't you?'

'Shops!' I cried. 'What on earth for?'

'Well, you see,' said he, 'by the time we're
finished it will be like a town, anyhow – an

' "But, look here," said the white mouse'

animal town – with a principal street, I suppose,
and the houses and clubs either side. A few shops
where the squirrels could buy nuts and the mice
could get acorns and grains of wheat – don't you
see? – it would liven things up a bit. Nothing
cheers a town up so much as good shops. And I
think a restaurant or two where we could go and
get our meals if we came home late and hadn't
time to get our own supper – yes, that's a good
notion – we should surely have a restaurant or
two.'

'But who are you going to get to run these shops?'
asked Polynesia. 'Stores and cafés don't run
themselves, you know.'

'Oh, that's easy,' laughed the white mouse. 'I
know lots of mice – and rats, too – who would
jump at the chance to run a nut store or a
restaurant. They just have a natural gift for
business, especially catering.'

'Maybe, for the rats and mice,' said Polynesia.
'But they're not the only ones in the zoo,
remember. This isn't just a rat and mouse town.'

'Well, I imagine it will probably separate itself
into districts, anyway,' said the white mouse. 'You
won't forget, Tommy, that you've promised us the
top end, near the gate, for our club? I have that
whole section laid out complete in my mind's eye.
And it is going to be just the neatest little
neighbourhood you ever saw.'

Well, after a tremendous amount of planning
and working out we finally got the new zoo going.
The list of public institutions with which it began
was as follows: the Rabbits' Apartment House
(this consisted of an enormous mound full of rabbit

holes with a comon lettuce garden attached), the Home for Cross-Bred Dogs, the Rat and Mouse Club, the Badgers' Tavern, the Foxes' Meeting House, and the Squirrels' Hotel.

Each of these was a sort of club in its way. And we had to be most particular about limiting the membership, because from the outset thousands of creatures of each kind wanted to join. The best we could do for those who were not taken in was to keep their names on a waiting list, and as members left (which was very seldom) admit them one by one. Each club had its president and committee who were responsible for the proper organization and orderly carrying on of the establishment.

As the white mouse had prophesied, our new animal town within the high walls of the old bowling green did naturally divide itself up into districts. And the animals from each, while they often mingled in the street with those from other quarters of the town, minded their own business, and no one interfered with anybody else.

This we had to make the first and most important rule of the Dolittle Zoo: within the walls of the town all hunting was forbidden. No member of the Home for Cross-Bred Dogs was allowed to go ratting – in the zoo. No fox was permitted to chase birds or squirrels.

And it was surprising how, when the danger of pursuit by their natural enemies was removed, all the different sorts of animals took up a new, freer and more open kind of life. For instance, it was no unusual thing in Animal Town to see a mother squirrel lolling on her veranda, surrounded by her

'Buying their Sunday dinner from a large rat'

children, while a couple of terriers walked down
the street within a yard of them.

The shops and restaurants, of course, were
mostly patronized by the rats and mice, who had
a natural love for city life, and the majority of
them were situated in the section at the north end
of the enclosure which came to be known as Mouse
Town. Nevertheless, at the main grocery on a
Saturday night we often saw foxes and dogs and
crows, all mixed up, buying their Sunday dinner
from a large rat. And the mouse errand boys who
delivered goods at the customers' houses were not
afraid to walk right into a bulldog's kennel or a
fox's den.

Chapter Six
POVERTY AGAIN

OF course it would be quite too much to expect that with lots of different kinds of animals housed in the same enclosure there would be no quarrels or disputes. It was in fact part of the Doctor's plan to see what could be done in getting different creatures who were born natural enemies to live together in harmony.

'Obviously, Stubbins,' said he, 'we can't expect foxes to give up their taste for spring chickens, or dogs their love of ratting, all in a moment. My hope is that by getting them to agree to live peaceably together while within my zoo, we will tend towards a better understanding among them permanently.'

Yes, there *were* fights, especially in the first few months before the different communities got settled down. But, curiously enough, many of the quarrels were among animals of the same kind. I think the badgers were the worst. In the evenings at their tavern they used to play games. Neither the Doctor nor I could ever make out what these games were about. One was played with stones on a piece of ground marked out with scratches. It

was almost like drafts. The badgers used to take
this game quite seriously – the badger is rather a
heavy type of personality, anyway. And there
seemed to be championships played and great
public interest taken in the outcome of matches.
Frequently these ended in a quarrel. And in the
middle of the night a frightened squirrel would
come and wake me or the Doctor and tell us there
was a fight going on in the Badgers' Tavern and
the whole town was being disturbed.

In the end, at the white mouse's suggestion (he
was more proud and important than ever, now
that he had been elected first Mayor of Animal
Town), this led to the Doctor instituting the Zoo
Police Force. Two dogs, two foxes, two squirrels,
two rabbits and two rats were elected as constables, with a bulldog for captain and a fox as
head of the Secret Service. After that woe betide a
quarrelsome member who tried to start a brawl in
the Badgers' Tavern! He promptly found himself
being trotted down the street under arrest to
spend the night in the town jail.

One of the first arrests to be made by the zoo
police was that of poor Gub-Gub. Having noticed
that the vegetable garden attached to the Rabbits'
Apartment House was promising a nice harvest of
early lettuce, he made a descent on it one night
secretly. But the chief of the fox detectives spotted
him and he was handcuffed (or trotter-cuffed)
before he could say Jack Robinson. It was only on
the Doctor's forbidding him entrance to the zoo
compound and guaranteeing his good behaviour
that he was dismissed the following morning with
a caution.

'Next time,' said His Honour the Mayor (the
white mouse who was acting as magistrate), 'we
will give you six days' hard labour in the rabbits'
garden – with a muzzle on.'

Besides the Rat and Mouse Club, of which I shall
speak further later on, the other more important
department in the new zoo was the Home for
Cross-Bred Dogs. This was an institution which
Jip had long pestered John Dolittle to establish.
Ever since the days of the Canary Opera, when Jip
had tried to run a Dogs' Free Bone Kitchen in the
East End of London, he had been hoping that the
Doctor would discover a way to give all the strays
and outcasts of dogdom a decent home. Now, in the
seventh heaven of contentment, he, with Toby and
Swizzle, was very busy working out the details of
the new club.

'Now some dogs,' said Jip to me, 'like to live in
kennels – prefer to be private, you know – and
others like to live in houses. So we'll have to have
a lot of kennels and at least one good house.'

Thereupon he persuaded me and Bumpo to build
a house according to his, Swizzle's and Toby's
directions. Toby, always a fussy, bossy little dog,
had a whole heap of ideas, mostly for the benefit of
the small dogs who were to come. You would think
they were surely the most important. And when
we finally had it finished I am bound to say the
Dogs' House was quite an unusual building. All
doors were made to open just with a lift of the nose-
latch and a push. The fireplaces were built
especially wide, so that at least a dozen dogs could
find room to lie in front of each one. All sofas (of
which there were many) were made low enough so

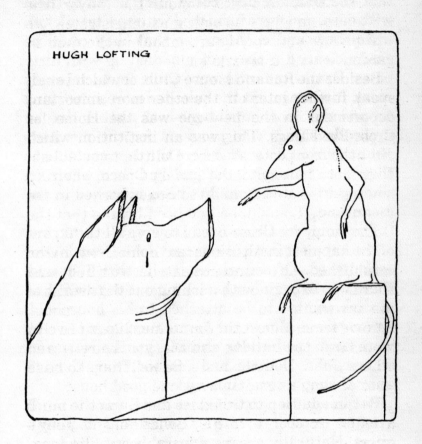

HUGH LOFTING

' "Next time we'll give you six days' hard labour" '

that the smallest dogs could jump up on to them
with ease, and were furnished with special oilcloth
upholstery and cushions, so that they could be
easily cleaned if they got muddied up with dirty
paws. Drinking bowls were to be found in every
room. It was against the rules to leave bones lying
around the floor, but a bone-rack (rather like an
umbrella stand) was provided for the members
near the front door. And here the dogs could leave
their bones on going out and find them again on
coming in — if they hadn't been borrowed in the
meantime.

The Home for Cross-Bred Dogs was, I think, one
of the happiest institutions that John Dolittle ever
established. Of course, as the Doctor had said,
there was to begin with a long list of dogs who had
always wanted to be attached to his household.
Among these almost the first to turn up at the club
were Grab the bulldog and Blackie the retriever,
whom John Dolittle had rescued from Harris's
animal shop a long time ago.

But in addition to this class there was the much
greater number of Jip's friends and acquaint-
ances. Naturally a very charitable dog, Jip loved
to go out and hunt round the streets for homeless
vagabonds. Every day he would bring home one or
two, till very soon the club had about as many
members as it would hold. And even when the
Doctor told him he would have to stop, he would,
if he found a particularly deserving case, as he
called it, sneak in with him after dark and see that
at least he got a square meal and a night's lodging.
From the outside the gate to the zoo could only be
opened by a secret latch. This was worked by

pulling a string carefully hidden in a ditch. All members of the zoo were specially instructed in this by the Doctor and made to promise not to give the secret away. And I am bound to say they were very conscientious about it. During the whole of the zoo's career no outsider ever learned the secret of the gate. But when Jip brought his 'deserving cases' home after dark he always made them turn their backs while he pulled the secret latch-string.

As soon as it became known in dog society that John Dolittle had formed a club, many dogs who had perfectly good homes of their own just left them and came here – for no other reasons than that they preferred living with the Doctor and because they loved the club and the good company. And more than one angry owner called at the Doctor's house and was all for having him arrested because, he or she said, he had lured the dog away.

Of course the cost of the upkeep of the new zoo was considerable, especially for the supply of food for the Home for Cross-Bred Dogs. And about six weeks after it had been established Dab-Dab and Too-Too came to me, both looking very serious.

'It is just as I thought it would be,' squawked Dab-Dab, throwing out her wings in a gesture of despair. 'We are already practically at the end of our money again. I don't know how many thousand pesetas it was you brought back with you, but it's nearly all gone. Too-Too and I have been going over accounts and we calculate we have about enough to last for another week. Jip has no sense. The Doctor is bad enough himself, goodness

'More than one angry owner called'

knows, the way he spends money – just regard-
less. But nobody in the world would be rich enough
to keep all the stray mongrels Jip has been bringing in the last few weeks. Well, here we are, penniless again. I don't know what we're going to do,
I'm sure.'

Chapter Seven
THE BADGER'S TOOTH

OF course, when I came (with Dab-Dab, Too-Too, and Polynesia) to the Doctor to report the condition of the family bank account he, as usual, took the matter very lightly.

'Don't bother me with such things now,' he said. 'Some money will come in somehow, I have no doubt — it generally does. I'm dreadfully busy.'

But though we managed to collect a few pounds which were due him from people who published his books on natural history, that did not last us long. And soon we were as badly off as ever. Dab-Dab was terribly angry and kept insisting that the Doctor get rid of the zoo, which was almost as expensive to run as all the rest of the household put together.

But John Dolittle was right; something did turn up, and, curiously enough, it turned up inside the zoo itself and saved that institution from extinction as well as the Dolittle household from bankruptcy. This is how it happened: one night, just as the Doctor was going to bed after a hard day's work with his new book on oceanography, a member of the Badgers' Tavern knocked on the

'We came to the Doctor to report'

door asking to see him. He said he had a terrible toothache and wanted the Doctor, if he would, to look at it at once. This, of course, the Doctor did. He was very clever at animal dentistry.

'Ah!' said he. 'You've broken a corner off that tooth. No wonder it hurts. But it can be filled. Open your mouth a little wider, please. . . . That's better – why, how curious! Did I ever fill any teeth for you before?'

'No,' said the badger. 'This is the first time I've come to you for treatment of any kind. I'm very healthy.'

'But you have gold in your teeth,' said the Doctor. 'How did that come there if you haven't been to some dentist?'

'I'm sure I don't know,' said the badger. 'What is gold?'

'Look, I'll show you in the mirror,' said the Doctor. 'Stubbins, give me that hand-glass, will you, please?'

I got it and brought it to the Doctor, who held it in front of the badger's face while he pointed to a place in his teeth with a small instrument.

'There,' said John Dolittle, 'you see that yellow metal sticking between your teeth? That's gold.'

'Oh!' said the badger, peering into the mirror, very pleased with his own handsome reflection. 'I and my wife were digging a hole out by Dobbin's Meadow and we chewed up a whole lot of that stuff. That's what I broke my tooth on.'

Polynesia, who was in the surgery at the time, was more interested in this statement of the badger's than was the Doctor. She flew across the room and from one of her hanging rings she peered

into the animal's open mouth where John Dolittle
was at work on the broken tooth. Then she came
back to me and whispered:

'Well, of all things! He's been eating gold. *Eating*
it, mind you – and us as poor as church mice.
Tommy, we will speak with this gentleman as
soon as the Doctor has done with him.'

John Dolittle did not take long over making his
patient comfortable. In spite of his podgy fat hands
he had the quickest and nimblest fingers in the
world.

'I have put a dressing in your tooth which will
stop the pain for the present, and you'll have to
come back and see me again tomorrow,' he said as
the badger closed his mouth and waddled down off
the table. 'You must be careful what you chew up
when you're digging holes. No teeth will stand
biting on metal, you know – not even yours. Good-
night.'

As the patient left the surgery Polynesia made
a sign to me, and we followed him.

'Where did you say you were digging this hole?'
asked Polynesia as we walked beside him toward
the zoo enclosure.

'Over near Dobbin's Meadow,' said the badger;
'just a bit to the north of it. We were tunnelling
into a bank – as much for exercise as anything
else. It was a cold day. But we did hope we might
find some pig nuts. Also, we need a refuge hole
or two up in that direction. Some of these dogs
the Doctor has here in such numbers now are
getting much too cheeky. They never touch us
while we are in the zoo, it is true, but if they get
wind of us when we're outside they think it is

funny to chase us all over the landscape. Our
committee down at the Badgers' Tavern thought
we ought to have a refuge hole up in that
neighbourhood.'

'What is a refuge hole?' I asked.

'Oh, it's just a public hole,' said he. 'We have
them stuck around all over the place. But we all
know where they are. They're just holes where
any badger can take refuge if chased by dogs. We
dig them very deep, and sometimes provision
them with food in case the dogs should besiege us
for a long time. We have to protect ourselves, you
know. Our pace is slow.'

'Well, now, look here,' said Polynesia, as we
reached the zoo gate, 'Tommy and I would like to
make an appointment with you for tomorrow
morning early – very early. We want to see this
place where you broke your tooth. Suppose we
meet you at the north end of Dobbin's Meadow at,
say, five o'clock.'

'All right,' said the badger. 'But that isn't early
for me. This time of year it has been broad
daylight for more than a quarter of an hour by five.
We don't go by the clock, you know; we go by the
sun. We prefer to travel before dawn. I'll meet you
there at daybreak.'

The following morning Polynesia had me out of
bed and dressing by candle-light before the cocks
had given their first crow.

'But don't you see, Tommy,' said she, in answer
to my sleepy grumbling at this unearthly hour for
rising, 'it's frightfully important that we get there
and do what exploring is necessary before there
are people about.'

I found it hard to be enthusiastic, even over the prospect of discovering gold, so early.

'But what are you expecting to find?' I asked. 'Do you fancy that old badger has run into a mine? There aren't any gold mines in England.'

'I've no more idea than you have,' said she impatiently. 'But just because no gold mines have been discovered so far, that doesn't mean that none ever will be. The fact remains that that blessed animal ran into gold of some kind, or he wouldn't have it sticking in his teeth. Hurry up and get your coat on. I think I see the dawn beginning to show in the east.'

Downstairs Polynesia made me collect a spade from the tool shed and the Doctor's mineral hammer from his study before we started away through the chilly morning twilight for Dobbin's Meadow.

The old badger was there, sure enough, waiting for us. And he promptly lumbered off alongside a hedge to lead us to the place where he had dug the hole. This, when we came to it, proved not to be in the Dobbin property at all, but on the other side of the hedge, in a wide, open piece of heathland, known as Puddleby Common.

Chapter Eight
THE PUDDLEBY GOLD RUSH

'THIS is lucky,' whispered Polynesia as we came to a halt before the hole which the badger had dug. 'Puddleby Common, public property — don't you see, Tommy? Even if anyone does see us digging here they can't stop us. Just the same, we must not give the show away. Get your spade now and go to work.'

I was still very sleepy. But little by little the fascination of hunting in the earth for treasure took hold of me. And before long I was working away as though my life depended on it, and, despite the chill of the morning air, the perspiration was running down my forehead in streams.

We had explained to the badger what we were after, and his assistance was very helpful. He began by going down to the bottom of the hole and bringing up several shapeless pieces of gravelly metal. These, when I cut into them with a penknife, showed the soft yellow gold of which they were composed.

'That's the piece I broke my tooth on,' said the badger 'and it is the last of it. Is the stuff any good?'

'Why, my gracious!' said Polynesia, 'of course it

'Before long I was working away as though my
life depended on it'

is. Are you sure this is all there is? If we can get enough we will have made the Doctor a rich man for life.'

The badger went back and dug the hole still deeper, and with my spade I cut away the bank all around and levelled out tons of gravel, which we searched and raked over diligently. But not another nugget could we find.

'Well, just the same,' said Polynesia, inspecting the array of pieces which I had laid out on my open handkerchief, 'we have a tidy little fortune as it is. Now let's get away before anyone sees what we've been up to.'

When we told the Doctor about it at breakfast he was much more interested in it from the geological, the scientific point of view, than he was from that of money or profit.

'It is most extraordinary,' he said, examining the specimens I had brought home in the handkerchief. 'If you had found old gold coins it would not have been so surprising. But these look like nuggets – native gold. Geologically, this is something quite new for England. I would like to see the place where you found it.'

'In the meantime,' said Dab-Dab, 'leave these nuggets with me, will you? I know a safe place to keep them till we can turn them into cash.'

When the Doctor set out with me and Polynesia to examine the place where the gold had been found, Jip and Gub-Gub, though they had not been invited, came along too.

Our prospecting exploration was very thorough. We searched the whole length of that gravel bank, digging and sifting and testing. Gub-Gub caught

the fever, and Jip, too. They burrowed into the
slope like regular prospectors, Gub-Gub using his
nose as though he were digging for truffles and Jip
scraping out the earth with his front paws the way
he always did when he was going after rats.

But we found no more gold.

'It's very puzzling,' said the Doctor, 'very. Quite
a geological mystery. This is not really gold-
bearing gravel at all. And yet that gold is exactly
as it would be found *in* gravel – in nugget form.
The only explanation I can think of is that it was
dug up elsewhere by some very early miners and
then buried here for safekeeping.'

But if we were not successful in finding a real
gold mine, we were successful in starting a prospecting boom. By the time the Doctor had finished
his survey of the ground it was quite late in the
morning. As we left the Common and started on
our way home we noticed that one or two people
had been watching us. Later we questioned
Matthew Mugg and Bumpo, who had accompanied
the expedition, and they swore they never told
anyone. Nevertheless, it apparently leaked out
that gold had been found in a gravel bank on
Puddleby Common. And by four o'clock that afternoon the place was crowded with people armed
with picks, shovels, garden trowels, firetongs –
every imaginable implement – all hunting for
gold.

The whole of Puddleby had gone prospecting
mad. Nursemaids with perambulators left their
charges to bawl while they scratched in the
ground with button-hooks and shoehorns for gold.
Loafers, poachers, gipsies, pedlars, the town

'Gub-Gub used his nose as though he were
digging for truffles'

tradesmen, respectable old gentlemen, school children – they came from all ranks and ages.

One rumour had it that the Doctor had discovered a lot of ancient Roman goblets, made of gold, and several old saucepans and kettles were dug up by the prospectors and taken away to be tested to see what they were made of.

After the second day the poor Common looked as though a cyclone or an earthquake had visited it. And the Town Council said they were going to prosecute the Doctor for the damage he had brought to public property.

For over a week the gold boom continued. People came from outside, real mining experts from London, to look into this strange rumour which had set everyone agog.

Gub-Gub, who of all the Doctor's household had the prospecting fever the worst, could hardly be kept away from the Common. He was sure he had found his real profession at last.

'Why,' said he, 'I can dig better holes with my nose than any of those duffers can with a spade – and quicker.'

He kept begging to be allowed to go back to continue the hunt. He was so afraid these other people might any minute discover a real mine which ought to be the property of the Dolittle household.

'You need not be worried, Gub-Gub,' said the Doctor. 'It isn't a mineral-bearing gravel at all. The gold we got came there by accident. The badger was probably right – there is no more than just that little hoard, which must have been specially buried there ages and ages ago.'

But Gub-Gub, while the boom continued, was

'Prospecting for raisins in the rice pudding'

not to be dissuaded, and his mining fever got
worse rather than better. When the Doctor would
not allow him to go back to the Common (he went
several times secretly at night) he consoled
himself by prospecting in the kitchen garden for
mushrooms. He even brought his new profession
to the table with him and went prospecting for
raisins in the rice pudding.

By whatever means the gold had come, Dab-Dab
was very pleased that Polynesia's business-like
attention had secured it all for the Doctor. Left to
himself he would most likely not have profited by
it at all. The Town Council insisted that he give it
up as Crown property. And this he willingly consented to do. But the wily Matthew Mugg consulted a solicitor and found that under ancient law
the finder was entitled to half of it. Even this sum,
when the gold was weighed, proved to be quite
considerable.

'Well,' sighed Dab-Dab, 'as the Doctor would say,
"it's an ill wind that blows nobody any good". That
old badger breaking his tooth was a stroke of luck.
It was just in time. I really didn't know where the
next meal was coming from. Now, thank goodness,
we shan't have to worry about the bills for another
six months, anyhow.'

Chapter Nine
THE MOUSE CODE

THERE had been a good deal of anxiety for some time past in the various departments of the zoo over Dab-Dab's constant demand that the Doctor should close the whole place up. Seeing how expensive it was to run, her argument sounded reasonable enough, and the members had all felt a bit selfish over continuing their clubs and other institutions when the cost was such a burden to the Doctor.

So with the news that half of the treasure found on the Common had been awarded to John Dolittle by the courts, the greatest rejoicing broke out in Animal Town – all the way from the Home for Cross-Bred Dogs at one end to the Rat and Mouse Club at the other. Even the timid pushmi-pullyu, who had now made his home within the peaceful, pleasant retirement of the zoo enclosure, joined in the jubilation, as did what few foreigners we still had, like the Russian minks and the Canadian woodchucks. I never heard such a pandemonium in my life. The information was brought to the zoo about supper-time by Toby and Swizzle. Immediately a demonstration began in every quarter.

All the citizens spilled out of the clubs into the
street cheering, or making noises which to them
were the same as cheering.

'The Doctor's rich again!' passed from mouth to
mouth, from door to door. The mixture of barks,
squeals, grunts and squawks was so extraordinary
that a policeman, passing on the Oxenthorpe Road
outside, knocked at the Doctor's door and asked if
everything was all right.

A little later the animals began organizing
parades and went walking up and down the main
street of Animal Town singing what they called
songs. The white mouse, as Mayor of the town, was
in charge – frightfully important – and he suggested, as it was now quite dark, that Mousetown
should have a torchlight procession. He asked me
to get a box of those very small candles which they
put on birthday cakes and Christmas trees. Then
he insisted that I should fix up a banner with
'Hooray! The Doctor's Rich Again!' on it in large
letters. And fifty-four mice and fifty-four rats
formed themselves up, two by two, each pair carrying a candle, and they marched round Mousetown
from eight o'clock till midnight, singing the most
extraordinary songs you ever heard. Every once in
a while they would come to a halt and yell in
chorus: 'Hooray! The Doctor's rich again! –
Hooray! Hooray!'

A little extra excitement was added when one
pair of torchbearers had an accident with their
candle and set light to the Squirrels' Hotel. And as
that building was largely made of dry leaves it not
only burned to the ground in no time at all, but
very nearly set the whole zoo in flames as well.

' "The Doctor's rich again!" passed from mouth
to mouth, from door to door'

However, no one was injured (the squirrels were all out celebrating), and after the entire town had formed itself into a fire brigade the blaze was quickly put out. Then everyone set to on the work of reconstruction and the Squirrels' Hotel was rebuilt in a night.

'It was a grand occasion,' declared the white mouse when it was all over. 'And the bonfire was almost the best part of it.'

Indeed, the white mouse was naturally of a cheerful, pleasure-loving disposition. And after the success of this first celebration he was continually wanting to organize club parties, city fêtes, processions, and entertainments of one kind or another. This, while the Doctor was always glad to see the animals enjoying themselves, could not be encouraged too far, because a lot of noise was usually a most important part of Animal Town festivities. And although the zoo stood well within the Doctor's own land, the racket which the Home for Cross-Bred Dogs made on these occasions could be heard miles away.

Many new and interesting features developed quite naturally in the zoo, for example, the Animals' Free Library. Shortly after I had visited my parents on our return from abroad, the Doctor had asked me to try to organize and arrange the tremendous quantity of material which he had collected and written on animal language. He had one whole bedroom above his study simply packed with books, manuscript notes and papers on this subject. It was all in great disorder, and the task of getting it straightened out was a heavy one.

But Polynesia and the white mouse helped me.

We got Matthew Mugg to make us a lot of book-
cases. And after a week of sorting and cataloguing
and listing we had arranged the extraordinary
collection in something like order. I think it was a
surprise even to the Doctor himself, when we
finally invited him into the little room above the
study and showed him the bookshelves running
all round the walls, to realize what a tremendous
amount of work he had done on the science of
animal languages.

'Why, Doctor,' squeaked the white mouse, gazing round the shelves, 'this is a regular animal
library you have here! It ought to be down in the
zoo, where the animals could make use of it,
instead of here.'

'Yes, there's something in that,' said the Doctor.
'But most of these writings of mine are only *about*
animal languages — dictionaries and so forth —
very few are actually story books written *in*
animal language. And then, besides, so few of you
can read, anyway.'

'Oh, but we could soon learn,' said the white
mouse. 'If you got one or two of us taught we could
quickly teach the rest. Oh, I do think an important
institution like the Rat and Mouse Club ought to
have a library of its own. Yes, indeed!'

Well, in spite of the objection which the Doctor
had advanced, the white mouse stuck to his idea of
an Animal Public Library for the Dolittle Zoo. He
pointed out that so far as the rats and mice were
concerned (and the dogs, badgers and squirrels,
too, for that matter) there was nothing they
enjoyed as much as stories.

'I would be delighted to do it for you,' said the

' "Why, Doctor, this is a regular animal library,"
said the white mouse'

Doctor, 'but in rat and mouse talk, for instance, there are no letters — there *is* no written language.'

'But we can soon invent one, can't we?' asked the white mouse. 'Why, there must have been a time when there wasn't any human written language. Listen, Doctor, you invent a sign alphabet for mice — simple, you know — we don't want any physics or skizzics to begin with — and teach it to me. I'll promise to teach the whole of the Rat and Mouse Club in a week. They're awfully keen about learning new things. What do you say?'

Of course such a suggestion, one might be sure, would always interest John Dolittle, who had given so many years of his life to animal education. He at once set to work and with the white mouse's co-operation devised a simple alphabet in rat and mouse language. There were only ten signs, or letters, in all. The Doctor called it the Mouse Code, but Polynesia and I called it the Squeaker-B-C, because it was all in squeaks of different kinds, and each letter had two different meanings, according to whether you let your squeak fall or rise at the end.

Then came the business of printing and binding the books. This the Doctor turned over to me as soon as he had established the alphabet or code. Of course, the volumes had to be terribly, terribly tiny in order that even the young mice could read and handle them with ease. The white mouse was most anxious that the young folk should be able to take advantage of the new education. What we called our 'Mouse Octavo' size of book was just slightly smaller than a postage stamp. The

**'Our "Mouse Octavo" was slightly smaller than
a postage stamp'**

binding had to be all hand-sewn and only the finest thread could be used. The pages were so small that I had to have a watchmakers' magnifying eyeglass to do my printing with, which was, of course, also all hand work. But no matter how tiny the letters were made, they were none too small for mouse eyes, which can pick out single grains of dust with the greatest ease.

We were very proud of our first book printed in mouse language. Although it was mostly the work of the Doctor, I, as printer and publisher, felt just as important as Caxton or Gutenberg as I put the name of my firm into the title page: 'Stubbins & Stubbins. Puddleby-on-the-Marsh' (I didn't know who the second 'Stubbins' was, but I thought it looked better and more business-like that way).

'This is a great occasion, Tommy,' said the white mouse as we officially declared the edition (one copy) off the press. 'The first volume printed in the mouse code! We are making history as well as books.'

Chapter Ten
THE NEW LEARNING

AS the white mouse had prophesied, the new education was taken up with great enthusiasm by all classes of rat and mouse society. The famous and truly rare first book from the press of Stubbins & Stubbins did not survive to be handed down to posterity. It was torn to shreds in the first week by the zealous public, who thronged the Animal Public Library in the Dolittle Zoo.

For the white mouse had insisted that the book be put into the library, and that institution officially opened with great pomp and ceremony. This was an occasion also for another of his favourite celebrations. But the more serious purpose was to attract public attention in Animal Town towards education and reading generally.

But the rats and mice continued to be the most keen to learn for themselves. There was a mystery about this new art that appealed to their natural inquisitiveness. The others – dogs, badgers, squirrels, foxes and rabbits – were quite content to be read to aloud. And for the first part of its career the Public Library chiefly did duty as a general recreation room where the white mouse read aloud every afternoon to a mixed and motley company.

The demand for books in the mouse code was enormous. The public, curiously enough, seemed to be very keen about poetry — especially comic poetry. The institution of the Public Library and of the Rat and Mouse Club Library (which was established a little later) seemed to encourage this art tremendously. And many rats and mice who had no idea of being poetic heretofore suddenly, with the new education, blossomed forth into verse.

Another thing that greatly encouraged the new zest for education was the mouse magazine which the Doctor established. It was called *Cellar Life*, and was issued on the first of every month. This, too, was a semi-comic periodical, and besides giving the latest news and gossip of the zoo, it contained jokes and funny pictures.

Now, on the mantelpiece of the Doctor's old waiting-room, disused ever since he had given up his practice, a miniature had always stood. It was a tiny portrait painted on ivory of John Dolittle as a young man, and for years it had never been moved from its place between the Empire clock and a Dresden china shepherdess. But one day the miniature disappeared and no one could account for it. The Doctor asked Dab-Dab, and that good housekeeper said she had seen it the previous day when she had given the waiting-room its weekly dusting, but had no idea at what hour it had disappeared nor what could have become of it.

The Doctor asked Jip, Too-Too, Chee-Chee, Polynesia and me, but none of us could throw any light on the mystery. John Dolittle valued the picture only because his mother had had it painted by a well-known artist the year he had graduated in medicine. However, he had a great many things to keep him occupied, and after a few more inquiries, which met with no better success, he dismissed the matter from his mind.

It was about two weeks after the opening of the Animal Public Library that the white mouse called on the Doctor one evening, when he and I were busy over a new book he was writing on deep-sea plants.

'I have something I would like to speak to you about, Doctor,' said the Mayor of Animal Town, stroking his white whiskers. 'I've come on behalf of the house committee to invite you and Tommy here to our club's Mooniversary Dinner.'

'*Mooniversary!*' the Doctor murmured. 'Er — what does that mean?'

'Yes, it's a new word,' said the white mouse, rather proudly. 'But then all languages have special words, haven't they, which the other languages haven't? So why shouldn't the mouse code have a word or two of its own? It happened this way: the house committee was having a meeting and the Railway Rat — he's one of the members, lived in a railway station, decent fellow, but he smells of kerosene — the Railway Rat got up and proposed that since the club had now been going on successfully for some time we ought to have an anniversary dinner to celebrate.'

'The Railway Rat got up'

'You're always celebrating,' muttered Dab-Dab from the fireside.

'Then,' the white mouse continued, 'the Hansom Cab Mouse – he's another member, lived under the floor of an old cab, knows London like a book – he gets up and he says, "Anniversary means a year. The club hasn't been going for a year. A year's a long time in a mouse's life. I suggest we call it the Club's Mooniversary Dinner, to celebrate our month's birthday, not our year's birthday."

'Well, they argued about it a good deal, but the suggestion was finally accepted – that our celebration banquet should be called the Mooniversary Dinner. Then the Church Mouse – he's another member, lived in a church, awful poor, fed on candle wax mostly, kind of religious type, always wants us to sing hymns instead of comic songs – he gets up and he says, "I would like to suggest to the committee that the Mooniversary Dinner would not be complete without the presence of Doctor John Dolittle, through whose untiring efforts" (he rather fancies himself as a speaker, does the Church Mouse – I suppose he's heard an awful lot of sermons) – "through whose untiring efforts," says he, "for the welfare of rat and mouse society this club first came into being. I propose we invite the Doctor to the Mooniversary Dinner – also that strange lad called Thomas Stubbins, who has made a very good assistant manager to the Dolittle Zoo."

'That motion was carried, too, without any question. And they chose me to come and present the club's invitation. The dinner's tomorrow night,

Doctor. You won't have to change or anything.
Wear just whatever clothes you happen to have
on. But say you'll come.'

'Why, of course,' said John Dolittle, 'I shall be
delighted — and I'm sure Stubbins will, too.'

Chapter Eleven
THE RAT AND MOUSE CLUB

WITHOUT doubt the Rat and Mouse Club was the only building of its kind in the world. At the beginning the clubhouse had been no more than two and a half feet high; but as the list of members had been enlarged, first from fifty to three hundred, and then from three hundred to five thousand, it became necessary to enlarge the premises considerably.

At the time when the Doctor and I were invited to attend the Mooniversary Dinner the building was about the height of a person and just about as broad – and as long – as it was high. The architecture was very unusual. In shape the clubhouse was rather like a large bee-hive, with a great number of tiny doors. It was fourteen stories high. The upper floors were reached by outside staircases, in the manner of Italian houses. In the centre of the building, inside, there was a large chamber called The Assembly Room which ran the entire height of the structure from ground-floor to roof. Ordinarily this was used for concerts, theatricals, and for the general meetings of the club when all the members came together to vote

'The architecture was very unusual'

on some new proposal or to celebrate birthdays or occasions of importance. The whole thing was thus a sort of thick hollow dome, in the shell of which were the living-rooms, furnished apartments, private dining-saloons, committee-rooms, etc.

The entrances were all, of course, very small — just big enough for a rat to pass through. But for this special occasion the white mouse had got the badgers to dig a tunnel down under the foundations through which the Doctor and I could reach the Assembly Room inside.

When we arrived at the mouth of this tunnel we found the white mouse and a regular committee on hand to greet us. Moreover, every doorway, all the way up the building, was thronged with rat and mouse faces waiting to witness the great man's arrival. After the white mouse, as president of the club, had made a short speech of welcome, we began the descent of the tunnel.

'Be careful how you go, Doctor,' I said. 'If we bump the top of the tunnel with our backs we're liable to throw the whole building over.'

Without mishap we reached the Assembly Room, where there was just about space enough for the two of us to stand upright, very close together. The white mouse said he wanted to show the Doctor over the clubhouse. But of course as none of the rooms, except the one in which we were standing, was big enough for a man to get into, being 'shown over' the building consisted of standing where he was and peering through the tiny holes called doors. Some of the rooms were along passages, and one could not see them direct from the Assembly Room. But to provide for this the

white mouse had got me to bring the Doctor's
dentist's mirror, so he could poke it down the
passages and see into the rooms around the corners, the same as he would look at the back of a
person's tooth.

John Dolittle was tremendously interested in
examining the tiny rooms which these highly
civilized rats and mice had designed, set out and
furnished for themselves. For this building with
all it contained was (excepting the few things
which I and Bumpo had done for them) entirely
their own work. The Chief Mouse Architect — he
was also the stonemason — was on hand and he
took great pride in pointing out to the distinguished visitor the whys and the wherefores of all
the details of design.

While the Doctor was poking round among the
passages and holes with his tooth-mirror he suddenly got quite excited.

'Why, Stubbins,' he cried, 'come and look here. I
don't know whether I'm dreaming or not. But isn't
that a human face I see down there? Look in the
mirror. It reminds me of myself.'

I looked into the mirror. Then I laughed.

'No wonder it reminds you of yourself, Doctor,' I
said. 'It *is* yourself. That's the missing miniature
of John Dolittle as a young man.'

At this moment I heard the white mouse, who
had left us for a moment, scolding the architect in
whispers behind the Doctor's back.

'Didn't I tell you,' said he furiously, 'to miss the
Committee Room and show the Doctor the Ladies'
Lounge instead? — Blockhead! Now we'll lose our
best painting.'

' "Didn't I tell you?" said he furiously'

'But how did the miniature get here?' asked John Dolittle.

'Well,' said the white mouse, 'we didn't exactly steal it, Doctor. It was the Prison Rat's idea – he's one of the members, has always lived in jails, sort of an unscrupulous customer, but has a great sense of humour and knows no end of interesting stories, crime stories. Well, as I was saying, it was his idea. We were having a meeting about the layout of the new Committee Room and how it should be furnished and decorated. You see, although it's small, it is in a way the most important room in the club. All the big decisions are made there. And someone got up and said we ought to have a picture on the wall over the president's chair. Then the Church Mouse arose and said, "Brethren," says he, "I think we should have a motto there, some message of good counsel, like, *Love One Another*'." "Well, I don't," said the Prison Rat, short like. "We can love one another all we want without boasting about it or writing it up on the wall." Then the Railway Rat gets up and says, "No, we ought to have a picture there. We don't want any sloppy mottoes. We want something cheerful. Let's put up one of the comic pictures out of *Cellar Life*." At that the Prison Rat gets up again and says, "I believe in being lighthearted, but I think a comic picture is hardly the thing – not – er – dignified enough for our Committee Room. What we ought to have is a portrait of the founder of our club, Doctor John Dolittle – and I know where I can get one, the right size to fit that place." So the motion was carried – and so was the picture, by the Prison Rat who went up to your house that very night and – er – borrowed it off the mantelpiece in your waiting-room. Will you want to take it away again, Doctor?'

'No, I don't suppose so,' said John Dolittle, smiling. 'It looks very well where it is. And it is quite a compliment that you want to keep it there. I will gladly present it to the club, provided you will take care of it. But you had better not let Dab-Dab know.'

'You may be sure we won't,' said the white mouse. 'And now, Doctor, if you and Tommy will take your seats I will call in the members who are all waiting for the signal to assemble. We had to keep the hall clear till you got seated because, as you will see for yourself, there isn't very much room.'

Thereupon the Doctor and I sort of folded ourselves up and sat down in the cramped space to this strangest banquet table that ever was laid. Our chairs were empty biscuit-tins borrowed from the Home for Cross-Bred Dogs. The table was egg-shaped, about three feet across and five feet long. The dishes, tiny little messes of cheese, nuts, dried fish, fried bread-crumbs, apple-seeds, the kernels of prune-stones, etc. were all gathered in the centre of the table, leaving a large outside ring clear for the diners to sit on. For in Mousetown one always sat, or stood, on the table at meal-times, even in the best society.

As soon as we were seated the white mouse gave a signal somewhere and then a very curious thing happened: hundreds and thousands of rats and mice suddenly poured out of holes all around us, squeaking and squealing with glee.

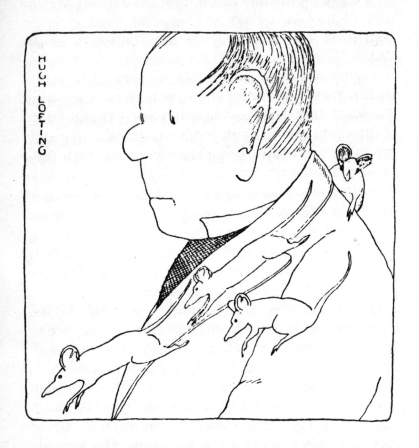

'Ran around the Doctor's collar and down on to
the table'

'You must excuse them, Doctor,' whispered the president, as a dozen rats ran around John Dolittle's collar and down his sleeve on to the table. 'Their manners are not usually so atrocious. I expected a rush for the places nearest to you – it is a great honour for them, you know, they want to boast that they sat beside you – that's why I kept them out till you were seated. Every single member of the club bought a ticket for the dinner – five thousand, you see, as well as some extra guests from out of town. So you mustn't mind a little crowding.'

Chapter Twelve
THE MOONIVERSARY DINNER

THE Mooniversary Dinner was a very great success. Of course neither the Doctor nor I could say afterwards that we had dined heartily. There were a vast number of dishes, it was true; but the plates were only walnut-shells, and clearly it would need a tremendous number of helpings of that size to make a square meal for a person. The drinks were served in acorn-cups.

However, the banquet was so interesting and unusual in other respects that neither of us noticed very much whether we were hungry or not. To begin with, it was quite a novel sensation to be dining, shut up in a room into which we only just fitted, with five thousand rats and mice. Once we got seated and the scramble for places near the great man was over, the members were very well-behaved. There were two sets of waiters, one on the table and the other off the table. Those on the table carried the dishes from the centre to the diners, who had seated themselves in a ring about twenty deep around the edge. The other lot were kept busy swarming up and down the legs of the table, running between the kitchen and the

'The drinks were served in acorn-cups'

Assembly Room to replenish the supply of such dishes as ran out.

'More apple seeds up!' the head waiter on the table would yell. And a couple of mice down below would hustle off to the kitchen, where the cooks would give them an eggshell full of apple seeds to bring to the table. It was all excellently managed. The kitchen staff was kept very busy; for although a mouse or rat may not eat a great deal at one meal, when you have five thousand diners to feed it means considerable work.

At one of the upper doorways a small mouse orchestra played tunes throughout the dinner. Their instruments were invented by themselves and consisted of drums of different kinds and shapes and harps made by stretching threads across nutshells. One mouse had a straw which he played in the manner of a flute. Their idea of music was rather peculiar and very faint – indeed with the enormous chatter of squeaky conversation going on all around they could hardly be heard at all.

When the last course had been finished the white mouse knocked on the table for silence. Immediately the chorus of conversation died down and several members shooed the waiters who were making a noise clearing away the walnut-shells and acorn-cups. Finally, after the door into the pantry had been stopped up with a banana skin to keep out the clatter of the washing-up, His Honour the Mayor, First President of the Rat and Mouse Club, cleared his throat with a dignified cough and began a very fine after-dinner speech.

I was sorry afterwards that I had never learned

shorthand so that I could have taken down the
white mouse's address word for word; for it was in
its way the most remarkable I have ever listened
to.

He began by telling the Doctor on behalf of the
whole club how glad they were to see him seated
at their board. Then he turned back to the vast
throng of members and sketched out briefly what
John Dolittle had done for mouse civilization and
what it was to be hoped his efforts would lead to in
the future.

'The majority of people,' said he, 'would never
believe it if they were told of the general advance,
organization and culture which this club, through
Doctor John Dolittle, has brought into rat and
mouse society.' (Cries of 'Hear, hear!') 'This is the
first time in history that our great race has been
given a chance to show what it could do.' (The
white mouse pounded the table with his tiny fist
and grew quite earnest and eloquent.) 'What has
our life always been heretofore?' he asked. 'Why,
getting chased, being hunted – flight, conceal-
ment, that was our daily lot. Through the Doctor's
farsightedness the rat and mouse peoples have
here, in Animal Town, been able to think of other
things besides keeping out of the jaws of a cat or
a dog or a trap. And, I ask you, what has been the
result?'

The president paused and for a silent second
twirled his white whiskers, while his spellbound
audience sat breathless, waiting for him to go on.

'Why, this,' he continued, waving his hand
round the lofty walls of the Assembly Room: 'this
great institution called the Rat and Mouse Club;

' "The majority of people," said he'

your education; the education of your children; all
the things which our new civilization has given
us, these are the results which John Dolittle has
brought into rat and mouse society by removing
the constant anxiety of our lives and giving us
comfortable peace and honest freedom in its
place. I, myself, look forward – as, I am sure, you
all do – to the time when rat and mouse civilization shall be at least on a level with that of
humans; to the time when there shall be rat and
mouse cities all over the world, rat and mouse
railway trains, steamship lines, universities, and
grand opera. I propose that we give the Doctor,
who has honoured us with his presence here
tonight, a vote of thanks to express our appreci-
ation of all he has done for the welfare of rats and
mice.'

At the conclusion of the president's speech a
great tumult broke loose. Every single one of the
five thousand members sprang to his feet, cheering and waving, to show that he agreed with the
sentiments of the speaker. And I could see that the
Doctor was quite affected by the extraordinary
demonstration in his honour.

There was a slight pause, during which it
became quite evident that the guest of honour was
expected to make some kind of an address in reply.
So rising with great care lest he wreck his hosts'
clubhouse, John Dolittle made a short speech
which was also received with great applause.

Then followed a considerable number of personal introductions. Of course the Doctor knew
many members of the club personally. But hundreds of rats and mice who had never met him

were now clamouring to be presented to the great
man.

Among those who came forward there were some
very interesting characters. First there were those
whom the white mouse had already spoken of to
the Doctor: the Prison Rat, the Church Mouse, the
Railway Rat and the Hansom Cab Mouse. But
besides these there were many more. They did not
all live permanently at the club. Several used to
drop in there two or three times a week, usually in
the evening, and then go back again to their
regular homes about midnight. And there were
some who came from quite a long way off attracted
by the reputation of this extraordinary establishment, which was now getting to be known all over
the country.

For instance, there was the Museum Mouse,
who had made his home in a natural history
museum up in London and who had travelled all
the way down from the city (the Railway Rat had
put him on a goods train which he knew was coming to a town near Puddleby) just to be present at
this important banquet. He was a funny little
fellow who knew a whole lot about natural history
and what new animals were being stuffed by the
museum professors. John Dolittle was very
interested in the news he brought with him from
the scientific world of London.

Then there was the Zoo Rat who had also come
from London especially for the occasion. He lived
in the Zoological Gardens in Regent's Park, and
boasted that he had often been into the lion's den
– when the lion was asleep – to steal suet. There
was the Tea-house Mouse, the Volcano Rat and

HUGH LOFTING

'The Prison Rat and the Church Mouse'

the Ice-box Mouse (who had very long fur which he
had specially grown from living constantly in cold
temperatures). Then there was the Ship's Rat, the
same old fellow who had warned the Doctor at the
Canary Islands about the rottenness of the ship he
was travelling in. He had now retired permanently from the sea and come to settle down in
Puddleby to club life and a peaceful old age. There
was the Hospital Mouse and the Theatre Mouse
and several more.

Of course, with so many, it was only possible for
the Doctor to talk a few moments to each. But as
the president brought them up and briefly told us
who they were, I realized that an assembly of rats
and mice could be just as interesting, if you knew
about their lives and characters, as any gathering
of distinguished people.

Chapter Thirteen
THE HOTEL RAT

WHEN most of the introductions were over the Doctor surprised me (as he often did) by his remarkable and accurate memory for animal faces. Out of the thousands of rats and mice who were all staring at him in rapt admiration he suddenly pointed to one and whispered to the white mouse:

'Who is that rat over there — the one rubbing the side of his nose with his left paw?'

'That's the Hotel Rat,' said the white mouse. 'Did you want to speak to him?'

But the rat in question had already noticed the Doctor pointing to him and, most proud to be recognized, came forward.

'Your face is very familiar,' said the Doctor. 'I have been wondering where I saw it before.'

'Oh, I'm the rat who was brought to you half dead, you recollect? About four years ago. My two brothers had to wake you up at six in the morning. It was an urgent case. I was quite unconscious.'

'Ah, yes,' said the Doctor. 'Now I remember. And you were taken away again the following morning before I was up. I never got a chance to talk to

' "Your face is very familiar," said the Doctor'

you. How did you come to get so badly smashed up?'

'I was run over,' said the rat, a far-away look of reminiscence coming into his eyes, 'by a perambulator containing two heavy twins. It happened – well, it's a long story.'

'I'd like to hear it,' said the Doctor. 'After dinner is a good time for stories.'

'I would gladly tell it,' said the Hotel Rat, 'if the company has time for it.'

At once a little buzz of pleased expectant excitement ran through the big crowd as everyone settled down to listen in comfort. There is nothing that rats and mice love more than stories, and something told them that this one would likely be interesting.

'It was about five years ago,' the Hotel Rat began, 'that I first started living in hotels. Some rats say they're dangerous places to make your home in. But I don't think, once you get used to them, they are any more unsafe than other places. And I love the changeful life you meet with there, folks coming and going all the time. Well, I and a couple of brothers of mine found a nice old hotel in a country town, not far from here, where the cooking was good, and we determined to settle down there. It had fine rambling big cellars; and there was always lots of food lying around, from the oats in the horses' stables across the yard to the scraps of cheese and bread on the dining-room floor. With us another rat came to live – a very peculiar character. He was not quite – er – respectable, as people call it. None of the ordinary rat colonies would let him live with them. But I happened to save his life from a dog once, and ever after that he followed me round. Leery, he was called. And he had only one eye.

'Leery was a wonderful runner. They said he cheated at the races. But I never quite believed that part of his bad reputation, because with a wind and a lightning speed like his, he didn't have to cheat — he could win everything easily without. Anyway, when he asked me if he could live with us I said to my older brother, "Snop," I said (my brothers' names were Snip and Snop), "I think there's a lot of good in Leery. You know how people are: once a rat gets a bad name they'll believe anything against him and nothing for him. Poor Leery is an outcast. Let's take him in."

' "Well," said Snop, "I suppose it will mean that most of our friends will refuse to know us. And Leery certainly is a tough-looking customer. He's only got one eye, and that's shifty. Still, I don't care about society's opinions. If you want to have him to live with us, Snap" (that was my nickname in the family, Snap), "take him in by all means."

'So Leery became part of our household in the little old country-town hotel. And it was a very good thing for me he did, as you will see later on. Now there was one subject on which Leery and I never agreed. He was quite a philosopher, was Leery. And he always used to say, "Rely on yourself — on your wits. That's my motto." While I, I always pinned my faith to the protection of a good hole. You know there are an awful lot of dangers in a hotel — any number of dogs, two or three cats at least, plenty of traps and rat-poison, and a considerable crowd of people coming and

'Leery, the outcast'

going all the time. The hole I had made for myself (it joined up with those of my brothers, but it only had one door which we all used) was the nicest and snuggest I have ever been in. It was alongside the back of the kitchen chimney and the bricks were always warm from the fire. It was a wonderful place to sleep on winter nights.

' "Well, Leery," I would say, "myself, I always feel safe when I get back to the home hole. I don't care what happens so long as I'm in my own comfortable home."

'Then Leery would screw up his one shifty eye and blink at me.

' "Just because it's familiar to you," he said — "because you know everything in it and love everything there, that doesn't mean it's a safe place, or a protection, at all."

' "Well, I don't know, Leery," said I. "In a way it's like a friend, one who will help defend you."

' "Oh, fiddlesticks!" said he. "You've got to carry your defence with you. A good hole won't save you always. You've got to rely on yourself; that's my motto — rely on your wits."

'Now there were two cats living at the hotel. Mostly they'd snooze before the parlour fire. They got fed twice a day. And of course we hotel rats knew their habits and their daily programme hour by hour. We weren't really afraid of them because they were lazy and overfed. But about once a month they'd decide to go on a rat and mouse hunt together. And they knew where our holes were just as well as we knew what their habits were.

'Well, one day the Devil got into those two cats, and they went on a rat hunt that lasted for three

days. We got word that they were out on the war-
path from one of our scouts – we had scouts on
duty day and night, of course we had to, with all
those dogs and cats and people about. And from
then on we took no chances on being caught too far
from a hole of some sort. But my own policy, as I
told you, had always been to count on reaching my
own hole. I didn't trust any others – not since I
dived into a strange hole one day to get away from
a dog and found a weasel in it who nearly killed
me. However, to go back: late in the afternoon,
returning home, I ran into both the cats at once.
One was standing guard over the hole and the
other made straight for me. I kept my head. I had
been chased lots of times before, but never by two
cats at once. There was no hope of my getting into
my hole, so I turned about and leapt clean through
the open window into the street.'

The Hotel Rat paused a moment to cough
politely behind his paw; while the whole of the
enormous audience, who had experienced the
thrill of similar pursuits themselves, leaned forward in intense expectation.

'I landed,' he said at length, with a grimace of
painful recollection, 'right under the wheels of a
baby-carriage. The rear wheel passed over my
body; and I knew at once that I was pretty badly
hurt. The nursemaid gave a scream – "Ugh! A
rat!" – and fled with the carriage and babies and
all. Then I expected the cats would descend on me
and polish me off right away. I was powerless; my
two back legs wouldn't work at all, and all I could
do was to drag myself along by my front paws at
about the speed of a tortoise.

HUGH LOFTING

'I leapt clean through the open window'

'However, my luck wasn't entirely out. Before the cats had time to spring on me a dog, attracted by the commotion, arrived on the scene at full gallop. He didn't even notice me. But he chased those two cats down the street at forty miles an hour.

'But my plight was bad enough in all conscience. I didn't know what was wrong, only that I was in terrific pain. Inch by inch, expecting to be caught by some enemy any moment, I began to drag myself back towards the window. Luckily it was a sort of cellar window, on a level with the street. If it hadn't been, of course I could never have got through it. It was only about a yard away from the spot where I had been injured, but never shall I forget the long agony of that short journey.

'And all the time I kept saying to myself over and over, "The hole! Once I'm back there I'll be all right. I must reach the home hole before those cats return." '

Chapter Fourteen
LEERY, THE OUTCAST

'**M**ORE dead than alive,' the Hotel Rat went on, 'I did finally reach my home hole, crawled to the bottom of it and collapsed in a faint.

'When I came to, Leery was bending over me.

' "Ah, Snap," said he with tears in his eyes, "this is one place where your philosophy doesn't work."

' "What's the matter with me?" I asked. "What's broken?"

' "Both your hind legs," said he. "We've got to get you to Doctor Dolittle, over to Puddleby. Your home hole is no help to you this time."

'My two brothers were there, Snip and Snop; and the three of them put their heads together to work out a way to get me to the Doctor's. They found an old slipper somewhere which they said would do for a stretcher or a sort of sleigh-ambulance. They were going to put me in it and drag it along the ground.'

'What, not all the way to Puddleby?' cried the Doctor.

'No,' said the Hotel Rat. 'They had done some

HUGH LOFTING

'Leery was bending over me'

scouting outside. All the rats in most of the colonies around had heard about the accident and had helped with their advice and in any other way they could. And a farm wagon had been found loaded with cabbages, standing in an inn yard down the street. It was going to Puddleby first thing in the morning. Their idea was to drag me to the yard in their shoe-ambulance, hide me among the cabbages, and at Puddleby watch their opportunity to get me across to your house.

'Well, everything was in readiness, and they had me tucked up in the ambulance, when Leery comes running back from the mouth of the hole swearing something terrible.

' "We can't go yet," he whispered. "Those horrible cats have come back and they've mounted guard outside the hole. They know well enough we've only got one entrance. I nearly walked right into their paws just now. We're nicely trapped! Give me the open, town or country, any day."

'So, there was nothing to do but to wait. My legs were getting worse and worse all the time and I had an awful high fever. Leery annoyed me by keeping on talking about relying on yourself.

' "This shows you," says he: "What's the good of a fine hole now? We want to get out of it and we can't. You've got to rely on your wits, on yourself. That's my motto."

' "Oh, be quiet!" I cried. "Such a comfort you are to have at a sick-bed! My head feels red-hot. Pour some cold water over it. You'll find a thimbleful over there in the corner."

'But if Leery's bedside manner was not as

cheerful as it might be, still in the end he saved my
life – and nearly lost his own in doing it. The best
part of a day went by and those horrible cats still
kept watch at the mouth of the hole. I was so bad
now that I was only conscious in short spells – and
even then sort of delirious with fever.

'In one of my clear moments, after Leery had
been watching me for a few minutes he turned to
my brothers and said: "There's only one thing to be
done. Those cats may stick on at the mouth of the
hole for another couple of days. Snap can't last
much longer. If we can't get him to the Doctor
soon, it's all up with him. He saved my life once,
did Snap. Now's the time I can pay back the debt
– or try to. I'm going to give those cats a run."

' "What," cried my brothers, "you mean to try
and draw them off?"

' "Just that," said Leery, winking with his one
shifty eye. "I'm the fastest rat in the country. If I
can't do it, no one can. You pull the shoe up to the
mouth of the hole and stand ready. In a little while
it will be late enough so that the streets are nearly
empty. I'll give them a run right round the town.
Get Snap down to that inn-yard. There's a cart full
of cabbage leaves there every morning just about
daylight. If I'm lucky I can keep those two mean
brutes busy till you've had time to get him in
among the cabbages."

' "There are two cats, remember," said my
brothers. "Look out! If you get caught we'll only be
one less to get him to the Doctor's."

'Well, they drew my shoe-ambulance up to
within about three inches of the mouth of the hole.
Then Leery, one-eyed outcast, champion runner

'They drew my shoe-ambulance quietly up'

and faithful friend, went up to the entrance. The light of the street-lamps, coming in through the window, shone down into the hole and lit up his ugly face. You could see, too, the shadows of those beastly cats, waiting – waiting with the patience of the Devil.

'It was indeed a dramatic moment. Leery was a born gambler; I had often seen him bet all he had on any reckless chance, apparently for the fun of the thing. And so, I think, in his own strange way he rather enjoyed this theatrical situation.

'With a little wriggle of his hind quarters he made ready for the leap – the most daring leap of his life.

'Then, *zip!* – he was gone!

'Instantly we heard a scuffle as the two cats wrenched around and started off in pursuit.

'Then for a whole hour Leery played the most dangerous game a rat can play, hide-and-seek with two angry cats, touch-and-go with double death. First he led them down the street at full speed. He had his whole programme mapped out in his own mind, with every stop, trick, and turnabout. There was a little yard behind a house he knew of. In that yard there was a small duck-pond; and in the pond a cardboard box was floating. Leery led the chase into the yard, leapt the pond, using the box as a sort of stepping-stone. The cat who was farthest ahead followed him, but found out too late that the floating box would take a rat's weight but not a cat's. With a gurgle she went down out of sight and was kept busy for the rest of the night getting herself dry. She, for one, had had enough of hunting.

'He leapt across to a clothes-line'

'But the other, realizing that she had a clever quarry to deal with, took no chances. She stuck to Leery like a leech – which was exactly what Leery wanted, so long as he could keep out of her clutches. He would slip into a hole just an inch ahead of her pounce. Then he'd get his breath while she waited, swearing, outside. And just as she was thinking of giving him up as a bad job and coming back to our hole after me, he'd pop out again and give her another run.

'All round the town he went: down into cellars; up on to roofs; along the tops of break-neck walls. He even led her up a tree, where she thought she'd surely get him in the upper branches. But right at the top he took a flying leap across on to a clothes-line – from which he actually jeered at her and dared her to follow.

'In the meantime Snip and Snop were trundling me along the road in my shoe-ambulance. I never had such a dreadful ride. Twice they spilled me into the gutter. At last they reached the inn-yard and somehow got me up into the wagon and stowed me away among the cabbages. As daylight appeared the wagon started on its way. Oh dear, how ill I felt! Luckily that load of cabbages came into Puddleby by the Oxenthorpe Road. They dropped me off the tail of the cart right at the Doctor's door – only just in time to save my life. But without Leery the outcast it could never have been done. One of my brothers, Snip, hustled back at once to the hole and hung about for hours waiting for Leery, worried to death that he might have paid the price of his life to save mine. For both of them realized now that even if Leery was an outcast from rat society, he was a hero just the same. About eight o'clock in the morning he strolled in chewing a straw as though he had spent a pleasant day in the country. . . .

'Well, after all, I suppose he was right: in the end you have to rely on your wits, on yourself.'

Chapter Fifteen
THE VOLCANO RAT

THE adventure related by the Hotel Rat reminded various members of things of interest in their own lives — as is often the case with stories told to a large audience. And as soon as it was ended a buzz of general conversation and comment began.

'You know,' said the Doctor to the white mouse, 'you rats and mice really lead much more thrilling and exciting lives than we humans do.'

'Yes, I suppose that's true,' said the white mouse. 'Almost every one of the members here has had adventures of his own. The Volcano Rat, for instance, has a very unusual story which he told me a week or so ago.'

'I'd like to hear some more of these anecdotes of rat and mouse life,' said the Doctor. 'But I suppose we ought to be getting home now. It's pretty late.'

'Why don't you drop in again some other night — soon?' said the white mouse. 'There's always quite a crowd here in the evenings. I've been thinking it would be nice if you or Tommy would write out a few of these life-stories of the members and make

' "Why don't you drop in again soon?" said
the white mouse'

them into a book for us, a collection. We'd call it, say, "Tales of the Rat and Mouse Club".'

At this suggestion quite a number of rats and mice who had been listening to our conversation joined in with remarks. They were all anxious for the honour of having their own stories included in the club's book of adventures. And before we left that night it was agreed that we should return the following evening to hear the tale of the Volcano Rat.

Considerable excitement and rejoicing were shown when it became known that we had consented to the plan. It was at once arranged that a notice should be put up on the club bulletin-board, in the room called the Lounge, showing which member was chosen to tell his story for each night in the week. And as we carefully rose from our seats and made our difficult way down the tunnel into the open air, we heard rats and mice all round us assuring one another they would be certain to come tomorrow night.

When he arose amid a storm of applause the following evening to address the large audience gathered to hear his story, the Volcano Rat struck me at once by his distinctly foreign appearance. He was the same colour as most rats, neither larger nor smaller; but there was something Continental about him – almost Italian, one might say. He had sparkling eyes and very smooth movements, yet clearly he was no longer young. His manner was a rather curious mixture of gaiety and extreme worldliness.

'Our president,' he began with a graceful bow towards the white mouse, 'was speaking last night

of the high state of civilization to which, through
Doctor John Dolittle and our club, this community
has reached. Tonight I would like to tell you of
another occasion – perhaps the only other occasion in history – when our race rose to great
heights of culture and refinement.

'Many years ago I lived on the side of a volcano.
For all we knew, it was a dead volcano. On its
slopes there were two or three villages and one
town. I knew every inch of the whole mountain
well. Once or twice I had explored the crater at the
top – a great mysterious basin of sponge-like rock,
with enormous cracks in it running way down into
the heart of the earth. In these, if you listened
carefully, you could hear strange rumbling noises
deep, deep down.

'The third occasion when I went up to the crater
I was trying to get away from some farm dogs who
had been following my scent through the
vineyards and olive groves of the lower slopes. I
stayed up there a whole night. The funny noises
sort of worried me; they sounded so exactly like
people groaning and crying. But in the morning I
met an old, old rat who, it seemed, lived there
regularly. He was a nice old chap and we got to
chatting. He took me all round the crater and
showed me the sights – grottoes, steaming
underground lakes and lots of queer things. He
lived in these cracks in the mountain.

'"How do you manage for food?" I asked.

'"Acorns," he replied "There are oak trees a little
way down the slope. And I lay in a good big store
each autumn. And then for water there's a brook
or two. I manage all right."

'On its slopes there were two or three villages'

' "Why, you live like a squirrel!" I said "storing up your nuts for the winter. What made you choose this place for a home?"

' "Well, you see," said he, "truth is, I'm getting old and feeble. Can't run like I used to. Any cat or dog could catch me in the towns. But they never come up here to the crater. Superstitious! They're afraid of the rumbling voices. They believe there are demons here."

'Well, I lived with the old Hermit Rat for two days. It was a nice change after the noisy bustling life of the town. It was a great place just to sit and think, that crater. In the evenings we would squat on the edge of it, looking down at the twinkling lights of the town far, far below — and the sea, a misty horizon in blue-black, far out beyond.

'I asked the old rat if he didn't often get lonely, living up there all alone.

' "Oh, sometimes," said he. "But to make up for the loneliness, I have peace. I could never get that down there."

'Every once in a while, when the rumbling voices coming out of the heart of the mountain got louder, he'd go down a crack and listen. And I asked him what it was he expected to hear. At first he wouldn't tell me and seemed afraid that I might laugh at him or something. But at last he told me.

' "I'm listening for an eruption," says he.

' "What on earth is that?" I asked.

' "That's when a volcano blows up," says he. "This one has been quiet a long time, many years. But I've listened to those voices so long that I can understand 'em. Yes, you needn't laugh," he added, noticing I was beginning to grin. "I tell you

'We would squat on the edge'

I've an idea that I shall know – for certain – when this mountain is going to blow up. The voices will tell me."

'Well, of course I thought he was crazy. And after I had grown tired of the lonely life myself, I bade him goodbye and came back to live in the town.

'It was not long after that that the citizens imported a whole lot of cats of a new kind. Us rats had got too plentiful and the townsfolk had made up their minds to drive us out. Well, they did. These cats were awful hunters. They never stopped; went after us day and night. And as there were thousands of them, life for us became pretty nearly impossible.

'After a good many of our people had been killed some of the leaders of the colonies got together in an old cellar one night to discuss what we should do about it. And after several had made suggestions which weren't worth much, I started thinking of my old friend the hermit and the peaceful life of his crater home. And I suggested to the meeting that I should lead them all up there, where we could live undisturbed by cats or dogs. Some didn't like the idea much. But beggars can't be choosers. And it was finally decided that word should be passed round to all the rats in the town that at dawn the next day I would lead them forth beyond the walls and guide them to a new home.'

Chapter Sixteen
THE VOICES IN THE EARTH

'S O,' the Volcano Rat continued, 'the following day a great departure of rats took place from that town. And the old hermit of the mountain-top had the surprise of his life when from his crow's-nest look-out he saw several thousand of us trailing up the slope to share his loneliness.

'Fortunately the autumn was not yet over and there were still great quantities of acorns lying beneath the oak trees. These we harvested into the many funny little underground chambers with which the walls of the crater were riddled.

'Because I had led them out of danger into this land of safety I came to be looked upon as a sort of leader. Of course after the first excitement of the migration was over a good deal of grumbling began. It seems people always have to grumble. Many young fellows who thought themselves clever made speeches to those willing to listen. They told the crowd that I had led them into as bad a plight as they were in before. Rat and mouse civilization had gone backwards, they said, instead of forwards. Now they were no better than

'A great departure of rats took place'

squirrels living on stored-up acorns. Whereas in the towns, though they may have had the constant dangers that always had to be faced in cities, life at least had some colour and variety; they hadn't got to eat the same food *every* day; and if they wanted to line their nests with silk or felt, they knew where to find it, etcetera, etcetera, and a whole lot more.

'These discontented orators got the common mass so worked up against me that for a time my life was actually in danger from the mob. Finally – though I am a rat of few words – I had to make a speech on my own account in self-defence. I pointed out to the people that the life we were now leading was nothing more nor less than the original life of our forefathers. "After the Flood," I told them, "this was how you lived, the simple outdoor life of the fields. Then when the cities of humans arose with their abominable crowding you were tempted by the easy life of cellars and larders. We rats," I said proudly, "were at the first a hardy race of agriculturists, living by corn and the fruits of the earth. Lured by idleness and ease, we became a miserable lot of crumb-snatchers and cheese-stealers. I gave you the chance to return to your healthy, independent, outdoor life. Now, after you have listened to these wretched cellar-loungers, you long to go back to the sneaking servitude of the dwellings of humans. Go then, you fleas, you parasites!" (I was dreadfully cross.) "But never," I said, "never ask me to lead you again!"

'And yet Fate seemed to plot and conspire to make me a leader of rats. I didn't want to be. I never had any taste or ambition for politics. But no sooner had I ended my speech, even while the cheers and yells of the audience were still ringing in my ears (for I had completely won them over to my side), the old hermit came up behind me and croaked into my ear, "The eruption! The voices in the earth have spoken. Beware! We must fly!"

'Something prompted me to believe him – though even to this day I don't see how he could have known, and I thought I had better act, and act quickly, while I had the crowd on my side.

' "Hark!" I shouted, springing to my feet once more. "This mountain is no longer safe. Its inner fires are about to burst forth. All must leave. Do not wait to take your acorns with you. For there is no time to lose."

'Then like one rat they rose up and shouted, "Lead us and we will follow. We believe in you. You are the leader whom we trust!"

'After that came a scene of the wildest kind. In a few minutes I had to organize a train of thousands of rats and mice and get it down that mountain-side the quickest possible way. Somehow or other I managed it – even though darkness came on before I started them off and the route was precipitous and dangerous. In addition to everything else, I had to make arrangements for six rats to carry the old hermit, who couldn't walk fast enough to keep up with the rest.

'So, through the night, past the walls of the town – the town which had turned us out – we hurried on and on and on, down, down into the valley. Even there, tired though we all were, I would not let them halt for long, but hurried the train on after a few moments' rest across the valley, over the wide river by a stone bridge and up the slopes of another range of hills twenty miles away from the spot we had started from. And even as I wearily shouted the command to halt, the volcano-top opened with a roar and sent a funnel of red fire and flying rocks hurtling into the black night sky.

'Never have I seen anything as terrifying as the anger of that death-spitting mountain. A sea of red-hot stones and molten mud flowed down the slopes, destroying all in its path. Even where we stood and watched, twenty miles away across the valley, a light shower of ashes and dust fell around us.

'The next day the fire had ceased and only a feather of smoke rising from the summit remained. But the villages were no more; the town, the town that had turned us out, could not be seen.

'Well, we settled down to country life and for some years lived in peace. My position as leader, whether I willed it or no, seemed more than ever confirmed now that I had led the people out of further dangers.

'And so time passed and the Second Migration was declared a great success. But presently, as always seemed to be the way, I foresaw that before long we would have to move again. Our trouble this time was weasels. Suddenly, they cropped up in great numbers all over the countryside and made war on rats, mice, rabbits, and every living thing. I began to wonder where I would lead the people this time. Often I had looked across the valley at our old mountain, our old home. The hermit had told me that he was sure that the

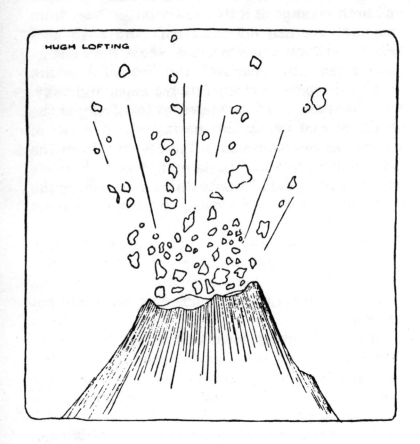

'The volcano opened with a roar'

volcano would not speak again for fifty years. He had been right once: he probably would be again. One day I made up my mind to go back across the valley and take a look around. Alone I set off.

'Dear me, how desolate! The beautiful slopes that had been covered with vineyards, olive groves and fig trees were now grey wastes of ashes, shadeless and hot in the glaring sun. Wearily I walked up the mountain till I came to about the place where I reckoned the town had stood. I began wondering what the buildings looked like underneath. I hunted around and finally found a hole in the lava; through it I made my way downward. Everything of course, after all these years, was quite cold; and to get out of the sun into the shade beneath the surface of the ground was in itself a pleasure. I started off to do some subterranean exploring.

'Down and down I burrowed. In some places it was easy and in some places it was hard. But finally I got through all that covering of ashes and lava crust and came into the town beneath.

'I almost wept as I ran all over it. I knew every inch of the streets, every stone in the buildings. Nothing had changed. The dead city stood beneath the ground, silent and at peace, but in all else just as it had been when the rain of fire had blotted it out from the living world.

' "So!" I said aloud, "here I will bring the people – back to the town that turned us out. At last we have a city of our own!" '

Chapter Seventeen
THE UNITED RAT STATES REPUBLIC

THE white mouse, seeing that the Volcano Rat seemed a little hoarse, motioned to a club waiter to fetch water – which was promptly done.

With a nod of thanks to the chairman the Volcano Rat took a sip from the acorn-cup and then proceeded.

'On my return I called the people together and told them that the time had come for our Third Migration. Many, when they found out whither I meant to lead them, grumbled as usual – this time that I was taking them back to the place from which we had already once taken flight.

' "Wait!" I said. "You complained years ago that I had set your civilization back, that I had reduced you to the level of squirrels. Well, now I'm going to give you a chance to advance your civilization to a point it never dreamed of before. Have patience."

'So, once more under the protection of darkness, I led the people across the valley and up the slopes of the sleeping mountain. When I had shown them where to dig, holes were made by the hundred, and through them we entered into possession of our subterranean town.

'It took us about a month to get the place in working order. Tons of ashes had to be removed from doorways, a great deal of cleaning up was needed, and many other things required attention. But it would take me more than a month to tell you in detail of the wonderful Rat City we made of it in the end. All the things which humans had used were now ours. We slept in feather beds. We had a marble swimming pool, built originally by the Romans, to bathe in. We had barbers' shops furnished with every imaginable perfume, pomade and hair-oil. Fashionable rat ladies went to the manicure establishments and beauty-parlours at least twice a week. And well-groomed dandies promenaded of an evening up and down the main street. We had athletic clubs where wrestling, swimming, boxing and jumping contests were held. All the best homes were filled with costly works of art. And an atmosphere of education and culture was everywhere noticeable.

'Of course much of the food which was in the town when the catastrophe happened had since decayed and become worthless. But there were great quantities of things that were not perishable, like corn, raisins, dried beans, and what not. These at the beginning were taken over by me and the Town Council as city property; and for the first month every rat who wanted an ounce of corn had to work for it. In that way we got a tremendous lot of things done for the public good, such as cleaning up the streets, repairing the houses, carrying away rotting refuse, etc.

**'Fashionable rat ladies went to the manicure
establishments'**

'But perhaps the most interesting part of our new city life was the development of professions and government. In our snug town beneath the earth we were never disturbed by enemies of any kind, except occasional sickness; and we grew and flourished. At the end of our first year of occupation a census was taken, and it showed our population as ten and three-quarter millions. So you see we were one of the largest cities in history. For such an enormous colony a proper system of government became very necessary. Quite early we decided to give up the municipal plan and formed ourselves into a city republic with departments and a Chamber of Deputies. Still later, when we outgrew that arrangement, we reorganized and called ourselves The United Rat States Republic. I had the honour of being elected the first Premier of the Union Parliament.

'After a while, of course, rats from outside colonies got to hear of our wonderful city, and tourists were to be seen on our streets almost any day in the week looking at the sights. But we were very particular about whom we took in as citizens. If you wanted citizenship you had to pass quite serious examinations both for education and for health. We were especially exacting on health. Our Medical College – which turned out exceptionally good rat doctors – had decided that most of our catching diseases had been brought in first by foreigners. So after a while a law was passed that not even tourists and sightseers could be admitted to the town without going through a careful medical examination. This, with the exceptionally good feeding conditions, the

'A popular interest in sports and athletics'

freedom of the life and the popular interest in sports and athletics, made the standard of physical development very high. I don't suppose that at any time in the whole history of our race have there been bigger or finer rats than the stalwart sons of the United Rat States Republic. Why, I've seen young fellows in our high-school athletic teams as big as rabbits and twice as strong.

'Building and architecture were brought to a very fine level, too. In order to keep the lava and ashes from falling in on us we constructed in many places regular roofs over the streets and squares. Some rats will always love a hole, even if you give them a palace to live in. And many of us clung to this form of dwelling still.

'One morning I was being measured for a new hole by a well-known digging contractor when my second valet rushed in excitedly waving the curling-irons with which he used to curl my whiskers.

'"Sir," he cried, "the Chief of the Street Cleaning Department is downstairs and wants to be admitted at once. Some men have come. They are digging into the mountain-side above our heads. The roof over the Market Square is falling in and the people are in a panic!"

'I hurried at once with the Chief of the Street Cleaning Department to the Market Square. There I found all in the greatest confusion. Men with pick-axes and shovels were knocking in the roof of lava and ashes which hid our city from the world. The moment I saw them I knew it was the end. Humans had returned to reclaim the lost town and restore it to its former glory.

'Some of our people thought at first that the new-comers might only dig for a little while and then go away again. But not I. And sure enough, the following day still more men came and put up temporary houses and tents and went on digging and digging. Many of our hot-headed young fellows were for declaring war. A volunteer army, calling itself *The Sons of Rat Freedom*, three million strong, raised itself at the street-corners overnight. A committee of officers from this army came to me the third day and pointed out that with such vast numbers they could easily drive these few men off. But I said to them:

' "No. The town, before it was ours, belonged to humans. You might drive them off for a while; but they would come back stronger than ever, with cats and dogs and ferrets and poison; and in the end we would be vanquished and destroyed. No. Once more we must migrate, my people, and find ourselves new homes."

'I felt terribly sad, as you can easily imagine. While I was making my way back through the wrecked streets to my home, I saw some of the men preparing to take away a statue of myself carved by one of our most famous rat sculptors. It had been set up over a fountain by the grateful townsfolk to commemorate what I had done for them. On the base was written, *"The Saviour of His People – The Greatest of All Leaders"*. The men were peering at the writing, trying to decipher it. I suppose that later they put the statue into one of their museums as a Roman relic or something. It was a good work of art – even if the rat sculptor did make my stomach too large.

'The men were peering at the writing'

Anyhow, as I watched them I determined that I would be a leader of rats no more. I had, as it were, reached the top rung of the ladder; I had brought the people to a higher pitch of civilization than they had ever seen before. And now I would let someone else lead them. The Fourth Migration would be made without me.

'Sneaking quietly into my home I gathered a few things together in a cambric handkerchief. Then I slipped out and by unfrequented back streets made my way down the mountain-side — suddenly transformed from a Prime Minister of the biggest government, the greatest empire our race had ever seen, into a tramp-rat, a lonely vagabond.'

Chapter Eighteen
THE MUSEUM MOUSE

AS the Volcano Rat ended his story there followed a queer little silence. That final picture of the great leader leaving the wonderful civilization he had built up and journeying forth alone rather saddened the audience. John Dolittle was the first to speak.

'But what became of the rest of your people?' he asked.

'I did not hear until much later,' the Volcano Rat replied. 'I took to the sea. I boarded a ship in the first harbour I came to and sailed away for foreign shores. A year or more afterwards I learned from some rats I met — when I was changing ships to come here — that several of the young wild volunteers had succeeded in getting the people to go to war. The results had been just about what I had prophesied. In the first battle between humans and rats, the rats had easily won and driven the enemy from the mountain-side. But a week later the humans came back armed with shot-guns, smoke-pots, and other engines of war; and in their train came cats and dogs and ferrets. The slaughter of rats was apparently just horrible.

'I boarded a ship'

Millions were wiped out. Panic seized the rest and
a general mad flight followed. The slopes were
simply grey with rats as the whole population left
the underground city and ran for the valley. There
were far too many for the dogs and cats to kill and
so quite a few reached safety; but they were widely
scattered. And no attempt was made to reorganize
the remnant of a great race under another government. The United Rat States Republic was no
more.'

The white mouse now arose from the presidential
chair and after thanking the Volcano Rat for his
story reminded the members that tomorrow night,
Tuesday the fifteenth, the Museum Mouse had
promised to entertain them. The meeting was
then declared adjourned and everyone went
home.

The next evening, in spite of the fact that both
the Doctor and I were very busy, we were in our
places in the Assembly Room by eight o'clock
because we did not want to miss the adventures of
the Museum Mouse. We knew him to be quite a
personality. He had already interested us considerably by his observations on natural history.
He looked something like a little old professor
himself. He had tiny beady black eyes and a funny
screwed-up look to his sharp-nosed face. His
manner was cut and dried.

'I've lived all my life in natural history
museums,' he began. 'Main reason why I like them
is because when they're closed to the public you
have the place to yourself — from six in the evening to ten o'clock the next morning, and till two in

the afternoon on Sundays. This story is mainly
concerned with the nest of the Three-ringed Yah-
yah, a strange East Indian bird who builds a
peculiar home; and Professor Jeremiah
Foozlebugg, one of the silliest animal-stuffers I
ever knew.

'Why, just to show you how stupid that professor
was: one day he was putting together the skeleton
of a prehistoric beast, the Five-toed Pinkidoodle –'

'The *what?*' cried the Doctor, sitting up.

'Well, I was never good on names,' said the
Museum Mouse. 'It was a five-toed something.
Anyway, while he was out of the room a moment
his dog dragged in an old ham-bone and left it
among the parts of the skeleton. And would you
believe it? Jeremiah Foozlebugg spent days and
nights trying to fit that ham-bone into the
skeleton of the five-toed – er – thingimajigg and
wondering why there was one bone left over.

'Now, when I was first married I took my wife for
a wedding trip to the Natural History Museum.
And after I had shown her all over it she thought
she'd like to settle down there. And we began to
look about to decide where in the building we
would make our home.

' "It must be a snug, warm place, Nutmeg," says
she, "on the children's account. It's a risky
business raising young mice where there are
draughts and cold winds."

' "All right, Sarsparilla," I said. "I know the very
spot. Come with me."

'Now, what we called the Stuffing Room was a
long workshop downstairs where Foozlebugg and
his assistants stuffed birds and animals and

'Professor Jeremiah Foozlebugg'

prepared specimens of plants and butterflies and things to be brought up later and put in the glass cases for the public to look at. All natural history museums have more collections and specimens presented to them than they can possibly use. And our Stuffing Room was always littered up with everything from elephants' tusks to fleas in bottles. Among all this junk there was a collection of birds' nests – many of them with the limb of the tree in which they had been built. For months and months this collection had lain upon a dusty shelf – nests of all sizes, shapes and sorts. One was quite peculiar. It was the nest of the Three-ringed Yah-yah. In form it was quite round, like a ball, and had for entrance one little hole – just big enough for a mouse to slip through. When you were inside no one would know you were there.

'I showed it to Sarsparilla and she was delighted. Without further delay we got some extra scraps of silk, which Foozlebugg had been using for some of his stuffing business, and lined it soft and snug – although it was already well padded with horsehair and thistledown by the Three-ringed Yah-yah who had built it. Then for several days we led a peaceful and happy life in our new home. During regular hours in the workshop we lay low and often had hard work stopping our giggles as we watched Professor Foozlebugg stuffing animals all out of shape and calling on his assistants to admire them.

'Well, the children came and then we were very glad about our selection of a home. For no place could have been more ideal for baby mice than was that old bird's nest with its round walls and draught-proof ceiling and floor. Now, there is one disadvantage in living in museums: you have to go out for all your meals. There's practically nothing to eat in the building, and what there is, like waxes and things of that sort, you soon learn to leave strictly alone, because those old professors use strong poisons on all their stuffing materials to keep the moths from getting into them. Of course even with all the doors locked any mouse can find his way in and out of a building somewhere. But occasionally, when the weather is bad, it is very inconvenient to have to go out for every single thing you eat. And now with a family of youngsters to feed this problem became more serious than usual.

'So Sarsparilla and I used to take it in turns to look after the youngsters while the other went out foraging for food. Sometimes we had to go a long way and to bring crumbs from various places to the lobby of the building before we hauled them down to the Stuffing Room. Well, one night I had been up very late foraging for food and didn't get in until nearly daylight. I was dog-tired, but even then I didn't get any sleep because the children were querulous and fretful and they kept me awake. As soon as evening came Sarsparilla left me in charge and started out on her food hunt. Shortly after she had gone the children settled down quietly, and right away, worn out with fatigue, I fell into a deep sleep.

'When I awoke the sunlight was streaming in through the entrance-hole of our nest. I supposed I must have long over-slept. But I never remembered the direct rays of the sun to have

'I peeped out cautiously'

shone in at our door like this before. I got up and peeped out cautiously.

'I could hardly believe my eyes. *Our nest was no longer in the Stuffing Room!* Instead, we were in a glass case in one of the main halls of the museum. Around us, on various twigs and stands and things, were the other nests of the old collection which had lain so long on the dusty shelf. Our house had been put on show for the public, shut up tight in a glass case; and that stupid old duffer Foozlebugg who had put it there was still standing outside, displaying his handiwork with great pride to a fat woman and two children who were visiting the museum!'

Chapter Nineteen
PROFESSOR FOOZLEBUGG'S MASTERPIECE

'WELL,' sighed the Museum Mouse, 'you can imagine how I felt. There I was with a whole family of youngsters, shut up in a glass case. I dared not show myself outside the nest, hardly, because, even when that ridiculous Professor Foozlebugg had moved away with the fat woman, odd visitors in ones and twos were always browsing by and looking in. It would be difficult to think of a more uncomfortable unprivate home than ours had become.

'However, there were moments when that end of the hall was free from visitors and attendants. And during one of these I suddenly saw Sarsparilla with a wild look in her eye frantically hunting about outside for her lost family. Standing at the door of the nest, I waved and made signs to her and finally caught her attention. She rushed up to the glass and called through it:

' "Get the children out of there, Nutmeg. Get them out at once!"

'That was the last straw.

' "Sarsparilla," I called back, "don't be a fool. Do you think I brought the nest and the children here

'Visitors were always browsing by'

myself? How am I to get them out! I can't bite through glass."

' "But they must be fed!" she wailed. "It is long past their morning meal-time."

' "Bother their morning meal-time!" said I. "What about my morning meal-time? They'll have to wait. We can't do anything till the museum closes to the public — at five o'clock. You had better get away from there before you are seen."

'But Sarsparilla just kept running up and down outside the glass, moaning and wringing her hands.

' "Can't you give them some of that stuffed duck there, on the shelf above your head?" she moaned.

' "I could *not*," I said. "Stuffed museum duck is full of arsenic. Don't worry. They can manage until five — the same as me."

'Sarsparilla would have gone on arguing all day, I believe, if an attendant hadn't come strolling down to that end of the wing and made it necessary for her to hide.

'The rest of the day I had my hands full. For the children, having missed two meals, suddenly got as lively as crickets. They were all for climbing out of the nest — though they hadn't had their eyes open more than a few days. I could have slapped them.

' "Where's Ma?" they kept on saying. "What's happened to Ma? I'm hungry. Where's Ma? Let's go and find her."

'I tell you they had me busy, dragging them down from the hole one after another. *They* didn't care how many people were looking in the glass cage. All that they cared about was that they were hungry and wanted Ma – the stupid little things!

'Never was I so glad in all my experience of museum routine to see the attendants clearing the people out of the halls and locking up the doors. I knew all those old fellows in uniform well. It was a funny life they led – generally pleasant enough. One of the things they had to do was to look out for bomb-throwers. Why people should want to throw bombs or set infernal machines in museums, of all places, I don't know. But they do – or, at all events, it is always expected that they will. That's why the attendants won't allow visitors to bring in parcels: they are afraid they may contain dynamite.

'One of these old men regularly brought his lunch with him and ate it behind the stuffed elephant when nobody was looking – he wasn't supposed to, you see. And the few crumbs he left upon the floor were the only food that I ever managed to get *in*side the museum. As he changed his coat this evening some crusts fell out of the paper in which his bread and cheese had been wrapped. I knew that if I didn't get them that night the charwoman would sweep them up in the morning. But while I was still gazing at them hungrily out of my glass prison Sarsparilla came and collected them and brought them over to the case.

' "Nutmeg, I want to get these in to the children," she said.

' "Oh, for Heaven's sake, have some sense!" I snapped back. "The first thing we've got to do is to find a way in – or rather a way out."

' "I knew the old fellow well" '

' "Gnaw a hole through the floor," said she – "quite simple. You needn't be afraid of anyone seeing you now. The night watchman won't be stirring for another hour yet."

' "Don't you know," I said wearily, "that all these cases are zinc-lined? I can't bite through zinc any more than I can through glass."

'That started her off again. She threw up her hands.

' "Why, the children will starve to death!" she cried. And she recommenced her running backwards and forwards like a crazy thing.

'I saw I wasn't going to get any helpful ideas from her, so I began to look over the situation myself with an eye to working something out. First, I climbed all around the whole case, carefully inspecting the joints in the walls, the floor and the roof, to see if I could find a weak spot anywhere. Then I examined each shelf in turn to see if by chance I might come upon anything that could help me. And finally on the top shelf I discovered something that suggested a plan of escape.

'It was this: among the collection of birds' nests there were some of sea-birds. These were set among stones, just as certain gulls and such build – just a rough hollow of twigs and seaweed laid on the shingle of the beach. Here Professor Foozlebugg had quite surpassed himself in the art of tastefully displaying specimens. He had the whole top shelf set out like a scene on a lonely island where sea-birds would build. At the back there was a picture of the sea painted, with lighthouses and sailing ships and everything. And

'There were nests of sea-birds'

in front of this there were several stuffed birds and
nests set among the stones of the beach. The
stones were mostly round, of all sizes. And it occurred to me that I might very easily roll some of the
larger ones off the top shelf. Then, if they struck
something slanting when they reached the bottom
of the case, they would fly against the glass wall
and break it.

'I wasted no time in getting to work. It was
necessary to prepare a bouncing place where the
stone would fall if my plan was to be a success. I
slid down to the bottom of the case and gathered
together a large pile of stiff twigs which I took
from the other nests. It was hard work, because
most birds put their nests together pretty firmly.
I made a frightful mess of the collection before I
was done.

'In the meantime, not being able to keep the
children in order while I was at work, I had let
them follow their own sweet wills. Every one of
the little beggars had got out of the nest; and now
having seen "Ma" outside the case, they too were
running up and down alongside the glass and
careering all over the place trying to find a way
out. If Professor Foozlebugg had come in at that
moment to inspect his latest work of art he would
have had a great shock.

'Well, when all was ready I went down below and
chased all the children up on to the upper shelves
so they wouldn't get hurt by falling stones or
flying glass. Then I explained to Sarsparilla, in
shouts, what I was going to do.

' "Stand by," I yelled, "to get the youngsters to a
place of safety. They're not easy to handle."

' "All right," she called back. "I'll take three and you take three. And for pity's sake be careful how you get them through the hole in the broken glass."

'Then, just as I was about to put my shoulder under the round stone and topple it down, there came another shout from my wife:

' "Look out! Night watchman coming! Hide the children, quick!"

'It was all very well for Sarsparilla to say, "Hide the children, quick!" They had no intention of being hidden. They had seen "Ma" and they meant to get to her as soon as possible. And as soon as she disappeared again they went entirely crazy, rushing all over the place crying, "Where's Ma gone? We're hungry. What's become of Ma?"

'Oh dear! I never had such a time! I had no sooner caught a couple of them and hidden them behind a stuffed bird or something, before they would pop out again while I was running after the next pair.

'Luckily the night watchman was not a very wide-awake old man at the best of times, and as it happened tonight he did not swing his lantern near our case.

'When he had gone Sarsparilla appeared again outside the glass and I got ready to try my plan once more.

'*Crash!*

'It worked all right and no mistake. The stone knocked a hole in the front of the case big enough for a bulldog to get through. In fact everything would have gone splendidly if it hadn't been for those half-witted children of mine. With the

'I got ready to try my plan again'

crashing of the glass they just ran about like
lunatics and we couldn't catch a single one of
them. We had time to get away easily. But while
we were still falling all over the place trying to get
the family together, alarm bells in every corridor
of the museum started ringing violently. The next
thing, the night watchman came running through
the hall shouting:

' "A bomb, a bomb! Hey! Help! Fire! Police! A
bomb's gone off somewhere! HELP!"

' "It's no use, Sarsparilla," I said. "We can't
manage it now. Bring in one of those crusts of
bread with you and come inside until the excitement dies down. Was anyone ever blessed with
such children? Help me get them into the nest,
quick! With you here, they'll be quieter and more
manageable. Later, if luck is still with us, we may
get away."

'And we only just got those little nuisances
stowed out of sight in time. In less than five
minutes from the crash of the glass people began
running in. First came a policeman with a
notebook from the beat outside the museum's
main entrance; then six firemen came rushing in
dragging a hose; next, the watchman's wife carrying bandages and a bottle of brandy.

'And all of them stood around the broken glass
case asking about the "bomb". Yes, the watchman
was quite sure it was a bomb. Look how it had
wrecked all the nests inside!

'Then they gave their opinions, one after
another: "Russian nihilists"; "suffragettes"; "East
End anarchists," etc, etc. While all the time we,
who were responsible for the whole thing, sat

inside the home of the Three-ringed Yah-yah and listened to their silly chatter.

'Finally the great Professor Foozlebugg arrived on the scene, summoned from his bed – for it was now nearly midnight – by a messenger from the watchman. He nearly wept when he saw his latest work of art – his masterpiece – knocked all to pieces. He was much more upset about his beautiful scene on the seashore than he was over the museum's narrow escape from being blown up by an infernal machine. He was about to wade into the wreckage then and there and put it to rights, but – fortunately for us – one of the policemen warned him off.

' "Don't touch it, sir, please. With these infernal machines, one never knows. A second, and more serious, explosion, sir, is liable to follow the moment you lay a finger on it. We will get the bomb experts from Police Headquarters. They know how to handle these things, sir."

'Well, just that saved us from a pretty serious situation. After a little more discussion between the firemen and the constable it was decided to let well alone until the morning – when the bomb experts from Police Headquarters would take charge of affairs. Meanwhile the policeman, the firemen and the professor felt they might as well go back to bed. As for the old watchman, he was so scared of that second explosion that the policeman had spoken of, that the moment the rest of them had departed he locked up the doors and left that hall severely to itself.

'Which, of course, was exactly what we wanted. We had seven peaceful hours before us – before

'The great Professor Foozlebugg arrived'

the charwoman would come to sweep – in which to do our moving. The first thing we did, after we had all the children safely lifted out through the broken glass, was to sit down in the middle of the hall and eat a hearty meal off the crusts which the old attendant had left behind. Then we herded the children down below by easy stages to the Stuffing Room. And there Sarsparilla kept them together while I hunted up a new home among the lumber and stuff with which the shelves were littered.

'But this time, you may be sure, I did *not* pick a bird's nest, nor anything else that was likely to get put on exhibition while we slept.'

Chapter Twenty
THE STABLE MOUSE

MY book, entitled *Tales of The Rat and Mouse Club*, was by now beginning to look somewhat thick and bulky. Of course rewritten, or rather printed, as it would be in the bound volume itself, it would not take up as much space as it did in my rough copy. Nevertheless I could see that only about one more story could be included in the book. I told this to the white mouse.

'Well,' said he, 'of course I see that you can't make the book too thick, otherwise it would be too heavy for the mouse readers to handle — and the rats have most of the volumes in the club library as it is. But there will be a terrible lot of disappointment. There are no less than nine members still hoping that their stories will be included — and I thought myself that you'd be able to get in another two, anyway.'

'Who are the members whose stories are still to be heard?' asked the Doctor.

'Oh, heavens, there's hundreds — hoping!' said the white mouse. 'But there are nine whom I had sort of half promised they would stand a chance. Out of that nine we shall now have to pick one —

HUGH LOFTING

' "There's hundreds – hoping," said the
white mouse'

and of course there will be hard feelings. I tell you what I'll do: I'll get them all to give me a rough outline of their stories and I'll pick the one which I think is the best and relate it at the club tomorrow night, eh?'

'All right,' said the Doctor. 'And you can tell the others that maybe there will be a second volume of *The Tales of the Rat and Mouse Club* – later – which they can all be in.'

To our surprise, when the Doctor and I took our places in the Assembly Room of the Rat and Mouse Club the following evening, we found that none of the nine whom the President had spoken of last night had been selected to tell the last story for the book. Instead, a mouse whom neither of us had seen or heard of before got up and was introduced as the Stable Mouse.

'Her story was rather different, I thought,' the white mouse whispered in my ear. 'We want variety in the book. And those others were all jealous of one another. So I decided I'd take a new member altogether.'

The Stable Mouse was a quiet, lady-like little individual – rather shy. And at the beginning she had to be asked several times to speak louder, because some of the members at the back of the hall (a few of the old-age pensioners who lived in the club) could not hear her.

'This story is mostly about my first husband, Corky,' she began, 'a good-natured mouse, but the most frivolous-minded mate that anybody was ever asked to live with. It was largely on Corky's account that I became a stable mouse – thinking it was a safer place for him, one where he would be

less likely to get into mischief and hot water.
Stables are generally very good places for mice to
live. There are always oats, which after all form
the most nourishing and digestible food that can
be found anywhere. And it is pleasant in the evenings when the horses come home from their work
to sit up in the rafters and listen to them gossip
about the day's doings.

'But even in a stable that husband of mine could
find plenty of occasions to get himself into trouble
and to keep me worried to death. One day he found
a large watering hose in a corner of the stable. And
he thought it would be great fun to get into it and
run up and down inside, as though it were a tunnel
– sort of switchback idea. He was a regular child
– I see that now: he never really grew up. Well,
while he was playing this game, sliding and
whooping round the loops of the hose, one of the
stable-boys came and turned the water on to wash
the stable floor. And of course, with the terrific
force of the water, my husband was shot out of the
hose like a bullet from a gun. His switchback gave
him a much bigger ride than he expected. As it
happened, the stable-boy had the hose pointed out
into the yard when the water first rushed forth.
And I suddenly saw Corky, gasping and half-
drowned, flying over the pig-house roof. He landed
in the pigs' trough on the other side – and very
nearly got eaten by a large hog who mistook him
for a floating turnip before he scrambled out to
safety.

'Often I used to think that that light-headed
husband of mine used to deliberately get himself
into hot water – just for sheer devilment. And no

'He was shot out like a bullet from a gun'

amount of hard lessons seemed to teach him any sense. How it was that he wasn't killed in the first year of his life I don't know.

'Would you believe it? Time after time he used to get into the horses' nose-bags to steal their oats while they were actually eating! I told him often that one of these days he would get chewed up. What usually happened was that his moving around in the bags would tickle the horses' noses until they sneezed and blew him out on to the floor like a piece of chaff.

'One day this happened when the farmer who owned the place was standing in the stable with his wife. But this time the horse sneezed so hard that Corky was shot right up, nearly to the rafters. And when he came down he landed on the farmer's hat. The farmer thought it was just a drop of water leaking from the roof – it was raining at the time – and didn't take any notice. But presently, while his wife was talking to him, she suddenly saw Corky's nose peering over the brim of her husband's hat – wondering how he was going to get down to solid ground. Being, like many people, terrified of mice, she just lost her head, screamed and struck at Corky with her umbrella. She didn't hit him, but she nearly brained her husband – who, of course, thought that she had suddenly gone crazy. And in the general excitement that followed Corky, as usual, got away.

'But one day he had a very narrow escape, and if I hadn't been there to come to his assistance it would certainly have been the end of his adventurous career. Now, there was an old jackdaw who used to hang about that stable-yard. Corky took a

dislike to him from the start. And I am bound to
say that he certainly was a churlish, grouchy cur-
mudgeon of a bird. He used to watch from the
stable roof, and if the farmer's wife threw out any
nice titbits of food he would be down on them
before we ever got a chance to start out for them.
If we did get there first he would drive us off
savagely with that great scissors-like bill of his. It
didn't matter how much food there was, he
wouldn't let us get any. The largest rats were
scared of him, for he was worse than a game-cock
to fight with. Even the cat wouldn't face him. She
would try to pounce on him when his back was
turned, but she would never face a duel with that
terrible bill.

'The result was that Mr Jackdaw – Lucifer we
called him – got to be the boss of the roost round
that stable-yard. He knew it, too. And everybody
hated him.

'Well, one day Corky came to me just brimming
over with news and excitement.

' "What *do* you think?" says he. "You know that
new stable-lad, the cross-eyed one with red hair?
Well, he's making a trap to catch Lucifer. I saw
him myself."

' "Oh," I said, "don't get excited over that. He'll
never catch him. That bird knows every kind of
trap that was ever invented."

'Nevertheless Corky was very hopeful. And he
used to spend hours and days watching that red-
headed lad trying to bag Mr Jackdaw. First the
boy used a sieve and a string, baiting the arrangement with raw meat. But Lucifer gave that clumsy
contrivance one glance and never even looked at it

'He would drive us off savagely'

again. Next the lad rigged up various sorts of nets
into which he hoped the bird would fly or could be
driven. Corky kept running to me with reports,
two or three times a day, to keep me posted on how
things were going. Then horsehair nooses were
tried — and paper bags with raisins and treacle
inside.

'But, as I had told Corky, Lucifer was a wily bird
and he seemed to know just as much about traps
as the boy did. What was more, he soon got on to
the fact that Corky was watching the proceedings
with great interest. Because one morning he
chased him away from some soup-meat on the
garbage heap, saying,

' "Hoping to see me get trapped, eh? You little imp!
Get out of that before I nip the tail off you!"

' "You may get caught yet, you big black bully,"
Corky threw back at him as he ran for a hole. "And
I hope you do!"

' "Oh, hah, hah!" croaked the jackdaw as he set
to on the meat. "That red-haired bumpkin couldn't
catch me if he tried for a lifetime."

'But the red-haired bumpkin was a persevering
lad and not so stupid as he looked. He had made up
his mind that he was going to have that jackdaw
in a cage for a pet. And after a good many failures,
instead of giving up, he set to work observing the
quarry and his habits and trying to find just why
it was that he hadn't caught him. And among
other things he noticed that the jackdaw had one
favourite drinking place, a little pool under a tap
in a corner of the stable-yard. Also he noticed that
the bird never flew down to settle where anything
new had been set up or anything old taken away.

'He used a sieve and a string'

'In other words, the stable-lad had stumbled upon the truth that birds, like mice, are afraid of anything unfamiliar. That's their great protection. They've a keen sense of observation; and whenever a yard or a corner of a garden has anything new or changed about it, they are at once suspicious and on their guard.

'So, having learned this, the bumpkin went about his job differently. He saw that whatever was changed, whatever he put out to catch the jackdaw must be changed or put out gradually. He began by laying a twig down near the watering-place – just one. Lucifer, when he came, eyed it suspiciously. But finally he decided it was innocent, walked around it and took his drink. The next morning the boy had two twigs there. Lucifer behaved in the same way. Three mornings later there were four or five twigs there. And so on, until a regular little bank of twigs surrounded the tiny pool beneath the tap; and the jackdaw couldn't get at the water without stepping on them.

'But at this point Mr Lucifer became very wary. He walked all around the twigs several times and finally flew away. He had gone to find another drinking-place.

'Corky came to me in despair.

' "You are right," he said dolefully. "That bird is related to the Devil, I do believe. I'm afraid he'll never be caught."

'But suddenly the weather came to the assistance of our red-headed trapper. It was late November; and one morning we woke up to find the ground and everything covered with a white

'Lucifer eyed it suspiciously'

mantle of snow and every puddle, pool and stream topped with ice. Mr Jackdaw came into the stable-yard looking for breakfast – as usual. There wasn't any. Everything was covered, cold and silent. He looked in at the stable door. There he saw us, nibbling oats on the top of the bin. He would have come in, only he was afraid.

' "You vermin," he sneered from the door, "are well off, guzzling in shelter, dry and warm, while honest folk can starve outdoors, with every blade of grass buried in the snow. A pest on the weather!"

' "We would throw you some oats," said I, "if you hadn't always been such a mean, selfish grouch to us, driving us from every titbit even when there was enough for all. Yes, you're right: it *is* bad weather – for folks who've gone through life making no friends." '

Chapter Twenty-one

THE CUNNING OF LUCIFER, THE JACKDAW

AT this point some of the old pensioners at the back of the hall made another request that the Stable Mouse should speak a little louder. John Dolittle suggested that she should be given a tea-canister or something to stand on, so that her voice would carry to the rear of the Assembly Room. After a short delay an empty mustard tin was found, which served the purpose very well. And as soon as she had climbed up on to it and overcome her embarrassment the speaker continued:

'The jackdaw made some vulgar remark in answer to what I had said and hopped away from the door. We got on to the windowsill and watched him flopping across the yard through the deep, loose, fluffy snow. I felt sort of sorry for him. I could see he was hungry; and in that weather he might not find a scrap to eat in a whole day. I was about to call him back and give him some oats, but Corky wouldn't let me.

'"Don't worry," said he. "He'll take care of himself. Serve him right, the mean bully!"

'As he passed his old drinking-place the jackdaw

'Flopping through the deep fluffy snow'

just glanced at it, expecting to find it frozen like all the other water out of doors. But behold! It wasn't. As a matter of fact the red-haired lad had specially come and broken the ice even before Mr Jackdaw was abroad.

'Lucifer was just as thirsty as he was hungry. He floundered, half flying through the snow, towards the tap. Corky got dreadfully excited as he watched him. We both guessed that those twigs were some sort of trap – though how they worked neither of us knew as yet. This morning they were half covered with snow and looked like a regular innocent part of the landscape. The water was very tempting. Lucifer hopped nearer. And Corky got even more worked up.

'Finally Mr Jackdaw jumped up on to the mound of twigs and took a long, long drink. Corky was disappointed. Nothing seemed to happen. It looked as though whatever machinery the twigs contained had failed to go off. And it was only when the bird started to leave the drinking-place that we realized what the trap was. The mound he was standing on stuck to his feet. The twigs had been covered with birdlime.

'Dear me, how he floundered and flopped and fluttered! And the more he fought and pulled and worked, the more the sticky twigs got gummed up with his feathers. We could see now that there were a whole lot of them beneath the snow; and by the time that the jackdaw had them all stuck to him it was quite clear that for the present he stood no chance whatever of flying or getting away.

'Then suddenly a door opened across the yard and the red-haired lad triumphantly came forth

and took possession of the helpless Mr Lucifer.
Whereupon Corky proceeded to do somersaults of
joy all over the stable.

'Well, you can be sure there was general rejoicing throughout the stables and the farm-yard. For
not only had Lucifer made himself objectionable to
us, but he was thoroughly unpopular with every
living thing in the whole neighbourhood.

'The lad put him in a wicker cage whose bars
were reinforced with wire; and he put the cage —
of all places — on a windowsill in our stable. I am
bound to say that once more I felt sorry for the
bird. It was bad enough to be caught and
imprisoned; but then to be put where other
creatures, of whom he had made enemies, could
look at him all day while they rejoiced in their
freedom, did seem to me a bit too much.

'And, oh, what a state he was in, poor wretch!
The birdlime had made all his sleek plumage
messy, so that he looked like some old silk hat
brought in off the dust-heap. And for the first day
he did nothing but bang his head against the bars
trying to get out, so that he rubbed all the feathers
off the top of his head and looked worse than ever.

'Corky, the heartless little imp, had a grand time
sitting outside his cage and laughing at him. He
had had to run away from Lucifer so often when he
was free, he was determined to make up for it now
that he had a chance. I thought this was mean and
I told Corky so.

' "Besides," I said, "I'm still scared of him — even
now."

' "Oh," said Corky, laughing, "What can he do,
the big bully? He's caught now for good."

HUGH LOFTING

'Corky sat outside the cage and laughed at him'

' "Just the same," I said, "be careful. He's clever, don't forget."

'All day long the jackdaw never said a word, not even in answer to Corky's most spiteful remarks. There was something dignified, as well as pathetic, in his downfall. He had now given up beating himself against the bars and just sat there, all huddled up at the bottom of his cage, the picture of despair. The only thing about him that seemed alive at all was his gleaming eyes full of bitter hatred. They looked like coals of fire as they followed every movement of Corky and the other mice who were taunting him outside the cage.

'It is curious how heartless some creatures can be. After Lucifer had subsided like that, those little monkeys, Corky and his friends, got up on top of the cage and started dropping bits of mortar and putty down on the jackdaw's head. I tried my best to stop them, but there were too many of them and they wouldn't listen to me. Before long there must have been a good dozen gathered on top of the cage laughing and throwing things at their old enemy, the one-time bully of the stable-yard. Truly Lucifer was paying a terrible price for a selfish life.

'And, alas! my fears proved right. That terrible bird was still dangerous, even when he was shut up in a cage. While those little fools were playing their heartless game one afternoon I was cleaning up our home under the hay-loft floor. Suddenly I heard a dreadful shriek. I rushed out of the hole and bounded down through a trap door into the stable below.

'Corky's friends were all standing around the

jackdaw's cage on the windowsill, their eyes popping out of their heads with horror. I looked for Corky among them. He wasn't there. On coming nearer I found that he was *inside* the cage firmly held in the jackdaw's right claw! As usual, he had been more daring than the rest. And as he had crawled over the cage he had come just a fraction of an inch too near the bird he was teasing. Like a flash – he told me this afterwards – Lucifer had thrust his long beak between the bars, caught him by the tail and pulled him inside. When I came up Corky was still bawling blue murder at the top of his voice.

' "Be quiet!" said the jackdaw. "Stop struggling or I'll kill you right away. Where's his wife?" he asked, turning to the others.

' "Here I am," said I, stepping up to the cage.

' "Good!" said he "You are just in time to save your husband's life. I want a hole gnawed through the bottom of this cage right away – one big enough for me to get out of. Mice can eat through wood. I can't. There is room for you to get under – the legs of the cage are high enough. But please waste no time. That lad is likely to come back any moment."

' "But," I began, "it would take . . ."

' "Don't argue!" said he shortly. "If a hole isn't made in the bottom of this cage large enough for me to escape through before nightfall, I'll bite your husband's head off."

'Well, I could see he meant it. And the only thing for me to do was to obey – unless I wanted to be left a widow. Luckily, the other mice were still standing around. I knew I could never nibble a

'Lucifer caught him by the tail and pulled him
inside'

hole alone, in so short a time, big enough for that great hulk to pass through. And, scared to death as Corky's brave friends were, I finally persuaded them to help me.

'With the jackdaw still firmly clutching him Corky watched us as we slipped under the floor of the cage and set to work.

'It wasn't easy. And if my husband's life hadn't depended on it I doubt very much whether it would have been done in time. The main difficulty was in getting started. As you all know — but perhaps the Doctor and Tommy do not — to begin biting a hole in the middle of a flat board is, even for a mouse, an almost impossible task. To chew off a corner, or to widen an old hole that has been already begun, that's different.

'However, I was desperate; and somehow — my teeth were sore for weeks afterwards — I got four holes started in the bottom of that cage, one in each corner, in the first quarter of an hour. Then I got eight other mice, two to each hole, to continue the work. As soon as one mouse's jaws got tired I took him off the job and put a fresh mouse on. I even went down into the foundations of the stables and gathered together all the mice I could find. Corky had always been popular with the neighbourhood; and as soon as they heard that his life was in danger they were willing enough to assist. In this way I had continuous relays of fresh help at work.

'Before very long we had those four holes very nearly joined up. There was only a little strip of wood scarcely wider than a pencil keeping the bottom of that cage from falling right out, whole.

'The jackdaw still clutched his wretched victim'

'The old jackdaw, still clutching his wretched victim, watched the work with an eagle eye. His plan was, as soon as the bottom fell, to turn the cage over on its side. This he could easily do directly he got his feet on the windowsill, because the cage wasn't very heavy.

'Well, we only just finished in time – in time for Corky, that is. Because I'm certain that if we had been interrupted before we had it done the jackdaw would have killed him. As the bottom of the cage clattered out Lucifer let go his victim at last, and with one twist of his powerful bill, not only threw the cage on its side, but hurled it right down to the stable floor – with Corky inside it.

'At that moment the lad came in and saw his precious pet standing, free, on the windowsill. He leapt to grab him. But Lucifer, with one curving swoop, skimmed neatly over his head and out through the stable door into the wide world; while all around the bewildered lad the mice, who had freed the bird whom they hated worse than poison, scuttled and scattered to safety.'

Chapter Twenty-two
MOORSDEN MANOR

AT this point, before anyone was quite certain whether the Stable Mouse had finished her story or not, some sort of a commotion started at the back of the hall. There was a great deal of excited whispering and we could see that some new arrival had just turned up in a very breathless state. He seemed to be demanding to speak to the Doctor at once.

The white mouse, as president and chairman of the meeting, started for the back of the hall to see what all the excitement was about. But the newcomer was apparently in much too great a hurry to stand on ceremony, and before the white mouse had more than got out of his seat he could be seen elbowing his way through the crowd making for John Dolittle.

'Doctor,' he cried, 'there's a fire over at Moorsden Manor. It's in the cellar. And everybody's asleep and no one knows anything about it.'

'Good gracious!' cried the Doctor, rising and looking at his watch. 'Asleep! Is it as late as that? Why, so it is. Nearly an hour past midnight. What's in the cellar — wood, coal?'

'The chairman started for the back of the hall'

'It's chock full of wood,' said the mouse. 'But the fire hasn't got to it yet — thank goodness! My nest, with five babies in it, is right in the middle of the wood pile. The wife thought the best thing I could do would be to come and tell you. Nobody else understands our language, anyway. She's staying with the children. The fire started in a heap of old sacks lying in a corner of the cellar. The place is full of smoke already. There is no chance of our carrying the babies out because there are too many cats about. Once the fire reaches the wood it's all up with us. Won't you come — quickly, Doctor?'

'Of course I will,' said John Dolittle. He was already scrabbling his way out through the tunnel, nearly wrecking the Rat and Mouse Club on the way. 'Stubbins,' he called as he reached the top, 'go and wake Bumpo — and send Jip along to Matthew's house. We'd better get all the help we can. If the blaze hasn't gone too far we can probably get it under control all right. Here's a note that Jip can give to Matthew, for the fire brigade — but it always takes them an eternity to get on the scene.'

He hastily scribbled a few words on an old envelope, with which I dashed off in one direction, while he disappeared in another.

For the next fifteen minutes I was occupied in getting Jip and then Bumpo aroused and informed of the situation. Bumpo was always the slowest man in the world to wake up. But after a good deal of hard work I managed to get him interested in clothes — and fires. Jip, I had already sent trotting down the Oxenthorpe Road with his note to fetch Matthew to the scene.

Then I clutched Bumpo (still only half dressed and half awake) firmly by the hand and hurried off after the Doctor in the direction of the fire.

Now Moorsden Manor was the largest and most pretentious private residence in Puddleby. Like the Doctor's home, it was on the outskirts of the town and was surrounded by a large tract of its own land. Its present owner, Mr Sidney Throgmorton, was a middle-aged man who had only recently come into the property. His millionaire father had died the year before, leaving him this and several other handsome estates in different parts of England and Scotland. And many people had expressed surprise that he remained at the Manor all the year round when he had so many other castles and fine properties to go to.

The main gates to the estate were guarded by a lodge. And when I arrived I found the Doctor hammering on the door trying to wake up the lodge-keeper. The gates, of course, were locked; and the whole of the grounds were enclosed by a wall which was much too high to climb over.

Almost at the same moment that Bumpo and I got there, Matthew Mugg, led by Jip, also arrived.

'Good gracious!' the Doctor was saying as he thumped the door with his fist. 'What sleepers! The whole place could burn down while we're standing here. Can it be that the lodge is empty?'

'No,' said Matthew. 'The keeper's here – or his wife. One of them is always on duty. That I know. I'll throw a stone against the window.'

It was only a small pebble that he threw, but the

cats'-meat-man put such force behind it that it
went right through the pane with a crash.

Indignant shouts from inside told us that at last
we had succeeded in arousing someone. And a few
moments later a man in a nightshirt, with a
shotgun in one hand and a candle in the other,
appeared at the door. As the Doctor stepped forward he quickly set the candle down and raised
the gun as if to shoot.

'It's all right,' said John Dolittle. 'I've only come
to warn you. There's a fire up at the Manor – in
the cellar. The people must be roused at once. Let
me through, please.'

'I will not let you through,' said the man stub-
bornly. 'I heard tell of hold-up gangs playing that
game afore. The cheek of you, coming breaking
into my windows this time of night! And how do
you come to know what's going on up at the
Manor?'

'A mouse told me about it,' said the Doctor. Then
seeing the look of disbelief coming over the man's
face, he added:

'Oh, don't argue with me! I *know* there's a fire
there. Won't you please let us in?'

But the man had apparently no intention
whatever of doing so. And I cannot say that he
should be altogether blamed for that. For with
Bumpo and Matthew we certainly must have
seemed a queer delegation to call in the middle of
the night.

Goodness only knows how long we would have
stood there while the fire in the Manor cellar went
on growing, if Matthew hadn't decided to deal with
the situation in his own peculiar way. With a

'A man in a nightshirt appeared at the door'

whispered word to Bumpo he suddenly ducked
forward and wrenched the shotgun out of the
lodge-keeper's hands. Bumpo grabbed the candle
that stood beside the door. And the fort was in our
possession.

'Come on, Doctor,' said the cats'-meat-man.
'There's another door through here which leads
into the grounds. We can't wait to talk things over
with him. Maybe when the brigade comes along in
an hour or so he will believe that there really is a
fire.'

Bumpo had already found and opened the second
door. And before the astonished keeper had had
time to get his breath we were all through it
and running up the drive that led to the big
house.

'I suppose it will take us another age to get
anyone awake here,' gasped the Doctor, as we
arrived breathless before the imposing portico and
gazed up at the high double doors.

'No, it won't,' said Matthew. And he let off the
lodge-keeper's shotgun at the stars and started
yelling 'Fire!' at the top of his voice. This din the
Doctor, Bumpo and I added to by hammering on
the panels and calling loudly for admittance.

But we did not have long to wait this time. The
shotgun was a good alarm. Almost immediately
lights appeared in various parts of the house.
Next, several windows were thrown open and
heads popped out demanding to know what was
the matter.

'There's a fire,' the Doctor kept shouting. 'A fire
in your house! Open the doors and let us in.'

A few minutes later the heavy bolts were shot

'Let off the gun, yelling *"Fire!"* '

210 DOCTOR DOLITTLE'S ZOO

back and an old manservant with a candle opened the door.

'I can't find the master,' he said to the Doctor. 'He isn't in his room. He must have fallen asleep in some other part of the house. All the rest have been woken up. But I can't find the master.'

'Where's the cellar?' asked the Doctor, taking the candle and hurrying by him. 'Show me the way to the cellar.'

'But the master wouldn't be in the cellar, sir,' said the old man. 'What do you want in the cellar?'

'A family of mice,' said the Doctor, 'young ones. They're in great danger. Their nest is in the wood-pile. Show me the way, quickly!'

Chapter Twenty-three
THE FIRE

I THINK that, for both the Doctor and myself, that was one of the most extraordinary nights we ever experienced. John Dolittle, as everyone knows, had for a long time now taken no part whatever in the neighbourhood's human affairs. Ever since he had given up his practice as an ordinary doctor and come to be looked upon as a crank naturalist, he had accepted the reputation and retired from all social life. While he was pleasant and kind to everyone, he avoided his neighbours even more than they avoided him.

And now suddenly, through this alarm of fire brought by the mouse from the Manor cellar, he found himself pitchforked by Fate, as it were, into a whole chain of happenings and concerns which he would have given a great deal to stay out of.

When Matthew, Bumpo and I followed him into the hall of the great house we found things in a pretty wild state of confusion. In various stages of dress and undress people were running up and down stairs, dragging trunks, throwing valuables over the banisters and generally behaving like a hen-roost in a panic. The smell of smoke was

'People were throwing valuables over the banisters'

strong and pungent; and when more candles had
been lit I could see that the hall was partly filled
with it.

There was no need for the Doctor now to ask the
way to the cellar. Over to the left of the hall there
was a door leading downward by an old-fashioned
winding stair. And through it the smoke was pouring upwards at a terrible rate.

To my horror, the Doctor tied a handkerchief
about his face, dashed through this doorway and
disappeared into the screen of smoke before
anyone had time to stop him. Seeing that Bumpo
and I had it in our minds to follow, Matthew held
out his hand.

'Don't. You'd be more trouble than help to him,'
he said. 'If you were overcome, the Doctor would
have to fetch you up too. Let's get outside and
break the cellar windows. It must be full of smoke
down there – more smoke than fire, most likely.
If we can let some of it out, maybe the Doctor can
see what he's doing.'

With that all three of us ran for the front door.
On the way we bumped into the old manservant,
who was still wandering aimlessly around, wringing his hands and wailing that he couldn't find 'the
master'. Matthew grabbed him and shoved him
along ahead of us into the front garden.

'Now,' said he, 'where are the cellar windows?
Quick, lead us to 'em!'

Well, finally we got the poor old doddering
butler to take us to the back of the house where,
on either side of the kitchen door, there were two
areas with cellar windows in them. To his great
astonishment and horror we promptly proceeded

to kick the glass out of them. Heavy choking
smoke immediately belched forth into our faces.

'Hulloa there! Doctor!' gasped Matthew. 'Are
you all right?'

The cats'-meat-man had brought a bull's-eye
lantern with him. He shone it down into the reeking blackness of the cellar. For a few moments,
which seemed eternally long, I was in an agony of
suspense waiting for the answering shout that
didn't come. Matthew glanced upwards over his
shoulder.

'Humph!' he grunted with a frown. 'Looks as
though we'll have to organize a rescue party by the
stair.'

But just as he was about to step up out of the
area I clutched him by the arm.

'Look!' I said, pointing downwards.

And there in the beam of his lantern a hand
could be seen coming through the reeking hole in
the broken window. It was the Doctor's hand. And
in the hollow of the half-open palm five pink and
hairless baby mice were nestling.

'Well, for the love of Methuselah!' muttered
Matthew, taking the family and passing them up
to me.

The Doctor's hand withdrew and almost immediately reappeared again, this time with the
thoroughly frightened mother-mouse – whom I
also pocketed.

But Matthew didn't wait for the Doctor's hand
to go back for anything else. He grabbed it by
the wrist and with a mighty heave pulled John
Dolittle, with the window-sash and all, up into the
area. We saw at once that he was staggering and

HUGH LOFTING

'We stretched him out flat and undid his collar'

in pretty bad condition, and we half dragged, half lifted him out away from the choking smoke, to a lawn near by. Here we stretched him out flat and undid his collar.

But before we had time to do anything else for him he began to struggle to his feet.

'I'm all right,' he gasped. 'It was only the smoke. We must get a bucket chain started. The fire has just reached the wood pile. If it's allowed to get a good hold the whole place will burn down.'

There is not the least doubt that that mouse who brought the news of the fire to the Doctor saved Moorsden Manor from total destruction — and possibly several lives as well. Certainly if it had not been for our efforts the place would never have been saved by those living there, even if they had been awakened in time. I never saw such an hysterical crew in my life. Everybody gave advice and nobody did anything. And the head of the servants, the old white-haired butler, continued to dodder around getting in everyone's way, still asking if the master had been seen yet.

However, without waiting for assistance from anyone else, the Doctor, Matthew, Bumpo and I formed a bucket line on our own, and by it we conveyed from the kitchen sink a continuous supply of water to those burning sacks and firewood. And before very long nothing remained of what had promised to be a very serious conflagration but a charred and hissing mass.

In addition to this Matthew discovered a tap in the garden, and with the help of a hose which we got out of the stable we brought another stream into the cellar through the broken window, which

'He accosted the Doctor in a distinctly unfriendly
manner'

could be kept in constant readiness if the fire
should break out again.

While we were attaching the hose in the garden
a man suddenly appeared out of a shrubbery and
accosted the Doctor in a distinctly unfriendly
manner.

'Who are you?'

'I?' said the Doctor, a little taken aback. 'I'm
John Dolittle. Er – and you?'

'My name is Sidney Throgmorton,' said the man.
'And I would like to know what you mean by
breaking into my lodge at this hour of night,
smashing windows and assaulting the keeper.'

'Why, good gracious!' said the Doctor. 'We
wanted to warn you about the fire. We hadn't time
to stand on ceremony. The keeper wouldn't let us
in. As it was, we only just got here in time. I think
I can assure you that if we *hadn't* got here the
house would have been burned to the ground.'

I now saw in the gloom behind the man's
shoulder that the lodge-keeper was with him.

'You have acted in a very high-handed manner,
sir,' said Sidney Throgmorton. 'My lodge-keeper
has his orders as to whom he shall, and whom he
shall not, admit. And there is a fire department in
the town whose business it is to look after con-
flagrations. For you to thrust your way into my
home in this violent and unwarrantable manner,
in the middle of the night, is nothing short of a
scandal, sir – for which I have a good mind to have
you arrested. I will ask you and your friends to
leave my premises at once.'

Chapter Twenty-four
THE LEATHER BOXES

FOR a moment or two the Doctor was clearly about to reply. I could see by the dim light of Matthew's lantern the anger and mortification struggling in his face. But finally he seemed to feel that to a man of this nature no words of explanation or justice would mean anything.

And certainly this Throgmorton person was an extraordinary individual. From his speech he seemed fairly well educated. But the whole of his bloated, red-faced appearance was as vulgar and as unprepossessing as it could be.

'My coat is in your cellar,' said the Doctor quietly at last. 'I will get it. Then we will go.'

To add insult to injury, the man actually followed us down into the cellar, as though we might steal something if we were not watched. Here lamps were still burning which we had lit to help us in making sure that there were no sparks of fire left that might smoulder up again. The man muttered some expression of annoyance beneath his breath when he saw the water which flooded the floor.

At this last show of ingratitude for what we had

done, Bumpo could contain his indignation no
longer.

'Why, you discourteous and worm-like boor!' he
began, advancing upon Throgmorton with battle
in his eye.

'*Please!* Bumpo!' the Doctor interrupted. 'No
further words are necessary. We will go.'

By the brighter light of the lamps I now saw that
Throgmorton carried beneath his arm several
small leather boxes. In climbing up over the wood
pile, in order to see what damage we might have
done on the other side, he laid these down for a
moment on top of a wine cask. I was close to
Matthew. In the fraction of a second, while
Throgmorton's back was turned, I saw the cats'-
meat-man open the upper one of the boxes, glance
into it and shut it again.

The box contained four enormous diamond shirt-
studs.

As soon as he had his coat the Doctor wasted no
further time, but made his way, with us following
him, up the stairs and out of the house which he
had saved from destruction.

The keeper accompanied us to the lodge and let
us out. Matthew, like Bumpo, was just burning to
speak his mind even to this representative of the
establishment which had shown us such
discourtesy. But the Doctor seemed determined
that there should be no further controversy and
checked him every time he tried to open his
mouth.

However, at the gate we met the fire brigade
coming to the rescue. This was too much for
Matthew's self-control, and he called to them as we

**'The box contained four enormous diamond
shirt-studs'**

stepped out on to the road: 'Oh, turn around and go back to bed! We put that fire out before you'd got your boots on.'

Outside the boundaries of the Moorsden Manor estate not even the Doctor could stay the tide of Matthew's and Bumpo's indignant eloquence.

'Well, of all the good-for-nothing, mangy, low-down ingrates,' the cats'-meat-man began, 'that stuffed pillow of a millionaire takes the prize! After all we've done for him! Getting up out of our beds, working like hosses — all to keep his bloomin' mansion from burning down. And then he tells us we've ruined his cellar by pouring water into it!'

'Such a creature,' said Bumpo, 'would make anyone feel positively rebellious. In Oxford he would not be allowed, under any circumstances, to proceed farther with his obnoxious existence. It was only with the greatest difficulty that I restrained myself from hitting him on the bono publico.'

'Enough,' said the Doctor. 'Please don't say any more. I am trying to forget it. The whole affair is just one of those incidents which it is no use think-ing about or getting yourself worked up over afterwards. I'm often very grateful that life has made it possible for me to keep away from my neighbours and mind my own business. This occa-sion couldn't be helped — but it has made me more grateful still. Thank goodness, anyway, that we got the mice out all right before the fire reached them. You have them safely in your pocket, Stubbins, have you not?'

'Yes,' said I, putting my hand in to make sure.

'He kept muttering to himself'

'Oh, but, Doctor, your hat? Where is it? You've left it behind.'

John Dolittle raised his hand to his bare head.

'Dear me!' said he. 'What a nuisance! Well, I'll have to go back, that's all.'

I knew how he hated to. But the well-beloved headgear was too precious. In silence all four of us turned about.

The gate was still open from the arrival of the fire brigade. Unchallenged, we walked in and down the drive towards the house.

Half-way along the avenue the Doctor paused.

'Perhaps it would be as well,' said he, 'if you waited for me here. After all, there is no need for four of us to come to fetch a hat.'

He went on alone while we stood in the shadow of the trees. The moon had now risen and we could see more plainly.

I noticed that Matthew was restless and fidgety. He kept muttering to himself and peering after the Doctor down the drive. Presently in a determined whisper he jerked out: 'No. I'm blessed if I let him go alone! I don't trust that Mr Throgmorton. Come on, you chaps. Let's follow the Doctor. Keep low, behind the trees. Don't let yourselves be seen. But I've a notion he may need us.'

I had no idea what was in Matthew's mind. But from experience I knew that usually when he acted on impulse, without rhyme or reason like this, he acted rightly. I always put it down to some mysterious quality he inherited with his gipsy blood.

So like a band of Indian scouts, scuttling from

'Like Indian scouts scuttling from tree to tree'

tree to tree, we shadowed the Doctor up the
avenue drive till he came to the clearing before the
house. Here the fire brigade, with a great deal of
pother and fuss, was in the act of departing – after
its captain had made sure that the fire was really
out. The big door lamps, either side of the portico,
had been lighted and the courtyard was fairly well
illumined. Mr Throgmorton could be seen dismiss-
ing the firemen and their worthy captain. We saw
John Dolittle go up to him, but he pretended to be
too busy to attend to anything but the business of
the fire brigade.

And it was only after the engine and fire-escape
had clattered noisily away, leaving the courtyard
empty save for him and the Doctor, that he
deigned to notice John Dolittle's presence. This
time he did not wait for the Doctor to speak.

'You here again!' he shouted. 'Didn't I tell you to
get off the premises? Clear out of here, or I'll set
the dogs on you.'

'I've come back for my hat,' said the Doctor, con-
trolling himself with truly wonderful restraint.
'It's in the hall.'

'Get out of here!' the other repeated threaten-
ingly. 'I'll have no more of you suspicious
characters messing round my place tonight. I find
you smashed the windows in the cellar as well as
the lodge. Clear out, unless you want the dogs
after you.'

'I will not go,' said the Doctor firmly, 'until I have
my hat.'

('My goodness! But I'd love to give that fellow a
crack on the jaw!' whispered Matthew, who was
standing behind the same tree as myself.)

The Doctor's answer seemed to infuriate Throgmorton beyond all bounds. He drew a whistle from his pocket and blew upon it loudly. An answering shout came from somewhere in the darkness of the gardens.

'Let go Dina and Wolf!' called Throgmorton.

('That's his two man-killing mastiffs,' chuckled Matthew in my ear. 'I know 'em — regular savages. He keeps 'em to defend the place. Now we'll see some fun.')

Chapter Twenty-five
THE WATCH-DOGS

NEXT moment we heard a scraping rush of paws upon the gravel and two gigantic dogs bounded out of the gloom into the lighted courtyard.

'Grab 'im! Go get 'im!' shouted Throgmorton. Together the two dogs hurled themselves towards the figure of the stranger. Then Mr Throgmorton got a great surprise. The stranger did not run or indeed show any panic whatever. But as he turned his face in the direction of the oncoming dogs he made some curious sounds, almost like another kind of growl answering theirs.

At this the two hounds behaved in a most curious manner. Instead of grasping their prey by the throat, they wagged their tails, licked his hand and generally carried on as though he were no stranger at all, but a very old and dear friend of theirs. Then, in response to an order he gave them, they disappeared into the darkness from which they had come.

Beside me, behind the tree, Matthew covered his face with his hand to keep from laughing.

'I will now get my hat,' said the Doctor. And he walked calmly into the house.

'Two gigantic dogs bounded out'

As for Throgmorton, he was just speechless with rage. It had been his proud boast that these two mastiffs, Dina and Wolf, had, between them, killed a burglar who had once attempted to rob the Manor. To be made ridiculous like this by such a quiet small person was more than he could bear.

Within the hall the Doctor could now be seen on his way out – with the precious hat. Throgmorton withdrew into the shadow of a door-column and waited.

'Yes, I thought so!' muttered Matthew. And he slid like a shadow out from behind the tree and crept towards the figure of the waiting Throgmorton.

John Dolittle, unaware of anything beyond the fact that he was anxious to get away from this disagreeable establishment as soon as possible, stepped briskly forth on to the gravel. An enormous weight landed on his shoulders and bore him to the ground.

'I'll teach you,' growled Throgmorton, 'to walk in and out of my house as though you–'

But he got no further, for Matthew had landed on top of him just as he had landed on the Doctor.

But Sidney Throgmorton, in spite of his bloated, unwholesome appearance, was a heavy, powerful man. He rose and threw Matthew off as though he were a fly. And he was just about to aim a kick at the Doctor lying on the ground when he suddenly found himself gripped from behind and lifted off his feet like a doll.

Indeed Bumpo not only lifted him, but was now proceeding to carry his portly victim bodily away towards the building.

'Well!' said the Doctor, rising and brushing his clothes, 'what an offensive person! Who would ever have thought he'd do that! The man must be out of his senses.'

'I'll have you all in jail for this,' grunted Throgmorton, as Bumpo let him fall heavily, like a large sack of potatoes, to the ground.

'If you take my tip,' grinned Matthew, 'you'll keep your silly mouth shut. There's three witnesses here saw you make that attack on the Doctor – slinkin' up and waitin' for him behind the door-post. And don't forget, his honesty is as well known as yours, you know – maybe better – even if folks do call him a crank. Your money can't do everything.'

'And I have witnesses, too,' spluttered the other, 'who saw you all breaking into my lodge and using violence on the keeper.'

'Yes, to save your hide and your house from burning,' added Matthew. 'Go on and do your worst. I dare you to take it to any court.'

'Come, come!' said the Doctor, herding us away like children. 'Let us be going. No more, Matthew – please! Come, Bumpo!'

And leaving the fuming, spluttering master of the Manor to pick himself up from the gravel, we walked down the drive.

On the return walk all four of us were silent – also a little tired, for, as Matthew had said, we had worked hard at our thankless task. And we must have been more than half-way to the house before anyone spoke. It was the cats'-meat-man.

'You know,' said he, breaking out suddenly, 'there's something fishy about the whole thing. That's my opinion.'

'There's something fishy about the whole thing'

'How do you mean?' said the Doctor sleepily, trying to show polite interest.

'About his ingratitude,' said Matthew, 'his wanting to get us off the place in such a hurry and – and, well, his general manner. I don't believe he ever thought we were suspicious characters at all – maybe the lodge-keeper might have, but not the owner. Why, everyone in Puddleby knows you, Doctor – even if you don't mix in with the society tea-parties and the afternoon muffin-worries. . . . And then the way things was run, up at the house there: nobody in charge unless the "master" is on the job. And the master wasn't. . . . Why wasn't he? What was he doing all that time while old Moses was runnin' round hollerin' for him? . . . And why –'

'Oh, Matthew,' the Doctor broke in, 'what's the use of guessing and speculating about it? Personally, I must confess I don't care what he was doing – or what he ever will do. Thank goodness, the whole stupid affair is over!'

But Matthew was much too wrapped up in his subject to dismiss it like that. And though he kept his voice low, as if he were talking to himself, he continued a quite audible one-man conversation for the rest of the way home.

'Yes, there's a mystery there, all right. And if anybody was to get to the bottom of it I'll bet they'd get a shock. . . . Why, even the lodge-keeper – there's another queer thing: supposing he *was* scared by the way we woke him up, just the same, no man in his senses – orders or no orders – is going to take no notice of a fire alarm. If he didn't want to let us in, he could anyway call to his wife and send her up to the Manor to find out. And then when he does follow us up to the house, and sees that there really is a fire, does he do anything to help us put it out? No, he does not. He goes and tells the precious "master" how badly we treated him getting in to save 'em all from burning to death. And, by the way, that's still another queer thing: how did he know where to find the master? The old butler didn't know — no, nor nobody else.'

The Doctor sighed gratefully as we finally reached the little gate. After this hard and trying night the thought of a good bed was very pleasant — as was also the prospect of getting a respite from Matthew's thinking aloud.

Chapter Twenty-six
THE SCRAP OF PARCHMENT

THE rescued mouse family which I had brought home in my pocket were given quarters in the club. The white mouse personally saw to it that the very best furnished suite was given to them. And, of course, they immediately became public heroes in Mouse Town. The thrilling story they had to tell of the fire; the father-mouse's midnight gallop for help; their perilous rescue by John Dolittle himself; and finally the Doctor's treatment at the hands of the churlish owner of the Manor, was undoubtedly the sensation of the season.

Many of the members were so infuriated over the discourtesy shown to the Doctor that they wanted to organize a campaign of revenge – which would, I believe, have utterly ruined the Manor if they had been allowed to carry it out. For they planned to chew up the curtains, drill the panelling, eat holes in the tapestries, break the wine glasses, and a whole lot of other mischief which rats and mice can easily accomplish if they want to. But to their indignation, as to Matthew's, the Doctor turned a deaf ear. He wanted to forget it.

Nevertheless, in the Rat and Mouse Club Throgmorton's ingratitude and his scandalous behaviour continued for a long time the principal topic of conversation. And any mice from the Manor who dropped in of an evening were always the centre of attention while they stayed, so great was the public interest in gossip from that quarter.

And it was through this that the poor Doctor, despite his earnest desire to stay out of the affairs of Sidney Throgmorton or any other neighbours, found himself finally forced by circumstances to take further part in matters which he insisted were 'none of his business'.

It began by the white mouse coming to me one night and saying: 'There's a mouse just run over from the Manor who has lived up there for some time. He has something he wants to show the Doctor. But the poor man is always so busy I thought I'd speak to you first. Will you come down to the club and see him?'

'All right,' I said. And I left what I was doing and went down right away.

When I got into the Assembly Room I found a whole crowd of members gathered around a mouse who seemed quite pleased with the sensation he was creating. They were all staring at a torn scrap of paper about the size of a visiting-card.

'I thought this might be of importance,' said the mouse to me. 'Of course I can't read what it says on it. But it is made of a very unusual kind of paper. That's a subject I do know something about, paper. I wondered whether the Doctor ought to see it. Perhaps you can tell us.'

HUGH LOFTING

'He seemed quite pleased with the sensation he
was creating'

I examined the slip. It was nibbled irregularly all round the edges like any piece of paper would be that had been part of a mouse's nest. But it was true: the paper itself was of a special kind. It was real parchment. Then I read the few words which were written in four lines across the scrap of parchment.

Well, after that I decided that the Doctor ought to see it. And without further ado I took it to him and told him so.

Matthew happened to be with him in the study at the time. And in spite of the fact that he couldn't read, he became quite interested as soon as he heard where the paper had come from.

'But what made the mouse think it would be of importance?' asked the Doctor, as he took it from me and put on his spectacles.

'On account of the nature of the paper,' I said. 'It's real parchment, the kind they use for special legal documents.'

While the Doctor was reading the few words written on the torn scrap I watched his face carefully. And I felt sure from his expression that he guessed what I had guessed. But he evidently wasn't going to admit it. Rather hurriedly he handed it back to me.

'Yes, er – quite interesting, Stubbins,' said he, turning to his work at the table. 'I'm rather busy just now. You'll excuse me, won't you?'

This was his polite way of telling me to go away and not bother him. And in the circumstances I felt there wasn't anything else for me to do but go.

Matthew's interest, on the other hand, was growing rather than diminishing. And as I left the

HUGH LOFTING

'I examined the slip'

room he followed me out. 'What do you make of that, Tommy?' he asked as soon as we had closed the door behind us.

'Why, between ourselves, Matthew,' said I, 'I think it's a will – or rather a piece of one. What's more, I believe the Doctor thinks so, too. But it is quite clear that he doesn't want to have anything to do with it. And nobody can blame him, after all he had to put up with from that horrible Throgmorton.'

'A will?' said Matthew. 'Whose will?'

'We don't know,' I said. 'This is all we have, just a corner of it.'

'A will, eh?' he muttered again. 'I wonder where that would fit in. . . . Humph!'

'What do you mean, fit in?' I asked.

'Into the puzzle,' he said, staring at the floor rapt in thought.

'I don't understand you, Matthew,' said I, rather impatiently. 'What puzzle?'

'I'll tell you later,' said he, 'after I've found out a little more. But I knew I was right. There *was* a mystery in that house. Keep that piece of paper carefully.'

And at that he left me, with the scrap of parchment in my hand, pondering over his words.

Chapter Twenty-seven
THE COMING OF KLING

FOR several days after that I saw nothing of Matthew. Moreover, while I was deeply interested in what he had said, I had very little time to think further of his 'mystery'. For I was kept exceptionally busy with my ordinary duties as Assistant Manager of the Dolittle Zoo, in general – and in particular with the arrival of Kling.

Kling, who later came to be known among us as 'The Dog Detective', was such an unusual animal that I feel I ought to devote a little space to telling how he came to join the zoo.

One day while Jip was wandering around the streets on his own, as he often did, he came upon a mongrel terrier who was evidently very ill. He was lying in a corner by a wall, groaning pitifully.

'What's the matter?' said Jip, going up to him.

'I've just eaten a rat,' said the dog. 'And I have a dreadful stomach-ache.'

'My gracious!' said Jip. 'Eating rats at this season! Don't you know any better than that? You should never eat rats when there isn't an *R* in the month. Why, they're rank poison!'

'Kling'

'What's the *R* mean?' asked the mongrel, groaning again.

'Why, *Rats* of course,' said Jip. 'Come along to the Doctor at once. He'll soon give you something that will put your stomach right. What's your name?'

'Kling,' said the mongrel. 'Thanks, but I'm afraid I'm too ill to walk.'

'All right, Kling,' said Jip. 'You wait here and I'll go and get the Doctor.'

Jip dashed away at top speed, muttering to himself that he must speak to John Dolittle about instituting a Dog Ambulance for urgent cases of this kind.

When he got to the house he found that the Doctor was out. So he came to me instead. Together we hurried off at once to the rescue of the sick mongrel.

I saw right away that the patient was pretty far gone and that it would need very prompt treatment to save him. I gathered him up in my arms, sent Jip off to scour the town for the Doctor and hurried back as fast as I could to the house.

There I found that John Dolittle had returned during my absence. I rushed the patient into the surgery, where the Doctor immediately examined him.

'It's a case of poisoning,' he said. 'Very likely the rat you ate had been poisoned. But we can put you right again. You had better stay here for a few days. You can sleep in the parlour – where I'll be able to keep an eye on you. Here, drink this. Now, Stubbins, carry him in to the sofa and put some blankets over him. He has a temperature and mustn't get chilled. Tell me, Kling, how did you come to eat a rat?'

'I was starving,' said the mongrel rather shame-facedly. 'Hadn't had a meal for two days.'

'Well, next time,' said the Doctor, 'come round to our zoo – the Home for Cross-Bred Dogs, you know. You can always get a meal there. But please, *don't* eat rats.'

Quite early the following morning I heard a most extraordinary noise in the Doctor's bedroom. It sounded as though he were moving every piece of furniture from its usual position and generally turning the place upside down. I was about to go up to see what was the matter, when he opened his door and called to me.

'Oh, Stubbins, have you seen anything of a boot of mine? I can't find it anywhere – the left one.'

'No, Doctor,' I said, 'I haven't.'

'It's most peculiar,' said he. 'I could have sworn I left it – both of them – beside the bed last night, just where I always take them off.'

My own first duty that morning was, of course, to see how the new patient, Kling, was getting on. And as soon as I got downstairs I went straight to the parlour. Imagine my astonishment to find the sofa empty and the patient gone!

Utterly puzzled, I wandered out through the French window into the garden. And there, in the middle of the lawn, I found not only Kling, but the Doctor's boot as well – which the new patient was thoughtfully chewing. As I ran to him, the Doctor also arrived, with his remaining boot on one foot and a bright red slipper on the other.

'Good gracious!' said John Dolittle. 'You made a

quick recovery, Kling. I didn't give you permission
to get up yet. What are you doing with my boot?'

There was really no need to ask. Even before the
Doctor stooped and picked it up anyone could see
that the dog had chewed a large hole in the side.

'Dear me!' said John Dolittle. 'Just look at that!
Now what shall I do?'

'Oh, did you want those boots?' said Kling
apologetically. 'I'm dreadfully sorry, Doctor. I
thought they were an old pair you had thrown
away.'

'Oh, no,' said the Doctor. 'They're my best boots
– my only boots, in fact. Listen, Stubbins: after
breakfast, would you mind running down with
this to your father? Give him my compliments
and ask him if he would be good enough to patch
it while you wait. I've got to go up to town
tonight to address a meeting of the Zoological
Society, and I can't very well go in red slippers. . . . But tell me, Kling: how comes it that
you still chew boots? You're no longer a puppy,
you know.'

'No,' said Kling, 'that's true. But I've never got
out of the habit since my childhood days. It is
strange, I know. My mother always said it meant
I was a genius; but my father said it was clearly a
sign I was just a plain fool and would never grow
up.'

'Well, Kling,' said the Doctor, 'I suppose I'll have
to get you a pair of shoes of your own to chew. I
can't let you have mine, you know. Er – would you
prefer brown or black?'

'Brown, please,' said Kling. 'They usually taste
better. And would you mind if I had them buttoned

instead of laced. I find chewing the buttons off almost the best part – very soothing.'

'Certainly,' said the Doctor. 'But we may find it hard to get brown buttoned boots in Puddleby. It's not a very up-to-date shopping centre, you understand. Perhaps you had better come with me. It's no use my buying you a pair of shoes that doesn't suit you. And I doubt if they will change them after you've tried them on – on your teeth, I mean.'

So that was how John Dolittle added yet another story to his reputation in the neighbourhood for eccentricity and craziness. After breakfast, while I took his damaged boot to my father's to be repaired, he took the mongrel Kling to the largest shoe shop in the town to buy him a pair of boots. The salesman was somewhat slow in getting it into his head that the customer (who was wearing slippers) wanted the shoes for the dog and not for himself. And for a whole week afterwards he entertained the neighbouring shopkeepers by telling them how the Doctor had requested that all the brown buttoned boots in the shop be set out in a row on the floor; and how this ill-conditioned, half-bred dog had then, at the Doctor's invitation, gone down the line and made his selection.

Kling himself insisted that his rapid recovery from the severe attack of ptomaine poisoning was largely aided by the soothing effect of chewing brown shoe leather. And certainly by that evening he seemed entirely himself and was frisking round the garden as lively as a puppy.

'Chewing a new pair of boots always makes me feel young again,' said he, leaping over the flower beds.

The whole of the Doctor's household as well as all the members of the Home for Cross-Bred Dogs and the Dolittle Zoo took to Kling at once. And both the Doctor and I agreed that we had never met a more interesting personality in dogs – in spite of his juvenile fondness for boots. He was a good example of that rule which John Dolittle had more than once maintained: that the mongrels often have more character than the thorough-breds. And it was, I think, greatly to the credit of our whole establishment that none of the other animals showed the least jealousy over the great popularity that Kling enjoyed from the first day of his joining the zoo.

Chapter Twenty-eight
THE MYSTERY OF MOORSDEN MANOR

OF course it was not long after I had taken the scrap of torn parchment to John Dolittle that the white mouse came to me demanding to know what the Doctor had said about it. I had to disappoint him terribly by telling him that he had refused to show any interest in it whatever.

Jip was in my room at the time that the white mouse called. He had never quite forgiven me for having him sent back home the night of the fire – especially after he had learned later that there had been a fight and that his beloved Doctor had been treated discourteously by Throgmorton.

It was after supper, about half-past eight. And while the white mouse and I were talking the cats'-meat-man also dropped in. I had not seen him for several days.

'Well, Matthew,' I said, 'how are you getting on with your mystery?'

'Humph!' he muttered, sinking into an arm-chair. 'It's still a mystery all right.'

Jip cocked up his ears at that and wanted to know what we were talking about. I explained to him, in dog language, that Matthew Mugg was

sure from certain things he had observed that
night at the Manor that there was some mystery
connected with the house and its owner.

'Tommy,' said Matthew, 'I can't get much for-
rarder until we find the rest of that will.'

'I'm afraid that may be hard,' said I, 'from the
inquiries I've made.'

'Listen,' the white mouse whispered to me: 'I can
get that mouse from the Manor for you any time
you want.'

'All right,' I said. 'Send for him, will you, please?
There's always a chance that he may have found
out something since.'

Thereupon the white mouse disappeared, and
Matthew and I went on with our conversation.

But it could not have been more than a quarter
of an hour before the white mouse was back at my
elbow again. And with him he had the mouse who
had brought us the scrap of parchment.

'Tell me,' I said to the Manor mouse, 'did you
ever find out anything more about the rest of that
paper?'

'As it happens,' said he, 'I did – tonight. The
scrap, as I told you, had been in a mouse nest – an
old one which I had discovered by accident and
taken to pieces. You see, I was going to rebuild it
into a new one for myself. Well, this evening I met
the owner of that old nest.'

'Ah!' I said. 'That sounds like news. And what
did he tell you?'

'Well,' said the Manor mouse, 'the reason I
hadn't met him before – as you know, I had made
inquiries of all the rats and mice in the mansion
– was that he had moved out of the house to a sort

of potting-shed place in the garden. I happened to
go out there looking for last year's chestnuts; and
that's how I ran into him. He's very, very old –
quite feeble in fact. But he had lived longer in the
Manor than any of us.'

'Yes,' I said, 'but get on to the business of the
parchment. What did he tell you about that?'

'It seems that it was in the days of this Mr
Throgmorton's father when, he told me, he had
lived in the old man's study on the first floor. He
was building a nest for himself and his wife, and
he made it behind the panelling – between the
panelling and the wall. Nesting materials were
hard to find. And he got into old Mr Throgmorton's
desk – by drilling a hole through the back – and
went through all the drawers looking for stuff he
could use to make a nest of. Papers and red tape
were about all he could find. And among the
papers he chewed corners off, there was this large
sheet which the old man kept locked up in the top
drawer. My friend used it for a foundation for his
nest because he saw it was nice and thick and
would keep the draughts out. It seems the old man
considered the paper important, because when, a
few days later, he opened the drawer and found
the corner chewed off, he swore and carried on
something dreadful. This mouse was watching
from behind the clock on the mantelpiece, and he
says he never saw anyone get so angry. The old
man saw right away that it was the work of mice,
from the way in which the paper was nibbled. He
hunted high and low for that missing corner –
turned all the furniture in the whole room inside
out. But of course he didn't find it because it was

behind the panelling in my friend's nest. At last he gave it up and took the larger piece of the parchment away and hid it somewhere else.'

'Where?' I asked, rising half out of my chair.

'The old mouse said he didn't know. But wherever it was, it wasn't in the study.'

I sank back disappointed.

'Do you think,' I asked, 'that if all the mice in the house went to work on it they could find it for us?'

The Manor mouse shook his head.

'As a matter of fact,' said he, 'we have tried. As soon as we learned from the gossip at the Club that you were interested in the paper we began a search on our own. But no trace of it could we find.'

I translated for Matthew's benefit what the Manor mouse had said, and his disappointment was even greater than mine.

'But tell me, Matthew,' I said, 'didn't you succeed in finding anything out yourself? When last I saw you you were going to do some investigating on your own account.'

'It wasn't so easy,' said he, 'for this reason: when the old man died and this Mr Throgmorton came into the property, all the servants were changed. That's suspicious in itself, of course. So trying to find out much about the family from gossip and hearsay was kind of hard. I learned some things, but nothing that seemed to help solve the problem.'

At this point Jip came up to my chair and nudged my knee beneath the table.

'Tommy,' said he, 'for solving problems the best hands I know are Cheapside and Kling.'

'Humph!' I muttered. 'Cheapside I could under-

stand, because he is in touch with the gossip of the
street sparrows. But why Kling? Why should he be
good at solving problems?'

'Why, my gracious!' said Jip. 'He knows an awful
lot about crime and the – er – underworld and all
that. He belonged to a thief once.'

'To a thief!' I cried.

'Yes. You ought to get him some time to tell you
the story of his life. You never heard anything so
thrilling. When he was quite a puppy he was
stolen by a sort of tramp person who specially
trained him in all sorts of queer dodges. This
tramp used to walk through the streets with Kling
on a string. And to anybody passing who looked
well-off, he'd say, "Do you want to buy a dog?" And
they would usually say "Yes" in the end, because
Kling had been taught all manner of cunning
tricks with which to fascinate them. Then Kling,
after he'd been sold, would run away from the new
owner and come back to the tramp. He was trained
to do that too, you see. And then the tramp would
take him away to a new town and sell him over
again. Kling says that man once sold him twelve
times in one month. But later the tramp invented
another way to make money even faster. He
trained Kling to learn the geography of the new
houses he went to, and especially where the silver
and valuables were kept. And the tramp would
come later and rob the house, Kling acting as
guide for him and showing him over the place.
Then together they would go off again to a new
town.'

'Goodness me!' I said. 'What an awful record!'

'Yes,' said Jip. 'But Kling had no idea he was

doing wrong, until one day he got talking about his adventures to a parson's dog, who was highly scandalized and persuaded him to give up the life of crime. So Kling, in spite of the fact that the tramp had always treated him kindly, ran away the first chance he got and never went back to him again.

'Oh my, yes, Kling's awfully well up on crime! You see, in his life with the tramp he fell in with many queer birds, regular gangs of crooks, you know. And in that way he learned a lot about the tricks and dodges of different kinds of criminals. And then later he got a job as a police dog in Belgium and he was used to hunt down lawbreakers. Why, in Brussels, I understand, he was known as 'The Dog Detective'. Had no end of a reputation. But he didn't care for that work, and after a year or so he ran away again. Then for a while he was a tramp himself – a dog tramp – said he wanted to see the world. He's had a wonderful career. And you'd never think it – unassuming and quiet, the way he is. On first meeting him one might almost think he was stupid, dragging that chewed-up shoe of his round. But I feel sure that if you and Matthew have a problem you want to solve you couldn't do better than to consult Kling.'

'Yes, I believe you're right, Jip,' I said. 'Go and ask him if he'll come and talk to us, will you? Don't say anything about it to the other members of the Home for Cross-Bred Dogs. You know how enthusiastic they get. But if you happen to see Cheapside in the garden ask him to drop in too, will you?'

While Jip was gone I explained to Matthew roughly what it was we proposed to do. Kling hadn't met Matthew yet, having arrived during the few days while the cats'-meat-man had been off 'investigating', as he called it.

But when, followed by Jip, the Dog Detective strolled into the room carrying one of his new chewing-boots, I thought I saw Matthew start almost uneasily. Kling too behaved in a rather odd manner. He stared hard at Matthew a moment through half-closed lids, as though he were trying to remember something. Then with a shake of his shoulders he settled down on the floor and began turning his boot over between his paws to find a good place to chew. Jip shot a glance at me that spoke volumes.

Knowing that Matthew didn't understand dog talk, I began by asking Kling if he had ever seen him before.

The mongrel thoughtfully pulled a button off his boot before answering.

'Oh, well,' he said, 'what does it matter! He's a friend of yours – and the Doctor's. I've met an awful lot of people, you know. After all, a man's past is his own. I believe in letting bygones be bygones. . . . Jip tells me you have something you wanted to see me about.'

'Yes,' I said. 'We have a problem – a sort of a mystery. Ah! Here's Cheapside, too. Good! We'll be glad to have his opinion as well.'

Chapter Twenty-nine
THE DOG DETECTIVE

THEN from beginning to end, leaving out nothing that I thought might be helpful, I told Kling the story of our midnight summons to the fire at Moorsden Manor and all that followed it.

Jip was right when he said that anyone might at first sight think that Kling was stupid. While I talked he went on chewing his boot as though his whole attention was absorbed in that and not in what I was saying. But I soon found out that he had not only heard what I had said, but that he remembered it, every word.

'Well,' he began when I was done, 'in a case like this the first thing I would do is to build up a story. By that I mean you lay the mystery out – you solve it before you begin, by guesswork, in other words. Then you go to work and see if you are right or not. Tell me: when you finally found Mr Throgmorton – or, rather, when he found you – had he anything with him?'

'Yes,' I said, 'some small leather boxes.'

'Did you by any chance find out what they contained?'

'Yes,' I said again. 'Matthew opened one when

Throgmorton wasn't looking. It had four large diamond studs in it.'

Kling nodded thoughtfully.

'And these two ferocious watch-dogs,' he went on presently, 'weren't they usually kept *in*side the house? Perhaps Matthew knows.'

I questioned the cats'-meat-man.

'Yes,' said he. 'And that's still another queer thing I hadn't thought of before. The dogs were always brought into the house after dark and left loose to roam where they would. When they killed that burglar, they caught him just as he was opening the silver drawer in the butler's pantry. I heard that from one of the gardeners. Yes, it was queer that that night Dina and Wolf were not inside the house at all. They were being kept by someone. It seemed as though they came from the stable.'

I interpreted to Kling. And he nodded again as though it all fitted in with his picture.

'Well, then,' he said, after a moment's thought, 'let us begin and build. Perhaps for the benefit of Matthew you had better explain to him once in a while what I am saying, so we can see whether he agrees with it or not. We will start off by supposing that since Mr Throgmorton was so annoyed with you – you who came to put the fire out – *that he lighted it himself.'*

I jumped slightly. It was such a startling idea.

'Just a minute, Kling,' I said. 'I'll put that to Matthew.'

The cats'-meat-man, when I told him, also jumped.

'Why, that's a notion!' said he. 'A notion and a

half, by Jiminy! And yet it fits in with some things, all right. I'd been thinking all the time that he was trying to get us off the place because he was doing something up there he hadn't oughter. I never thought of his setting fire to his own mansion — must be worth thousands and thousands of pounds, that place, with all the stuff in it. And then he kicked because we'd broken the windows. That don't sound as though he didn't care about the house. . . . Just the same, it's an idea worth followin' up. Tell the dog to go on.'

'You see,' Kling continued, 'the fact that Sidney Throgmorton had his jewellery with him, also that this was the only night that the dogs were not kept in the house, makes it look as though he expected the fire.'

'Yes,' I said, 'that's so. But his loss would have been enormous just the same.'

'Wait,' said Kling. 'Maybe we'll find that his loss would have been still more enormous if he didn't have the fire. . . . Well, to proceed: now, having supposed that Throgmorton set fire to his own house — it has been done before, I've known cases myself — the next question is: what did he want to burn it down for? He wanted to get rid of something, we'll say. What did he want to get rid of? Had he any people in it he wanted to kill?'

I questioned Matthew. The answer was: none that he knew of.

'Any brothers or sisters?' asked Kling.

'None,' said Matthew. 'That I know for sure.'

'Very well,' Kling went on, 'then he wanted to destroy some*thing*, since people are out of the question. Why didn't he find the thing and get rid

of it, instead of burning down a valuable house?
Because he had tried and couldn't find it? Possibly.
And almost certainly, if it was—'

'A will?' I broke in.

'Exactly,' said Kling, nodding. 'Yet why destroy
a will? Because in it he knew, or guessed, that his
father had left the property, not to him, the son,
but to some other parties. If there was no will he
would get all the property because he was the only
child. So, guessing there had been a will made;
almost certain it was in that house; unable to find
it himself, but terrified that someone else might —
don't forget that he got rid of all the old servants
and bought two ferocious watch-dogs to keep
people out — finally he determines to burn the
whole place up and the will with it. What does that
loss matter when he had a dozen other houses and
estates — which he never visited, fearing to leave
the Manor lest someone find the will while he is
gone!'

Chapter Thirty
OLD MR THROGMORTON

'IT fits, it fits!' cried Matthew, jumping up in his excitement when I had explained what Kling had said. 'The gardener told me the father and son could never get along together. And that's why Sidney Throgmorton stayed abroad most of the time till after the old man died. And the father didn't want it known that they couldn't agree, see? So of course he would keep the will dark. It all fits like a glove. The dog's a wizard. But listen: we ought to do something quickly. That man is liable to try and burn the house down again any minute.'

One would have thought, to hear the cats'-meat-man talk, that it was he who would lose most by the will's destruction. And I must confess that the fascination of the mystery and the desire to frustrate the iniquitous Sidney Throgmorton had me also in its grip by this time.

'Oh, I don't think he'll make another attempt in a hurry,' I said. 'It would look fishy. After all, he has got to be careful, you see. If he knows there was a will, then what he tried to do was a criminal offence – goodness, I don't wonder he was furious with us!'

'The next step for you, I should say,' Kling went on, 'is to try and find out to whom the old Throgmorton would have been most likely to leave his money.'

At that Cheapside, whom in our interest we had forgotten all about, hopped on to the table and started talking.

'Folks,' said he, 'I think I can help you there, maybe. I saw a good deal of the old Mr Throgmorton, and a mighty fine gentleman he was. It wasn't at Moorsden Manor that I saw him, because he only spent a week or two out of every year here. But to one of his other places, Bencote Castle, down in Sussex, I used to go regular, at one time, in the early autumn. The old man, as perhaps you know, retired from business when he was getting on in years. And 'e spent 'is old age, pleasant like, raisin' prize stock, cows, sheep, and horses – specially heavy draught-horses. He was good to animals all round, was old Jonathan T. Throgmorton. He had bird-fountains put out in all his gardens, nesting-boxes in the trees and everything. And he gave one of his footmen the special job of throwing out crumbs every morning for the sparrows and wild birds. Some days, when the old man was well enough, he used to do it himself. That's how I came to know him. Besides all that, he did a whole lot towards making life easier for working animals – paid to have drinking-troughs put up for horses, and kept extra help-teams, at his own expense, on all the steep hills in more than one town where he had homes. He was a friend to animals and a fine old gent, if ever there was one. I shouldn't wonder, Tommy, if he left part of this fortune to the same cause, the happiness of animals.

Before Cheapside had quite finished speaking I got out my pocket-book in which I had carefully preserved the scrap of parchment. I spread the fragment out and re-read the few words which had been nibbled from the will. They were in four lines. The first line ran: *'trustees who shall have —'* The second line, beginning a new paragraph, was: *'I bequeath —'* The third: *'by said party or parties —'* And the last: *'an Association for the Pre —'*

To everyone's astonishment I suddenly sprang up and said: 'Let's all go and see the Doctor — just as quickly as we possibly can.'

The Manor mouse excused himself, saying that he ought to be getting back home as it was late and his wife might be anxious. As we left the room the white mouse told me he would accompany his friend as far as the gate and would rejoin me in a minute or two. Together the rest of us, Matthew, Jip, Kling, Cheapside and I, proceeded at once to the study, where we found John Dolittle, as usual, at work on his books.

'Doctor,' I cried, bursting in, 'I'm dreadfully sorry to interrupt you, but I really feel you ought to hear this.'

With a patient sigh he laid down his pen as I poured forth my tale.

'Now, don't you see, Doctor,' I ended, showing him the scrap of parchment again, 'it is practically certain that when this piece is joined to the rest that last line will read, *"an Association for the Prevention of Cruelty to Animals,"* or some such

title. For that is the cause in which this man had
already spent great sums of money while he was
alive. And that is the cause which the wretched
son Sidney Throgmorton has robbed of probably a
large fortune. Doctor, it is the *animals* who have
been cheated.'

We all watched the Doctor's face eagerly as he
pondered for a silent moment over my somewhat
dramatic harangue. At length I thought I saw
from his expression signs of sympathy, if not
agreement.

'But, Stubbins,' said ·he quietly, 'aren't you
basing most of this on guesswork, conjecture –
though I admit it sounds plausible enough. Tell
me: what do you want me to do?'

'Doctor,' I said, 'we've got to get that will.'

'Yes, yes, I quite see that,' said he. 'But how?
Even if we got into the house – risking arrest for
burglary and all that – what chance would we
stand of finding it, if Sidney Throgmorton, living
there all the time and hunting for it ever since his
father's death, couldn't find it?'

I saw at once that he was right. The difficulties
of the task I proposed were enormous. But while I
stood there silent, discouraged and perplexed, I
suddenly heard the white mouse out in the
passage squeaking at the top of his voice: 'Tommy,
Tommy! They've found it. They've found it! The
mice have found the will!'

Chapter Thirty-one
THE SECRET CUPBOARD

THE white mouse was so breathless with running when he appeared at the study door that he could hardly talk. I lifted him to the table, where between puffs he finally managed to give us his message.

Apparently, just as he was seeing the Manor mouse off at the gate, a rat had run up and said that they had at last located the document. The old man had hidden it, it seemed, in a secret cupboard on the top floor of the house. They couldn't get the will out because it was a large heavy roll of parchment; and the hole which they had made into the cupboard (through the brickwork at the back) was very, very small. Indeed, it was so tiny that the two rats who had made it couldn't get through it. But they could see that there were papers of some sort inside. So they had got the very smallest mouse in the Manor and sent him in to make an examination and give them a report. And they were now quite certain that the document was the will, because it was made of the same kind of parchment and had a corner missing corresponding to the one in my possession.

Well, as you can imagine, the excitement among us was tremendous. And when, a moment later, the rat in question himself appeared, confirmed the story, and offered to lead the Doctor at once to the secret cupboard, I could see that the thrill of the Moorsden Manor Mystery was beginning to take hold of John Dolittle himself. Matthew was all for starting right away.

'No, now wait a minute,' said the Doctor. 'Not so fast. This is a serious thing. If we should be wrong and get caught we will have hard work to explain our actions — especially with Sidney Throgmorton anxious to put us all in jail, anyway. We must proceed carefully and make as few mistakes as possible. Let me see: what time is it? Eleven forty-five. We couldn't attempt it before two o'clock in the morning, anyhow. We must be sure everyone's abed first. Listen, Jip: you run over there to the Manor and tell — by the way, could you get into the grounds, do you think?'

'Oh, yes,' said Jip. 'I can slip through the bars of that big gate easily.'

'Well,' said the Doctor, 'don't be seen, for Heaven's sake. They might shoot you. Then just nose quietly round the house till you get a chance to speak to those two watch-dogs, Dina and Wolf. Tell them to expect me about two o'clock. Goodness knows how I'm going to get into the house. That I'll have to find out when I get there. Anyway, tell them not to be worried or give any alarm if they hear latches being forced or anything like that. Do you understand?'

'All right,' said Jip. And he hopped through the

open window into the darkness of the garden and was gone.

'Now, the next thing,' said the Doctor, 'we'll need a rope. See if you can find my alpine rope up in the attic, Stubbins, will you please?'

'Shall we be taking Bumpo along, Doctor?' asked Matthew. 'Better, don't you think? He's a handy man in a tight place.'

'Er – yes, I suppose so,' said John Dolittle.

'Then I'll go and start getting him woke up,' said the cats'-meat-man. 'It's a long job as a rule.'

Well, although we had two and a quarter hours in which to make our preparations it did not seem any too long. One after another the Doctor, Matthew, Kling, Cheapside, and the white mouse and I would keep thinking of things we ought to take, or do, to ensure success to the expedition. And when John Dolittle finally looked at his watch and said that we ought to be starting, it did not seem as though more than a few minutes had elapsed since he had made up his mind to embark upon the venture.

Fortunately there would be no moon till somewhere about three o'clock in the morning. So, to begin with anyhow, we had the protection of pretty complete darkenss.

In spite of the fact that I shared Polynesia's confidence in the Doctor's luck and success, I must confess I felt quite thrilled by the risks ahead of us as we quietly opened the gate and trailed down to the road.

The Doctor and Matthew had worked out most of the details of our campaign before we left and had assigned to each of us what parts we were to play.

So there was no talking as we plodded silently
along the road towards the Manor.

At a point where the limb of a large ash tree
overhung the high wall of the estate we halted and
the Doctor uncoiled his rope. With the aid of a
stone tied to a long length of twine, we got the
rope's end hauled up over the branch and down to
the road again. Up this we all swarmed in turn.
Meanwhile Cheapside kept watch in the branches
above to see that no one surprised us on the Manor
side, and Kling below kept an eye open for late
wayfarers that might pass along the road.

When all of us were inside the grounds and the
rope hauled over after us, Kling went off to enter,
like Jip, through the bars of the gate.

When I got down out of the tree the first thing I
noticed was Jip's white shadow flitting across the
sward to meet us.

'It's all right,' he whispered to the Doctor. 'I've
told Dina and Wolf. They say they will be on the
look out for you and will show you round the place
when you get in.'

'Yes, but it is the getting in that is going to be
the job, I'm afraid,' muttered John Dolittle.
'Listen, Jip: from here I've no idea of even where
the house lies – through all this shrubbery and
parkland. Lead us to it, will you? And bring us up
on the wooded side. We don't want to cross any
open spaces.'

'Very good,' said Jip. 'I'll take you to the kitchen-
garden side. You'll have cover all the way up. But
if you should get spotted and have to run for it, tell
everyone to follow me. I know the easiest and
shortest way out.'

Then in single file we trailed after Jip, who kept us behind bushes and hedges for what seemed like a good ten minutes' walk. Suddenly we found ourselves against the wall of the house itself. Here I noticed for the first time that Kling had rejoined us.

'Listen,' I heard him whisper to the Doctor, 'you've got that rat in your pocket still, haven't you – the one who lives here?'

'Yes,' said John Dolittle. 'And the white mouse, too.'

'Well, that rat is your best chance for getting in,' said Kling. 'If you let Matthew force a lock you're liable to have complications with the police afterwards. Send the rat into the house through a hole – he'll know lots of them leading down into the cellar. And tell him to get you the master's latchkey. It'll be in his bedroom, on the dressing-table, you may be sure.'

'Splendid!' whispered the Doctor. And he at once took the rat from his pocket and explained to him what Kling had said. Then he let him go upon the ground and we waited.

It was about five minutes later, I should say, when I felt something small and sharp hit me on the head. Even through my cap it stung. From my head it bounced to the ground. And by the dim starlight I could see it shining dully where it lay. I picked it up. It was a small key. Apparently the master's bedroom window was directly above our heads; and the rat, to save time, had thrown the key out to us.

I slipped it into the Doctor's hand and in silence we moved round towards the front of the house.

Chapter Thirty-two
THE WILD RIDE OF THE WHITE MOUSE

IT had been agreed that only Matthew should accompany the Doctor to the top floor. I was to remain downstairs in the hall; and Bumpo was to stay outside the house. His and my parts in the plot were mostly those of watching and standing on guard. In case of emergency we had signals arranged and were to assemble at a certain point.

As the Doctor very, very quietly opened the front door with the latchkey I got my first real scare of the evening. With uncanny suddenness, both together, the two great ferocious heads of the watch-dogs popped out to greet him.

Within the hall, where the darkness was quite intense, I confess that I was quite glad that my duties carried me no farther. As we had arranged, I sat down on the floor by the front door and began my watch. Jip, thank goodness, stayed with me. Matthew and the Doctor, each with a hand on the collar of one of the guiding watch-dogs, were led away swiftly and silently through the inky blackness, up the carpeted stairs, to the rooms above.

It seemed a perfect eternity that they were

gone. Before the evening was over I decided that I didn't care for the profession of burglary a bit. It was a little too thrilling. Every time the breeze rattled a window or swung a curtain whispering across the floor, I was certain that we had been discovered and someone was coming after us with a pistol or a club. It was a great temptation to open the front door and let in the little light of the starry sky without. But I had been told to keep it closed lest the draught be detected by any of the household.

At last Jip whispered: 'Don't get scared now if someone bumps into you. They're coming down the stairs again. I can smell 'em.'

A moment later the wet muzzle of Dina, leading the Doctor across the hall, dabbed me in the ear. It was a good thing Jip had warned me – I should probably have started hitting out in all directions if he hadn't. I rose and carefully swung open the front door. The dim forms of the Doctor and Matthew passed out. I followed. With a pat of thanks John Dolittle turned and shut the two dogs in behind us, letting the tongue of the night-latch gently into its socket with the key. Then he took the rat from his pocket, gave him the key and set him on the ground. From somewhere out of the general gloom of the garden Bumpo's huge figure emerged and joined us.

Once more under Jip's guidance we began the journey across the park towards the walls. I was simply burning up to ask the Doctor if he had succeeded, but I managed to restrain my curiosity till we stood again beneath the ash tree. Then at last I felt it was safe to whisper: 'Did you get it?'

'Yes,' he said. 'It's in my pocket. Everything

went all right. We were able to open the cupboard
and close it again too, leaving it so no one would
know we were there. But, of course, I haven't had
a chance to read the will yet. Come along now,
where's that rope?'

Again, one by one, we swarmed to the top of the
wall, transferred the dangling rope to the other
side and slid quietly down into the roadway.

With a general sigh we set off towards home. As
we passed the gate we noticed the grey of the dawn
showing in the east. Like silent ghosts Kling and
Jip slipped out through the bars and dropped in
behind the procession.

On reaching the house we all hurried to the
study. I got some candles lighted while the Doctor
spread the will out on the table. It was a tense
moment for all of us as we leant over his shoulder.

Sure enough, a piece had been bitten out of the
document at the corner. And when I added the
fragment I had in my pocket it fitted perfectly.
Then, without going through the preliminary
preamble of the document, the Doctor traced that
paragraph with his finger. This is what he read
out: 'I bequeath the sum of One Hundred Thousand Pounds for the endowment of an Association
for the Prevention of Cruelty to Animals. The
Trustees will select—'

But he was not permitted to get any farther.
Matthew, Bumpo and I suddenly started cheering
and dancing round the table. And it was quite
some minutes before our enthusiasm had let off
enough steam to allow us to listen to any more.

As we settled down into our chairs again I noticed
the Doctor staring fixedly at something Matthew

was turning over in his fingers. I started as I saw what it was – one of the diamond shirt-studs from Sidney Throgmorton's little leather box.

'Er – where – did you get that, Matthew?' asked the Doctor, in a low, somewhat fearful voice.

'Oh, this?' said the cats'-meat-man, trying hard not to look guilty. 'This is a little souvenir I brought along from the Manor.'

For a moment the Doctor seemed too horrified to speak.

'Well,' Matthew went on, 'it wasn't his, you know, after all, with him robbin' the animals of that whole fortune what was coming to them accordin' to the will.'

'But when, how, did you take it, Matthew?' asked the Doctor. 'I thought you were with me all the time.'

'Oh, I just dropped into his bedroom to take a look around, as we passed his door going up the stairs,' said Matthew. 'These pretty playthings was in a box on the dressin'-table, and I couldn't resist the temptation of bringin' one along as a souvenir.'

With his hand to his head the Doctor sank into a chair as if stunned.

'Oh, Matthew, Matthew!' he murmured. 'I thought you had promised me to give up that – that sort of thing for good.'

For a moment we were all silent. Finally the Doctor said: 'Well, I don't know what we are to do now, really I don't.'

The white mouse crawled up my sleeve from the table and whispered in my ear: 'What's the matter with the Doctor? What has happened?'

I explained to him as quickly and as briefly as I could.

'Give me that stud, Doctor,' said he, suddenly darting across the table to John Dolittle. 'I'll get it back into its box before you can say Jack Robinson.'

'Goodness! Do you think you could?' cried the Doctor. Immediately all cheered up. 'Oh, but look: the daylight is here now. The disappearance of the diamond is most likely already discovered. And think of the time it would take you to travel there – at your pace!'

'Doctor, it wouldn't take long if he rode on my back,' Jip put in. 'If I carry him as far as the house he can soon pop in through a hole and slip upstairs. It's worth trying.'

'All right,' said the Doctor. 'Any port in a storm.'

And to Matthew's great disappointment he leant across the table, took the valuable jewel out of his hands and gave it to the white mouse.

'You'll save us from a terrible mess,' he said 'if you can get it there in time. Good luck to you!'

The white mouse took the stud in his paws, jumped on to Jip's back and disappeared through the garden window at a gallop.

After he had gone there was an embarrassed, uncomfortable pause. Finally the Doctor said: 'Er – Stubbins and Bumpo: you will not of course – supposing that this matter ends satisfactorily – mention it, ever, to a living soul.'

Ill at ease, but very much in earnest, we nodded our promise of silence.

'As for you, Matthew,' the Doctor went on, 'I must warn you now, once and for all, that if any other occurrence of er – this sort takes place we shall have to sever relations permanently. I know I can trust you where my own property is concerned, but I must feel secure that you will regard the property of others in the same way. If not, we can have nothing further to do with one another. Do you understand?'

'Yes, I understand, Doctor,' said Matthew in a low voice. 'I ought to have known I might be putting you in an awkward situation. But – well, no more need be said.'

The Doctor turned as though to go into the garden. He looked about him for his hat. And suddenly a look of horror came slowly into his face.

'Stubbins!' he gasped. 'Where is it?'

'Don't tell me,' I cried, 'that you left it again – *in the Manor!*'

Chapter Thirty-three
OUR ARREST

IT was true. In the thrill and excitement of our nocturnal adventure none of us had noticed whether the Doctor had come away from the Manor bareheaded or with his hat on. But now that we came to think of it we could all recall that he had worn it on the way there. Next, he himself remembered clearly that in getting into the secret cupboard he had laid it aside on a chair because it was in the way.

'Dear me!' he sighed, shaking his head. 'That's the kind of a burglar *I* am — leave my hat behind me, the one thing that everybody in the neighbourhood would recognize as mine. . . . Hah! It would be funny if it wasn't so serious. Well, more than ever depends on the white mouse now. Dear, dear! Anyhow,' he added as Dab-Dab appeared at the door, 'let's not meet our troubles half-way. Breakfast ready, Dab-Dab?'

'No,' said the housekeeper, coming forward into the room and lowering her voice. 'But there are three men walking up the garden path. One is carrying your hat. And one is a policeman.'

At that Matthew sprang up and in a twinkling

was half out of the garden window. Then, apparently changing his mind, he stopped.

'No, Doctor,' said he, coming back into the room, 'I ain't goin' to skedaddle and leave you to face the music. I've bin in jail before. I'll tell 'em I've done it.'

'Look here, Matthew,' said John Dolittle firmly: 'I want you to do one thing only throughout the rest of this business, and that is keep your mouth closed tight – unless I ask you to talk. Stubbins, will you please let them in?'

I went and opened the door. I knew all three men by sight. One was Sidney Throgmorton; the other his lodge-keeper; and the third our local police sergeant. The sergeant's manner was distinctly apologetic. He knew John Dolittle, and this duty was distasteful to him. Throgmorton's behaviour, on the other hand, was offensive from the start. He brushed by me before I had invited him to come in and walked straight to the Doctor's study.

'Ah!' he cried. 'We have the whole lot here, sergeant – the same party exactly that came pretending to put the fire out when they wanted to learn their way around the house they meant later to rob. Put them all under arrest and bring them at once to the Manor.'

The sergeant, while he was somewhat impressed by Throgmorton's position in the community, knew what his duties were without being told. He addressed himself to John Dolittle.

'This gentleman has brought a charge, Doctor,' he said. 'A valuable diamond was stolen from his house last night and your hat was found on the

premises this morning. I shall have to ask you to
come up to the Manor, please.'

We were all glad that the early hour gave us
practically empty streets to walk through. For certainly our party with the sergeant for escort would
have set gossip running all over Puddleby if there
had been many abroad to see us.

Hardly a word was said the whole way by
anyone except Throgmorton, to whose indignant
fumings no one seemed to want to make any reply.

At the house the old manservant let us in and we
went straight upstairs to the master's bedroom.
Here Throgmorton at once plunged into a dramatic
recital, for the sergeant's benefit, of how he had
arisen at his usual hour of six and had at once
noticed that his stud-box had been moved from the
place where he had left it the night before. He
opened it, he said, and found one stud missing.
After the servants had been summoned and a
search made of the house, the Doctor's hat had
been found in a room on the top floor. This, and the
fact that we had all behaved in a suspicious
manner the night of the fire, at once convicted us
in his mind as the culprits.

'Just a minute,' said the Doctor. 'Is the box now
in the exact place where you found it when you got
up?'

'Yes,' said Throgmorton.

'Well, would you show us, please, just how you
went to the dressing-table and opened it?'

'Certainly,' said Throgmorton. 'I walked from
the bed, like this, and first threw back the curtains
of the window, so. Then one glance at the dressing-
table told me something was wrong. I stepped up

to it – so – lifted the box and opened it. Like
this. . . . What the–'

At that last exclamation of astonishment we all
four breathed a secret sigh of relief. For it told us
that the white mouse had done his work. I shall
never forget Throgmorton's face as he stood there,
staring into the box he had taken up to
demonstrate with. In it there were not three studs,
as he had expected, but the complete set of four.

The sergeant looked over his shoulder.

'There's been some mistake, sir, hasn't there?'
said he quietly.

'There's b-b-b-been some trickery,' cried
Throgmorton, spluttering. Indeed his discomfited
indignation was understandable enough in the
circumstances. He would much sooner have got
John Dolittle into jail than have recovered his
stud. And this small quiet man seemed to have a
knack for making a fool of him at the most
dramatic moments.

'If you didn't do it,' he snarled, swinging round
on the Doctor and pointing a fat accusing finger
at him, 'how did your hat come to be in my
house?'

'I think,' said the Doctor, 'it would be best if I
gave you an answer to that question in private.'

'No,' snapped Throgmorton. 'If it's the truth
there's no harm in the police sergeant hearing it.'

'As you wish,' said the Doctor. 'But I thought you
would prefer it that way. It has to do with a will
whose existence we discovered by accident.'

Astonishment, fear, hatred flitted across
Throgmorton's face in quick succession during the
short moment that passed before he answered.

'All right,' he said sullenly at last. 'We will go down to the library.'

In a silent, very thoughtful procession we returned down the several flights of stairs. At the tail of it came Matthew and myself.

'Thank goodness for the white mouse, Tommy!' he whispered in my ear. 'But I don't like trusting that fellow alone with the Doctor.'

'Don't worry,' I answered. 'We'll be outside the door. He'll hardly dare to start any violence with the sergeant here as a witness. His game's up.'

I heard the big grandfather clock in the hall strike as the Doctor and Throgmorton went into the library and closed the door behind them. And it was exactly three-quarters of an hour before they came out.

Throgmorton was very white, but quite quiet. He immediately addressed himself to the policeman.

'The charge is withdrawn, sergeant,' he said. 'A mistake – for which I tender my apologies to – er – all concerned. I'm sorry I got you up here so early when there was no need.'

Again in silence we trailed across the wide carpeted hall and out into the gravel court.

At the gate we bade farewell to the sergeant, whose direction was a different one from ours. I noticed that the Doctor made no comment upon the matter to him.

When he was well out of earshot Matthew asked eagerly: 'But, Doctor, how did you explain your hat's being there?'

'I didn't,' said John Dolittle. 'But I told him that all four of us were convinced he lit that fire himself. And after that he was much more anxious that I should keep my mouth shut than that I should do any explaining. He has got rather scared of me now, I imagine. And he probably thinks that I can prove he lit the fire. Which I can't. But it is just as well that he should think so, because I feel sure he did. He is going back to Australia now.'

'To Australia!' cried Matthew. 'Why?'

'Well, he has to earn a living, you see,' said the Doctor. 'The will left not only the hundred thousand pounds for the prevention of cruelty to animals, but when I came to read it through I found that it left the rest to other charities.'

When the outcome of the Moorsden Manor mystery became generally known in the Dolittle Zoo, jubilation and rejoicing broke forth and lasted two whole days. Accustomed as it was to celebration, Animal Town admitted it had never seen the like before. The white mouse's genius for parade organization surpassed itself; and he was elected to a second term of office as mayor on the strength of it.

He felt that since animals in general had by the Doctor's victory come into such a considerable fortune, this occasion should be made a larger and more important one than any in the history of the zoo. So for the second day's celebrations he got the Doctor's permission to send out an invitation to all the creatures of the neighbourhood who wished to come. An enormous amount of preparation was made in expectation of a large attendance. The whole zoo was most gaily decorated, with ribbons and bunting by day and with lanterns and fireworks by night. Great quantities of all sorts of

things to eat and drink were bought and set out at
several buffets in the enclosure.

But the crowd that actually did come was even
vaster than had been anticipated. All the regular
members of the Rat and Mouse Club, the Rabbits'
Apartment House, the Home for Cross-Bred Dogs,
the Badgers' Tavern, the Squirrels' Hotel and the
Foxes' Meeting House had to set to and do duty as
hosts. So did Gub-Gub, the pushmi-pullyu, Chee-
Chee, Too-Too, Dab-Dab, and Polynesia. And even
with this extra help it was only by working like
bees that they managed to feed and entertain that
enormous crowd of visitors.

As for the Doctor, Matthew, Bumpo and me, we
were kept busy running between the house and
the town for more, and still more, refreshments, as
the ever-increasing attendance did away with
what we had already. Too-Too, the accountant,
told me afterwards that according to his books we
had bought more than a wagon-load of lettuce,
three hundred-weight of corn and birdseed, close
on a ton of bones and meat, four large cheeses and
two dozen loaves — besides a great number of
delicacies in smaller quantity.

Within the old bowling-green it was almost
impossible to move along the lawns, so thronged
were they with hedgehogs, moles, squirrels,
stoats, rats, badgers, mice, voles, otters, hares,
and what not. At frequent intervals cheers for the
Doctor, old Mr Throgmorton, or his Association for
the Prevention of Cruelty to Animals, would
break out in some corner and be rapidly taken up
all over the vast assembly. Every tree and shrub
in the zoo enclosure — and throughout the whole

of the Doctor's garden, too — was just packed and laden with perching birds of all kinds and sizes, from wrens to herons. The din of their chatter was constant and terrific.

Before the day was over the grass of the bowling-green was all worn away by the continuous passing of those millions of feet. And after the guests had departed it took the members of the Dolittle Zoo another whole day to clear away the scraps and put the place in order.

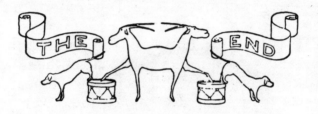

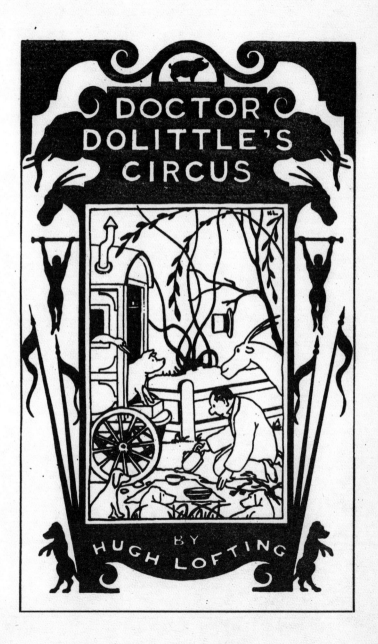

DOCTOR
DOLITTLE'S
CIRCUS

BY HUGH LOFTING

Contents

Illustrations

PART I

Chapter One
THE FIRESIDE CIRCLE

THIS is the story of that part of Doctor Dolittle's adventures which came about through his joining and travelling with a circus. The Dolittle party, Jip the dog, Dab-Dab the duck, Too-Too the owl, Gub-Gub the pig, the pushmi-pullyu (the extraordinary two-headed animal that the doctor had brought back with him from Africa), and the white mouse, had returned at last to the little house in Puddleby-on-the-Marsh after their long journey from Africa. It was a large family to find food for. And the Doctor, without a penny in his pockets, had been worried over how he was going to feed it. However, the thoughtful Dab-Dab had made them carry up from the ship such supplies as remained in the larder after the voyage was done. These, she said, should last the household – with economy – for a day or two at least.

The animals' delight on getting back home had banished every care or thought of the morrow from the minds of all – except Dab-Dab. That good housekeeper had gone straight to the kitchen and set about the cleaning of pots and the cooking of

food. The rest of them, the Doctor included, had
gone out into the garden to re-explore all the well-
known spots. And they were still roaming and
poking around every nook and corner of their
beloved home when they were suddenly summoned to luncheon by Dab-Dab's dinner bell — a
frying pan beaten with a spoon. At this there was
a grand rush for the back door. And they all came
trundling in from the garden, gabbling with
delight at the prospect of taking a meal again in
the dear old kitchen where they had in times past
spent so many jolly hours together.

'It will be cold enough for a fire tonight,' said Jip
as they took their places at the table. 'This
September wind has a chilly snap in it. Will you
tell us a story after supper, Doctor? It's a long time
since we sat around the hearth in a ring.'

'Or read to us out of your animal storybooks,'
said Gub-Gub, 'the one about the fox who tried to
steal the King's goose.'

'Well, maybe,' said the Doctor. 'We'll see. We'll
see. What delicious sardines these are! From
Bordeaux, by the taste of them. There's no mistaking real French sardines.'

At this moment the Doctor was called away to
see a patient in the surgery — a weasel who had
broken a claw. And he was no sooner done with
that when a rooster with a sore throat turned up
from a neighbouring farm. He was so hoarse, he
said, he could crow only in a whisper, and nobody
on his farm woke up in the morning. Then two
pheasants arrived to show him a scrawny chick
that had never been able to peck properly since it
was born.

'He could crow only in a whisper'

For, although the people in Puddleby had not yet learned of the Doctor's arrival, news of his coming had already spread among the animals and the birds. And all that afternoon he was kept busy bandaging, advising, and giving out doses of medicine, while a huge motley crowd of creatures waited patiently outside the surgery door.

'Ah me! – just like old times,' sighed Dab-Dab. 'No peace. Patients clamouring to see him morning, noon and night.'

Jip had been right: by the time darkness came

that night it was very chilly. Wood enough was
found in the cellar to start a jolly fire in the big
chimney. Round this the animals gathered after
supper and pestered the Doctor for a story or a
chapter from one of his books.

'But look here,' said he. 'What about the circus?'

During his recent African voyage, the Doctor
had borrowed a sailor's boat. Unfortunately, the
boat was wrecked, but Doctor Dolittle was persuaded by his animal friends to bring back that
rarest of animals, the pushmi-pullyu. The
animals' idea was that they would join a circus and
put the pushmi-pullyu on display. By that means,
the Doctor could earn enough money to pay the
sailor for his boat, and even have some money left
over for his own household.

'If we're going to make money to pay the sailor
back we've got to be thinking of that. We haven't
even found a circus to go with yet. I wonder what's
the best way to set about it. They travel all over
the place, you know. Let me see: who could I ask?'

'Sh!' said Too-Too. 'Wasn't that the front doorbell
ringing?'

'Strange!' said the Doctor, getting up from his
chair. 'Callers already?'

When John Dolittle had lit the candles in the
hall he opened the front door. And there standing
on the threshold was the cat's-meat man.

'Why, it's Matthew Mugg, as I'm alive!' he cried.
'Come in Matthew, come in. But how did you know
I was here?'

'I felt it in my bones, Doctor,' said the cat's-meat
man, stumping into the hall. 'Only this morning I
says to my wife, "Theodosia," I says, "something

' "Why, it's Matthew Mugg!" '

tells me the Doctor's got back. And I'm going up to
his house tonight to take a look." '

'Well, I'm glad to see you,' said John Dolittle.
'Let's go into the kitchen where it's warm.'

Although he said he had only come on the
chance of finding the Doctor, the cat's-meat man
had brought presents with him: a knucklebone off
a shoulder of mutton for Jip; a piece of cheese for
the white mouse; a turnip for Gub-Gub and a pot
of flowering geraniums for the Doctor. When the
visitor was comfortably settled in the armchair

before the fire John Dolittle handed him the
tobacco jar from the mantelpiece and told him to
fill his pipe.

'I got your letter about the sparrow,' said Matthew. 'He found you all right, I s'pose.'

'Yes, and he was very useful to me. He left the
ship when we were off the Devon coast. He was
anxious to get back to London.'

'Are you home for a long stay now?'

'Well – yes and no,' said the Doctor. 'I'd like
nothing better than to enjoy a few quiet months
here and get my garden to rights. It's in a shocking
mess. But unfortunately I've got to make some
money first.'

'Humph,' said Matthew, puffing at his pipe.
'Meself, I've bin trying to do that all my life. Never
was very good at it. But I've got twenty-five shillings saved up, if that would help you.'

'It's very kind of you, Matthew, very. The fact
is I – er – I need a whole lot of money. I've got
to pay back some debts. But listen: I have a
strange kind of new animal – a pushmi-pullyu.
He has two heads. The monkeys in Africa
presented him to me after I had cured an epidemic
for them. Their idea was that I should travel with
him in a circus – on show, you know. Would you
like to see him?'

'I surely would,' said the cat's-meat man. 'Sounds
like something very new.'

'He's out in the garden,' said the Doctor. 'Don't
stare at him too hard. He isn't used to it yet. Gets
frightfully embarrassed. Let's take a bucket of
water with us and just pretend we've brought him
a drink.'

When Matthew came back into the kitchen with the Doctor he was all smiles and enthusiasm.

'Why, John Dolittle,' said he, 'you'll make your fortune – sure as you're alive! There's never bin anything seen like that since the world began. And anyway, I always thought you ought to go into the circus business – you, the only man living that knows animal language. When are you going to start?'

'That's just the point. Perhaps you can help me. I'd want to be sure it was a nice circus I was going with – people I would like, you understand.'

Matthew Mugg bent forward and tapped the Doctor on the knee with the stem of his pipe.

'I know the very concern you want,' said he. 'Right now over at Grimbledon there's the nicest little circus you ever saw. Grimbledon Fair's on this week and they'll be there till Saturday. Me and Theodosia saw 'em the first day they was on. It isn't a large circus but it's a good one – select like. What do you say if I take you over there tomorrow and you have a chat with the ringmaster?'

'Why that would be splendid,' said the Doctor. 'But in the meantime don't say anything to anyone about the idea at all. We must keep the pushmi-pullyu a secret till he is actually put on show before the public.'

Chapter Two
THE DOCTOR MEETS A
FRIEND – AND A RELATIVE

NOW, Matthew Mugg was a peculiar man. He loved trying new jobs — which was one reason, perhaps, that he never made much money. But his attempts to get into some new kind of work usually ended in his coming back to selling cat's meat and rat-catching for farmers and millers around Puddleby.

Matthew had already at Grimbledon Fair tried to get a job with the circus and been refused. But now that he found the Doctor was going into the business — and with such a wonderful exhibition as a pushmi-pullyu — his hopes rose again. And as he went home that night he already in imagination saw himself in partnership with his beloved doctor, running the biggest circus on earth.

Next day he called at the little house early. After Dab-Dab had made them up some sardine sandwiches to take with them for lunch, they set out.

It was a long walk from Puddleby to Grimbledon. But after the Doctor and the cat's-meat man had been trudging down the road a while, they heard a sound of hoofs behind them.

They turned round; and there was a farmer coming towards them in a trap. Seeing the two travellers upon the road, the farmer was going to offer them a ride. But his wife did not like the ragged looks of the cat's-meat man, and she forbade her husband to stop for them.

'What d'yer think of that for Christian charity?' said the cat's-meat man as the cart went spinning by them. 'Sit comfortable in their seats and leave us to walk! That's Isidore Stiles, the biggest potato-grower in these parts. I often catches rats for him. And his wife, the snobby old scarecrow! Did yer see that look she give me? A rat-catcher ain't good enough company for her!'

'But look,' said the Doctor. 'They're stopping and turning the trap around.'

Now this farmer's horse knew the Doctor very well both by sight and reputation. And as he had trotted by he had recognized the little man tramping along the road as none other than the famous John Dolittle. Delighted to find that his friend had returned to these parts, the horse had then turned around of his own accord, and was now trotting back — in spite of his driver's pulling — to greet the Doctor and inquire about his health.

'Where are you going?' asked the horse as he came up.

'We're going to Grimbledon Fair,' said the Doctor.

'So are we,' said the horse. 'Why don't you get into the back of the trap beside the old woman?'

'They haven't invited me,' said the Doctor. 'See, your farmer is trying to turn you around again

towards Grimbledon. Better not anger him. Run
along. Don't bother about us. We'll be all right.'

Very unwillingly the horse finally obeyed the
driver, turned about, and set off once more for the
fair. But he hadn't gone more than half a mile
before he said to himself, It's a shame the great
man should have to walk while these bumpkins
ride. I'm hanged if I'll leave him behind!

Then he pretended to shy at something in the
road, swung the trap around again suddenly, and
raced back towards the Doctor at full gallop. The
farmer's wife screamed and her husband threw all
his weight on the reins. But the horse took not the
slightest notice. Reaching the Doctor he started
rearing and bucking and carrying on like a wild
colt.

'Get into the trap, Doctor,' he whispered. 'Get in,
or I'll spill these boobies into the ditch.'

The Doctor, fearing an accident, took hold of
the horse's bridle and patted him on the nose.
Instantly he became as calm and gentle as a
lamb.

'Your horse is a little restive, sir,' said the Doctor
to the farmer. 'Would you let me drive him for a
spell? I am a veterinary surgeon.'

'Why, certainly,' said the farmer. 'I thought I
knew something about horses meself. But I can't
do a thing with him this morning.'

Then, as the Doctor climbed up and took the
reins, the cat's-meat man got in behind and,
chuckling with delight, sat beside the indignant
wife.

'Nice day, Mrs Stiles,' said Matthew Mugg. 'How
are the rats in the barn?'

'The Doctor took hold of the bridle'

They reached Grimbledon about the middle of the morning. The town was very full and busy and holidayfied. In the cattle market fine prize pigs, fat sheep, and pedigree draft horses with ribbons in their manes filled the pens.

Through the good-natured crowds that thronged the streets the Doctor and Matthew made their way patiently towards the enclosure where the circus was. The Doctor began to get worried that he might be asked to pay to go in, because he hadn't a single penny in his pockets. But at the entrance to the circus they found a high platform erected, with some curtains at the back. It was like a small outdoor theatre. On this platform a man with an enormous black moustache was standing. From time to time various showily-dressed persons made their appearance through the curtains; and the big man introduced them to the gaping crowd and told of the wonders they could perform. Whatever they were, clowns, acrobats or snake charmers, he always said they were the greatest in the world. The crowd was tremendously impressed; and every once in a while people in ones and twos would make their way through the throng, pay their money at the little gate, and pass into the circus enclosure.

'There you are,' the cat's-meat man whispered in the Doctor's ear. 'Didn't I tell yer it was a good show? Look! People going in by hundreds.'

'Is that big man the manager?' asked the Doctor.

'Yes, that's him. That's Blossom himself – Alexander Blossom. He's the man we've come to see.'

The Doctor began to squirm his way forward through the people, with Matthew following behind. Finally he reached the front and started making signs to the big man on the platform above to show that he wanted to speak to him. But Mr Blossom was so busy bellowing about the wonders of his show that the Doctor – a small man in a big crowd – could not attract his attention.

'Get up on the platform,' said Matthew. 'Climb up and talk to him.'

So the Doctor clambered up on the corner of the

stage and then suddenly got frightfully embarrassed to find himself facing so large a gathering of people. However, once there, he plucked up his courage and, tapping the shouting showman on the arm, he said, 'Excuse me.'

Mr Blossom stopped roaring about the 'greatest show on earth' and gazed down at the little round man who had suddenly appeared beside him.

'Er – er—' the Doctor began.

Then there was a silence. The people began to titter.

Blossom, like most showmen, was never at a loss for words and seldom missed an opportunity of being funny at somebody else's expense. And while John Dolittle was still wondering how to begin, the manager suddenly turned to the crowd again and, waving his arm towards the Doctor, shouted, 'And this, Ladies and Gentlemen, is the original Humpty-Dumpty – the one what gave the king's men so much trouble. Pay your money and come in! Walk up and see 'im fall off the wall!'

At that the crowd roared with laughter and the poor Doctor got more embarrassed than ever.

'Talk to him, Doctor, *talk* to him!' called the cat's-meat man from down below.

Soon, when the laughter had subsided, the Doctor made another attempt. He had just opened his mouth when a single piercing cry rang from amidst the crowd – '*John!*'

The Doctor turned and gazed over the heads of the people to see who was calling him by name. And there on the outskirts of the throng he saw a

woman waving violently to him with a green
parasol.

'Who is it?' said the cat's-meat man.

'Heaven preserve us!' groaned the Doctor, shame-
facedly climbing down off the stage. 'What'll we do
now? Matthew – *it's Sarah!*'

Chapter Three
BUSINESS ARRANGEMENTS

'WELL, Well, Sarah!' said John Dolittle when he had finally made his way to her. 'My, how well and plump you're looking!'

'I'm nothing of the sort, John,' said Sarah severely. 'Will you please tell me what you mean by gallivanting around on that platform like a clown? Wasn't it enough for you to throw away the best practice in the West Country for the sake of pet mice and frogs and things? Have you no pride? What were you doing up there?'

'I was thinking of going into the circus business,' said the Doctor.

Sarah gasped and put her hand to her head as though about to swoon. Then a long lean man in parson's clothes who was standing behind her came and took her by the arm.

'What is it, my dear?' said he.

'Launcelot,' said Sarah weakly, 'this is my brother, John Dolittle. John, this is the Reverend Launcelot Dingle, rector of Grimbledon, my husband. But, John, you can't be serious. Go into the circus business! How disgraceful! You must be joking – and who is the person?' she

added as Matthew Mugg shuffled up and joined
the party.

'This is Matthew Mugg,' said the Doctor. 'You
remember him, of course?'

'Ugh! – the rat-catcher,' said Sarah, closing her
eyes in horror.

'Not at all. He's a meat merchant,' said the
Doctor. 'Mr Mugg, the Reverend Launcelot
Dingle.' And the Doctor introduced his ragged,
greasy friend as if he had been a king. 'He's my
most prominent patient,' he added.

'But listen, John,' said Sarah, 'if you do go
into this mad business, promise me you'll do it
under some other name. Think what it would
mean to our position here if it got known that
the rector's brother-in-law was a common showman!'

The Doctor thought a moment. Then he smiled.
'All right, Sarah, I'll use some other name. But I
can't help it if someone recognizes me, can I?'

After they had bidden farewell to Sarah, the
Doctor and Matthew again sought out the
manager. They found him counting money at the
gate, and this time were able to talk to him at
their ease.

John Dolittle described the wonderful animal
that he had at home and said he wanted to join the
circus with him. Alexander Blossom admitted he
would like to see the creature and told the Doctor
to bring him there. But John Dolittle said it would
be better and easier if the manager came to
Puddleby to look at him.

This was agreed upon. And after they had
explained to Blossom how to get to the little house

on Oxenthorpe Road, they set out for home again, very pleased with their success so far.

'If you do go with Blossom's circus,' Matthew asked, as they tramped along the road chewing sardine sandwiches, 'will you take me with you, Doctor? I'd come in real handy, taking care of the caravan, feeding and cleaning and the likes o' that.'

'You're very welcome to come, Matthew,' said the Doctor, 'But what about your own business?'

'Oh, that,' said Matthew, biting viciously into another sandwich. 'There ain't no money in that. Besides, it's so tame, handing out bits of meat on skewers to overfed poodles! There's no . . . no what d'y' call it?' – he waved his sandwich towards the sky – 'no adventure in it. I'm naturally venturesome – reckless like – always was, from my cradle up. Now the circus: that's real life! That's a man's job.'

'But how about your wife?' asked the Doctor.

'Theodosia? Oh, she'd come along. She's venturesome, like me. She could mend the clothes and do odd jobs. What do you think?'

'What do I think?' asked the Doctor, who was staring down at the road as he walked. 'I was thinking of Sarah.'

'Queer gent, that what she married, ain't he,' said Matthew, 'the Reverend Dangle?'

'*Dingle*,' the Doctor corrected. 'Yes. He's venturesome too. It's a funny world! Poor dear Sarah! Poor old Dingle! Well, well.'

Late that night, when the Grimbledon Fair had closed, Mr Blossom, the ringmaster, came to the Doctor's house in Puddleby.

'He waved his sandwich towards the sky'

After he had been shown by the light of a lantern the pushmi-pullyu grazing on the lawn, he came back into the library with the Doctor and said, 'How much do you want for that animal?'

'No, no, he's not for sale,' said the Doctor.

'Oh, come now,' said the manager. 'You don't want him. Anyone could see you're not a regular showman. I'll give you twenty pounds for him.'

'No,' said the Doctor.

'Thirty pounds,' said Blossom.

Still the Doctor refused.

'Forty pounds – fifty pounds,' said the manager. Then he went up and up, offering prices that made the cat's-meat man, who was listening, open his eyes wider and wider with wonder.

'It's no use,' said the Doctor at last. 'You must either take me with the animal into your circus or leave him where he is. I have promised that I myself will see he is properly treated.'

'What do you mean?' asked the showman. 'Ain't he your property? Who did you promise?'

'He's his own property,' said the Doctor. 'He came here to oblige me. It was to himself, the pushmi-pullyu, that I gave my promise.'

'What! Are you crazy?' asked the showman. Matthew Mugg was going to explain to Blossom that the Doctor could speak animals' language. But John Dolittle motioned to him to be silent.

'And, so, you see,' he went on, 'you must either take me *and* the animal or neither.'

Then Blossom said no, he wouldn't agree to that arrangement. And to Matthew's great disappointment and grief he took his hat and left.

But he had expected the Doctor to change his mind and give in. And he hadn't been gone more than ten minutes before he rang the doorbell and said that he had come back to talk it over.

Well, the upshot of it was that the showman finally consented to all the Doctor asked. The pushmi-pullyu and his party were to be provided with a new wagon all to themselves and, although travelling as part of the circus, were to be entirely free and independent. The money made was to be divided equally between the Doctor and the manager. Whenever the pushmi-pullyu wanted a

'Hooray for the circus!'

day off he was to have it, and whatever kind of food he asked for was to be provided by Blossom.

When all the arrangments had been gone into, the man said he would send the caravan there next day, and prepared to go.

'By the way,' he said, pausing at the front door. 'What's your name?'

The Doctor was just about to tell him, when he remembered Sarah's request.

'Oh, well, call me John Smith,' said he.

'All right, Mr Smith,' said the showman. 'Have

your party ready by eleven in the morning. Good
night.'

'Good night,' said the Doctor.

As soon as the door had closed Dab-Dab, Gub-
Gub, Jip, Too-Too, and the white mouse, who had
been hiding and listening in various corners of the
house, all came out into the hall and started chattering at the top of their voices.

'Hooray!' grunted Gub-Gub. 'Hooray for the
circus!'

'My,' said Matthew to the Doctor, 'you're not
such a bad businessman after all! You got Blossom
to give in to everything. He wasn't going to let the
chance slip. Did you see how quickly he came back
when he thought the deal was off? I'll bet he
expects to make a lot of money out of us.'

'Poor old home,' sighed Dab-Dab, affectionately
dusting off the hat rack. 'To leave it again so soon!'

'Hooray—' yelled Gub-Gub, trying to stand on
his hind legs and balance the Doctor's hat on his
nose. 'Hooray for the circus! Tomorrow! *Whee!*'

Chapter Four
THE DOCTOR IS DISCOVERED

VERY early the next morning Dab-Dab had the whole house astir. She said breakfast must be eaten and the table cleared before seven, if everything was to be got in readiness for their departure by eleven.

As a matter of fact, the diligent housekeeper had the house closed and everybody waiting outside on the front steps hours before the wagon arrived. But the Doctor, for one, was still kept busy. For up to the last minute animal patients were still coming in from all parts of the countryside, with various ailments to be cured.

At last Jip, who had been out scouting, came rushing back to the party gathered in the garden.

'The wagon's coming,' he panted, '. . . all red and yellow . . . it's just around the bend.'

Then everybody got excited and began grabbing parcels. Gub-Gub's luggage was a bundle of turnips, and just as he was hurrying down the steps to the road, the string broke and the round white vegetables went rolling all over the place.

The wagon, when it finally came in sight, was certainly a thing of beauty. It was made like a

'Waiting on the front steps'

Gypsy caravan, with windows and door and chimney. It was very gaily painted and quite new.

Not so the horse; he was quite old. The Doctor said that never had he seen an animal so worn out and weary. He got into conversation with him and found out that he had been working in the circus for thirty-five years. He was very sick of it, he said. His name was Beppo. The Doctor decided he would tell Blossom that it was high time Beppo should be pensioned off and allowed to live in peace.

They reached the Grimbledon fairgrounds about

two o'clock in the afternoon and entered the circus
enclosure by a back gate. Inside they found the
great Blossom himself waiting to welcome them.

He seemed quite surprised, on the van's being
opened, to find the odd collection of creatures the
Doctor had brought with him – he was particularly astonished at the pig. However, he was so
delighted to have the pushmi-pullyu that he didn't
mind.

He at once led them to what he called their stand
– which, he said, he had had built for them that
very morning. This the Doctor found to be similar
to the place where he had first spoken with
Blossom. It was a platform raised three feet from
the ground, so that the board and canvas room
on the top of it could be seen. It had steps up to it,
and a little way back from the front edge of the
platform, curtains covered the entrance to the
room, so no one could see inside unless they paid
to go in.

Across the front of it was a sign:

THE PUSHMI-PULLYU!
COME AND SEE THE MARVELLOUS
TWO-HEADED ANIMAL
FROM THE JUNGLES OF AFRICA!
ADMISSION: SIXPENCE

The red and yellow wagon (in which the Doctor's
party, with the exception of the pushmi-pullyu,
were to live) was backed behind the 'stand'. And
Dab-Dab immediately set about making up beds
and arranging the inside so it would be homelike.

Blossom wanted to have the pushmi-pullyu put

on show at once, but the Doctor refused. He said any wild animal would need to rest after the journey from Puddleby. And he wished the timid beast to get used to the noisy bustle of circus life before he was stared at by a crowd of holiday-makers.

Blossom was disappointed, but he had to give in. Then, to the animals' delight, he offered to show the Doctor around the circus and introduce him to the various performers. So after the pushmi-pullyu had been moved to his new home in the stand and the Doctor had seen that he was provided with hay and water and bedding, the Puddleby party started out to make a tour of the circus under the guidance of the great Alexander Blossom, ringmaster.

The main show took place only twice a day (at two in the afternoon and at six-thirty at night), in a big tent in the middle of the enclosure. But all around this there were smaller tents and stands, most of which you had to pay extra to get into. Of these the Doctor's establishment was now to form one. They contained all manner of wonders: shooting galleries, guessing games, wild men of Borneo, bearded ladies, merry-go-rounds, strong men, snake charmers, a menagerie, and many more.

Blossom took the Doctor and his friends to the menagerie first. It was a dingy third-rate sort of collection. Most of the animals seemed dirty and unhappy. The Doctor was so saddened he was all for having a row with Blossom over it. But the cat's-meat man whispered in his ear, 'Don't be starting trouble right away, Doctor. Wait awhile.

After the boss sees how valuable you are with performing animals, you'll be able to do what you like with him. If you kick up a shindy now, we'll maybe lose our job. Then you won't be able to do anything.'

This struck John Dolittle as good advice. And he contented himself for the present with whispering to the animals through the bars of their cages that later he hoped to do something for them.

Just as they had entered, a dirty man was taking around a group of country folk to show them the collection. Stopping before a cage where a small furry animal was imprisoned, the man called out, 'And this, ladies and gents, is the famous hurri-gurri, from the forests of Patagonia. 'E 'angs from the trees by 'is tail. Pass on to the next cage.'

The Doctor, followed by Gub-Gub, went over and looked in at 'the famous hurri-gurri'.

'Why,' said he, 'that's nothing but a common opossum from America. One of the marsupials.'

'How do you know it's a ma soupial, Doctor?' asked Gub-Gub. 'She hasn't any children with her. Perhaps it's a pa soupial.'

'And this,' roared the man, standing before the next cage, 'is the largest elephant in captivity.'

'Almost the smallest one I ever saw,' murmured the Doctor.

Then Mr Blossom suggested that they go on to the next show, Princess Fatima, the snake charmer. And he led the way out of the close, evil-smelling menagerie into the open air. As the Doctor passed down the line of cages he hung his head, frowning unhappily. For the various

'One of the marsupials'

animals, recognizing the great John Dolittle, were all making signs to him to stop and talk with them.

When they entered the snake charmer's tent there were no other visitors there for the moment but themselves. On the small stage they beheld the Princess Fatima, powdering her large nose and swearing to herself in cockney. Beside her chair was a big shallow box full of snakes. Matthew Mugg peeped into it, gasped with horror, and then started to run from the tent.

'It's all right, Matthew,' the Doctor called out. 'Don't be alarmed. They're quite harmless.'

'What d'yer mean, harmless?' snorted the Princess Fatima, glaring at the Doctor. 'They're king cobras, from India – the deadliest snakes livin'.'

'They're nothing of the sort,' said the Doctor. 'They're American blacksnakes – non-poisonous.' And he tickled one under the chin.

'Leave them snakes alone!' yelled Fatima, rising from her chair – 'or I'll knock yer bloomin' 'ead orf.'

At this moment Blossom interfered and introduced the ruffled princess to Mr Smith.

The conversation that followed (Fatima was still too angry to take much part in it) was interrupted by the arrival of some people who had come to see the snake charmer perform. Blossom led the Doctor's party off into a corner, whispering, 'She's marvellous, Smith. One of the best turns I've got. Just you watch her.'

Behind the curtains at the back somebody started beating a drum and playing a pipe. Then Fatima arose, lifted two snakes out of the box, and wound them around her neck and arms.

'Will ze ladies and ze gentlemen step a little closair,' she cooed softly to her audience. 'Zen zay can see bettair – zo!'

'What's she talking like that for?' Gub-Gub whispered to the Doctor.

'Sh! I suppose she thinks she's speaking with an Oriental accent,' said John Dolittle.

'Sounds to me like a hot-potato accent,' muttered Gub-Gub. 'Isn't she fat and wobbly!'

' "You leave them snakes alone!" '

Noticing that the Doctor did not seem favourably impressed, the circus master led them out to see the other side-shows.

At the next booth a large audience was gathered and yokels were gasping in wonder as the strong man lifted enormous weights in the air. There was no fake about this show. And John Dolittle, deeply interested, joined in the clapping and the gasping.

The strong man was an honest-looking fellow, with tremendous muscles. The Doctor took a liking to him right away. One of his tricks was to lie on the stage on his back and lift an enormous

dumb-bell with his feet till his legs were sticking
right up in the air. It needed balance as well as
strength because if the dumb-bell should fall the
wrong way the man would certainly be injured.
Today when he had finally brought his legs into an
upright position the crowd was whispering in
admiration, suddenly there was a loud crack. One
of the boards of the stage had given way.
Instantly, down came the big dumb-bell right
across the man's chest.

The crowd screamed and Blossom jumped up on
the platform. It took two men's strength to lift the
dumb-bell off the strong man's body. But even
then he did not arise. He lay motionless, his eyes
closed, his face a deathly white.

'Get a doctor,' Blossom shouted to the cat's-meat
man. 'Hurry! He's hurt hisself – unconscious. A
doctor, quick!'

But John Dolittle was already on the stage,
standing over the ringmaster, who knelt beside
the injured man.

'Get out of the way and let me examine him,' he
said quietly.

'What can you do? He's hurt bad. Look, his
breathing's queer. We got to get a doctor.'

'I am a doctor,' said John Dolittle. 'Matthew, run
to the van and get my black bag.'

'You a doctor!' said Blossom, getting up off his
knees. 'Thought you called yourself *Mr Smith*.'

'Off course he's a doctor,' came a voice out of the
crowd. 'There wur a time when he wur the best
known doctor in the West Country. I know un.
Dolittle's his name – John Dolittle, of Puddleby-
on-the-Marsh.'

Chapter Five
THE DOCTOR IS DISCOURAGED

THE Doctor found that two of the strong man's ribs had been broken by the dumb-bell. However, he prophesied that with so powerful a constitution the patient should recover quickly. The injured man was put to bed in his own caravan and until he was well again the Doctor visited him four times a day and Matthew slept in his wagon to nurse him.

The strong man (his show name was Hercules) was very thankful to John Dolittle and became greatly attached to him – and very useful sometimes, as you will see later on.

So the Doctor felt, when he went to bed that first night of his circus career, that if he had made an enemy in Fatima, the snake charmer, he had gained a friend in Hercules, the strong man.

Of course, now that he had been recognized as the odd physician of Puddleby-on-the-Marsh, there was no longer any sense in his trying to conceal who he was. And very soon he became known among the circus folk as just 'the Doctor' or 'the Doc'. On the very high recommendation of Hercules, he was constantly called upon for the

cure of small ailments by everyone, from the
bearded lady to the clown.

The next day, the pushmi-pullyu was put on
show for the first time. He was very popular. A
two-headed animal had never before been seen in
a circus and the people thronged up to pay their
money and have a look at him. At first he nearly
died of embarrassment and shyness, and he was
forever hiding one of his heads under the straw so
as not to have to meet the gaze of all those staring
eyes. Then the people wouldn't believe he had
more than one head. So the Doctor asked him if he
would be so good as to keep both of them in view.

'You need not look at the people,' he said. 'But
just let them see that you really have two heads.
You can turn your back on the audience – both
ends.'

But some of the silly people, even when they
could see the two heads plainly, kept saying that
one must be faked. And they would prod the poor,
timid animal with sticks to see if part of him was
stuffed. While two country bumpkins were doing
this one day the pushmi-pullyu got annoyed, and
bringing both his heads up sharply at the same
time, he jabbed the two inquirers in the legs. Then
they knew for sure that he was real and alive all
over.

But as soon as the cat's-meat man could be
spared from nursing Hercules (he turned the job
over to his wife) the Doctor put him on guard
inside the stall to see that the animal was not
molested by stupid visitors. The poor creature had
a terrible time those first days. But when Jip told
him how much money was being taken in, he

determined to stick it out for John Dolittle's sake. And after a little while, although his opinion of the human race sank very low, he got sort of used to the silly, gaping faces of his audiences and gazed back at them – from both his heads – with fearless superiority and the scorn that they deserved.

Poor Dab-Dab was busier than ever now. For in addition to the housekeeping duties she always had to keep one eye on the Doctor; and many were the scoldings she gave him because he would let the children in for nothing when she wasn't looking.

At the end of each day Blossom, the manager, came to divide up the money. And Too-Too, the mathematician, was always there when the adding was done, to see that the Doctor got his proper share.

Although the pushmi-pullyu was so popular, the Doctor saw very early in his new career that it would take quite a time to earn sufficient money to pay the sailor back for the boat – let alone to make enough for himself and his family to live on besides.

He was rather sorry about this, for there were a lot of things in the circus business that he did not like and he was anxious to leave it. While his own show was a perfectly honest affair, there were many features of the circus that were fakes; and the Doctor, who always hated fake of any kind, had an uncomfortable feeling that he was part of an establishment not strictly honest. Most of the gambling games were arranged so that those who played them were bound to lose their money.

'Too-Too was always there'

But the thing that worried the Doctor most was the condition of the animals. Their life, he felt, was in most cases an unhappy one. At the end of his first day with the circus, after the crowds had gone home and all was quiet in the enclosure, he had gone back into the menagerie and talked to the animals there. They nearly all had complaints to make: their cages were not kept properly clean; they did not get exercise or room enough; with some, the food served was not the kind they liked.

The Doctor heard them all and was so indignant

he sought out the ringmaster in his private caravan right away and told him plainly all the things he thought ought to be changed.

Blossom listened patiently until he had finished and then he laughed.

'Why, Doc,' said he, 'if I was to do all the things you want me to, I might as well leave the business! I'd be ruined. What, pension off the horses? Send the hurri-gurri back to his home? Keep the men cleaning out the cages all day? Buy special foods? Have the animals took out for walks every day, like a young ladies' academy? Man, you must be crazy! Now, look here: you don't know anything about this game – nothing, see! I've given in to you in all you asked. I'm letting you run your part of the show your own way. But I'm going to run the rest of it my way. Understand? I don't want no interference. It's bad enough to have the strong man on the sick list. I ain't going to go broke just to please your Sunday school ideas. And that's flat.'

Sad at heart, the Doctor left the manager's quarters and made his way across to his own caravan. On the steps of his wagon, he found the cat's-meat man smoking his evening pipe. Close by, Beppo, the old horse, was cropping the scrubby grass of the enclosure by the light of the moon.

'Nice night,' said Matthew. 'You look kind of worried, Doctor. Anything wrong?'

'Yes,' said John Dolittle, sitting down miserably on the steps beside him. 'Everything's wrong. I've just been talking to Blossom about improving conditions in the menagerie. He won't do a single thing I ask. I think I'll leave the circus.'

'Oh, come now,' said Matthew. 'Why, you ain't hardly begun, Doctor! Blossom doesn't know yet that you can talk animal language even! Circuses don't have to be bad. *You* could run one that would be a new kind. Clean, honest, special — one that everybody in the world would come to see. But you got to get money first. Don't give up so easy.'

'No, it's no use, Matthew. I'm doing no good here and I can't stay and see animals unhappy. I never should have gone into the business.'

At this moment the old horse, Beppo, hearing his friend's voice, drew near and pushed his muzzle affectionately into the Doctor's ear.

'Hulloa,' said John Dolittle. 'Beppo, I'm afraid I can be of no help to you. I'm sorry — but I am going to leave the circus.'

'But, Doctor,' said the old horse, 'you're our one hope. Why, only today I heard the elephant and the talking horse — the cob who performs in the big show — they were saying how glad they were that you had come. Be patient. You can't change everything in a minute. If you go, then we'll never get anything we want. But we know that if you stay, before long you will be running the whole show the way it should be run. We're not worried as long as you're with us. Only stay. And mark my words, the day will come when the new circus, "the Dolittle Circus", will be the greatest on earth.'

For a moment the Doctor was silent. And Matthew, who had not understood the conversation with the horse, waited impatiently for him to speak.

At last he arose and turned to go into the caravan.

'Well,' said the cat's-meat man anxiously, 'are
you going to stay?'

'Yes, Matthew,' said the Doctor. 'It seems I've got
to. Good night.'

At the end of that week the Grimbledon Fair was
over and the circus had to move on to the next
town. It was a big job, this packing up a large show
for a long journey by road. And all day Sunday the
enclosure was a very busy place. Men ran around
everywhere shouting orders. The big tent and the
little tents were pulled down and rolled up. The
stands were taken apart and piled into wagons.
The large space that had looked so gay was
quickly changed into a drab, untidy mess. It was
all very new to the Doctor's pets; and though Dab-
Dab joined in the general hustle of packing, the
rest of them enjoyed the excitement and the
newness of it no end.

Then in a long procession of caravans the circus
set out upon the road. The next town to be visited
was fifty miles off. This journey could not, of
course, be covered in a single day, going at a walk.
Jip got lots of fun chasing the rats out of the
ditches along the road and often going off across a
meadow on the scent of a fox.

The nights were spent camping out by the roadside or in whatever convenient clear spaces could
be found. This part of the life, the halting for sleep,
seemed to be enjoyed by all. When the kettle was
put on to boil over the roadside fire everyone
cheered up and got talkative. Jip's two friends, the
clown's dog, Swizzle, and Toby, the Punch-and-
Judy dog, always came around as soon as the procession stopped for the night and joined the

HUGH LOFTING

'On the scent of a fox'

Doctor's party. They, too, seemed to be much in favour of John Dolittle's taking charge of the show or running a circus of his own. And when they weren't amusing the family circle with wonderful stories of a show-dog's life they kept telling the Doctor that a real Dolittle Circus would, to their way of thinking, be a perfect institution.

John Dolittle had always said that there were just as many different characters and types among dogs as there were among people – in fact, more. He had written a book to prove this. He called it

Dog Psychology. Most metaphysicians had pooh-poohed it, saying that no one but a hairbrain would write on such a subject. But this was only to hide the fact that they couldn't understand it.

Certainly these two, Swizzle, the clown's dog, and Toby, the Punch-and-Judy dog, had very different personalities. Swizzle (to look at, he was nothing but a common mongrel) had a great sense of humour. He made a joke out of everything. This may have been partly on account of his profession – helping a clown make people laugh. But it was also part of his philosophy. He told both the Doctor and Jip more than once that when he was still a puppy he had decided that nothing in this world was worth taking seriously. He was a great artist, nevertheless, and could always see the most difficult jokes – even when they were made at his own expense.

It was Swizzle's sense of humour that gave the Doctor the idea for the first comic papers printed for animals – when later he founded the Rat-and-Mouse Club. They were called *Cellar Life* and *Basement Humour* and were intended to bring light entertainment to those who live in dark places.

Toby, the other, was as different from his friend Swizzle as it is possible to be. He was a small dog, a dwarf white poodle. And he took himself and life quite seriously. The most noticeable thing about his character was his determination to get everything that he thought he ought to get. Yet he was not selfish, not at all. The Doctor always said that this shrewd business-like quality was to be found in most little dogs – who had to make up for their small size by an extra share of cheek. The

'Toby and Swizzle'

very first time Toby came visiting to John Dolittle's caravan he got on the Doctor's bed and made himself comfortable. Dab-Dab, highly scandalized, tried to put him off. But he wouldn't move. He said the Doctor didn't seem to mind and he was the owner of the bed. And from that time on he always occupied this place in the caravan's evening circle when he came to visit. He had won a special privilege for himself by sheer cheek. He was always demanding privileges, and he usually got them.

But there was one thing in which Toby and
Swizzle were alike, and that was the pride they
took in their personal friendship with John
Dolittle, whom they considered the greatest man
on earth.

One night on the first trip between towns the
procession had stopped by the side of the road as
usual. There was a nice old-fashioned farm quite
near and Gub-Gub had gone off to see if there
were any pigs in the sty. Otherwise the Doctor's
family circle was complete. And soon after the
kettle had been put on to boil, along came Toby
and Swizzle. The night was cool; so instead of
making a fire outside, Dab-Dab was using the
stove in the caravan, and everybody was sitting
round it chatting.

'Have you heard the news, Doctor?' said Toby,
jumping up on the bed.

'No,' said John Dolittle. 'What is it?'

'At the next town – Ashby, you know, quite a
large place – we are to pick up Sophie.'

'Who in the world is Sophie?' asked the Doctor,
getting out his slippers from behind the stove.

'She left us before you joined,' said Swizzle.
'Sophie's the performing seal – balances balls on her
nose and does tricks in the water. She fell sick and
Blossom had to leave her behind about a month
ago. She's all right now, though, and her keeper is
meeting us at Ashby so she can join us again. She's
rather a sentimental sort of girl, is Sophie. But she's
a good sport, and I'm sure you will like her.'

The circus reached Ashby about nine o'clock on
a Wednesday evening. It was to open to the public

'Climbed wearily from his bed'

the first thing the following morning. So all
through that night, by the light of flares, the men
were busy hoisting tents, setting up booths, and
spreading tan-bark. Even after the pushmi-
pullyu's stand was put together and the Doctor's
family retired to rest, no one got any sleep, for the
ground still shook with the hammers driving pegs
and the air was full of shouts and the spirit of
work, till the dusk of dawn crept over the roofs of
Ashby and showed the city of canvas that had been
built in a night.

John Dolittle decided, as he climbed wearily from his bed, that circus life took a lot of getting used to. After breakfast, leaving Matthew in charge of his stand, he set out to make the acquaintance of the performing seal.

Chapter Six
SOPHIE, FROM ALASKA

SOPHIE'S keeper, like the rest of the showmen, had by this time got his part of the circus in readiness to open to the public. The seal was accustomed to perform in the big tent twice a day, following the Pinto brothers (trapeze acrobats) and the talking horse. But during the rest of the day she was a sideshow like the pushmi-pullyu. Here in an enclosed tank she dived after fish for the amusement of anyone who paid threepence to come and see her.

This morning – it was still quite early – Sophie's keeper was eating his breakfast outside on the steps when the Doctor entered the stand. Inside, a tank about twelve feet across had been let into the ground, and around it was a platform with a railing where visitors stood to watch the performance. Sophie, a fine five-foot Alaskan seal, with sleek skin and intelligent eyes, was wallowing moodily in the water of the tank. When the Doctor spoke to her in her own language, and she realized who her visitor was, she burst into a flood of tears.

'What is the matter?' asked John Dolittle.

The seal, still weeping, did not answer.

'Calm yourself,' said the Doctor. 'Don't be hysterical. Tell me, are you still sick? I understood you had recovered.'

'Oh, yes, I got over that,' said Sophie through her tears. 'It was only an upset stomach. They *will* feed us this stale fish, you know.'

'Then what's the matter?' asked the Doctor. 'Why are you crying?'

'I was weeping for joy,' said Sophie. 'I was just thinking as you came in that the only person in the world who could help me in my trouble was John Dolittle. Of course, I had heard all about you through the post office and the *Arctic Monthly*. In fact, I had written to you. It was I who contributed those articles on underwater swimming. You remember? The Alaskan Wiggle – you know – double overhand stroke. It was printed in the August number of your magazine. We were awfully sorry when you had to give up the *Arctic Monthly*. It was tremendously popular among the seals.'

'But what was this trouble you were speaking of?' asked the Doctor.

'Oh, yes,' said Sophie, bursting into tears again. 'That just shows you how glad I am; I had forgotten all about it for the moment. You know, when you first came in I thought you were an ordinary visitor. But the very first word of sealish that you spoke – and Alaskan sealish at that – I knew who you were: John Dolittle, the one man in the world I wanted to see! It was too much, I—'

'Come, come!' said the Doctor. 'Don't break down again. Tell me what your trouble is.'

'Well,' said Sophie, 'it's this: while I—'

At that moment there was a noise outside, the rattling of a bucket.

'Sh! It's the keeper coming,' whispered the Doctor quickly. 'Just carry on with your tricks. I'm not letting them know I can talk to the animals.'

When the keeper entered to swab the floor, Sophie was frisking and diving for an audience of one: a quiet little fat man with a battered high hat on the back of his head. The keeper just glanced at him, before setting to work, and decided that he was quite an ordinary person, nobody in particular at all.

As soon as the man had finished his mopping and disappeared again, Sophie continued:

'You know,' said the seal, 'when I fell sick we were performing at Hatley-on-Sea, and I and my keeper — Higgins is his name — stayed there two weeks while the circus went on without us. Now, there's a zoo at Hatley — only a small one — near the esplanade. They have artificial ponds there with seals and otters in them. Well Higgins got talking to the keeper of these seals one day and told him about my being sick. And they decided I needed company. So they put me in the pond with the other seals till I should recover. Among them there was an older one who came from the same part of the Bering Straits as I did. He gave me some very bad news about my husband. It seems that ever since I was captured he has been unhappy and refused to eat. He used to be leader of the herd. But after I was taken away he had worried and grown thin and finally another seal was elected leader in his place. Now he wasn't expected to live.' Quietly Sophie began to weep again. 'I can quite understand it. We were devoted to one another. And although he was so big and strong and no other seal in the herd ever dared to argue with him, without me, well, he was just lost, you know – a mere baby. He relied on me for everything. And now – I don't know what's happening to him. It's just terrible – terrible!'

'Well, wait a minute,' said the Doctor. 'Don't cry. What do you think ought to be done?'

'I ought to go to him,' said Sophie, raising herself in the water and spreading out her flippers. 'I ought to be by his side. He is the proper leader of the herd and he needs me. I hoped I might escape at Hatley, but not a chance did I get.'

'Humph!' muttered the Doctor. 'It's an awful long way to the Bering Straits. How on earth would you get there?'

'That's just what I wanted to see you about,' said Sophie. 'Overland, of course, my rate of travel is very slow. If I could only have got away at Hatley I'd have been all right. Because, of course,' she added with a powerful swish of her tail that slopped half the water out of the tanks, 'once I reached the sea I'd be up to Alaska in no time.'

'Ah, yes,' the Doctor agreed, as he shook the water out of his boots. 'I see you are a powerful swimmer. How far are we from the coast here?'

'About a hundred miles,' said Sophie. 'Oh, dear! Poor Slushy! My poor, poor Slushy!'

'Poor who?' asked the Doctor.

'Slushy,' said the seal. 'That's my husband's name. He relied on me in everything, poor, simple Slushy. What shall I do! What *shall* I do?'

' "I ought to go to him" '

'Well, now listen,' said John Dolittle. 'This is no easy matter, to smuggle you to the sea. I don't say it's impossible. But it needs thinking out. Perhaps I can get you free some other way – openly. In the meantime I'll send word up to your husband by bird messenger and tell him to stop worrying because you are all right. And the same messenger can bring us back news of how he is getting on. Now, cheer up. Here come some people to see you perform.'

A schoolmistress with a band of children

entered, accompanied by Higgins, the keeper. As they came in a little fat man went out, smiling to himself. Soon the children were laughing with delight at the antics of the big animal in the tank. And Higgins decided that Sophie must now be feeling entirely recovered, for he had never seen her so sprightly or so full of good spirits before.

Chapter Seven
THE MESSENGER FROM THE NORTH

LATE that night the Doctor took Too-Too with him and went to visit the seal again. 'Now, Sophie,' said he when they had reached the side of the tank, 'this owl is a friend of mine, and I want you to describe to him just where in Alaska your husband can be found. Then we'll send him off to the seashore, and he will hand on your message to the gulls who are going north-westward. Let me introduce you: Sophie, this is Too-Too, one of the cleverest birds I know. He is particularly good at mathematics.'

The owl sat on the rail while Sophie told him exactly how Slushy could be reached and reeled off a long and loving message for her husband. When she had ended he said, 'I think I'll make for Bristol, Doctor. It is about the nearest coast town. There are always plenty of gulls to be found in the harbour. I'll get one to take this and pass it on to its destination.'

'Very good, Too-Too,' said the Doctor. 'But we want to hurry it all we can. If you can find some seabird who is willing to take it the whole way as a special favour to me, it would be better.'

'All right,' said Too-Too, preparing to depart. 'Leave the window of the caravan open, so I can get in. I don't suppose I shall be back much before two in the morning. So long!'

Then the Doctor returned to his wagon and rewrote the last part of his new book, which was called *Animal Natation*. Sophie had given him a lot of helpful hints on good swimming style, which made it necessary for him to add three more chapters.

He got so interested in this he did not notice how the time was passing till, somewhere between two and three in the morning, he suddenly found Too-Too, the night bird, standing on the table before him.

'Doctor,' said he, speaking low so he would not wake the animals. 'You could never guess whom I met. You remember the gull who brought you the warning about Cape Stephen Light? Well, I ran into him in Bristol harbour. I hadn't seen him since the good old houseboat days. But I recognized him at once. I told him I was hunting for someone to take a message up to Alaska; and when he heard it was you who sent me, he said he would attend to it himself with pleasure. He doesn't expect to be back under five days, though – at best.'

'Splendid, Too-Too, splendid!' said the Doctor.

'I am returning to Bristol on Friday,' said the owl, 'and if he isn't back then, I'll wait till he comes.'

The following morning John Dolittle told Sophie that her message had been sent on, and she was very pleased. For the present there was nothing further to be done but to wait for the gull's return.

On Thursday (a day before the time Too-Too had planned to return to Bristol) the Doctor's whole party was seated around the table in the caravan listening to a story from Toby, the Punch-and-Judy dog. Just as Toby paused breathless at the most exciting part, there came a gentle tapping on the window.

'*Booh!*' said Gub-Gub. 'How spookish!' And he crawled under the bed.

John Dolittle rose, drew back the curtains, and opened the window. On the sill stood the gull who months before had brought him another message by night when he lived in the houseboat post office. Now, weather-beaten and weary, he looked more dead than alive. Gently the Doctor lifted him from the windowsill, and set him down on the table. Then they all drew near, staring at him in silence, waiting for the exhausted bird to speak.

'John Dolittle,' said the gull at last, 'I didn't wait for Too-Too to meet me in Bristol because I thought you ought to know at once. The seal herd to which Sophie and her husband belonged is in a bad way — very bad. And it has all come about because Sophie was taken away and her husband, Slushy, lost the leadership. Winter has set in up there early this year — and my, such a winter! Blizzards, mountainous snowdrifts, the seas frozen months ahead of the usual time. I nearly died of the cold myself — and you know we gulls can stand awful low temperatures. Well, leadership for the seal herds is tremendously important in bad weather. They're not much different from sheep — same as all animals that travel and live

'He crawled under the bed'

in packs. And without a big, strong boss to lead them to the open fishing and the protected wintering places, they're just lost, that's all – helpless. Now, it seems, ever since Slushy started to mope they've had one leader after another – and none of them any good. Rows and little revolutions going on in the herd all the while. And in the meantime the walruses and sea lions are driving them out of all the best fishing and the Eskimo seal hunters killing them right and left. No seal herd can last long against the fur hunters up there

if they haven't got a good leader with wits enough
to keep them out of danger. Slushy was the best
they ever had, as strong as an ox. Now all he does
is lie on an iceberg, mooning and weeping because
his favourite wife's been taken away. He's got hundreds more, just as good-looking, but the only one
he wants is Sophie, and there you are. The herd's
just going to pieces. In the days of Slushy's leadership, they tell me, it was the finest seal herd in the
Arctic Circle. Now, most likely, with this extra
bad winter setting in, it'll be wiped right out.'

For fully a minute after the gull finished his long
speech silence reigned in the caravan.

Finally John Dolittle said, 'Toby, does Sophie
belong to Blossom or to Higgins?'

'To Higgins, Doctor,' said the little dog. 'He does
something the same as you do; in return for letting
the seal perform in the big ring, Higgins gets his
stand in the circus free and pockets whatever
money he makes on her as a sideshow.'

'Well, that *isn't* the same as me at all,' said the
Doctor. 'The big difference is that the pushmi-
pullyu is here of his own accord and Sophie is kept
against her will. It is a perfect scandal that
hunters can go up to the Arctic and capture any
animals they like, breaking up families and upsetting herd government and community life in this
way – a crying shame! Toby, how much does a seal
cost?'

'They vary in price, Doctor,' said Toby. 'But I
heard Sophie say that when Higgins bought her in
Liverpool from the men who had caught her he
paid twenty pounds for her. She had been trained
on the ship to do tricks before she landed.'

'How much have we got in the money box, Too-Too?' asked the Doctor.

'All of last week's gate money,' said the owl, 'except one shilling and threepence. The threepence you spent to get your hair cut and the shilling went on celery for Gub-Gub.'

'Well, what does that bring the total to?'

Too-Too, the mathematician, cocked his head on one side and closed his left eye — as he always did when calculating.

'Two pounds, seven shillings,' he murmured, 'minus one shilling and threepence leaves — er — leaves — two pounds, five shillings, and ninepence, cash in hand, net.'

'Good Lord!' groaned the Doctor, 'barely enough to buy a tenth of Sophie! I wonder if there's anyone I could borrow from. That's the only good thing about being a people's doctor. When I had a practice I could borrow from my patients.'

'If I remember rightly,' muttered Dab-Dab, 'it was more often your patients that borrowed from you.'

'Blossom wouldn't let you buy her even if you had the money,' said Swizzle. 'Higgins is under contract — made a promise — to travel with the circus for a year.'

'Very well, then,' said the Doctor. 'There's only one thing to be done. That seal doesn't belong to those men, anyhow. She's a free citizen of the Arctic Circle. And if she wants to go back there, back she shall go. Sophie must escape.'

Before his pets went to bed that night the Doctor made them promise that for the present they would say nothing to the seal about the bad news

the gull had brought. It would only worry her, he
told them. And until he had helped her to get
safely to the sea there was no need for her to
know.

Then, until the early hours of the morning, he
sat up with Matthew making plans for Sophie's
flight. At first the cat's-meat man was very much
against the idea.

'Why, Doctor,' said he, 'you'll get arrested if
you're caught. Helping that seal escape from her
owner! They'll call it stealing.'

'I don't care that much,' said the Doctor snapping
his fingers. 'Let them call it what they like. Let
them arrest me – if they catch me. If the case is
taken to the courts, at least I'll get a chance to say
a word for the rights of wild animals.'

'They won't listen to you, Doctor,' said Matthew.
'They'll say you're a sentimental crank. Higgins
would win easy. Rights of property and all that. I
see your point, but the judge wouldn't. He'd tell
you to pay Higgins his twenty pounds for a lost
seal. And if you couldn't, you'd go to jail.'

'I don't care,' the Doctor repeated. 'But listen,
Matthew: I wouldn't want you to get mixed up in
it if you don't think it's right. I shall have to use
deception if I'm to be successful. And I should be
very sorry to get you into trouble. If you would
prefer to stay clear of it, say so now. But for my
part, my mind is made up: Sophie is going to
Alaska even if I have to go to jail – that will be
nothing new. I've been in jail before.'

'So have I,' said the cat's-meat man. 'Was you
ever in Cardiff Jail? By Jingo! that's a rotten one!
The worst I was ever in.'

' "I don't care that much" '

'No,' said the Doctor. 'I've only been in African jails – as yet. They're bad enough. But let us get back to the point. Would you sooner not help me in this? It's against the law – I know – even if I think the law is wrong. Understand, I shan't be the least offended if you have conscientious objections to aiding and abetting me. Eh?'

'Conscientious objections, me eye!' said the cat's-meat man, opening the window and spitting accurately out into the night. 'O' course, I'll help you, Doctor. That old sour-faced Higgins ain't got no right to that seal. She's a free creature of the seas. If he paid twenty pounds for her, more fool him. What you say goes, Doctor. Ain't we kind of partners in this here circus business? I think it's a good kind of a lark meself. Didn't I tell you I was venturesome? Lor' bless us! I done worse things than help a performin' seal to elope. Why, that time I was telling you of, when I was jailed in Cardiff – do you know what it was for?'

'No, I have no idea,' said the Doctor. 'Some slight error, I have no doubt. Now let us—'

'It was no slight error,' said Matthew, 'I—'

'Well, never mind it now,' said John Dolittle quickly. 'We all make mistakes, you know.' ('It was no mistake, neither,' muttered Matthew as the Doctor hurried on.) 'If you are quite sure that you will have no regrets about going into this – er – matter with me, let us consider ways and means. It will be necessary, I think, in order to avoid getting Blossom suspicious, for me to leave the circus for a few days. I will say I have business to attend to – which is quite true, even if I don't attend to it. But it would look very queer if I and Sophie disappeared the same night. So I will go first, leaving you in charge of my show. Then a day – or better, two days – later, Sophie will disappear.'

'Also on business,' put in Matthew, chuckling. 'You mean you'll leave me the job of letting her out of her tank after you're gone?'

'Yes, if you don't mind,' said the Doctor.

'It'll give me great pleasure,' said the cat's-meat man.

'Splendid!' said the Doctor. 'I'll arrange beforehand with Sophie where she is to meet me, once she's clear of the circus. And then—'

'And then your job will begin in earnest,' Matthew Mugg said with a laugh.

PART II

Chapter One
PLANNING THE ESCAPE

ALTHOUGH the plans for Sophie's escape were of course kept a strict secret from any of the people in Blossom's establishment, the animals of the circus soon got to know of them through Jip, Toby, and Swizzle. And for days before the flight took place it was the one subject of conversation in the menagerie, in the stables, and in the Doctor's caravan.

When John Dolittle returned from telling Blossom that he was about to leave the circus on business for a few days, he found his own animals seated about the table in the wagon talking in whispers.

'Well, Doctor,' said Matthew, who was sitting on the steps, 'did you speak to the boss?'

'Yes,' said the Doctor. 'I told him. It's all right. I'm leaving tonight. I felt frightfully guilty, and underhanded. I do wish I could do this openly.'

'You'd stand a fat chance of succeeding, if you did!' said Matthew. 'I don't feel guilty none.'

'Listen, Doctor,' said Jip. 'All the circus animals are tremendously interested in your scheme.

They've asked if there's anything they can do to help. When is Sophie going to get away?'

'The day after tomorrow,' said John Dolittle. 'Matthew, here, will undo the door of her stand just after closing time. But listen, Matthew: you'll have to be awfully careful no one sees you tinkering with the lock. If we *should* get caught we would indeed be in a bad fix then. Tinkering with locks makes it a felony instead of a misdemeanour, or something like that. Do be careful, won't you?'

'You can rely on me, Doctor,' said the cat's-meat man, proudly puffing out his chest. 'I've got a way of me own with locks, I have. No force, sort of persuasion like.'

'Get clear out of the way as soon as you have let her free,' said the Doctor, 'so you won't be connected with it at all. Dear me, how like a low-down conspiracy it sounds!'

'Sounds like lots of fun to me,' said Matthew.

'To me, too,' said Jip.

'It'll be the best trick that's been done in this show for a long while,' put in Swizzle. 'Ladies and gentleman: John Dolittle, the world-famous conjurer, will now make a live seal disappear from the stage before your eyes. Abracadabra, mumble-and-jabberer, hoopla, hey presto! *Gone!*'

And Swizzle stood on his hind legs and bowed to an imaginary audience behind the stove.

'Well,' said the Doctor, 'even though it sounds underhanded, I don't feel I'm doing anything wrong — myself. They've no right to keep Sophie in this slavery. How would you and I like it,' he asked of Matthew, 'to be made to dive for fish

'Swizzle bowed to an imaginary audience'

into a tub of dirty water for the amusement of loafers?'

'Rotten!' said Matthew. 'I never did care for fish – nor water, neither. But look here, have you arranged with Sophie where she's to meet you?'

'Yes,' said John Dolittle. 'As soon as she gets clear of the circus enclosure – and don't forget we are relying on you to leave the back gate open as well as Sophie's own door – as soon as she's out of the fence, she is to cross the road where she will find an empty house. Alongside of that there is a

little dark passage, and in that passage I will be
waiting for her. My goodness, I do hope everything
goes right! It's so dreadfully important for her –
and for all those seals in Alaska, too.'

'And what are you going to do then,' asked
Matthew, 'when she's got as far as the passage?'

'Well, it's no use trying to plan too far as to
detail. My general idea is to make for the Bristol
Channel. That's about our shortest cut to the sea
from here. Once there, she's all right. But it's
nearly a hundred miles as the crow flies; and as
we'll have to keep concealed most of the way I'm
not expecting an easy journey. However, there's
no sense in meeting your troubles half-way. I've no
doubt we shall get along all right once she's safely
away from the circus.'

Many of the Doctor's pets wanted to accompany
him on his coming adventure. Jip tried especially
hard to be taken. But in spite of his great desire to
have the assistance of his friends, John Dolittle
felt that he would arouse less suspicion if he left
his entire family with the circus just as it was.

So that night after a final talk with Sophie he set
out alone – on business. He took with him most of
what money he had, leaving a little with Matthew
to pay for the small needs of his establishment
while he was away. His 'business', as a matter
of fact, did not take him further than the next
town – which journey he made by a stagecoach. In
those days, you see, although there were railways,
to be sure, they were as yet very scarce. And most
of the cross-country travelling between the
smaller towns was still done in the old-fashioned
way.

On his arrival at the next town he took a room in an inn and remained there the whole time. Two nights later he returned to Ashby after dark and, entering the town from the far side, made his way through unfrequented streets till he reached the passage that was to be his meeting place with Sophie.

Now all his pets, though they had not been given any particular parts to play in the plot of Sophie's escape, were determined to do anything they could to help things on their own account – which, as you will see, turned out to be a good deal. And as they waited for the arrival of the appointed hour their excitement (which Gub-Gub, for one, had hard work to conceal) grew every minute.

About ten o'clock, when the circus was beginning to close up, Too-Too stationed himself on top of the menagerie where he could see everything that went on. He had arranged with the elephant and the animals of the collection to start a rumpus in the menagerie on a given signal – to attract, if necessary, the attention of the circus men away from the escaping seal. Gub-Gub gave himself the job of watching Blossom, and he took up a post underneath the ringmaster's private caravan.

There was a full moon, and even after the circus lamps were put out there was still a good deal of light. The Doctor would have postponed the escape on this account until later, but he realized that the state of affairs among the Alaskan seals made it necessary for Sophie to get away as soon as possible.

Well, about an hour after Blossom had locked up the fence gates and retired to his caravan,

'Made his way through unfrequented streets'

Matthew slipped away from the pushmi-pullyu's stand and sauntered off across the enclosure. Jip, also pretending he was doing nothing in particular, followed him at a short distance. Everyone seemed to be abed and not a soul did Matthew meet till he came to the gate the Doctor had spoken of. Making sure that no one saw him, the cat's-meat man quickly undid the latch and set the gate ajar. Then he strolled away towards Sophie's stand while Jip remained to watch the gate.

He hadn't been gone more than a minute when

along came the circus watchman with a lantern.
He closed the gate, and, to Jip's horror, locked it
with a key. Jip, still pretending he was just
sniffing around the fence after rats, waited till the
man had disappeared again. Then he raced off
towards Sophie's stand to find Matthew.

Now things had not turned out for the cat's-meat
man as easy as he had expected. On approaching
the seal's tank house, he had seen from a distance
the figure of Higgins sitting on the steps smoking
and looking at the moon. Matthew therefore
withdrew into the shadow of a tent and waited till
the seal's keeper should go away to bed.

Higgins, he knew, slept in a wagon close to
Blossom's on the other side of the enclosure. But
while he watched and waited, instead of Higgins
going away, another figure, the watchman's,
came, joined the man on the steps, sat down,
and started chatting. Presently Jip, smelling
out Matthew behind the tent, came up and tried
frantically to make him understand that the
gate he had opened had been closed again and
locked.

Jip had very little success in trying to make the
cat's-meat man understand him, and for nearly an
hour Matthew stayed in the shadow waiting for
the two figures on the steps of Sophie's stand to
move away and leave the coast clear for him to let
the seal free. In the meantime John Dolittle in his
narrow, dark passage outside the circus enclosure
wondered what the delay was and tried to read his
watch by the dim light of the moon.

Finally Matthew decided that the two men were
never going to bed. So, swearing under his breath,

he crept away from the shadow of the tent and set off to seek Theodosia, his wife.

On arrival at his own wagon he found her darning socks by the light of the candle.

'*Pst!* Theodosia,' he whispered through the window. 'Listen.'

'Good Lord!' gasped Mrs Mugg, dropping her needlework. 'What a fright you gave me, Matthew! Is it all right? Has the seal got away?'

'No, it's all wrong. Higgins and the watchman are sitting on the steps talking. I can't get near the door while they're there. Go up and draw 'em off for me, will yer? Tell 'em a tent's blown down or something – anything to get 'em away. They're going to sit there all night if something ain't done.'

'All right,' said Theodosia. 'Wait till I get my shawl. I'll bring them over here for some cocoa.'

Then the helpful Mrs Mugg went off and invited Higgins and the watchman to come to her husband's wagon for a little party. Matthew would be along to join them presently, she said.

As soon as the coast was clear the cat's-meat man sped up the steps of the seal's stand and, in a minute, his nimble fingers had the door unlocked. Just inside lay Sophie, all ready to start out upon her long journey. With a grunt of thanks she waddled forth into the moonlight, slid down the steps, and set off clumsily towards the gate.

Once more Jip tried his hardest to make Matthew understand that something was wrong. But the cat's-meat man merely took the dog's signals of distress for joy and marched off to join his wife's cocoa party, feeling that his share of the night's work had been well done.

'His nimble fingers soon had the door unlocked'

In the meantime Sophie had waddled her way laboriously to the gate and found it locked.

Jip had then gone all around the fence, trying to find a hole big enough for her to get through. But he met with no success. Poor Sophie had escaped the captivity of her tank only to find herself still a prisoner within the circus enclosure.

Everything that had happened up to this had been carefully watched by a little round bird perched on the roof of the menagerie. Too-Too, the listener, the night seer, the mathematician, was

more than usually wide-awake. And presently,
while Jip was still nosing around the fence, trying
to find Sophie a way out, he heard the whir of
wings over his head and an owl alighted by his
side.

'For heaven's sake, Jip,' whispered Too-Too,
'keep your head. The game will be up if you don't.
You're doing no good by running around like that.
Get Sophie into hiding – push her under the flap
of a tent or something. Look at her, lying out in the
moonlight there, as though this were Greenland!
If anyone should come along and see her we're lost.
Hide her until Matthew sees what has happened
to the gate. Hurry – I see someone coming.'

As Too-Too flew back to his place on the
menagerie roof, Jip rushed off to Sophie and in a
few hurried words explained the situation to her.

'Come over here,' he said. 'Get under the skirt of
this tent. So! Gosh! Only just in time! There's the
light of a lantern moving. Now lie perfectly still
and wait till I come and tell you.'

And in his little dark passage beyond the circus
fence John Dolittle once more looked at his watch
and muttered, 'What *can* have happened? Will she
never come?'

It was not many minutes after Matthew had
joined the cocoa party in his own wagon that the
watchman rose from the table and said he ought to
be getting along on his rounds. The cat's-meat
man, anxious to give Sophie as much time as possible to get away, tried to persuade him to stay.

'Oh, stop and have another cup of cocoa!' said he.
'This is a quiet town. Nobody's going to break in.
Fill your pipe and let's chat a while.'

'No,' said the watchman, 'thank ye. I'd like to, but I mustn't. Blossom give me strict orders to keep movin' the whole night. If he was to come and not find me on the job, I'd catch it hot.'

And in spite of everything Matthew could do to keep him, the watchman took his lamp and left.

Higgins, however, remained. And while the cat's-meat man and his wife talked pleasantly to him of politics and the weather, they expected any moment to hear a shout outside warning the circus that Sophie had escaped.

But the watchman, when he found the stand open and empty, did not begin by shouting. He came running back to Matthew's wagon.

'Higgins,' he yelled, 'your seal's gone!'

'Gone!' cried Higgins. *'Gone!'* said Matthew. 'Can't be possible!'

'I tell you she 'as,' said the watchman. " 'Er door's open and she ain't there.'

'Good heavens!' cried Higgins, springing up. 'I could swear I locked the door as usual. But if the gates in the fence was all closed, she can't be far away. We can soon find 'er again. Come on!'

And he ran out of the wagon – with Matthew and Theodosia, pretending to be greatly disturbed, close at his heels.

'I'll go take another look at the gates,' said the watchman. 'I'm sure they're all right. But I'll make double certain anyway.'

Then Higgins, Matthew, and Theodosia raced off for the seal's stand.

'The door's open, sure enough,' said Matthew as they came up to it. ' 'Ow very peculiar!'

' "Oh! Oh! I'm feeling faint!" '

'Let's go inside,' said Higgins. 'Maybe she's hiding at the bottom of the tank.'

Then all three of them went in and by the light of matches peered down into the dark water.

Meanwhile the watchman turned up again.

'The gates are all right,' he said, '– closed and locked, every one of them.'

Then at last Matthew knew something had gone wrong. And while Higgins and the watchman were examining the water with the lamp, he whispered something to his wife, slipped out, and ran for the gate, hoping Theodosia would keep the other two at the stand long enough for his purpose.

As a matter of fact she played her part very well, did Mrs Mugg. Presently Higgins said, 'There ain't nothing under the water. Sophie's not here. Let's go outside and look for her.'

Then just as the two men turned to leave, Theodosia cried, 'What's that?'

'What's what?' said Higgins, turning back.

'That – down there,' said Mrs Mugg, pointing into the dirty water. 'I thought I saw something move. Bring the lantern nearer.'

The watchman crouched over the edge of the tank; and Higgins, beside him, screwed up his eyes to see better.

'I don't see nothing,' said the keeper.

'Oh! Oh! I'm feeling faint!' cried Mrs Mugg. 'Help me. I'm going to fall in!'

And Theodosia, a heavy woman, swayed and suddenly crumpled up on top of the two crouching men.

Then, *splash! splash!* in fell, not Theodosia, but Higgins and the watchman – lamp and all.

Chapter Two
'ANIMALS' NIGHT' AT THE CIRCUS

THE white mouse was the only one of the Doctor's pets that witnessed that scene in Sophie's tank house when Mrs Mugg pushed the two men into the water by-accident-on-purpose. And for weeks afterwards he used to entertain the Dolittle family circle with his description of Mr Higgins, the seal keeper, diving for fish and coming up for air.

That was one of the busiest and jolliest nights the circus ever had – from the animals' point of view; and the two men falling in the water and yelling for help was the beginning of a grand and noble racket, which lasted for a good half hour and finally woke every soul in Ashby out of his sleep.

First of all, Blossom, hearing cries of alarm, came rushing out of his caravan. At the foot of the steps a pig appeared from nowhere, rushed between his legs, and brought him down on his nose. Throughout the whole proceedings Gub-Gub never let Blossom get very far without popping out from behind something and upsetting him.

'A small pig tripped him up'

Next Fatima, the snake charmer, ran from her
boudoir with a candle in one hand and a hammer
in the other. She hadn't gone two steps before a
mysterious duck flew over her head and, with one
sweep of its wing, blew the candle out. Fatima ran
back, relit the candle, and tried again to go to the
rescue. But the same thing happened. Dab-Dab
kept Fatima almost as busy as Gub-Gub kept
Blossom.

Then Mrs Blossom, hastily donning a dressing
gown, appeared upon the scene. She was met by

the old horse Beppo, who had a habit of asking
people for sugar. She tried to get by him and Beppo
moved out of her way. But in doing so he trod on
her corns so badly that she went howling back to
bed again and did not reappear.

But although the animals managed by various
tricks to keep many people occupied, they could
not attend to all the circus folk; and before long
the watchman and Higgins, yelling murder in the
tank, had attracted a whole lot of tent riggers and
other showmen to Sophie's stand.

Now, in the meantime, Matthew Mugg had
re-opened the gate in the fence. But when he
looked around for Sophie she was nowhere to be
seen. Jip and Too-Too, as a matter of fact, were the
only ones who really knew where she was. Jip,
however, with all this crowd of men rushing
around the seal's stand near the gate, was afraid
to give Sophie the word to leave her hiding place.
More of Blossom's men kept arriving and adding
to the throng. Several lanterns were lit and
brought on to the scene. Everybody was shouting,
one half asking what the matter was, the other
half telling them. Mr Blossom, after being thrown
down in the mud by Gub-Gub for the sixth time,
was hitting everyone he met and bellowing like
a mad bull. The hubbub and confusion were
awful.

At last Higgins and the watchman were fished
out of their bathtub and, highly perfumed with
kerosene and fish, they joined the hunt.

The watchman and everyone were sure that
Sophie must be somewhere near – which was
quite true: the tent, under the skirt of which she

was lying, was only thirty feet from her stand. But
the gate by which she was to pass out was also
quite near.

While Jip was wondering when the men would
move away so he could let her go, Higgins cried out
that he had found a track in the soft earth. Then
a dozen lanterns were brought forward, and the
men started to follow the trail that Sophie had left
behind on the way to her hiding place.

Luckily, with so many feet crossing and recross-
ing the same part of the enclosure, the flipper
marks were not easy to make out. Nevertheless,
even with Matthew doing his best to lead them off
on a wrong scent, the trackers steadily moved in
the right direction – towards the tent where poor
Sophie, the devoted wife, lay in hiding with a
beating heart.

John Dolittle, waiting impatiently in his little
passage, had heard the noise of shouting from the
circus. He knew that meant that Sophie had got
out from her stand. But as minute after minute
went by and still she did not come to the meeting
place, the Doctor's uneasiness increased a
hundredfold.

But his anxiety was no worse than Jip's. Closer
and closer the trackers came towards the spot
where he had hidden the seal. The poor dog was in
despair.

However, he had forgotten Too-Too the mathematician. From his lookout on the menagerie roof,
away off on the far side of the enclosure, the little
owl was still surveying the battlefield with a
general's eye. He was waiting only till he was sure
that all the circus folk had left their beds to join

the hunt and that there were no more to come. When he played his masterstroke of strategy he did not want any extra interference from unexpected quarters.

Suddenly he flew down to a ventilator in the menagerie wall and hooted softly. Instantly there began within the most terrible pandemonium that was ever heard. The lion roared, the opossum shrieked, the yak bellowed, the hyena howled, the elephant trumpeted and stamped his floor into kindling wood. It was the grand climax to the animals' conspiracy.

On the other side of the enclosure the trackers and hunters stood still and listened.

'What in thunder's that?' asked Blossom.

'Coming from the menagerie, ain't it?' said one of the men. 'Sounds like the elephant's broke loose.'

'I know,' said another: *It's Sophie.* She's got into the menagerie and scared the elephant.'

'That's it,' said Blossom. 'Lord, and us huntin' for 'er over here! To the menagerie!' And he grabbed up a lantern and started to run.

'To the menagerie!' yelled the crowd. And in a moment, to Jip's delight, they were all gone, rushing away to the other side of the enclosure.

All but one. Matthew Mugg, hanging back, pretending to do up his shoelace, saw Jip flash across to a small tent and disappear under the skirt.

'Now,' said Jip. 'Run, Sophie! Swim! Fly! Anything! Get out of the gate!'

Hopping and flopping, Sophie covered the ground as best she could, while Jip yelped to her to hurry and Matthew held the gate open. At last

'He stamped his floor into kindling wood'

the seal waddled out on to the road, and the cat's-meat man saw her cross it and disappear into the passage alongside the deserted house. He closed the gate again and stamped out her tracks at the foot of it. Then he leaned against it, mopping his brow.

'Holy smoke!' he sighed. 'And I told the Doctor I done worse things than help a seal escape! If I ever—'

A knock sounded on the gate at his back. With shaking hands he opened it once more; and there stood a policeman, his little bull's-eye lantern shining at his belt. Matthew's heart almost stopped beating. He had no love for policemen.

'I ain't done nothing!' he began. 'I—'

'What's all the row about?' asked the constable. 'You've got the whole town woke up. Lion broke loose or something?'

Matthew heaved a sigh of relief.

'No,' he said. 'Just a little trouble with the elephant. Got his leg caught in a rope and pulled a tent over. We 'ave 'im straightened out now. Nothing to worry about.'

'Oh, is that all?' said the policeman. 'Folks was going around asking if the end of the world was come. Good night!'

'Good night, constable!' Matthew closed the gate for the third time. 'And give my love to all the little constables,' he added under his breath as he set off for the menagerie.

And so at last John Dolittle, waiting, anxious and impatient, in the dark passage alongside the empty house, heard to his delight the sound of a peculiar footstep. A flipper-step, it should more properly be called; for the noise of Sophie travelling over a brick pavement was a curious mixture between someone slapping the ground with a wet rag and a sack of potatoes being yanked along a floor.

'Is that you, Sophie?' he whispered.

'Yes,' said the seal, hitching herself forward to where the Doctor stood.

'Thank goodness! What in the world kept you so long?'

'Oh, there was some mix-up with the gates,' said

Sophie. 'But hadn't we better be getting out of the
town? It doesn't seem to me very safe here.'

'There's no chance of that for the present,' said
the Doctor. 'The noise they made in the circus has
woken everybody. We dare not try and get
through the streets now. I just saw a policeman
pass across the end of the passage there — luckily
for us, just after you popped into it.'

'But then what are we going to do?'

'We'll have to stay here for the present. It would
be madness to try and run for it now.'

'Well, but suppose they come searching in here.
We couldn't—'

At that moment two persons with lanterns stopped at the end of the passage, talked a moment,
and moved away.

'Quite so,' whispered the Doctor. 'This isn't safe
either. We must find a better place.'

Now, on one side of this alleyway there was a
high stone wall, and on the other a high brick wall.
The brick wall enclosed the back garden belonging
to the deserted house.

'If we could only get into that old empty house,'
murmured the Doctor. 'We'd be safe to stay there
as long as we wished — till this excitement among
the townsfolk dies down. Can you think of any way
you could get over that wall?'

The seal measured the height with her eye.

'Eight feet,' she murmured. 'I could do it with a
ladder. I've been trained to walk up ladders. I do
it in the circus, you know. Perhaps—'

'Sh!' whispered the Doctor. 'There's the policeman's bull's-eye lantern again. Ah, thank goodness, he's passed on! Listen, there's just a chance

I may find an orchard ladder in the garden. Now
you wait here; lie flat and wait till I come
back.'

Then John Dolittle, a very active man in spite of
his round figure, drew back and took a running
jump at the wall. His fingers caught the top of it;
he hauled himself up, threw one leg over, and
dropped lightly down into a flower bed on the other
side. At the bottom of the garden he saw in the
moonlight what he guessed to be a toolshed. Slipping up to the door, he opened it and went in.

Inside his groping hands touched and rattled
some empty flower pots. But he could find no
ladder. He found a grass mower, a lawn roller,
rakes and tools of every kind, but no ladder. And
there seemed little hope of finding one in the dark.
So he carefully closed the door, hung his coat over
the dirty little cobwebby window, in order that no
light should be seen from the outside, and struck
a match.

And there, sure enough, hanging against the
wall right above his head, was an orchard ladder
just the right length. In a moment he had blown
out the match, opened the door, and was marching
down the garden with the ladder on his shoulder.

Standing it in a firm place, he scaled up and sat
astride the wall. Next he pulled the ladder up after
him, changed it across to the other side, and
lowered the foot end into the passage.

Then John Dolittle, perched astride the top of
the wall (looking exactly like Humpty-Dumpty),
whispered down into the dark passage below him,
'Now climb up, Sophie. I'll keep this end steady.
And when you reach the top get on to the wall

beside me till I change the ladder over to the garden side. Don't get flustered now. Easy does it.'

It was a good thing that Sophie was so well trained in balancing. Never in the circus had she performed a better trick than she did that night. It was a feat that even a person might well be proud of. But she knew that her freedom, the happiness of her husband, depended on her steadiness. And though she was in constant fear that any minute someone might come down the passage and discover them, it gave her a real thrill to turn the tables on her captors by using the skill they had taught her in the last grand performance to escape them.

Firmly, rung by rung, she began hoisting her heavy body upward. The ladder, fortunately, was longer than the height of the wall. Thus the Doctor had been able to set it at an easier, flattish slope instead of straight upright. With the seal's weight it sagged dangerously; and the Doctor on the wall prayed that it would prove strong enough. Being an orchard ladder for tree-pruning, it got very narrow at the top. And it was here, where there was hardly room enough for a seal's two front flappers to take hold, that the ticklish part of the feat came in. Then, from this awkward situation, Sophie had to shift her clumsy bulk on to the wall, which was no more than twelve inches wide, while the Doctor changed the ladder.

But in the circus Sophie had been trained to balance herself on small spaces, as well as to climb ladders. And after the Doctor had helped her by leaning down and hoisting her up by the slack of her sealskin jacket, she wiggled herself along the top of the wall beside him and kept her balance as easily as though it were nothing at all.

Then, while Sophie gave a fine imitation of a statue in the moonlight, the Doctor hauled the ladder up after her, swung it over – knocking his own high hat off in the process – and lowered it into the garden once more.

Coming down, Sophie did another of her show tricks: she laid herself across the ladder and slid to the bottom. It was quicker than climbing. And it was lucky she did slide. For the Doctor had hardly lowered the ladder to the lawn when they heard voices in the passage they had left. They had only just got into the garden in time.

'Thank goodness for that!' said the Doctor when the sound of footsteps had died away. 'A narrow squeak, Sophie! Well, we're safe for the present, anyway. Nobody would dream of looking for you here. Oh, I say, you're lying on the carnations. Come over here on to the gravel. So! Now, shall we sleep in the toolshed or the house?'

'This seems good enough to me,' said Sophie, wallowing into the long grass of the lawn. 'Let's sleep outdoors.'

'No, that will never do,' said the Doctor. 'Look at all the houses around. If we stay in the garden people could see us out of the top windows when daylight comes. Let's sleep in the toolshed. I love the smell of toolsheds – and then we won't have to break open any doors.'

'Nor climb any stairs,' said Sophie, humping along towards the shed. 'I do hate stairs. Ladders I can manage but stairs are the mischief.'

Inside the toolshed they found by the dim light

'He lowered the ladder into the garden'

of the moon several old sacks and large quantities
of bass-grass. Out of these materials they made
themselves two quite comfortable beds.

'My, but it's good to be free!' said Sophie, stretching out her great, silky length. 'Are you sleepy,
Doctor? I couldn't stay awake another moment if
you paid me.'

'Well, go to sleep then,' said the Doctor. 'I'm
going to take a stroll in the garden before turning
in.'

Chapter Three
IN THE DESERTED GARDEN

THE Doctor, always fascinated by any kind of a garden, lit his pipe and strolled out of the toolshed into the moonlight. The neglected appearance of the beds and lawns of this deserted property reminded him of his own beautiful home in Puddleby. There were weeds everywhere. John Dolittle could not abide weeds in flower beds. He pulled one or two away from the roots of a rose tree. Further along he found them thicker still, nearly smothering a very fine lavender bush.

'Dear me!' he said, tiptoeing back to the shed for a hoe and a basket. 'What a shame to neglect a fine place like this!'

And before long he was weeding away by moonlight like a Trojan – just as though the garden were his own and no danger threatened him within a thousand miles.

'After all,' he muttered to himself as he piled the basket high with dandelions, 'we are occupying the place – and rent free at that. This is the least I can do for the landlord.'

After he had finished the weeding he would have

got the mower and cut the lawn — only that he was afraid the noise might wake the neighbours.

And when, a week later, the owner of this property rented the place to his aunt, that good lady entirely puzzled her nephew by writing to congratulate him on the way he had had his garden kept!

The Doctor, going back to bed after a hard night's work, suddenly discovered that he was hungry. Remembering the apple trees he had noticed behind a wisteria arbour, he turned back. But no fruit could he find. It had all been gathered or taken by marauding boys. Knowing that he would not be able to move about the garden after daylight came, he then started hunting for vegetables. But in this he had no better luck. So, with the prospect of a foodless day before him tomorrow, he finally went to bed.

In the morning the first thing Sophie said when she woke up was, 'My! I've been dreaming about the dear old sea all night. It's given me a wonderful appetite. Is there anything to eat around, Doctor?'

'I'm afraid not,' said John Dolittle. 'We'll have to go without breakfast — and lunch, too, I fear. I dare not try to get out of here by daylight. As soon as it gets dark, though, I may be able to go by myself and bring you some kippers or something from a shop. But I hope that late tonight they'll have given up hunting for you and that we can both make for the open country and get on our way to the sea.'

Well, Sophie was very brave and made the best of it. But as the day wore on they both got ravenously hungry. Somewhere near one o'clock in the afternoon, Sophie suddenly said, 'Sh! Did you hear that?'

'No,' said the Doctor, who was looking for onions in a corner of the shed. 'What was it?'

'It's a dog barking in the passage – the other side of the garden wall. Come out from under the bench and you'll hear it. Goodness! I do hope they're not hunting me with dogs now. The game's up if they do.'

The Doctor crawled out from under a potting table, came to the door, and listened. A low, cautious bark reached his ears from over the wall.

'Good Heavens!' he muttered. 'That's Jip's voice. I wonder what he wants.'

Not far from the shed there was a thick, branchy pear tree standing close to the wall. Making sure no one saw him from the windows of houses overlooking the garden, the Doctor sped across and got behind the tree.

'What is it, Jip?' he called. 'Is anything wrong?'

'Let me in,' Jip whispered back. 'I can't get over the wall.'

'How can I?' said the Doctor. 'There's no door and I'm afraid the neighbours may see me if I move out in the open.'

'Get a rope and tie a basket on the end,' whispered Jip. 'Then throw it over the wall behind the tree and I'll get in it. When I bark, pull on the rope and haul me up. Hurry! I don't want to be seen around this passage.'

Then the Doctor crept back to the toolshed, found a planting line and tied the garden basket on the end of it.

Returning to the cover of the tree, he threw the basket over the wall, but kept the end of the line in his hand.

Presently a bark sounded from the passage and he started hauling in the rope. When the basket reached the top of the wall on the other side Jip's head appeared.

'Keep the rope tight, but tie it to the tree,' he whispered. 'Then spread your coat out like an apron. I want you to catch some things.'

The Doctor did as he was told. And Jip threw down to him the contents of the basket: four ham sandwiches, a bottle of milk, two herrings, a razor, a piece of soap, and a newspaper. Then he threw the empty basket on to the lawn.

'Now catch me,' said Jip. 'Hold your coat real tight. Ready? One, two, three!'

'My goodness!' said the Doctor as the dog took the flying dive and landed neatly in the coat. 'You could perform in the circus yourself.'

'I may take it up some day,' said Jip carelessly. 'Whereabouts in this place have you been living? In the cellar?'

'No. Over there in the toolshed,' whispered the Doctor. 'Let's slip across quietly and quickly.'

A minute later they were safe in the toolshed. Sophie was gulping a herring; and the Doctor was chewing hungrily on a ham sandwich.

'You're a marvel, Jip,' said he with his mouth full. 'But how did you know we were here — and in need of food? Both of us were just starving.'

'Well,' said Jip, throwing the seal another herring, 'after Sophie got out of the gate the excitement still went on inside the circus. Blossom and

'The dog took the flying dive'

his men hunted around all night. Then we decided, from the people's heads popping out of the windows, that the town, too, was pretty much disturbed by the rumpus.

'Too-Too was awfully worried. "I do hope," he kept saying, "that the Doctor has not tried to get out into the country. He'll surely be caught if he has. The thing for him to do for the present is to hide."

'So all night long we sat up, expecting any minute to see you and Sophie dragged back into the circus. Well, morning came and still you hadn't been captured – and, as far as I know, nobody suspects that you, Doctor, have had anything to do with it. But the circus folk were still searching even when daylight came, and Too-Too kept fussing and worrying. So I said to him, I said, "I'll soon tell you if the Doctor is still in Ashby or not."

'And I went off on a tour of inspection. It was a damp morning and a good one for smelling. I made a circular trip right round the outside of the town. I knew that if you had left it by any means except flying I could pick up your scent. But nowhere did I cross the Dolittle trail. So I went back to Too-Too and I said, "The Doctor hasn't left Ashby yet – unless he went by balloon."

' "Good," says he. "Then he's safe in hiding some place. He's got wits, has the Doctor – in some things. Now, nose him out – and come back and tell me where he is. In the meantime I'll have some food got ready for him. Both he and the seal will be hungry. They've neither of them had a thing probably since noon yesterday, and they'll certainly have to stay where they are till late tonight."

'So then I went smelling around *inside* the town and picked up your incoming trail from where the coach stops. And it led me first, as I expected, by roundabout side streets to the dark passage. But from there, to my surprise, it didn't go on – just stopped dead. Sophie's didn't go on any further either. Well, I knew you couldn't have crept down a rat hole or flown up in the air; and for a couple of minutes I was absolutely fogged. Then, suddenly, I got a whiff of tobacco smoke coming over the wall – I know the brand you smoke – and I was certain you were in the garden. But, if you ask me, I should say that both of you are pretty fine jumpers.'

The Doctor laughed as he started on a second sandwich, and even Sophie, wiping her fishy whiskers with the back of her flipper, smiled broadly.

'We didn't jump the wall, Jip,' said John Dolittle. 'We used that ladder over there. But how did you get this food here without being seen?'

'It wasn't easy,' said Jip, 'not by any means. Too-Too and Dab-Dab made up the sandwiches, and we got Sophie's herrings from Higgins' fish pail. The milk was delivered at our wagon by the usual dairyman. Then Too-Too said you'd surely like to see a newspaper – to pass the time – if you had to stay here all day; and I chose *The Morning Gazette,* which is the one we had often seen you reading. Then the white mouse said not to forget your razor and soap because you hated to go without shaving. And we put *them* in. But all this stuff together weighed quite a lot – too much for me to carry in one trip. So I made two, hiding the first load behind an ash barrel in the passage till I could fetch the second. On the first journey I got stopped by an old woman – you see, I had the things rolled up in the newspaper, so they wouldn't look so noticeable. "Oh, my," said the old lady, "look at the nice doggie carrying the news-paper for his master! Come here, clever doggie!"

'Well, I gave the old frump the slip and got away from her all right. And then on the second trip I met some more idiots – dog idiots. They caught

'Sophie smiled'

the scent of the herrings I was carrying for Sophie and started following me in droves. I ran all round the town trying to get away from them and nearly lost the luggage more than once. Finally I put my package down and fought the whole bunch of them . . . No, it wasn't an easy job.'

'Goodness!' said the Doctor, finishing his last sandwich and opening the milk. 'It's wonderful to have such friends. I'm awfully glad you thought of the razor. I'm getting terribly bristly around the chin . . . Oh, but I haven't any water.'

'You must use milk,' said Jip. 'Steady! Don't drink it all. We thought of that, too, you see.'

'Humph,' said the Doctor setting down the half-empty bottle. 'That's an idea. I never shaved with milk before. Ought to be splendid for the complexion. You don't drink it, Sophie, do you? No. Oh, well, now we're all fixed up.'

And he took off his collar and began to shave.

After he had finished, Jip said, 'Well, I must be leaving, Doctor. I promised them at the caravan I'd come and let them know how everything was going with you as soon as I could. If you don't succeed in getting away tonight I'll be back again the same time tomorrow with some more grub. The townsfolk have pretty much calmed down. But Higgins and Blossom haven't given up the hunt yet by any means. So you will be careful, won't you? You're all safe and snug here. Better stay two days, or even three more, if necessary, rather than run for it too soon and get caught.'

'All right, Jip,' said the Doctor. 'We'll be careful. Thank you ever so much for coming. Remember me to everyone.'

'Me, too,' said Sophie.

'And tell Too-Too and the rest we are ever so grateful for their help,' the Doctor added as he opened the door of the shed.

Then they slipped across to the pear tree again. And after he had climbed into the branches of it, the Doctor poked Jip, inside the basket, over the wall and let him down on the string into the passage.

Nothing further of excitement happened for some hours. And though, from time to time, they heard the voices of people hunting for them in the passage and the streets around, a pleasant afternoon was spent by the two fugitives, the Doctor reading the paper and Sophie lolling thoughtfully on her bed.

After darkness began to fall John Dolittle could no longer see to read, so he and Sophie took to chatting over plans in low tones.

'Do you think we'll be able to get away tonight, Doctor?' asked Sophie. 'Surely, they'll have given up hunting me by then, won't they?'

'I hope so,' said the Doctor. 'As soon as it's dark I'll go out into the garden and see if I hear anything. I know how anxious you are to be getting along on your trip. But try and be patient.'

About half an hour later the Doctor took the ladder and, mounting near the top of the garden wall, he listened long and carefully.

When he came back to Sophie in the toolshed he was shaking his head.

'There are still an awful lot of people moving about in the streets,' he said. 'But whether they are circus men hunting you, or just ordinary townsfolk walking abroad, I can't make out. We'd better wait a while longer, I think.'

'Oh, dear!' sighed Sophie. 'Are we never going to get further than this garden? Poor Slushy! I'm so worried.'

After another hour had gone by the Doctor went out again. This time, just as he was about to climb the ladder, he heard Jip whispering to him on the other side of the wall.

'Doctor, are you there?'

'Yes, what is it?'

'Listen! Higgins and the boss have gone off
somewhere with a wagon. Blossom just came and
told Matthew to take on some extra jobs with the
circus because he wouldn't be back for a while.
Too-Too thinks it's a grand chance for you to make
a dash for it and get out of the town. Start in an
hour, when the circus is in full swing and the men
are all busy. Have you got that?'

'Yes, I heard you. Thank you, Jip. All right.
We'll leave in an hour.' And the Doctor looked at
his watch. 'Which way did Blossom go?'

'East – towards Grimbledon. Swizzle followed
them out part of the way and came back and told
us. You make for the west. Turn to the left at the
end of this passage and then double to the left
again at the next corner. It's a dark by-street and
it leads you out on to the Dunwich Road. Once you
reach that you'll be all right. There aren't many
houses on it and you'll be in the open country in no
time. I'm leaving some more sandwiches here in
the passage for you. Pick them up on your way out.
Can you hear me?'

'Yes, I understand,' whispered the Doctor. Then
he ran back to the shed with the good news.

Poor Sophie, when she heard they were to leave
that night, stood up on her tail and clapped her
flippers with joy.

'Now listen,' said the Doctor: 'if we meet anyone
on the street – and we are pretty sure to – you lie
down by the wall and pretend you're a sack I'm
carrying – that I'm taking a rest, you see. Try and
look as much like a sack as you can. Understand?'

'All right,' said Sophie. 'I'm frightfully excited.
See how my flippers are fluttering.'

Well, the Doctor kept an eye on his watch; and long before the hour had passed he and Sophie were waiting at the foot of the ladder ready and impatient.

Finally, after looking at the time once more, the Doctor whispered, 'All right, I think we can start now. Let me go first so I can steady the ladder for you, the way I did before.'

But, alas, for poor Sophie's hopes! Just as the Doctor was halfway up, the noise of distant barking, deep-voiced and angry, broke out.

'John Dolittle paused'

John Dolittle paused on the ladder, frowning. The barking – many dogs baying together – drew nearer.

'What's that?' said Sophie in a tremulous whisper from below. 'That's not Jip or any of our dogs.'

'No,' said the Doctor, climbing down slowly. 'There's no mistaking that sound. Sophie, something's gone wrong. That's the baying of bloodhounds – bloodhounds on a scent. And they're coming this way!'

Chapter Four
THE LEADER OF THE BLOODHOUNDS

JIP, after his last conversation with the Doctor over the garden wall, returned to the caravan and his friends, feeling comfortably sure that now everything would go all right.

He and Too-Too were chatting under the table while Dab-Dab was dusting the furniture, when suddenly in rushed Toby, all out of breath.

'Jip,' he cried. 'The worst has happened! They've got bloodhounds. That's what Blossom and Higgins went off for. There's a man who raises them, it seems, in the next village. They're bringing 'em here in a wagon − six of 'em. I spotted them just as they entered the town over the tollbridge. I ran behind and tried to speak to the dogs. But with the rattle of the wagon wheels they couldn't hear me. If they put those hounds on Sophie's trail she's as good as caught already.'

'Confound them!' muttered Jip. 'Where are they now, Toby?'

'I don't know. When I left them they were crossing the marketplace on their way here at a trot. I raced ahead to let you know as quick as I could.'

'All right,' said Jip, springing up. 'Come with me.'

And he dashed out into the night.

'They'll try and pick up the trail from the seal's stand,' said Jip as the two dogs ran on together across the enclosure. 'Perhaps we can meet them there.'

But at the stand there were no bloodhounds.

Jip put his nose to the ground and sniffed just once.

'Drat the luck!' he whispered. 'They've been here already and gone off on the trail. Listen, there they are, baying now. Come on! Let's race for the passage. We may be in time yet.'

And away he sped like a white arrow towards the gate, while poor little Toby, left far behind, with his flappy ears trailing in the wind, put on his best speed to keep up.

Dashing into the passage, Jip found it simply full of men and dogs and lanterns. Blossom was there, and Higgins, and the man who owned the hounds. While the men talked and waved the lamps, the hounds, six great, droopy-jowled beasts, with long ears and bloodshot eyes, sniffed the ground and ran hither and thither about the alley, trying to find where the trail led out. Every once in a while they would lift their noses, open their big mouths, and send a deep-voiced howl rolling towards the moon.

By this time other dogs in the neighbourhood were answering their bark from every backyard. Jip ran into the crowded passage, pretending to join in the hunt for scent. Picking out the biggest bloodhound, who, he guessed, was the leader, he got alongside of him. Then, still keeping his eyes and nose to the ground, he whispered in dog language, 'Get your duffers out of here. This is the Doctor's business – John Dolittle's.'

The bloodhound paused and eyed Jip haughtily.

'Who are you, mongrel?' he said. 'We've been set to run down a seal. Stop trying to fool us. John Dolittle is away on a voyage.'

'He's nothing of the kind,' muttered Jip. 'He's on the other side of that wall – not six feet away from us. He is trying to get this seal down to the sea so she can escape these men with the lanterns – if you idiots will only get out of the way.'

'I don't believe you,' said the leader. 'The last I heard of the Doctor he was travelling in Africa. We must do our duty.'

'Duffer! Numbskull!' growled Jip, losing his temper entirely. 'I'm telling you the truth. For two pins I'd pull your long ears. You must have been asleep in your kennel the last two years. The Doctor's been back in England over a month. He's travelling with the circus now.'

But the leader of the bloodhounds, like many highly trained specialists, was (in everything outside his own profession) very obstinate and a bit stupid. He just simply would not believe that the Doctor wasn't still abroad. In all his famous record as a tracker he had never failed to run down his quarry once he took up a scent. He had a big reputation, and was proud of it. He wasn't going to be misled by every whippersnapper of a dog who came along with an idle tale – no, not he.

Poor Jip was in despair. He saw that the hounds

were now sniffing at the wall over which Sophie
had climbed. He knew that these great beasts
would never leave this neighbourhood while the
seal was near, and her fishy scent so strong all
about. It was only a matter of time before Blossom
and Higgins would guess that she was in hiding
beyond the wall and would have the old house and
garden searched.

While he was still arguing, an idea came to Jip.
He left the knot of bloodhounds and nosed his way
carelessly down to the bottom of the passage. The
air was now simply full of barks and yelps from
dogs of every kind. Jip threw back his head and
pretended to join in the chorus. But the message
he shouted was directed over the wall to the
Doctor:

'These idiots won't believe me. For heaven's sake
tell 'em you're here – *Woof! Woof! WOO —!*'

And then still another doggish voice, coming
from the garden, added to the general noise of the
night. And this is what it barked:

'It is I, John Dolittle. Won't you please go away!
Wow! Woof! Wow-ow!'

At the sound of that voice – to Blossom and
Higgins no different from any of the other yelps
that filled the air – the noses of all six bloodhounds left the ground and twelve long ears cocked up, motionless and listening.

'By ginger!' muttered the leader. 'It is he! It's the
great man himself.'

'What did I tell you?' whispered Jip, shuffling
towards him. 'Now lead these men off towards the
south – out of the town, quick – and don't stop
running till morning.'

Then the dog trainer saw his prize leader suddenly double around and head out of the passage. To his delight, the others followed his example.

'All right, Mr Blossom,' he yelled, waving his lantern. 'They've got the scent again. Come on, follow 'em, follow 'em! They're going fast. Stick to 'em! . . . Run!'

Tumbling over one another to keep up, the three men hurried after the hounds; and Jip, to help the excitement in the right direction, joined the chase, barking for all he was worth.

'They've turned down the street to the south,' shouted the owner. 'We'll get your seal now, never fear. Ah, they're good dogs! Once they take the scent they never go wrong. Come on, Mr Blossom. Don't let 'em get too far away.'

And in a flash the little dark passage, which a moment before was full and crowded, was left empty in the moonlight.

Poor Sophie, weeping hysterically on the lawn, with the Doctor trying to comfort her, suddenly saw the figure of an owl pop up on to the garden wall.

'Doctor! Doctor!'

'Yes, Too-Too. What is it?'

'Now's your chance! The whole town's joined the hunt. Get your ladder. Hurry!'

And two minutes later, while the hounds, in full cry, led Blossom and Higgins on a grand steeplechase over hill and dale to the southward, the Doctor led Sophie quietly out of Ashby by the Dunwich road, towards the westward and the sea.

'A steeplechase over hill and dale'

When Sophie and John Dolittle had travelled down the Dunwich Road as far as where the houses of Ashby ended and the fields of the country began, they both heaved a sigh of relief. What they had been most afraid of while still in the streets was being met by a policeman. The Doctor guessed that Higgins had probably applied to the police station and offered a reward for the return of his lost property. If he had, of course, all the town constables would be very much on the lookout for stray seals.

As they now plodded along the road between hedgerows, the Doctor could tell from Sophie's heavy breathing and very slow pace that even this bit of land travel had already wearied the poor beast. Yet he dared not halt upon the highway.

Spying a copse over in some lonely farming lands to his left, he decided that it would make a good, snug place in which to take a rest. He therefore turned off the road, found a hole in the hedge for Sophie to crawl through, and led her along a ditch that ran up towards the copse.

Arriving at the little clump of trees and brambles, they found it excellent cover and crawled in. It was the kind of place where no one would be likely to come in a month of Sundays — except perhaps stray sportsmen after rabbits, or children berry-picking.

'Well,' said the Doctor, as Sophie flopped down, panting within the protection of dense hawthorns and furze, 'so far so good!'

'My!' said Sophie, 'but I'm winded. Seals weren't meant for this kind of thing, Doctor. How far do you reckon we've come?'

'About a mile and a half, I should say.'

'Good Lord! Is that all! And it's nearly a hundred to the sea! I tell you what I think we ought to do, Doctor; let's make for a river. Rivers always flow to the sea. I can travel in water as fast as a horse can run. But much more of this highroad walking will wear holes in the sole of my stomach. A river's the thing we've got to make for.'

'Yes, I think you're right, Sophie. But where to

'He found a hole for Sophie to crawl through'

find one? That's the point. If we were anywhere near Puddleby now, I could tell you at once. But I don't know a thing about the geography of these parts. I ought to have remembered to bring a map with me. I don't want to be asking people – not yet, anyway. Because I'm still supposed to be miles away from here, attending to business.'

'Well, ask some animal, then,' said Sophie.

'Of course!' cried the Doctor. 'Why didn't I think of that before? Now, what kind of a beast could best give us the information we want?'

'Oh, any sort of water creature will do.'

'I know. We'll ask an otter. Otters are about your nearest relatives in England, Sophie. They travel and hunt in fresh water very much the way you do in salt. Now you stay here and take a good rest, and I'll go off and find one.'

It was about one o'clock in the morning when the Doctor returned to the copse. The noise he made entering woke Sophie out of a sound sleep.

With him he had brought a rather unusual animal. In odd, curving, graceful leaps this creature kept bounding up out of the high bracken that carpeted the copse to get a good look at Sophie. He seemed somewhat afraid of her, but very interested.

'Isn't she large, Doctor!' he whispered. 'Did you say she was related to us?'

'In a way, yes. Though, strictly speaking, she is a *pinniped,* while your people are *musteloids.*'

'Oh, well, I'm glad of it. She is so clumsy. And look, she hasn't any hind legs – just sort of stubby things. Are you sure she won't bite?'

Finally, the otter was persuaded that Sophie was harmless, and drawing close, he talked pleasantly with this other furred fisherman from foreign parts.

'Now,' said the Doctor, 'as I have told you, we are anxious to get down to the sea by the quickest and quietest way possible. And Sophie thinks that the best thing is make for some stream.'

'Humph!' said the otter. 'She's quite right, of course. But you've come to a pretty poor place for waterways. The only reason I stay in this neighbourhood is because there are no otter

hounds here. I live and do my fishing in a few
ponds. They're not much good, but at least I'm not
hunted by the packs. There are no decent rivers in
these parts – certainly none that *she* could swim
in to the sea.'

'Well, where do you recommend us to go, then?'
asked the Doctor.

'I really don't know,' said the otter. 'You see, I
travel so little myself. I was born in this district.
And my mother always told me that this was the
only safe place left in England for otters to live.
And so I've stayed here – my whole life.'

'Well, could you get us some fish, then?' asked
Sophie. 'I'm famished.'

'Oh, surely,' said the otter. 'Do you eat carp?'

'I'd eat anything just now,' said Sophie.

'All right. Wait a minute till I go down to my
pond,' said the otter, and he turned around and
bounded out of the copse.

In less than ten minutes he was back again with
a huge brown carp in his mouth. This Sophie
disposed of in a couple of gulps.

'Why don't you ask the wild ducks, Doctor?' said
the otter. 'They travel no end, following the waterways up and down to the sea, feeding. And they
always go by the quietest streams, where they
won't meet people. They could tell you.'

'Yes, I think you're right,' said John Dolittle.
'But where can I get hold of any?'

'Oh, that's easy. They're always flying by night.
Just go up on a hill somewhere and listen. When
you hear them passing overhead, call 'em.'

So, leaving Sophie and her fresh-water cousin
chatting quietly in the copse, the Doctor climbed

up a ridge till he came to a high field, from where he could see the moonlit sky all around him. And after a minute or two he heard, a long way off, a faint quacking and honking – wild ducks on the wing. Presently, high above his head, he could make out a V-shaped cluster of little dots, heading seawards.

Putting his two hands to his mouth, like a trumpet, he sent a call hurtling upward. The cluster paused, broke up, and started flying round in circles, coming downward – cautiously – all the time.

Presently, in the copse Sophie and the otter stopped chatting and listened tensely to the sound of approaching footsteps.

Then the figure of John Dolittle stepped into the hiding place, with a lovely green and blue duck tucked comfortably under each arm.

'Well,' said the ducks, after the Doctor had explained the situation to them and asked their advice, 'the nearest river big enough to be of any use to a seal is the Kippet. Unfortunately, there are no brooks or anything leading into it from here. To reach the valley of Kippet River you'll have to cross about forty miles of land.'

'Humph!' said the Doctor. 'That sounds bad.'

'Very bad,' sighed Sophie, wearily. 'Poor Slushy! Such a time I'm taking to get to him. What kind of land is this which we've got to cross?'

'It varies a good deal,' said the ducks. 'Some of it's hilly; some of it's flat; part of it's standing crops; part of it's heath. It's very mixed travelling.'

'Dear me!' groaned Sophie.

' "Yes," said the ducks'

'Yes,' said the ducks, 'it would be easier, as far as the river, if you went by road.'

'But don't you see,' said the Doctor, 'I'm afraid of being met and stopped? That's why we left the Dunwich Road. There are too many people who've heard of our escape round these parts.'

'But,' said the ducks, 'you wouldn't have to go back on to the Dunwich Road. Listen, if you follow the hedge on westwards, it will lead you down on to another road, the old Roman road from Igglesby

to Grantchester. Coaches use it, going north and
south. You're not likely to meet Ashby folks on
that. Well, if you go along that road for about forty
miles north you'll come to the Kippet River. The
highway crosses it at Talbot's Bridge – just before
you enter the town of Grantchester.'

'It sounds simple for a good walker,' said the
Doctor. 'But for Sophie it's another matter. Still, I
suppose it's the best. Follow the Grantchester
Road north as far as Talbot's Bridge, and there
take to the river, the Kippet – is that it?'

'That's right,' said the ducks. 'You can't go
wrong, once you reach the road. After you take to
the stream you'd better make some more inquiries
of other waterfowl because, although the Kippet
will lead you to the sea, there are places on it
where you must be careful.'

'Very good,' said the Doctor. 'You have been
most kind. I thank you.'

Then the ducks flew off about their business and
John Dolittle looked at his watch.

'It's now two o'clock in the morning,' said he. 'We
have three hours more before daylight comes.
Would you prefer, Sophie, to stay here and rest till
tomorrow evening, or shall we push on and get as
far as we can before dawn?'

'Oh, let's push on,' said Sophie.

'All right,' said the Doctor, 'come along.'

While they were making their way along the
hedge towards the road, the little otter went off
and got Sophie a large meal of fresh fish to help
strengthen her for her hard trip. About a mile
below, at the end of a long field, he showed them
a hole through another hedge, told them the road

was just the other side of it, and bade them fare-well.

Crawling through, they came out upon a fine highway that stretched away into the night on either hand, wide and well paved.

With a sigh of resignation from Sophie, they turned to the right and set off northwards.

Chapter Five
THE PASSENGERS FROM PENCHURCH

'OH, dear! Oh, dear!' said Sophie after they had travelled for about an hour. 'This road is just as hard and knobby and scrapy as the other one. How far have we come now?'

'About another mile,' said the Doctor.

Sophie began to weep big tears into the white dust of the road.

'Always "about another mile"! I'm afraid I'm being a dreadful nuisance to you, Doctor.'

'Oh, not at all,' said John Dolittle. 'Don't be down-hearted. We'll do it yet. It'll be easy going once we reach the river.'

'Yes, but we are still thirty-nine miles from that,' said Sophie. 'And I'm *so* worn out.'

The Doctor looked down at her and saw that, indeed, she was in a very exhausted state. There was nothing for it but to halt again.

'Come over here,' he said, 'off the road – so. Now lie down in this ditch, where you won't be seen, and take a rest.'

Poor Sophie did as she was told, and the Doctor sat down upon a milestone, thinking hard. Although he was doing his best to cheer Sophie

along, it was beginning to look, at this rate, as
though they could never get as far as the river.

While he was pondering drearily over the difficulties of the situation, Sophie suddenly said,
'What's that noise?'

The Doctor looked up and listened.

'Wagon wheels,' he said. 'You're quite safe where
you are. Just keep still till it passes. You'll never
be seen in the ditch.'

The rumbling noise drew nearer and presently,
round a bend in the road, a light came in sight.
Soon the Doctor could see that it was a closed carriage of some kind. As it drew level with him, the
driver stopped his horses and called out, 'Are you
waiting for the coach?'

'Er – er,' the Doctor stammered, ' – oh, are you
the coach?'

'We're one of 'em,' said the man.

'Where do you go to?' asked the Doctor.

'We are the local,' said the driver; 'Penchurch to
Anglethorpe. D'yer want to get in?'

While he hesitated over an answer, a wild idea
came into the Doctor's head.

'Have you got many passengers?' he asked.

'No, only two – man and his wife – and they're
asleep. Plenty o' room inside.'

The carriage, lit within by a lamp which shone
dimly through drawn curtains, had stopped a little
beyond the Doctor's milestone. The driver, from
where he sat, could see neither Sophie's hiding
place nor the back door of his own coach.

'Are your passengers from these parts?' asked
the Doctor, lowering his voice.

'No, we come from Penchurch, I told you. What

more would you like to know? If you want to get in, hurry! Can't stay talking all night.'

'All right,' said the Doctor. 'Wait just a second till I get my luggage.'

'Want any help?'

'No, no, no! Stay where you are. I can manage.'

Then the Doctor slipped behind the end of the coach and opened the door. A man and a woman, with their heads sunk upon their chests, were dozing in the far corner. Leaving the door open, the Doctor ran to the ditch, put his arms around Sophie, and lifted her huge weight bodily in his arms.

'We'll cover part of the ground this way, anyhow,' he whispered as he carried her to the coach. 'Keep as still and quiet as you can. I'm going to stow you under the seat.'

For entering the carrige, whose floor stood high above the level of the road, there were two little iron steps hung below the doorsill. As the Doctor looked in the second time, the passengers were still apparently sleeping. But in trying to mount the steps with his tremendous burden he stumbled noisily. The woman in the corner woke up and raised her head. The Doctor, Sophie's flippers still clinging about his neck, stared, speechless.

'*John!*'

It was Sarah.

Mrs Dingle fainted with a shriek into her husband's arms. The horses bolted. The Doctor lost his balance entirely. And the coach rattled off into the night, leaving him seated in the road, with Sophie on his lap.

'Heigh-ho!' he sighed, picking himself up wearily.

'He carried her to the coach'

'Of course it would be Sarah! It might have been anyone else in the world, but it *had* to be Sarah. Well, well!'

'But what did you mean to do?' asked Sophie. 'You could never have got me under the seat. There wasn't room there to hide a dog.'

'Oh, well, I just acted on the spur of the moment,' said the Doctor. 'I might have got you a few miles on your journey – if I hadn't stumbled and woken Sarah. Bother it! But, you know, Sophie, I think that the coach idea is our best scheme, anyhow.

Only we must arrange it a little differently; we must lay our plans with care. In one way it was a good thing it was Sarah. If it had been anyone else who had seen me carrying a seal, they might have talked and set people on our track. But Sarah and her husband are ashamed of my being in the circus business and they won't say anything, we may be sure.

'Now, listen: over in the east the sky is growing grey – look. It's no use our trying to get further today. So we'll hide you in those woods down there, and then I'll go on alone to the next village and find out a few things.'

So they moved along the highway a short distance to where some pleasant woods bordered the road.

Entering the cover of these preserves, they found a nice place for Sophie to lie hidden. Then, when he had made her comfortable, the Doctor set out down the road just as the cocks in the nearby farms began crowing their first greeting to the morning sun.

After a walk of about two miles he came to a village with a pretty little ivy-covered inn called The Three Huntsmen. Going in he ordered breakfast. He had not had anything to eat since he had left the deserted garden. A very old waiter served him some bacon and eggs in the taproom.

As soon as the Doctor had eaten he lit his pipe and began chatting to the waiter. He found out a whole lot of things about the coaches that ran up and down the Grantchester Road – what the different ones were like to look at, at what hour they were to be expected, which of them were usually crowded, and much more.

Then he left the inn and walked down the street till he came to the few shops the village had. One of these was a general clothier and haberdasher's. The Doctor entered and asked the price of a lady's cloak that was hanging in the window.

'Fifteen shillings and sixpence,' said the woman in charge of the shop. 'Is your wife tall?'

'My wife?' asked the Doctor, entirely bewildered. 'Oh, ah, yes, of course. Well – er – I want it long, anyway. And I'll take a bonnet, too.'

'Is she fair or dark?' asked the woman.

'Er – she's sort of medium,' said the Doctor.

'There's a nice one here, with red poppies on it,' said the woman. 'How would she like that?'

'No, that's too showy,' said the Doctor.

'Well, they do say them flowery ones is right fashionable up to London just now. How would this do?'

And the woman brought forward a large, plain, black bonnet. 'This is very genteel. I wear this kind myself.'

'Yes, I'll take that one,' said the Doctor. 'And now I want a lady's veil – a heavy one, please.'

'Oh, mourning in the family?'

'Er – not exactly. But I want it pretty thick – a travelling veil.'

Then the woman added a veil to the Doctor's purchases. And with a large parcel under his arm he presently left the shop. Next, he went to a grocery and bought some dried herrings for Sophie – the only kind of fish he could obtain in the village. And about noon he started back down the road.

' "How would this do?" '

'Sophie,' said John Dolittle, when he reached the seal's hiding place in the woods, 'I have a whole lot of information for you, some food, and some clothes.'

'Some clothes!' said Sophie. 'What would I do with clothes?'

'Wear them,' said the Doctor. 'You've got to be a lady — for a while, anyhow.'

'Great heavens!' grunted Sophie, wiping her whiskers with the back of her flipper. 'What for?'

'So you can travel by coach,' said the Doctor.

'But I can't walk upright,' cried Sophie, 'like a lady.'

'I know. But you can sit upright – like a sick lady. You'll have to be a little lame. Any walking there is to be done, I'll carry you.'

'But what about my face? It isn't the right shape.'

'We'll cover that up with a veil,' said the Doctor. 'And your hat will disguise the rest of your head. Now, eat this fish I've brought for you and then we will rehearse dressing you up. I hear that the Grantchester coach passes by here about eight o'clock – that is, the night one does; and we'll take that because it's less crowded. Now, it's about a four hours' ride to Talbot's Bridge. During all that time you'll have to sit up on your tail and keep still. Do you think you can manage that?'

'I'll try,' said Sophie.

'Perhaps you'll have a chance to lie down for a spell if we have the carriage to ourselves part of the way. Much will depend upon how crowded the coach is. It makes three stops between here and Talbot's Bridge. But being a night coach, I don't suppose it will take on many passengers – if we're lucky. Now, let me try these clothes on you and we'll see how you look.'

Then the Doctor dressed up Sophie, the performing seal, like a lady. He seated her on a log, put the bonnet on her head, the veil across her face, and the cloak over the rest of her.

After he had got her into a human sitting position on the log, it was surprising how natural she looked. In the deep hood of the bonnet her long nose was entirely concealed; and with the veil hung over the front of it, her head looked extraordinarily like a woman's.

'You must be careful to keep your whiskers inside,' he said. 'That's very important. The cloak is quite long, you see – comes right down to the ground – and while you are seated and it's kept closed in the front it will look quite all right in a dim light. You can keep it drawn together with your flippers – so. Now you look just as though you had your hands folded in your lap – that's the idea, splendid! So long as you can stay that way no one would take you for anything but a lady passenger. . . . Oh, look out! Don't wiggle your head or the bonnet will fall off. Wait till I tie the ribbons under your chin.'

'How am I supposed to breathe?' asked Sophie, blowing out the veil in front like a balloon.

'Don't do that,' said the Doctor. 'You're not swimming or coming up for air. You'll get used to it after a while.'

'I can't keep very steady this way, Doctor. I'm sitting on the back of my spine, you know. It's an awfully hard position for balancing – much worse than walking on a ladder. What if I should slip down on to the floor of the coach?'

'The seat will be wider than this log and more comfortable. Besides, I'll try to get you into a corner and I'll sit close beside you – so you'll be sort of wedged in. If you feel yourself slipping, just whisper to me and I'll hitch you up into a safer position. You look splendid – really, you do.'

Well, after a little more practice and rehearsing

'He put the veil across her face'

the Doctor felt that Sophie could now pass as a
lady passenger. And when evening came it found
him by the edge of the road, with a heavily veiled
woman seated at his side, waiting for the
Grantchester coach.

Chapter Six
THE GRANTCHESTER COACH

AFTER they had waited about a quarter of an hour, Sophie said, 'I hear wheels, Doctor. And look, there are the lights far down the road.'

'Yes,' said John Dolittle. 'But it isn't the coach we want. That's the Twinborough Express – a green light and a white light. The one we want has two white lights in front. Step back a little further into the shadow of the hedge. Try not to walk on your cloak. You mustn't get it muddy.'

A little while after the Twinborough Express had rattled by, along came another.

'Ah!' said the Doctor. 'This is ours, the Grant-chester coach. Now sit up by the side of the road here and keep perfectly still till I signal the driver. Then I'll lift you in, and let's hope we find a corner seat empty. Is your bonnet on tight?'

'Yes,' said Sophie. 'But the veil is tickling my nose most awfully. I do hope I don't sneeze.'

'So do I,' said the Doctor, remembering the cowlike bellow that seals make when they sneeze.

Then John Dolittle stepped out into the middle of the road and stopped the coach. Inside he found three passengers – two men at the far end and an old lady near the door. To his delight, the corner seat opposite the old lady was empty.

Leaving the door open, he ran back and got Sophie and carried her to the coach. The two men at the far end were talking earnestly together about politics. They took little notice as the lame woman was lifted in and made comfortable in the corner seat. But as the Doctor closed the door and sat beside his companion, he noticed that the old lady opposite was very interested in his invalid.

The coach started off, and the Doctor, after making sure that Sophie's feet were not showing below the long cape, got out a newspaper from his pocket. Although the light from the oil lamp overhead was too dim to read by, he spread out the paper before his face and pretended to be deeply absorbed in it.

Presently the old lady leaned forward and tapped Sophie on the knee.

'Excuse me, my dear—' she began in a kindly voice.

'Oh, er—' said the Doctor, looking up quickly. 'She doesn't talk – er – that is, not any English.'

'Has she got far to go?' asked the old lady.

'To Alaska,' said the Doctor, forgetting himself, 'er – that is, eventually. This journey, we're only going to Grantchester.'

Wishing people would mind their own business, the Doctor plunged again into his paper as though his life depended on his reading every word.

But the kindly passenger was not easily put off. After a moment she leaned forward once more and tapped the Doctor on the knee.

'Is it rheumatics?' she asked in a whisper,

' "Excuse me, my dear," she began'

nodding towards Sophie. 'I noticed that you had to carry her in, poor dear!'

'Er, not exactly,' stammered the Doctor. 'Her legs are too short. Can't walk. Can't walk a step. Been that way all her life.'

'Dear me!' sighed the old lady. 'How sad; how very sad!'

'I'm slipping,' whispered Sophie behind her veil. 'In a minute I'm going to slide on to the floor.'

While the Doctor was putting away his newspaper and getting ready to hitch Sophie up higher, the old lady spoke again. 'What a nice sealskin coat she's wearing!'

Sophie's knee was sticking out through the cloak.

'Yes. She has to be kept warm,' said the Doctor, busily wrapping his invalid up. 'Most important.'

'She'll be your daughter, I suppose?' asked the old lady.

But this time Sophie spoke for herself. A deep roar suddenly shook the carriage. The tickling of the veil had finally made her sneeze. The Doctor was now standing up, but before he could catch her she had slid down on to the floor between his feet.

'She's in pain, poor thing,' said the old lady. 'Wait till I get out my smelling bottle. She's fainted. I often do it myself, travelling. And this coach does smell something horrible — fishy like.'

Luckily for the Doctor, the old lady then busied herself hunting in her handbag. He was therefore able, while lifting the seal back on to the seat, to place himself in between Sophie and the two men, who were now also showing interest in her.

'Here you are,' said the old lady, handing out a silver smelling bottle. 'Lift up her veil and hold it under her nose.'

'No, thank you,' said the Doctor quickly. 'All she needs is rest. She's very tired. We'll prop her up snugly in the corner, like this — so. Now, let's not talk, and probably she'll soon drop off to sleep.'

Well, finally the poor Doctor got the little old lady to mind her own business and keep quiet. And for about an hour and a half the coach continued on its way without anything further happening. But it was quite clear that the men at the

other end were puzzled and curious about his
invalid. They kept glancing in her direction and
talking together in whispers in a way that made
him very uneasy.

Presently the coach stopped at a village to
change horses. The driver appeared at the door
and told the passengers that if they wished to have
supper at the inn (in whose yard they had halted)
they had half an hour to do so before they went on.

The two men left the coach, eyeing Sophie and
the Doctor as they passed on their way out; and
soon the old lady followed their example. The
driver had now also disappeared and John Dolittle
and his companion had the coach to themselves.

'Listen, Sophie,' the Doctor whispered. 'I'm getting uneasy about those two men. I'm afraid they
suspect that you are not what you pretend to be.
You stay here now, while I go in and find out if
they're travelling any further with us.'

Then he strolled into the inn. In the passage he
met a serving maid and asked the way to the
dining room. She showed him an open door with a
screen before it a little way down the passage.

'Supper will be served in a minute,' she said.
'Just walk in and sit down.'

'Thank you,' said the Doctor. 'By the way, do you
happen to know who those two men were who
came in off the coach just now?'

'Yes, sir,' said the maid. 'One of them's the
county constable and the other's Mr Tuttle, the
mayor of Penchurch.'

'Thank you,' said the Doctor, and passed on.

Reaching the screen door, he hesitated a
moment before entering the dining room. And

presently, he heard the voices of the two men seated at a table within on the other side of the screen.

'I tell you,' said the one in a low tone, 'there's not the least doubt. They're highwaymen, as sure as you're alive. It's an old trick, disguising as a woman. Did you notice the trick veil? As likely as not it's that rogue, Robert Finch himself. He robbed the Twinborough Express only last month.'

'I shouldn't wonder,' said the other. 'And the short, thick villain will be Joe Gresham, his partner. Now, I'll tell you what we'll do. After supper let's go back and take our seats as though we suspected nothing. Their plan, no doubt, is to wait till the coach is full and has reached a lonely part of the road. Then they'll hold up the passengers — money or your life! — and get away before the alarm can be raised. Have you got your travelling pistols?'

'Yes.'

'All right, give me one. Now, when I nudge you — you tear off the man's veil and hold a pistol to his head. I'll take care of the short one. Then we'll turn the coach about, drive back, and lodge them in the village jail. Understand?'

While the Doctor was still listening, the maid came down the passage again, with a tray full of dishes, and touched him on the back.

'Go on in, sir,' she said, 'and sit down. I'm just going to serve supper.'

'No, thank you,' said the Doctor. 'I'm not really hungry. I think I'll go out into the air again.'

Luckily, on reaching the yard, he found it

'He heard the voices of two men at a table within'

deserted. The horses had been taken out of the shafts and put into the stable. The new ones had not yet been hitched up to the coach. The Doctor sped across the yard and opened the door.

'Sophie,' he whispered, 'come out of that. They think we're highwaymen in disguise. Let's get away – quick! – while the coast is clear.'

Hoisting the seal's huge weight in his arms, the Doctor staggered out of the yard with her. On account of the lateness of the hour there was no one in the road. All was still and quiet but for the

rattle of dishes from the inn kitchen and the noise
of washing from the stables.

'Now,' said he, putting her down, 'we haven't far
to go. See, this place is the last in the village. Once
we reach those fields and get beyond the hedge we
should be all right. I'll go ahead and find a place
to get through, and you follow along as quick as
you can. Give me your cloak and bonnet — that's
it. Now you can travel better.'

A few minutes later they were safe behind a
high hedge, resting in the long grass of a meadow.

'My!' sighed Sophie, stretching herself out. 'It's
good to be rid of that wretched cloak and veil. I
don't like being a lady a bit.'

'That was a narrow escape,' said the Doctor. 'It's
a good thing I went in and overheard those men
talking. If we had gone on with them in the coach
we'd have been caught for sure.'

'Aren't you afraid they'll come hunting for us?'
asked Sophie.

'Oh, maybe. But they'll never look for us here.
They take us for highwaymen, you see. And by the
time they discover our escape they'll probably
think we've gone miles. We'll wait here till the
coach passes, and then we needn't worry.'

'Well,' said Sophie, 'even if we are safe it doesn't
seem to me we are much better off than we were
before.'

'But we're this much further on our way,' said
the Doctor. 'Have patience. We'll do it yet.'

'How far have we come now?' asked Sophie.

'That village was Shottlake,' said the Doctor.
'We've got only eighteen miles more to do to reach
Talbot's Bridge.'

'Well, but how are we going to travel? I can't walk it, Doctor; I simply can't – not eighteen miles.'

'Shh! Don't speak so loud,' whispered John Dolittle. 'They may be snooping around somewhere, looking for us. We'll find a way – don't worry. And once we reach the river, the worst will be over. We must first wait till the coach goes by, though, before we can stir.'

'Poor Slushy!' murmured Sophie, looking up at the moon. 'I wonder how he's getting on. . . .Will you try to take another coach, Doctor?'

'No. I think we'd better not. They may leave word at the inn and drivers will be on the lookout for a woman of your description.'

'Well, I hope they don't find us here,' said Sophie. 'It doesn't seem to me we're very well concealed. Good heavens! Listen – a footstep!'

The place where they lay was the corner of a pasture field. Besides the hedge that hid them from the road there was another, on their right, dividing their field from the next. Behind this they now heard a heavy footstep passing up and down.

'Keep still, Sophie!' whispered the Doctor. 'Don't move an inch.'

Presently the top branches of the hedge began to sway and the crackling of twigs reached their ears. 'Doctor,' said Sophie in a frightened whisper, 'they've discovered us. There's someone trying to get through the hedge!'

For a moment or two the Doctor was undecided whether to keep still or to run for it. He thought at first that if it were someone out looking for them he might not know exactly where they were anyway, and would, perhaps, if they kept quiet, go to some other part of the hedge easier to pass through.

But the crackling of branches grew louder — only a few feet away from them. Whoever it was, he seemed determined to enter the field at that place. So, with a whispered word to Sophie, the Doctor sprang up and started off, running across the meadow, with the poor seal flopping along at his side.

On and on they went. Behind them they heard a crash as the hedge gave way, and the heavy footsteps beating the ground in pursuit.

From the sound the pursuer, whoever he was, was gaining on them. And presently the Doctor, fearing that as highwaymen they might be fired upon without warning, turned to look back.

And there, lumbering along behind them, was an old, old plough horse!

'It's all right, Sophie,' panted the Doctor halting. 'It isn't a man at all. We've had our run for nothing. Good lord, but I'm blown!'

The horse, seeing them stop, slowed down to a walk and came ambling towards them in the moonlight. He seemed very decrepit and feeble; and when he came up Sophie saw with great astonishment that he was wearing spectacles.

'Heavens!' cried the Doctor. 'It's my old friend from Puddleby. Why didn't you call to me instead of chasing us across country? We expected you to shoot us in the back any minute.'

'Is that John Dolittle's voice I hear?' asked the old horse, peering close into the Doctor's face.

'Yes,' said the Doctor. 'Can't you see me?'

'Only very mistily,' said the plough horse. 'My sight's been getting awful bad the last few months. I saw fine for quite a while after you gave me the spectacles. Then I got sold to another farmer, and I left Puddleby to come here. One day I fell on my nose while ploughing, and after I got up my spectacles didn't seem to work right at all. I've been almost blind ever since.'

'Let me take your glasses off and look at them,' said the Doctor. 'Perhaps you need your prescription changed.'

Then John Dolittle took the spectacles off the old horse and, holding them up to the moon, peered through them, turning them this way and that.

'Why, good gracious!' he cried. 'You've got the lenses all twisted. No wonder you couldn't see! That right glass I gave you is quite a strong one. Most important to have them in proper adjustment. I'll soon set them right for you.'

'I did take them to the blacksmith who does my shoes,' said the old horse as the Doctor started screwing the glasses around in the frames. 'But he only hammered the rims and made them worse than ever. Since I was brought to Shottlake I couldn't come to you about them and, of course, our local vet doesn't understand horses' glasses.'

'There, now,' said the Doctor, putting the spectacles back on his old friend's nose. 'I've fixed them tight, so they can't turn. I think you'll find them all right now.'

'Oh, my, yes,' said the old horse, a broad smile spreading over his face as he looked through them. 'I can see you as plain as day. Goodness! How natural you look – big nose, high hat, and all! The

'John Dolittle peered through them'

sight of you does me good. Why, I can see the very
blades of grass by moonlight! You've no idea what
an inconvenience it is to be shortsighted, if you're
a horse. You spend most of your grazing time
spitting out the wild garlic that you chew by accident. . . . My, oh, my! You're the only animal doctor
there ever was!'

PART III

Chapter One
THE HIGHWAYMAN'S DOUBLE

'IS he a decent fellow, this farmer you're working for now?' asked the Doctor, seating himself in the grass of the meadow.

'Oh, yes,' said the old horse. 'He means well. But I haven't done much work this year. He's got a younger team for ploughing. I'm sort of pensioned off – only do odd jobs. You see, I'm getting pretty old – thirty-nine, you know.'

'Are you, indeed?' said the Doctor. 'You don't look it – nothing like it. Thirty-nine! Well, well! Yes, to be sure, now I recollect. You had your thirty-sixth birthday the same week I got you your spectacles. You remember the garden party we gave for you – in the kitchen garden – when Gub-Gub overate himself with ripe peaches?'

'Very well, I do. Ah, those were the days! Good old Puddleby! But what's this animal you have with you,' asked the plough horse as Sophie moved restlessly in the grass, 'a badger?'

'No, that's a seal. Let me introduce you: this is Sophie, from Alaska. We're escaping from the circus. She has to go back to her country on urgent business, and I'm helping her get to the sea.'

'Sh!' said Sophie. 'Look, Doctor, there's the coach going by.'

'Thank goodness for that!' murmured John Dolittle as the lights disappeared down the road.

'You know,' said he, turning to the old horse again, 'we've had a hard time getting even this far. Sophie has to keep concealed, and she can't walk much. We are making for the Kippet River, at Talbot's Bridge. We came by coach up to Shottlake, but we had to leave it. We were just wondering how we could continue our journey when you scared the life out of us behind that hedge.'

'You want to get to Talbot's Bridge?' said the old horse. 'Well, that should be easy. Listen you see that barn up on the skyline? Well, there's an old wagon in it. There's no harness but there's plenty of ropes. Let's run up there, and you can hitch me between the shafts, put your seal in the wagon, and we'll go.'

'But you'll get into trouble,' said the Doctor, 'taking your farmer's wagon off like that.'

'My farmer will never know,' said the old horse, grinning behind his spectacles. 'You leave the gate on the latch as we go out, and I'll bring the wagon back and put it where we found it.'

'But how will you get out of your harness alone?'

'That's easy. If you knot the ropes the way I tell you, I can undo them with my teeth. I won't be able to take you the whole way because I couldn't get back in time to put the wagon up before daylight comes. But I've got a friend about nine miles down the Grantchester Road, on the Redhill Farm. He gets put out to graze nights, like me. He'll take you

'He rigged up a kind of harness'

the rest of the way. It'll be easy for him to get back
to his place before anyone's about.'

'Old friend,' said the Doctor, 'you have a great
head. Let's hurry and get on our way.'

Then they climbed the hill to the barn. Inside
they found an old wagon. The Doctor dragged it
out. Then, getting down some ropes that hung
coiled against the wall, he rigged up a kind of
harness, with the help of an old collar, which he
found thrown up in the manger. And when the
plough horse had set himself between the shafts,

John Dolittle hitched him up, being careful to make all the knots exactly the way he was told.

Then he lifted Sophie into the wagon and they started off down the meadow towards the gate.

As they were going out the Doctor said, 'but suppose anyone should meet me driving a wagon in a high hat? Wouldn't it seem sort of suspicious? . . . Oh, look: there's a scarecrow in the next field. I'll borrow his hat.'

'Bring the whole scarecrow with you,' the old horse called after him as the Doctor started off. 'I'll need something as a dummy driver when I'm coming back. Folks would stop me if they thought I was straying around the country without a driver.'

'All right,' said the Doctor and he ran off.

In a few minutes he came marching back with the scarecrow on his shoulder. Then he set the gate on the latch so the old horse could push it open on his return, threw the scarecrow up into the wagon, and climbed in himself.

Next, he took the scarecrow's tattered hat and put it on his own head in place of his high one. Then he got into the driver's seat, lifted the rope reins in his hands, called 'Gee-up!' to his old friend between the shafts, and they started off.

'You better keep your cloak and bonnet ready to slip on, Sophie,' said he. 'Somebody might ask for a ride. And if we are compelled to give anyone a lift you'll have to be a lady again.'

'I'd sooner be almost anything in the world than a lady,' sighed Sophie, remembering the tickling veil. 'But I'll do it if you say so.'

Thus, driving his own farm-wagon coach, with a scarecrow and a seal for passengers, John Dolittle

'Came marching back with the scarecrow on his shoulder'

successfully completed the next stage in his
strange journey. They passed very few people, and
no one asked for a ride. They had one anxious
moment, however, when a gentleman armed with
pistols in his saddle holsters galloped up on a very
fine horse and asked if they had seen anything of
a man and a veiled woman along the road.

The Doctor, sitting on top of Sophie, leaned on
the side of his wagon, with his scarecrow hat
pulled well down over his eyes.

'I saw a couple getting into a field a few miles

back,' he said, trying to talk like a yokel. 'But I reckon they be a long ways from there by now.'

'That'll be they, sure enough,' said the man putting spurs to his horse: 'Finch and Gresham, the highwaymen. They boarded the coach below Shottlake. But they got away before we could arrest them. Never mind, we'll get 'em yet. Good night!'

And he galloped off down the road.

'Poor Mr Finch!' said the Doctor, as the old horse moved on. 'I'm afraid we are not improving his reputation for him.'

'It's a good thing I got you away from Shottlake,' said the old horse. 'I reckon that fellow will set the whole country busy hunting for you now.'

'Their hunting won't do us any harm back at Shottlake,' said the Doctor. 'Good thing if they're kept busy. But I hope you don't get into trouble on your return to the farm.'

'No, I don't suppose so,' said the old horse. 'Even if I'm seen they'll never guess how I got hitched up. Don't bother about me. I'll manage.'

A little further on the plough horse stopped.

'This is Redhill Farm on the right,' said he. 'Wait till I call Joe.'

Then he went close to the hedge beside the road and neighed softly. Presently there was a scampering of hoofs and his friend, a much younger horse, poked his head over the hawthorns.

'I've got John Dolittle here,' whispered the plough horse. 'He wants to get to Talbot's Bridge in a hurry. Can you take him?'

'Why, certainly,' said the other.

'You'll have to use a wagon of your own,' said the plough horse. 'I must get mine back to the barn before my farmer wakes up. Got a cart or something anywhere about the place?'

'Yes, there's a trap up in the yard. It'll be faster than a wagon. Come over this side of the hedge, Doctor, and I'll show you where it is.'

Then, hurrying lest daylight overtake them, they made the exchange. Madam Sophie was transferred from a farm wagon to a smart trap. The old plough horse, after an affectionate farewell from the Doctor, started back with his own wagon, driven by his scarecrow propped up on the front seat. At the same time John Dolittle and Sophie were carried at a good, swift pace in the opposite direction, towards the Kippet River.

On arriving at his own farm, the old horse found everyone in a great state of excitement. People were rushing wildly up and down the fields with lanterns. The scarecrow had been missed; so had the old wagon; so had the old horse. The farm labourers were following the wheel tracks across the meadow. As soon as the plough horse reached the gate he was surrounded by a mob with lamps and guns, all guessing and advising and chattering at once. But his owner, thinking he must have been stolen and harnessed by the highwaymen, did not blame him for the adventure.

In the meantime the Doctor and Sophie, in their trap, were spanking along the road in the direction of Talbot's Bridge. And, although the armed horseman (he was the county constable's assistant) turned and galloped after them as hard as he could, he never overtook them, with the good start they had gained.

On reaching the river, the Doctor lifted Sophie out of the trap and dropped her over the bridge into the stream. Telling the Redhill horse to go back to his farm by a different way, lest he be met by the search for the highwaymen too, John Dolittle leapt off the parapet of the bridge on to the bank. Then, while he ran along the stream beside her, Sophie, with gurgles of delight, plunged and darted through the river, catching all the fish she wanted on the way.

Chapter Two
TO THE SEA BY RIVER

AS they had expected, John Dolittle and Sophie now found that the worst part of their troublesome travelling was over. If they met anyone on the banks of the stream Sophie just ducked underwater till the danger was past, while the Doctor pretended he was fishing, with a willow wand for rod and a piece of string for line.

They still had a long way to go. The journey north to Talbot's Bridge, you see, had not brought them any nearer to the coast.

The country through which the Kippet flowed was pleasant and sometimes it passed close by a farm, where cattle drank. At these places the travellers would either wait till nightfall, lest they be seen, or if the depth of the river permitted, Sophie would do her swimming underwater while the Doctor would go around by the roads and meet her further down.

While the going was, for the most part, easy for a seal, it was by no means always simple for the Doctor. The hundreds of hedges he had to get through, the walls he had to climb, the bogs he had to cross made his part of the journey a hard and slow one. Sophie had to slacken her pace constantly and do a lot of loitering and waiting in order that he might keep up with her.

'Look here, Doctor,' said she, about the middle of the second day when John Dolittle was resting on the bank, 'it doesn't seem to me there is really any need for you to come further. This going is so easy for me I can do the rest of the journey by myself, can't I?'

'I think not,' said the Doctor, lying back and gazing up at the willows over his head. 'We don't know yet what sort of difficult places the river may run you into before it reaches the sea. We had better consult some other waterfowl, as the ducks said we should, before we go further.'

Just at that moment a pair of fine bitterns flew down into the stream not far away and started feeding. The Doctor called them and they came up at once to his side.

'Would you please tell us,' said John Dolittle, 'how much further the river runs before it reaches the sea?'

'Counting all the bends and wiggles,' said the bitterns, 'about sixty miles.'

'Dear me!' said the Doctor. 'Then we are barely halfway yet. What kind of country does it pass through? This seal wishes to swim all the way to the coast, and we must avoid having people see her on the way.'

'Well,' said the birds, 'you will have plain sailing for another ten miles yet. But after that there are several places pretty dangerous for a seal to travel. The first one is Hobb's Mill. It's a water mill, you understand, and the stream is dammed

up with a high dam, a weir, and a big waterwheel.
She'll have to leave the water at Hobbs's Mill and
join it again below.'

'All right,' said the Doctor, 'we can do that, I
imagine. Then, what's the next trouble?'

'The next is a town. It isn't a large one, but it has
machinery buildings in it on the riverbank. And
the river is made to run into pipes to turn these
machines, and if your seal went floating down the
pipes she'd get all mixed up in the machinery.'

'I understand,' said the Doctor. 'Then we'll have
to go round the town by land — after dark.'

'Go round to the *right*,' said the bitterns — 'to the
northward. On the other side the machinery-
men's houses spread out a long way.

'After that you'll be all right till you get very
nearly to the sea. But there you will meet with
another town — a port. Your seal can't possibly
swim through that town because the river flows
over many little waterfalls and rapids right where
the houses and bridges are thickest. So as soon as
you come in sight of the port you had better leave
the stream again, and make for the seashore at
some lonely place to the north of it. You won't have
far to go, but you'll have to do some stiff climbing,
for the coast thereabouts is all high cliffs. If you
get safely past the port without being caught your
troubles will be over.'

'Well, thank you very much,' said the Doctor.
'This knowledge will be most helpful to us. Now I
think we had better be getting on our way.'

Then after wishing John Dolittle good luck, the
bitterns went back to their feeding, and the Doctor
proceeded along the bank with Sophie swimming

'They reached Hobb's Mill just as evening was coming on'

in the river. They reached Hobbs's Mill just as
evening was coming on. As soon as the Doctor had
explored around the buildings to see that all was
quiet and nobody abroad, Sophie got out of the
stream and hobbled across a couple of meadows
and joined the river below the millrace on the
other side. There they waited till the moon rose,
and soon, with sufficient light for the Doctor to see
his way along the shore, they went on again.

Coming in sight of the machinery town of which
the bitterns had spoken, John Dolittle left Sophie

with orders to duck underwater if anyone should pass that way, and went forward into the town to explore and get some food for himself.

Although most of the shops were shut at this hour, he managed to buy some sandwiches and fruit at a hotel. In making these purchases he noticed that his supply of money was getting very low. Indeed, he had only just enough to pay for what he had bought. However, never having bothered much about money, this did not disturb him. And after spending his last twopence to get his boots cleaned – they were frightfully muddy from all this boggy walking – he proceeded to explore a way for Sophie to come round the town by land.

The journey she would have to make on foot proved to be quite a long one. But the Doctor found a way over a chain of ponds, waterlogged meadows, and a little brook that ran into the Kippet about two miles the other side of the town.

By the time he returned to Sophie the night was nearly passed, and they had to hurry to reach the river again before daylight came.

With Sophie safely back in the stream, John Dolittle decided he had better take a little sleep before going on. Sophie, too, was pretty weary, in spite of her anxiety to push on with all possible speed. So, asking a little moorhen, who had her nest in the bank of the stream, to mount guard and wake them on the approach of danger, they both took a nap – Sophie sleeping in the water, with her head poked out on to a stump, and the Doctor propped against a willow tree on the shore.

The sun was high in the heavens when he awoke to find the moorhen plucking at his sleeve.

'There's a farmer driving a team across the meadow,' whispered the little bird. 'He'll come right by here. He might not take any notice of you, but Sophie he couldn't miss. Get her to stick her head under the water. She's snoring like a foghorn, and I can't wake her up.'

After the Doctor had made Sophie disappear beneath the water, and the danger of discovery was past, they started off once more and travelled all day and the following night towards the sea.

Gradually the landscape changed and finally, on the evening of the next day, they saw the lights of the seaport town twinkling in the distance. The land either side of it sloped upwards to cliffs overlooking the Bristol Channel.

A little further down the stream roads ran either side of the river, presumably going into the town. Along these, every once in a while, coaches and carriages passed them on their way to the port.

Feeling that it would be unwise to go further by water, they now left the stream for the last time and hit out across country.

The Doctor made Sophie keep her bonnet on, and he had her cloak ready to throw over her at any minute because there were many roads to cross and farmhouses to pass upon the way.

About a mile had to be covered before they would reach the top of the long slope and come in sight of the sea beyond the cliffs. Picking out a line which would miss most of the barns on the downs, they proceeded steadily and slowly forwards. On this upland country they met with many stone walls. And though they were low enough for the Doctor to jump, they were too much for Sophie to manage and the Doctor had to lift her over.

She did not complain, but the uphill going was telling on her terribly. And when at last they came to a level stretch at the top, and the wind from the Channel beat in their faces, Sophie was absolutely exhausted and unable to walk another step.

The distance now remaining to the edge of the cliffs was not more than a hundred yards. Hearing the voices of people singing in a house nearby, the Doctor began to fear that they might yet be discovered – even with the end of their long trip in sight. So with poor Sophie in a state of utter collapse, he decided there was nothing for it but to carry her the remainder of the journey.

As he put the cloak about her he saw the door of the house open and two men came out. Hurriedly he caught the seal up in his arms and staggered with her towards the edge of the cliffs.

'Oh,' cried Sophie when they had gone a few yards, 'look, the sea! How fresh and nice it sparkles in the moonlight. The sea, the sea at last!'

'Yes, this is the end of your troubles, Sophie,' the Doctor panted as he stumbled forward. 'Give my regards to the herd when you reach Alaska.'

At the edge John Dolittle looked straight downwards to where the deep salt water swirled and eddied far below.

'Good-bye, Sophie,' he said with what breath he had left. 'Good-bye, and good luck!'

Then, with a last tremendous effort, he threw Sophie over the cliff into the Bristol Channel.

Turning and twisting in the air, the seal sped

'He threw Sophie into the Bristol Channel'

downwards – her cloak and bonnet, torn off her by the rushing air, floating more slowly behind. And as she landed in the water the Doctor saw the white foam break over her, and the noise of a splash gently reached his ears.

'Well,' he said, mopping his brow with a hand-kerchief, 'thank goodness for that! We did it, after all. I can tell Matthew that Sophie reached the sea and I *didn't* go to jail.'

Then a cold shiver ran down his spine. A heavy hand had grasped his shoulder from behind.

Chapter Three
SIR WILLIAM PEABODY, J. P.

JOHN DOLITTLE, turning about slowly, found a large man grasping his collar. He wore some kind of a sailor-like uniform.

'Who are you?' asked the Doctor.

'Coastguard,' said the man.

'What do you want? Let go of my coat.'

'You're arrested.'

'What for?'

'Murder.'

While the Doctor was still trying to recover from his astonishment he saw more people coming across the downs from the lonely house that he had already noticed. When they came close he saw they were two men and a woman.

'Have you got him, Tom?'

'Yes. Caught 'im right in the act.'

'What was it?'

'A woman,' said the coastguard. 'I grabbed him just as he threw her over the cliff. Jim, you run down to the station and get the boats out. You may be in time to save her yet. But I doubt it. I'll take him along to the jail. You come on down there or send me word if you find anything.'

'It'll be his wife,' said the woman, peering at the Doctor in awe and horror. 'Murdered his wife! You Bluebeard! He ought to be still more ashamed of 'isself,' said the woman – 'much more than if he'd been brought up to such habits – poor creature!' (She gazed over the edge of the cliff with a shudder.) 'I wonder will they find 'er. Seems to me almost as though I could see something floating on the water down there. Poor creature! Well, that's the end of her troubles. Maybe she's better off than she was, married to him, the brute!'

'It wasn't my wife,' said the Doctor sullenly.

'Who was it, then?' asked the coastguard. 'It was some woman – 'cause I seen you carrying her in your arms.'

To this the Doctor decided, after a moment of thought, to say nothing. Now that he was arrested he would probably have to admit in the end that it was Sophie he had thrown into the sea. But until he was compelled in court to tell the whole story it seemed wiser to keep silence.

'Who was it?' the man repeated.

Still the Doctor said nothing.

'It was his wife all right,' said the woman. 'He has a wicked eye. I'll bet he has five or six wives stowed away somewhere – waiting for their doom, pore things.'

'Well, he don't have to answer,' said the coastguard. 'It's my duty to warn you,' he said very grandly, turning to the Doctor, 'that anything you say may be used in evidence against you. Now let's go down to the court-house.'

Fortunately for the Doctor it was by this time well on into the early hours of the morning. And

' "You Bluebeard!" '

when after crossing the downs they finally made
their way into the town they found the streets
deserted. The woman had not accompanied them.
And the Doctor and his coastguard reached the
court-house without meeting a single soul.

Just as they were about to enter the police
station next door, Jim, the other coastguard man,
ran up and joined his companion, with Sophie's
wet cloak on his arm and her bonnet in his hand.

'We couldn't find the body, Tom,' said he, 'but
these clothes was floating at the foot of the cliff.

I've left Jerry Bulkley in the boat still searching. I brought these down to you 'cause I thought you might want 'em.'

'Yes, they'll be needed in evidence,' said the other, taking the things from him. 'Better go back and carry on with the search. I'll come and join you as soon as I've got the prisoner locked up.'

Then the poor Doctor was taken into the police station; and after his name and various particulars about him were written down in a big book, he was placed in a little stone cell with some bread and water and left to his meditations.

As the noise of the clanging door and rattling bolts died away, John Dolittle noticed the grey light of dawn creeping in at a little barred window at his elbow.

'Heigh-ho!' he sighed, gazing around the bare stone walls. 'Jail again! I congratulated myself too soon. I wonder, was Matthew ever in *this* prison.'

Where the morning sun fell in a patch upon the wall he noticed some letters and signs scratched in the stone by former prisoners. He crossed the cell and examined them. Among them he found a very badly made 'M.M.'

'Yes,' he said, 'Matthew's been here, too. Seems proud of it. Well, well — it's a funny world.'

Picking up the loaf that had been provided for him, he broke it in half and ate a couple of mouthfuls. He was very hungry.

'What good bread!' he murmured. 'Quite fresh. I must ask the jailer where he gets it. The bed isn't bad either,' he added, punching the mattress. 'I think I'll take a nap. Haven't had a decent sleep in I don't know how long.'

'He found a badly made "M. M." '

Then he took his coat off, rolled it up for a pillow, and lay down.

And when, about ten o'clock in the morning, the superintendent of police entered with a tall white-haired gentleman they found the prisoner stretched on his cot snoring loudly.

'Humph!' murmured the old gentleman in a low voice. 'He doesn't look very dangerous, does he, Superintendent?'

'Ah,' said the other, shaking his head, 'it only shows you, Sir William, what a life of crime will do. Fancy being able to sleep like that after throwing his poor wife into the sea!'

'Well, leave us alone for a little while,' said the older man. 'Come back in about a quarter of an hour. And, by the way, you need not mention my visit here to anyone – not for the present.'

'Very good, Sir William,' said the superintendent. And he went out, locking the door behind him.

Then the white-haired old gentleman went over to the cot and stood looking down a moment into the Doctor's peaceful face.

Presently he shook the sleeper gently by the shoulder.

'Dolittle,' he said. 'Here – John, wake up!'

Slowly the Doctor opened his eyes and raised himself on his elbow.

'Where am I?' he said drowsily. 'Oh, yes, of course, in jail.'

Then he stared at the man who stood beside him. And at last a smile spread over his face.

'Heavens above! It's Sir William Peabody,' said he. 'Well, well, William! What on earth brings you here?'

'I might still more reasonably ask you how *you* come to be here,' said the visitor.

'My goodness!' murmured the Doctor. 'It must be fifteen years since I've seen you. Let me see: the last time was when we both got pretty angry – you remember? – arguing for and against fox hunting. Have you given it up yet?'

'No,' said Sir William. 'I still hunt two days a week. That's all I can manage now with my court duties and other things. They made me a Justice of the Peace about five years ago.'

'Well, it ought to be stopped,' said the Doctor, with great earnestness, 'altogether. You can say what you like, but the fox is not given a square deal. One fox against dozens of dogs! Besides, why should he be hunted? A fox has his rights, the same as you and I have. It's absurd: a lot of grown men on horses, with packs of hounds, roaring across country after one poor little wild animal.'

The old gentleman sat down on the bed beside the Doctor, threw back his head, and laughed.

'Same old Dolittle,' he chuckled. 'Did anyone ever see the like? In jail, charged with murder, the first thing he does when I come to see him is try and open a discussion about fox hunting. Ever since I've known you, John – even when you were a scrubby little boy at school studying beetles under a magnifying glass – you've been the same. Listen, I haven't come here to argue about the rights of foxes. As I told you, I'm a J. P. You're due to appear before me for examination in about an hour. What I want to hear is your version of this charge that is brought against you. You are accused of murdering your wife. I happened to notice your name on the police book. From what I remember of you, I can well understand your killing any woman who was mad enough to marry you. But the part I don't believe is that you ever had a wife. What's it all about? They tell me you were seen throwing a woman into the sea.'

'It wasn't a woman,' said the Doctor.

'What was it then?'

The Doctor looked down at his boots and fidgeted

like a schoolboy caught doing something wrong.

'It was a seal,' he said at last, 'a circus seal dressed up as a woman. She wasn't treated properly by her keepers. And she wanted to escape, to get back to Alaska and her own people. So I helped her. I had the very dickens of a time bringing her across country all the way from Ashby. I had to disguise her as a woman so we could travel without arousing suspicion. And the circus folk were out after me. Then just as I got her here to the coast and was throwing her into the sea so she could swim back to her native waters, one of your coastguard men saw me and put me under arrest – what are you laughing about?'

Sir William Peabody, who had been trying to suppress a smile throughout the Doctor's story, was now doubled up with merriment.

'As soon as they said it was your wife,' he gurgled when he had partly recovered, 'I knew there was something fishy about it. And there was, all right! You do smell terrible.'

'Seals have to smell of fish,' said the Doctor in an annoyed tone. 'And I was compelled to carry her part of the way.'

'You'll never grow up, John,' said Sir William, shaking his head and wiping the tears of laughter from his eyes. 'Now tell me: how far back on this trip of yours were you and the lady you eloped with seen? Because although we can certainly get you out of the charge of wife murder, it may not be so easy to clear you on the charge of stealing a seal. Were you followed down here, do you think?'

'Oh, no. We were not bothered by the circus folk after we got away from Ashby. Then at Shottlake

we got taken for highwaymen and caused a little
sensation when we travelled by coach. But after
that nobody suspected anything till . . . till—'

'Till you threw your lady-love over the cliff,' Sir
William put in. 'Did anyone see you being brought
in here?'

'No,' said the Doctor. 'No one down here knows
anything about it except the three coastguards-
men and a woman – the wife of one of them, I suppose. The streets were quite empty when I was
brought to the jail.'

'Oh, well,' said Sir William, 'I think we can
manage it. You'll have to stay here till I can get
the charge withdrawn. Then get away from this
part of the country as quick as you can.'

'But what about the coastguard folk?' asked the
Doctor. 'Are they still hunting for the body?'

'No, they've given it up now,' said Sir William.
'They brought back your victim's cloak and bonnet.
That was all they could find. We'll say you were just
throwing some old clothes into the sea – which is
partly true. When I explain matters to them they
won't talk – and even if they do, it isn't likely their
gossip will ever reach your circus people. But
listen, Dolittle: do me a favour and don't bring any
more menageries down here to throw over our
cliffs, will you? It would get hard to explain if you
made a habit of it. Besides, you'll spoil the circus
business. Now you stay here till I've fixed things up
officially; and as soon as they let you out, get away
from this district. Understand?'

'All right,' said the Doctor. 'Thank you. But
listen, Will, about that fox hunting . . . Supposing
you were in the fox's—'

'No,' said Sir William, rising. 'I refuse to re-open the argument now, John. I hear the superintendent coming back. We have too many foxes in this country. They need to be kept down.'

'Quite a nice prison you have here, Will,' said the Doctor as the superintendent opened the door. 'Thanks for calling.'

When Sir William and the superintendent had disappeared the Doctor fell to walking up and down his cell for exercise. He began to wonder how things were getting on with his household in his absence. And he was still thinking over the animals' idea of a reformed circus when, about half an hour later, a police sergeant appeared at the door, extraordinarily polite and gracious.

'The superintendent presents his compliments, Doctor,' he said, 'and apologizes for the mistake that was made. But it was not our department's fault. It was the coastguards who made the arrest. Very stupid of them, very. The charge is now withdrawn, Sir, and you are free to go whenever you wish.'

'Thank you,' said the Doctor. 'I think I'll go now. It's a nice prison you have here — almost the best I was ever in. Tell the superintendent he needn't apologize. I've had a most refreshing sleep — so well ventilated. It would make a splendid place for writing — undisturbed and airy. But unfortunately I have matters to attend to and must leave right away. Good day to you.'

'Good day, Sir,' said the sergeant. 'You'll find the exit at the end of the passage.'

At the front door of the police station the Doctor paused.

' "Excellent bread you have here" '

'My goodness!' he muttered. 'I haven't any money to pay the coach back to Ashby. I wonder if Sir William would lend me a guinea.'

And he turned back. But at the superintendent's office he was told that the Justice of Peace had gone off hunting for the day and wouldn't be back till tomorrow morning.

Once more he set out to leave the station. But at the door he paused again.

'I might as well take the rest of my loaf with me,' he murmured. 'It belongs to me after all — and I'll need it if I'm to get to Ashby without a penny in my pockets.'

And he hurried back to his cell.

He found a policeman putting the place in order.

'Excuse me,' said the Doctor. 'Don't let me disturb your sweeping. I just came back for something I left behind me. Ah, there it is — my loaf! Thank you. Excellent bread you have here.'

And after inquiring at the superintendent's office on the way out for the name of the baker who supplied the police station, John Dolittle sallied forth to freedom with half a loaf under his arm.

Chapter Four
NIGHTSHADE THE VIXEN

PENNILESS, but happy, the Doctor walked through the seaport town till he reached the market-place in the centre. At this point three big highways met: one from the north, one from the south and one from the east.

After admiring the town hall – it was a very beautiful and ancient building – the Doctor was about to set off along the road to the eastward. But he had not gone more than a pace or two before he paused, thinking. It occurred to him that it would be wiser if he found some other way to return to Ashby than that by which he had come.

He, therefore, changed his direction and swung off along the road to the south, intending to work his way back around to Ashby by some route where he would run no risk of meeting the people who had seen him in the coach or the Shottlake inn.

It was a pleasant morning. The sun was shining, sparrows chirping; and he felt, as he strutted down the road with his loaf of bread under his arm, that in such weather it was a pleasure to be alive.

Before long he had left the last houses of

'He came to a crossroads'

the town behind and found himself in the open
country. About noon he came to a crossroads
where a signpost, pointing down a very pretty
little country lane, read **TO APPLEDYKE**, TEN
MILES.

That looks a nice road, said the Doctor to
himself. And it runs in the right direction for me.
I like the sound of Appledyke too.

So, although he was not very far yet from the
seaport town which he had left, he struck off
eastward along the country lane to Appledyke.

Soon he decided it was lunch time and looked about him for a brook where he might get a drink of clean water to wash down his dry-bread meal. Over to his right he saw a place where the land dipped downward into a hollow filled with trees and bushes.

'I'll bet there's a brook down there,' the Doctor murmured. 'It is certainly most delightful country, this.'

Then he climbed over a stile and set off across the meadows, that led down into the hollow.

He found his brook, all right; and the banks of it, shaded by the trees, formed the most charming picnicking ground anyone could wish for. After he had taken a drink the Doctor with a grateful sigh sank down on the grass at the foot of a spreading oak, took out his loaf, and began to eat.

Presently he saw a starling hopping around near him, and he threw him some crumbs. While the bird was eating them the Doctor noticed that one of his wings seemed queer, and on examining it he found that the feathers were all stuck together with tar. The tar had hardened and the wing would not spread open the way it should. John Dolittle soon put it right and the bird flew off about his business. After his lunch the Doctor felt that before going on with his journey he would like to rest a while in this pleasant spot. So he leaned back against the trunk of the oak tree and soon he fell asleep to the music of the murmuring brook.

When he awoke he found four foxes, a vixen with three cubs, sitting patiently beside him waiting till he should finish his nap.

'Good afternoon,' said the vixen. 'My name is Nightshade. Of course, I've heard a lot about you. But I had no idea you were in the district. I've often thought of coming all the way to Puddleby to see you. I'm awfully glad I didn't miss you on this visit. A starling told me you were here.'

'Well,' said the Doctor, sitting up, 'I'm glad to see you. What can I do for you?'

'One of these children of mine' – the vixen pointed towards her three round little cubs who were gazing at the famous Doctor in great awe – 'one of these children has something wrong with his front paws. I wish you would take a look at him.'

'Certainly,' said the Doctor. 'Come here, young fellow.'

'He has never been able to run properly,' said the mother as John Dolittle took the cub on his lap and examined him. 'It has nearly cost us all our lives, his slow pace, when the dogs have been after us. The others can run beautifully. Can you tell me what's the matter with him?'

'Why, of course,' said the Doctor, who now had the cub upside down on his knees with its four big paws waving in the air. 'It's a case of flat feet. That's all. The muscles of the pads are weak. He can get no grip on the ground without good pad muscles. You'll have to exercise him morning and night. Make him rise on his toes like this: One, two! One, two! One, two!'

And the Doctor stood up and gave a demonstration of the exercise which in a person strengthens the

' "It's a case of flat feet" '

arches of the feet and in a fox develops the muscles of the paw pads.

'If you make him do that twenty or thirty times every morning and every night I think you'll soon find his speed will get better,' said the Doctor.

'Thank you very much,' said the vixen. 'I have the greatest difficulty making my children do anything regularly. Now you hear what the Doctor says, Dandelion: every morning and every night, thirty times, up on your toes as high as you can go. I don't want any flat-footed cubs in my

family. We've always been – great heavens!
Listen!'

The mother fox had stopped speaking, the
beautiful brush of her tail straight and quivering,
her nose outstretched, pitiful terror staring from
her wide-open eyes. And in the little silence that
followed, from over the rising ground away off to
the northeastward, came the dread sound that
makes every fox's heart stand still.

'The horn!' she whispered through chattering
teeth. 'They're out! It's th – th – the huntsman's
horn!'

As he looked at the trembling creature John
Dolittle was reminded of the occasion that had
made him an enemy of fox hunting for life – when
he had met an old dog fox one evening lying half
dead with exhaustion under a tangle of black-
berries.

As the horn rang out again the poor vixen began
running round her cubs like a crazy thing.

'Oh, what *shall* I do?' she moaned. 'The children!
If it wasn't for them I could perhaps give the dogs
the slip. Oh, why did I bring them out in daylight
to see you? I suppose I was afraid you might be
gone if I waited till after dark. Now I've left our
scent behind us, all the way from Broad Meadows,
as plain as the nose on your face. And I've come
right into the wind. What a fool I was! What shall
I do? What shall I do?'

As the horn sounded the third time, louder and
nearer, joined by the yelping of hounds in full cry,
the little cubs scuttled to their mother and
cowered under her.

A very firm look came into the Doctor's face.

'What pack is this?' he asked. 'Do you know the name of it?'

'It's probably the Ditcham — their kennels are just the other side of Hallam's Acre. It might be the Wiltborough, over from Buckley Downs — they sometimes hunt this way. But most likely it's the Ditcham — the best pack in these parts. They were after me last week. But my sister crossed my trail just below Fenton Ridge and they went after her — and got her. There's the horn again! Oh, what a fool I was to bring these children out in daylight!'

'Don't worry, Nightshade,' said the Doctor. 'Even if it's the Ditcham and the Wiltborough together, they're not going to get you today — nor your children, either. Let the cubs get into my pockets — come on, hop in, young fellows — so. Now you, Nightshade, come inside the breast of my coat. That's the way — get further around toward the back. And you can stick your feet and your brush into the tail-pocket. And when I've buttoned it up like this — see? — you will be completely covered. Can you breathe all right back there?'

'Yes, I can breathe,' said the vixen. 'But it won't do us much good to be out of sight. The hounds can smell us — that's the way they run us down — with their noses.'

'Yes, I know,' said the Doctor. 'But the men can't smell you. I can deal with the dogs all right. But you mustn't be seen by the men. Keep as still as a stone, all four of you — don't move or try to run for it, whatever happens.'

And then John Dolittle, with his coat bulging

with foxes in all directions, stood in a little clearing in the wooded hollow and awaited the oncoming of the Ditcham Hunt in full cry.

The mingled noises of the dogs, men, horns and horses grew louder. And soon, peeping through the crossing branches of his cover, the Doctor saw the first hounds come in view at the top of the ridge. For a moment the leaders paused and sniffed the wind. Then in a beeline for the bottom of the hollow they came on down, stretched at full speed. Over the ridge and after them came the rest of the pack; and close behind the dogs rode the men in red coats on fine, swift horses.

Ahead of most of the huntsmen galloped one man, old, lean, and white-haired – Sir William Peabody, the Master of the Foxhounds. Halfway down the slope he turned in his saddle and called to a man on a grey mare close behind him.

'Jones, they're making for the spinney. Don't let the leaders break into it before we've got it surrounded. Watch Galloway; he's rods ahead. Mind, he doesn't put the fox out the other side – watch Galloway!'

Then the man on the grey mare spurted ahead, cracking a long whip and calling, 'Galloway! Here, Galloway!'

As the Doctor peered through the foliage he saw that the leading hound was now quite close. But, wonderfully trained to the huntsmen's command, Galloway suddenly slackened his pace within a few yards of the trees and remained, yelping and barking, for the others to come up.

Over the ridge more riders came pouring – fat parsons on stocky cobs, country squires on hacks,

ladies on elegant, dainty thoroughbreds – all the
gentry of the neighbourhood.

'My goodness!' murmured the Doctor. 'Was there
ever anything so childish? All this fuss for a poor
little fox!'

As the hounds, under the guidance of the men
with long whips, spread, yelping, around all sides
of the spinney, the people called and shouted to
one another and the noise was tremendous.

'We'll get him,' bellowed a fat farmer on a pony.
'Hounds have gone all around now and scent don't
go on. It's a killing, sure. Wait till Jones lets 'em
into the spinney. We'll get him!'

'Oh, no, you won't,' the Doctor muttered, the firm
look coming back into his face. 'Not today, my fat
friend – not today.'

The dogs, impatient and eager, sniffed and ran
hither and thither, waiting for permission to enter
the little patch of woods and finish the hunt.

Suddenly a command was given and instantly
they leapt into the underbrush from all sides.

John Dolittle was standing in his clearing, with
his hands over his pockets, trying to look all ways
at once at the moment when the hounds broke in.
But he had not known from which direction the
vixen had entered and left her scent behind. And
suddenly, before he knew it, four heavy dogs had
leapt on his back, and he went down on the
ground, simply smothered under a tangled pile of
yelping, fighting foxhounds.

Kicking and punching in all directions, the
Doctor struggled to his feet.

'Get away!' he said in dog language. 'Lead the
hunt somewhere else. This fox is mine.'

The hounds, spoken to in their own tongue, now had no doubt as to who the little man was that they had knocked down.

'I'm awfully sorry, Doctor,' said Galloway, a fine, deep-chested dog with a tan patch over one eye. 'We had no idea it was you. We jumped on you from behind, you know. Why didn't you call to us while we were outside?'

'How could I?' said the Doctor irritably, pushing away a dog who was sniffing at his pocket. 'How could I – with you duffers making all that din? Look out, here come the huntsmen. Don't let them see you smelling around me. Get the pack out of here, Galloway, quick.'

'All right, Doctor. But it smells to me as though you had more than one fox in your pockets,' said Galloway.

'I've got a whole family,' said the Doctor. 'And I mean to keep them, too.'

'Can't you let us have even one of them, Doctor?' asked the hound. 'They're sneaky little things. They eat rabbits and chickens, you know.'

'No,' said the Doctor, 'I can't. They have to get food for themselves. You have food given you. Go away – and hurry about it.'

At that moment Sir William Peabody came up.

'Great heavens! Dolittle!' he exclaimed. 'Haven't you left these parts yet? Did you see the fox? Hounds headed right down into this hollow.'

'I wouldn't tell you, Will, if I had seen him,' said the Doctor. 'You know what I think of fox hunting.'

'Funny thing!' muttered Sir William as he watched the dogs lurching about among the brush uncertainly. 'They can't have lost the scent, surely. They came down here as firm as you like. Curious! . . . Oh, heavens! I know what it is: they've followed your rotten fish smell — the sea! Good Lord!'

At that moment a cry came from the huntsmen that the hounds had found another scent and were going off to the southward. Sir William, who had dismounted, ran for his horse.

'Hang you, Dolittle!' he shouted. 'You've led the hounds astray. I should have kept you in jail.'

The few dogs remaining within the spinney were now melting away like shadows. One of the fox cubs stirred in the Doctor's pocket. Sir William had already mounted his horse outside.

'Goodness, I forgot again!' muttered the Doctor. 'I must get that guinea . . . I say, Will!'

Then John Dolittle, his pockets full of foxes, ran out of the spinney after the Master of the Hunt.

'Listen, Will!' he called. 'Would you lend me a guinea? I haven't any money to get to Ashby with.'

Sir William turned in his saddle and drew rein.

'I'll lend you five guineas — or ten — John,' said the magistrate, 'if you'll only get out of this district and stop putting my hounds on false scents. Here you are.'

'Thanks, Will,' said the Doctor, taking the money and dropping it in his pocket on top of one of the cubs. 'I'll send it back to you by post.'

Then he stood there by the edge of the spinney and watched the huntsmen, hallooing and

'Sir William turned and drew rein'

galloping, disappear over the skyline to the
southward.

'What a childish sport!' he murmured. 'I can't
understand what they see in it. Really, I can't.
Grown men rushing about the landscape on
horseback, caterwauling and blowing tin horns —
all after one poor little wild animal! Perfectly
childish!'

Returning to the side of the brook within the
shelter of the trees, the Doctor took the foxes out
of his pocket and set them on the ground.

'Well,' said the vixen, 'I had often heard that you were a great man, John Dolittle, but I never realized till now what a truly marvellous person you were. I don't know how to thank you. I'm all overcome – Dandelion, stop playing with my tail!'

' "Dandelion, stop playing with my tail!" '

PART IV

Chapter One
BACK TO THE CIRCUS

AND now, with money in his pocket to pay for a ride, John Dolittle set about finding a coach that would carry him back in the direction of Ashby.

At the village of Appledyke his little country lane led him on to a bigger highway running north and south. Making inquiries of the village blacksmith, he found that coaches plied this road and that he could expect one to pass in about half an hour. So, after buying some toffee at the one small shop which Appledyke could boast of, the Doctor settled down to wait, munching sweetmeats to pass the time.

About four o'clock in the afternoon a coach came along and took him to the next large town. From there he caught a night coach going east; and in the early hours of the following morning he was back within ten miles of Ashby again.

The remainder of the journey he thought he had better do on foot for safety's sake. So after he had a shave and a breakfast and a rest at an inn, he set out to walk the short remaining distance.

The way the Doctor first knew that he was

nearing the circus was by hearing Jip's bark in the distance. The sound was joined by two other barks. And presently, rounding a bend in the highway, he found Jip, Toby, and Swizzle all yapping about the foot of a tree, up which they had chased a black cat. Still further down the road he saw the tail end of the wagon train winding on its way.

As soon as he came in view the dogs forgot all about the cat and came racing down the road.

'Doctor! Doctor!' yelped Jip. 'How did everything go off? Did Sophie get away?'

Then the three of them jumped all over him, and he had to answer a hundred questions at once. From beginning to end he told the story of his adventurous journey to the sea. And when a little later he overtook the circus train and reached his own wagon he had to tell it all over again for the benefit of his delighted family.

Dab-Dab hustled around and prepared a meal right away — a sort of tea-and-supper-combined arrangement; and she kept the rest of the household busy pulling out the bed linen to be aired, so that the Doctor should have dry sheets to sleep in.

Then Matthew Mugg got wind of his great friend's arrival, and he came and joined the party, and the story had to be told a third time.

'It was a great piece of work, Doctor,' said he, 'couldn't have gone better. Blossom never got the least suspicious that you was in it at all.'

'What's happened to Higgins?' asked the Doctor.

'Oh, 'e's doing honest work now. Took a stableman's job in Ashby. Good thing, too! 'E's no loss to the circus business anyhow.'

'All yapping about the foot of an oak tree'

'Has Blossom put on any extra act to take Sophie's place?' asked the Doctor.

'No,' said Matthew. 'We were short 'anded for a bit. But Hercules the strong man is back on the job now and the show's as good as ever.'

'And we've made lots of money with our part of it, Doctor,' cried Too-Too. 'How much do you think the pushmi-pullyu took in last week?'

'I've no idea.'

'Twelve pounds, nine shillings, and sixpence!'

'Great heavens!' cried the Doctor. 'That's

enormous — twelve pounds a week! That's more
than I ever made in the best days of my practice. Why, we'll soon be able to retire at that
rate!'

'What do you mean, retire, Doctor?' asked
Toby, pushing his head up on to the Doctor's
knee.

'Well, we hadn't meant to stay in the business for
good, you know,' said John Dolittle. 'I have work
of my own to look after in Puddleby . . . and . . .
and . . . oh, heaps of things to attend to.'

'I see,' said Toby sadly. 'I thought you were going
to stay with us for quite a while.'

'But how about the Dolittle Circus, Doctor?'
asked Swizzle. 'Aren't you going to try that idea —
the reformed show we talked about?'

'It's a great notion, Doctor,' Jip put in. 'All the
animals are crazy about the scheme. They've been
working out the details of their own part of the
performance.'

'And what about our theatre, Doctor — the
Animals' Own Theatre?' Gub-Gub put in. 'I've
written a play for it since you've been gone. It's
called *The Bad Tomato*. I do the comic fat-lady's
part. I know my lines by heart already.'

'And what about the house in Puddleby? That's
what I'd like to know?' said Dab-Dab, angrily
brushing the crumbs off the table. 'All you
animals ever think of is having a good time. You
never think of the Doctor and what he wants. You
never think of the house going to ruin back there
and the garden turning into a jungle. The Doctor
has his own work and his own home and his own
life to attend to.'

A little silence followed the housekeeper's furious outburst, and Toby and Swizzle rather shamefacedly retired under the table.

'Well,' said the Doctor at last, 'there is something in what Dab-Dab says. I do think as soon as the pushmi-pullyu has made enough to pay back the sailor for his boat – and a little to spare – we ought to think about leaving the business.'

'Oh, dear!' sighed Toby. 'The Dolittle Circus would have been such a wonderful show!'

'Heigh-ho!' said Gub-Gub. 'And I would have been simply splendid as a fat lady. I always thought I ought to have been a comic actor.'

'Huh!' snorted Dab-Dab. 'Last week you said you ought to have been a greengrocer.'

'Well,' said Gub-Gub. 'I could be both – a comic greengrocer. Why not?'

That same night Blossom's circus entered the town of Stowbury. And, as usual, before dawn the next morning the tents had been set up and everything got in readiness for showing.

As soon as the news of the Doctor's arrival got about, Mr Blossom came to see him. And from all appearances John Dolittle decided that no suspicions had been aroused in the mind of the ringmaster by his 'business' trip.

Another caller at the Doctor's stand that morning was Hercules the strong man. Hercules had never forgotten the kind attention shown him at the time of his accident, and he was glad to find that his friend had returned. His pleasant chat was cut short, however, when he suddenly discovered that it was time for him to give his first

performance. The Doctor accompanied him back
to his stand.

While returning across the circus enclosure the
Doctor noticed, as he passed the tent of Fatima the
snake charmer, a strong odour of chloroform.
Fearing an accident might have happened, he
went inside and found that Fatima was out at the
moment. Within the tent the smell was stronger,
and it seemed to be coming from the snake box.
The Doctor looked into the box and found the six
snakes in an almost unconscious state from the
drug. One of them still had sense enough left to
tell the Doctor, in answer to his questions, that
Fatima always dosed them with chloroform on hot
days, when they were too lively, in order to make
them easier to handle for her performance. They
hated it, the snake said, because it gave them
headaches.

On this pleasant, sunny morning the Doctor had
forgotten, for a moment, the wretched condition of
many of the animals, which had so often sickened
him of the whole circus business. This piece of
senseless cruelty threw him into a boiling rage,
and he hurried off at once to look for Blossom.

He found him in the big tent and Fatima with
him. The Doctor firmly demanded that the custom
of chloroforming the snakes be forbidden. Blossom
merely smiled and pretended to be busy with other
matters, while Fatima hurled a lot of vulgar
language at the Doctor's head.

Discouraged and sad, John Dolittle left the tent,
intending to return to his own wagon. The gates
were now open and the crowds were coming in
thick and fast. The Doctor was wondering how

' "They hated it," the snake said'

American blacksnakes would manage in the English climate if he contrived their escape, when he noticed a throng of visitors collecting about a platform down at the other end of the enclosure.

At this moment Matthew came up and joined him, and together they started towards the platform. On this the Doctor now saw a man who advertised himself as Dr Brown, delivering a lecture about the wonders of his pills and ointments, which could cure, in one dose, all the ailments known to mankind.

'What arrangement has this fellow with Blossom?' the Doctor asked of Matthew.

'Oh, he pays him a rake-off,' said the cat's-meat man. 'Blossom gets so much on all he takes in. He's going on with us to the next three towns, I hear. Doing a good trade too, ain't he?'

Indeed, Dr Brown was very busy. Country yokels, after listening to his noisy medical lectures, were buying his wares right and left.

'Go and get me a pot of that ointment, will you, Matthew?' said the Doctor. 'Here's some money – and get me a box of the pills as well.'

'All right,' said Matthew with a grin. 'But I don't reckon you'll find them much good.'

The cat's-meat man returned with the purchases and the Doctor took them to his wagon. There he opened them, smelled them, examined them and tested them with chemicals from his little black bag.

'Rubbish and bunkum!' he cried when he had ended. 'This is just highway robbery. Why did I ever go into this rotten show business? Matthew, get me a step-ladder.'

The cat's-meat man went out, disappeared behind some tents, and presently returned with the step-ladder.

'Thank you,' said the Doctor, putting it on his shoulder and marching off towards the platform. There was a dangerous light in his eyes.

'What are you going to do, Doctor?' asked Matthew, hurrying after him.

'I'm going to give a medical lecture myself,' said the Doctor. 'Those people are not going to pay their money for quack rubbish if I can help it.'

Jip, who was sitting at the door of his wagon, suddenly pricked up his ears and sprang to his feet.

'Toby,' he called over his shoulder, 'the Doctor's going over to the patent-medicine man's platform. He's got a step-ladder. He looks awfully mad about something. There's going to be a row, I fancy. Get Swizzle and let's go and see the fun.'

John Dolittle, on reaching the crowd at Brown's lecture stand, set up his step-ladder right opposite the speaker, and Matthew Mugg cleared a space around it so the audience shouldn't knock it over while the Doctor climbed it.

At the moment of his arrival, Brown was holding up in his left hand a pot of ointment.

'This preparation which I 'old in my 'and, ladies and gentlemen,' he bawled, 'is the greatest remedy in the world for sciatica, lumbago, neuralgia, ague, and gout. It 'as been hendorsed by all the leadin' physicians. It is the same what is used by the royal family of Belgium and the Shah of Persia. One application of this marvellous remedy will—'

At this point another voice, still more powerful, interrupted the lecture. The people all turned around, and there behind them, perched on a step-ladder, stood a little round man with a battered high hat on his head.

'Ladies and gentleman,' said the Doctor, 'what this man is telling you is not true. His ointment contains nothing but lard mixed with a little perfume. His pills are no good either. I do not recommend you to buy any.'

For a moment there was a dead silence. While

Dr Brown was trying to think up something to say, the voice of a woman, Fatima the snake charmer, was heard from the edge of the crowd.

'Don't you listen to him,' she yelled, pointing a fat finger at John Dolittle. 'He's nothing but a showman. He doesn't know anything about medicines. Push 'im orf 'is ladder.'

'Just a minute,' said the Doctor, addressing the crowd again. 'It is true that I am in the show business – for the moment. But I am a medical graduate of the University of Durham. I am prepared to stand by what I have said. These preparations that this man is trying to sell you are worthless. Also I have grave doubts about his education in dentistry, and I do not advise any of you to have your teeth touched by him.'

The crowd now began to get restless. Several people had already purchased Brown's wares and these could now be seen making their way to the platform and demanding their money back. Brown refused it and tried to make another address to his audience in answer to the Doctor's statements.

'Listen,' yelled John Dolittle from his ladder, 'I challenge this man to produce a medical degree or credentials of any kind to prove that he is a qualified doctor or dentist. He is a quack.'

'You're a fake yourself,' yelled Brown. 'I'll have the law on you for libel.'

'Push 'im down!' howled Fatima. 'Mob 'im!'

But the people did not seem inclined to follow her orders. Presently the Doctor was recognized by one of his old patients among the audience – just as he had been in the case of the strong man's accident some weeks before. A little old lady suddenly waved an umbrella above the crowd.

'That's John Dolittle,' she shouted, 'who cured my son Joe of whooping cough back in Puddleby ten years ago. Like to die he was. He's a real doctor – none better in the West Country. T'other's a quack. Ye be fools if ye turn a deaf ear to what John Dolittle tells ye.'

Then other voices were heard here and there among the crowd. The general restlessness increased. More people struggled forward to Brown's platform to bring back the wares they had bought. A growing murmur arose.

'Mob 'im! Knock 'im down!' yelled Fatima, trying to make herself heard.

Dr Brown thrust aside two men who had climbed up on to his stand for their money, came to the edge of the platform, and opened his mouth to begin another medical lecture.

But a large, well-aimed turnip suddenly sailed across the heads of the audience and hit him squarely in the face. The mobbing had begun – but it wasn't directed against John Dolittle. Soon carrots, potatoes, stones, all manner of missiles, were flying through the air.

'Grab 'im!' yelled the crowd. 'He's a crook.'

And the next moment the whole audience surged towards the platform yelling and shaking their fists.

Chapter Two
THE PATENT-MEDICINE RIOTS

JOHN DOLITTLE himself grew a little alarmed as he saw what an ugly mood the crowd was now beginning to show. When he had first mounted his ladder and interrupted the quack doctor's lecture he had meant to do no more than warn the people against buying fake medicines. But as he watched the throng swarm over the platform, wrecking and smashing it on the way, he began to fear for Brown's safety.

When the riot was at its height the police arrived. Even they had considerable difficulty in calming the crowd. They had to use their clubs to make them listen at all. There were many broken heads and bloody noses. Finally the police saw that their only chance of restoring order would be to clear the circus enclosure altogether.

This was done – in spite of the people's objection that they had only just come in and wanted their admission money back before they left. Then the circus was ordered by the police to remain closed until further instructions.

It was not long before the further instructions were forthcoming. Much indignation had been aroused throughout the respectable town of Stowbury over the whole affair. And the mayor sent word to Blossom about noon that he and the aldermen would be obliged to him if he would pack up his circus and take it out of their town immediately.

Brown had escaped and got away across country long before this. But that wasn't the end of the affair so far as John Dolittle was concerned. Blossom, already annoyed, became so furious when the mayor's order was brought that everybody thought he was going to have a fit. Fatima had been railing against the Doctor to him all the morning; and on hearing the last bit of news, which meant considerable loss, he got almost black in the face.

Many of the showmen were with him when the policeman delivered the order. On them too Fatima had been working, trying to rouse bad feeling against the Doctor.

'Blast it!' yelled Blossom, rising to his feet and reaching for a thick walking stick that stood behind his wagon door. 'I'll teach him to get my circus closed up! Come on, some of you fellows!'

With waving fists Fatima and four or five of the showmen standing near followed the ringmaster as he marched off towards the Doctor's stand.

Both Jip and Matthew had also been hanging around Blossom's wagon. They too now departed, Jip running ahead to warn the Doctor and the cat's-meat man going off in a wholly different direction.

On their way to the Doctor's wagon Blossom and his party of vengeance were joined by several tent

riggers and others. By the time they arrived at his
door they numbered a good dozen. To their suprise
the Doctor came out to meet them.

'Good afternoon,' said John Dolittle politely.
'What can I do for you?'

Blossom tried to speak, but his anger was too
much for him – nothing more than spluttering
gurgles came from his throat.

'You've done enough for us already,' shouted one
of the men.

'We're going to do for you now,' screamed
Fatima.

'You've got the show turned out of the town,'
growled a third, 'one of the best places on the road.
You've cost us a week's pay.'

'You've been doing your best to put my show on
the blink,' snarled Blossom, finding his voice at
last, 'ever since you've been with us. But, by
jiminy, you've gone too far this time!'

Without further words the group of angry men,
led by the ringmaster, rushed upon the Doctor and
he went down under a football scrum of kicking
feet and punching fists.

Poor Jip did his best to drag them off. But it was
little help he could give against twelve such
enemies. He couldn't see the Doctor at all. He was
beginning to wonder where Matthew was when he
saw the cat's-meat man running towards the fight
from the other side of the enclosure. And beside
him ran an enormous man in pink tights.

On reaching the scrum the big man began pulling off the showmen by their feet or hair and tossing them aside as though they were wisps of straw.

Finally Hercules the strong man – for it was he

— had thinned the fight down to two, Blossom and the Doctor. These still rolled upon the ground trying to throttle one another. With a hand the size of a leg of mutton, Hercules grasped the ringmaster by the neck and shook him like a rat.

'If you don't be'ave yourself, Alexander,' he said quietly, 'I'll slap your face and knock your brains out.'

There was a little silence while the rest of the showmen picked themselves up from the grass.

'Now,' said Hercules, still grasping Blossom by

' "I'll slap your face" '

the collar, 'what's this all about? What are you all settin' on the Doc for? Ought to be ashamed – a good dozen of yer – and him the littlest of all!'

'He went and told the people that Brown's ointment wasn't no good,' said Fatima. 'Got 'em all worked up, asking for their money back. Called him a fake in front of the audience – and 'im the biggest fake that ever walked himself.'

'You're a nice one to talk about fakes!' said Hercules. 'Didn't I see you painting bands on your pore harmless snakes last week – to make 'em look like real deadly ones? This man's a good doctor. He couldn't 'ave mended my busted ribs for me if he wasn't.'

'He's got the show turned out of the town,' growled one of the men. 'We had our thirty-mile trip from Ashby for nothing – and another forty-mile one ahead of us before we take in a penny. That's what your precious *doctor* has done for you!'

'He's not going any further with my show,' spluttered Blossom. 'I've taken about all I'm going to stand from him.'

He wriggled himself out of the strong man's grasp and advancing towards the Doctor shook a finger in his face.

'You're fired,' he yelled. 'Understand? You leave my show today – now.'

'Very well,' said the Doctor quietly. And he turned away towards the door of his wagon.

'Just a minute,' Hercules called after him. 'Do you want to go, Doctor?'

John Dolittle paused and turned back.

'Well, Hercules,' he said doubtfully, 'it's rather hard to answer that question.'

'What he *wants* 'as got nothing to do with it,' said Fatima. 'The boss 'as fired him. That settles it. 'E's got to go.'

As the Doctor looked into the jeering eyes of this woman who hated him, he thought of the snakes who were in her care. Then he thought of several other circus animals whose condition he had hoped to improve – of Beppo, the old wagon horse who should have been pensioned off years ago. And while he hesitated Swizzle pushed his damp nose up into his hand and Toby plucked at the tail of his coat.

'No, Hercules,' he said at last. 'All things considered, I do not want to go. But if I'm sent away there's nothing I can do about it, is there?'

'No,' said the strong man. 'But there's something others can do about it. Look here' – he spun Blossom around by the shoulder and shook an enormous fist under his nose. 'This man's an honest man. Brown was a crook. If the Doctor goes, I go too. And if I go, my nephews, the trapeze acrobats, will come with me. And I've a notion that Hop the clown will join us. Now how about it?'

Mr Alexander Blossom, proprietor of the greatest show on earth, hesitated, chewing his moustache in dismay and perplexity. With Sophie the seal gone, deserted by the strong man, the trapeze brothers, his best clown, and the pushmi-pullyu, his circus would be sadly reduced. While he pondered, Fatima's face was a study. If looks could have killed, both Hercules and the Doctor would have died that day twice over.

'Well,' said the ringmaster at last in quite a different voice, 'let's talk this over friendly like.

HUGH LOFTING

' "He's bought six fat snakes with it!" '

There's no need for hard feelings – and no sense
in breaking up the show just because we've come
a cropper in one town.'

'If I stay,' said the Doctor, 'I insist that no more
fake medicines be sold while I am with you.'

'Huh!' snorted Fatima. 'See what he's goin' to do?
'E's beginnin' again. 'E's goin' to tell you how to
run your show.'

'Also,' said the Doctor, 'I shall require that
this woman no longer have the handling of snakes
or any other animals. If you want to keep me,

she must go. I will buy her snakes from her myself.'

Well, in spite of Fatima's screaming indignation, matters were at last arranged peaceably. But that night, when Too-Too was sitting on the steps of the wagon listening to a brother owl who was hooting to him from the town cemetery, Dab-Dab came out and joined him, with tears in her eyes.

'I don't know what we'll ever do with the Doctor,' she said wearily. 'Really I don't. He has taken every penny we had in the money box – the whole twelve pounds, nine shillings, and sixpence that we had saved up to go back to Puddleby with. And what do you think he has gone and spent it on? He's bought six fat snakes with it!' (Dab-Dab burst into a renewed flood of tears.) 'And he . . . he . . has put them in my flour bin to keep till . . . till he can get a proper bed for them!'

Chapter Three
NINO

AFTER the departure of Fatima the snake charmer, John Dolittle liked the life of the circus a good deal better. It had mostly been the thought that he was not doing anything to help the animals that had made him so often speak against it. But now that he had sent Sophie back to her husband, freed the snakes from a life of slavery and chloroform, and forbidden the selling of quack medicines, he began to feel that his presence here was doing good.

And then Blossom, ever since the medical lecture riot, had shown him a great deal more respect. The ringmaster had always known that he had a good thing in the pushmi-pullyu. And if it had not been for his blind rage at being turned out of the town by the mayor, and for Fatima's eternal nagging against the Doctor, he would never have dreamed of trying to get rid of him at all.

John Dolittle's own popularity with the circus people themselves was in the end improved greatly by the incident at Stowbury. In spite of the fact that she had successfully turned many of the showmen against the Doctor, Fatima herself had always been disliked by almost everyone. And when it became known that the Doctor had brought about her departure he was very soon forgiven for the loss caused by the circus being ordered out of the town.

However, his real power and influence with the show people did not properly begin until the day that the talking horse fell sick.

The circus had moved on to a town called Bridgeton, a large manufacturing centre, where good business was expected by Blossom. The animals and clowns and bareback riders and the rest had made their usual procession through the streets; big bills were posted all over the place. And when the enclosure was opened to the public, great throngs of people had crowded up to the gates. It looked like one of the best weeks the circus had ever known.

At two o'clock a large sign was set up showing the programme: Mademoiselle Firefly, the Bareback Rider; the Pinto Brothers, Daring Trapeze Artists; Hercules, the Strongest Man on Earth; Hop, the Side-Splitting Clown, and His Comedy Wonder-Dog Swizzle; Jojo, the Dancing Elephant, and (in large letters) NINO, the World Famous Talking Horse.

Now this Nino was just an ordinary, cream-coloured cob who had been trained to answer signals. Blossom had bought him from a Frenchman; and with him he had bought the secret of his so-called talking. In his act he didn't talk at all really. All he did was to stamp his hoof or wag his head a certain number of times to give

HUGH LOFTING

'They had made their usual procession through the streets'

answers to the questions Blossom asked him in
the ring.

'How many do three and four make, Nino?'
Blossom would say. Then Nino would stamp the
floor seven times. And if the answer was yes, he
would nod his head up and down, and if it was no,
he would shake it from side to side. Of course, he
didn't know what was being asked of him at all, as
a matter of fact. And the way he knew what
answers to give was from the signals that Blossom
made to him secretly. When he wanted Nino to say

yes, the ringmaster would scratch his left ear; when he wanted him to answer no, he would fold his arms, and so on. The secret of all these signals Blossom kept jealously to himself. But, of course, the Doctor knew all about them because Nino had told him how the whole performance was carried on.

Now, in advertising the circus Blossom always put Nino, the World-Famous Talking Horse, before all the other acts in importance. It was a popular performance and the children loved shouting questions down to the little plump cob and seeing him answer with his feet or his head.

Well, on the circus's first day in Bridgeton, a little before the show in the big tent was to begin, the Doctor and the ringmaster were in the clown's dressing room talking. Suddenly in rushed the head stableman in a great state of excitement.

'Mr Blossom,' he cried, 'Nino's sick! Layin' in his stall with 'is eyes closed. The show's due to begin in fifteen minutes and I can't do nothing with 'im – can't even get 'im on his feet.'

With a hearty curse Blossom rushed out and tore away in the direction of the stables, while the Doctor followed him on the run.

When they got to Nino's stall Blossom and the Doctor found the horse in a bad state. His breathing was fast and heavy. With difficulty he was made to stand up on his feet, but for walking even a few steps he seemed far too shaky and weak.

'Darn the luck!' muttered the manager. 'If he can't perform it will queer the whole week's showing. We've posted him as the star act. The crowd will want to know about it if they don't see him.'

'You'll have to make a speech and explain,' said the Doctor. 'That horse has a bad fever. I doubt if he can leave his stall today.'

'Good heavens, man, he'll have to!' cried Blossom. 'We'll likely have the audience asking for its money back if he don't appear. We can't have any more riots like—'

At that moment a boy came up.

'Five minutes to two, Mr Blossom. Pierce wants to know if you are all ready.'

'Hang it!' said the manager. 'I can't take the ring for the first act. I must get Nino fixed up before I can come on.'

'We ain't got nobody else, sir,' said the boy. 'Robinson 'asn't got back yet.'

'Lord, what a day!' groaned the manager. 'Well, the show can't open without a ringmaster, that's sure. And I can't leave Nino yet. I don't know what—'

'Excuse me, governor,' said a voice behind him. And turning, Blossom looked into the crossed eyes of Matthew Mugg.

'Couldn't I take your place, Boss?' said the cat's-meat man. 'I know your whole line of talk by heart. I could introduce the acts – same as you – and nobody know the difference.'

'Well,' said Blossom looking him up and down, 'you're about the scrubbiest ringmaster I ever see'd. But beggars can't be choosers. Come with me – quick – and I'll give you these clothes.'

Then, while the Doctor turned his attention to Nino, Blossom and Matthew made off on the run

for the dressing rooms. There, with the aid of
Theodosia (who put a large swift pleat in
Blossom's riding breeches) and a little rouge and
a false moustache from the clown's make-up box,
Mr Mugg was transformed from a cat's-meat man
into a ringmaster. The ambition of his life was
realized at last. And as he swaggered into the ring
and looked up at the sea of faces around him, his
chest swelled with dignity, while Theodosia, watching him through a slit in the tent flap, glowed
with wifely pride and prayed that the pleat in his
riding breeches would hold till the show was over.

In the meantime from an examination of Nino
the Doctor became certain that there was no hope
of his recovering in time to perform that day. He
went and got some large pills from his black bag
and gave him two. Presently Blossom, now dressed
in a jersey and flannel trousers, joined him.

'You can't have this horse perform today, Mr
Blossom,' said the Doctor, 'nor for a week, probably, at least.'

'Well,' said the ringmaster, throwing up his
hands in despair, 'we're just ruined — that's all —
ruined! That row up in Stowbury got into the
papers, and now if we have another frost here,
we're done for. And if Nino don't go on, the crowd's
going to ask for their money back, sure as you're
alive. He's the star act. We might manage if we
had another act to put on in his place, but I haven't
a blessed thing for an extra. And it was a short
programme anyhow. We're ruined. Darn it, I
never saw such a run of rotten luck!'

Poor Blossom seemed genuinely crestfallen.
While the Doctor looked at him thoughtfully, a

' "You can't have this horse perform today" '

horse in the stall next to Nino's neighed softly. It was Beppo, the veteran wagon horse. A smile came into the Doctor's face.

'Look here, Mr Blossom,' said he quietly, 'I think I can help you out of this trouble, but if I do you've got to promise me a few things. I know a good deal more about animals than you suppose I do. I've given up the best part of my life to studying them. You advertised that Nino understood you and could answer any questions you put to him. You and I know that's not so, don't we? The trick was done by a system of signals. But it took the public in. Now I'm going to tell you a secret of my own, which I don't boast about because nobody would believe me if I did. I can talk to horses in their own language and understand them when they talk back to me.'

Blossom was staring down moodily at the floor while the Doctor spoke. But at the last words he gazed up at John Dolittle frowning.

'Are you crazy?' he said, 'or didn't I hear straight? Talk to animals in their own language! Look 'ere, I've been in the show business thirty-seven years, knocked around with animals ever since I was a nipper. And I know there ain't no such thing as a man talking with a horse in horse language. You got a cheek to tell me a yarn like that – me, Alexander Blossom!'

Chapter Four
ANOTHER TALKING HORSE

'**I** AM not telling you a yarn,' said the Doctor quietly. 'I am telling you the truth. But I can see that you will not believe me till I prove it to you.'

'You bet I won't,' sneered Blossom.

'Well, there are five horses in this stable, aren't there?' asked the Doctor. 'And none of them can see me here where I stand, can they? Now if you will ask me to put some questions to any one of them I will endeavour to give you his answer.'

'Oh, you're crazy!' said Blossom. 'I ain't got time to fool with you.'

'All right,' said the Doctor. 'My intention was to help, as I told you. But, of course, if you don't want my assistance, then that ends the matter.'

He shrugged his shoulders and turned away. The noise of clapping sounded from the big tent.

'Ask Beppo,' said Blossom, 'what's the number of the stall he's in.'

Beppo's was the second from the end. On his door was marked a large '2' in white paint.

'Do you wish to have him tell me the answer in horse language?' asked the Doctor, 'or shall I have him tap the number?'

'Have him tap the partition with his foot, Professor,' sneered Blossom. 'I don't know no horse grammar; and I couldn't tell, t'other way, whether you was faking or not.'

'Very good,' said the Doctor. And from where he stood, quite invisible to Beppo, he made some snuffly breathing noises – rather as though he had a cold in his head. Immediately two taps sounded from stall No. 2.

Blossom's eyebrows went up in surprise. But almost immediately he shrugged his shoulders.

'Pshaw! Could easily 'ave been an accident. Maybe he just fell against the partition. Ask 'im – er – ask 'im 'ow many buttons I 'ave on my waistcoat – the one your cross-eyed assistant is wearing in the ring now.'

'All right,' said the Doctor. And he made some more snuffly noises, ending with a gentle whinny.

But this time, unintentionally, he did not include Beppo's name in his message. Now all the five horses in that stable knew Blossom's waistcoat very well, of course. And each one thought the question was being asked of him. Suddenly from every stall six sharp raps rang out, and even poor Nino lying in the straw with eyes closed, stretched a hind leg and weakly kicked his door six times. Mr Blossom's eyes looked as though they were going to pop out of his head.

'Now,' said the Doctor smiling, 'in case you should think that that was accidental too, I will ask Beppo to pull down the rag you see there hanging on his partition and to throw it up in the air.'

In response to a few more words of horse language the rag, whose end hung over the top of the partition, suddenly disappeared. The Doctor had not moved. Blossom ran down the stable to look inside stall No. 2. There he found the aged wagon horse tossing the rag up in the air and catching it – rather like a school girl playing with a handkerchief.

'Now do you believe me?' asked the Doctor.

'Believe you!' cried Blossom. 'I believe you're the man I want, all right. Come on down to the dressing room and let's put some togs on you.'

'Just a minute,' said the Doctor. 'What do you mean to do?'

'Dress you up,' said Blossom, 'of course. You're going to do an act for us, ain't yer? Why you could take any cab horse and make a Nino of him. You said you was going to help me?'

'Yes,' answered John Dolittle slowly, 'and I will – after, as I told you, you have promised me a few things. I am willing to make Beppo provide your ring with a talking horse on certain conditions. Nino's act doesn't come on till the end of the show. We have a half hour to talk this over in.'

'There's no need,' cried Blossom, all excited. 'I'll promise you any bloomin' thing. Why, if you can talk animals' language we'll make a fortune in a season! Lor' bless us! I never believed you could do it. You ought to 'ave joined the show business years ago. You'd 'ave bin a rich man by now – instead of a broken-down country doctor. Come on over and we'll pick you out some nifty togs. Can't go on in them baggy trousers; people 'ud think you'd never bin on a horse in your life.'

Blossom and the Doctor left the stable and made their way across to the dressing rooms, where out of some of the well-travelled trunks the ringmaster began pulling costume after costume and piling them on the floor. While he was going through the gaudy clothes the Doctor laid down the conditions under which he would give the performance.

'Now, Mr Blossom,' said he, 'ever since I have been with your concern I have noticed certain things that were distasteful to my ideas of honest business and the humanitarian treatment of animals. Some of these I have brought to your attention and in almost all cases you refused to listen to me.'

'Why, Doctor,' said Mr Blossom, yanking a pair of red Persian trousers out of a trunk, 'how can you say such a thing? Didn't I get rid of Brown and Fatima because you objected to 'em?'

'You parted with them because you had to,' said the Doctor, 'not to oblige me. I have felt very uneasy about being part of a show that I did not consider strictly honest. It would take a long time to go into all the details. For the present, the bargain I am going to strike with you is this: Beppo, the horse I will use for the talking act, is far too old to work. He has been in service now thirty-five years. I want him, as a reward for this help that he will give you, to be pensioned off for the remainder of his days, made comfortable, and given the kind of life he likes.'

'I agree. Now how would this do?'

Blossom held up a cavalier's jerkin against the Doctor's chest. 'No – too small. You ain't very high from the ground, but you're full-sized around the middle, all right.'

' "Why, Doctor, how can you say such a thing?" '

'The other thing I want you to do,' the Doctor went on, as Blossom turned back to the trunk for another costume, 'is to put your menagerie in proper order. The cages are not cleaned often enough; some of the animals have not sufficient space for their needs. And many of them never get the kinds of food they like best.'

'All right, Doc, we'll do anything in reason. I'll let you draw up a set of rules for the menagerie keeper and you can see that he toes the line. 'Ow would you like to be a western cowboy?'

'I wouldn't,' said the Doctor. 'They are inconsiderate to their cattle. And I don't approve of that silly business of flapping a hat in a horse's eyes to make him buck. Then, for the rest, I shall from time to time expect you to make many minor reforms for the animals' comfort. I shall expect you to treat my suggestions reasonably and co-operate with me for their welfare. What do you say?'

'I say it's a go, Doc,' said Blossom. 'We ain't begun yet. If you stay with my outfit for a year – with your gift of talking to animals – why? – I'll make every other circus look like a two-penny peepshow. Oh, my! 'Ere's the very thing – a cavalry uniform – Twenty-first Hussars. Just your size. Medals and all! Suits your complexion, too.'

This time Blossom held a bright scarlet tunic over the Doctor's bosom and beamed on him with delight.

'Ever seen anything so nifty?' he chuckled. 'My word! I tell yer – we'll make this town sit up! Could you get these things on your feet?'

'Oh, I daresay,' said the Doctor, taking a gaudy pair of military riding boots from the ringmaster and sitting down to unlace his own. At that moment the door opened and a stable boy came in.

'Joe, you're just in time,' said Blossom. 'Run over to the stables and give Beppo a rub down with the curry comb. He's going to do an act.'

'*Beppo!*' cried the boy incredulously.

'That's what I said, block'ead!' shouted Blossom. 'And put the green 'alter on 'im with the white rosettes – and braid 'is tail with a red ribbon. Hop about it!'

As the lad disappeared, the clown with Swizzle
entered for a short rest between acts. The Doctor,
in smart regimental breeches and top boots, was
now buttoning up the scarlet tunic about his chin.

"Ow's my cross-eyed understudy doing?' asked
Blossom.

'Governor, he's a wonder!' said Hop, sinking into
a chair. 'A born ringmaster. You never heard such
a voice. He's got a gift of the gab, all right. Ready
with a joke if anybody slips; cracking quips with
the audience − I tell you, governor, you've got to
look to your laurels if you leave him with the
ladies for long. Who's the military gentleman? My
hat, it's the Doctor! What's he going to do?'

At this moment another lad ran in.

'Only ten minutes before the last act goes on, Mr
Blossom,' he cried.

'All right,' said Blossom. 'We can do it. Here's
your sword belt, Doctor. How's the crowd, Frank?'

'Great!' said the boy. 'Pleased as Punch! They
brought the whole grammar school down at the
last minute. And the Soldiers and Sailors Home is
coming tonight. People standing two deep in the
aisles. It's the biggest business we've played to
this year.'

Chapter Five
THE STAR GIVES A GREAT PERFORMANCE

TREMENDOUS excitement now prevailed behind the scenes in Blossom's Mammoth Circus. As the clown, Hop, opened the dressing-room door to go back into the ring, mingled cheers and hand-clapping, the noise of a big audience's applause, reached the ears of John Dolittle and the manager.

'Listen, Hop,' said Blossom, 'pass the word to Mugg as you go back in that Nino is going to play anyway – in substitute – and the Doc here is doing the part of the trainer. Mugg can give 'em the introduction patter just the same. Tell 'im to lay it on thick. It's going to be the greatest little act we ever showed – better than Nino at his best.'

'All right, governor,' said the clown, grinning through his paint. 'But I wish you had picked a better-looking horse.'

At the last moment one of the Doctor's shoulder straps was found to be loose. Only two minutes now remained before his act was due. Someone flew off and found Theodosia and with frantic haste she put it right with a needle and thread.

' "Listen, Hop!" '

Then, complete in his gay and wonderful uniform, the Doctor ran out of the dressing room to join his partner, Beppo, whose bridle was being held at the entrance to the big tent by the boy, Frank.

Poor Beppo did not look nearly as smart as the Doctor. Years of neglect and haphazard grooming could not be remedied by one currycombing. His coat was long and dingy-looking, his mane straggly and unkempt. In spite of the smart green and white headstall and the red ribbon in his plaited tail, he looked what he was: an old, old servant who had done his work faithfully for many, many years and got little credit or thanks for it.

'Oh, I say, Beppo!' the Doctor murmured in his ear as he took the bridle from Frank. 'Anyone would think you were going to a funeral. Brace up! Draw your head back, high. That's it. Now blow out your nostrils. . . . Ah, much better!'

'You know, Doctor,' said Beppo, 'you mightn't believe it, but I come of a very good family. My mother used to trace her pedigree way back to the battle charger that Julius Caesar used – the one he always rode when he reviewed the praetorian guard. My mother was very proud of it. She took first prizes, she did. But when the heavy battle chargers went out of fashion all the big military horses got put to draft work. That's how we came down in the world. Oughtn't we to rehearse this act a bit first? I've no idea of what I'm expected to do.'

'No, we haven't time now,' said John Dolittle. 'We are liable to be called on any minute. But we'll manage. Just do everything I tell you – and put in any extras you think of yourself. Look out, you're drooping your head again. Remember your Roman ancestor. Chin up – that's the way. Arch your neck. Make your eyes flash. Look as though you were carrying an emperor who owned the earth. . . . Fine! That's the style! Now you look great.'

Within the big canvas theatre Mr Matthew Mugg, ringmaster for a day, was still covering himself with glory, bossing the greatest show on earth with creditable skill and introducing the performers with much oratory and unusual grammar. He was having the time of his life and making the most of it.

In between the acts of the Pinto brothers and the strong man, he saw Hop return into the ring and recommence his antics, which always so delighted the children. As the clown did a somersault past the ringmaster's nose, Matthew heard him whisper, 'The boss is putting on another talking horse, with the Doctor playing the trainer. He wants you to introduce him the same as Nino.'

'Right you are,' Matthew whispered back. 'I've got the idea.'

And when Jojo the dancing elephant had bowed himself out amidst a storm of applause, the ringmaster stepped to the entrance flap and himself led forward the next, the star, act.

For a moment old Beppo, accompanied by a short, stout man in cavalry uniform, seemed a little scared to find a sea of faces staring down at him.

Motioning to the strange-looking performers to remain by the edge of the ring a moment, Matthew advanced into the centre. With a lordly wave of the hand he silenced the wheezy band who were still finishing Jojo's last dance. And in the quiet that followed he looked up at the audience and filled his lungs for his last and most impressive speech.

'Ladies and gentleman,' roared Ringmaster Mugg, 'we 'ave now harrived at the last and most himportant act in our long and helegant programme. You 'ave all 'eard, I'm sure, of Nino — Nino, the world-famous talking horse, and his gallant owner, the dashing cossack cavalry

officer, Captain Nicholas Pufftupski. There they
are, ladies and gentlemen – you see them before
you in the flesh. Kings and queens have travelled
miles to witness their act. Only two months
ago, when we were playing in Monte Carlo, we 'ad
to turn away the Prime Minister of England
because we 'adn't got a seat for 'im in the
'ouse.'

'Oh, stop this nonsense, Matthew,' whispered
the Doctor, coming up to him, dreadfully embarrassed. 'There's no need to—'

But the eloquent ringmaster hurried on with a
thunderous voice:

'General Pufftupski is a modest man and he for-
bids me to tell you about 'is medals what was given
'im by the King of Sweden and the Empress of
China. I now pass on to the hextraordinary
hintelligence of the animal you see before you.
On 'is way back from chasing Napoleon out of
Russia, Count Pufftupski was took prisoner –
and 'is 'orse, the famous Nino, with 'im. During
their himprisonment they became very hintimate.
So much so that at the end of the two years while
they was captives of the French, Nino and 'is
owner could talk to one another freely – the same
as you and I might do. If you don't believe what I
say, you can prove it for yourselves. All you 'ave to
do is to ask any question of Nino through his
owner and it will be answered – if it 'as an answer.
Field Marshal Pufftupski will open 'is performance with this marvellous 'orse with a few tricks
just to show you what they can do. Ladies and
gentlemen, I 'ave great pleasure in introducing
to you the Archduke Nicholas Pufftupski,

' "The Commander-in-Chief of the Russian Army" '

Commander-in-Chief of the Russian Army, and 'is battle charger, the one and only, world-famous NINO.'

As the band played a few opening chords the Doctor and Beppo stepped forward to the centre of the ring and bowed. A tremendous burst of applause came from the people.

It was a strange performance, the only one of its kind ever given to a circus audience. The Doctor, when he entered the ring, had no definite idea of what he was going to do. Neither had Beppo. But the old, old veteran knew that the performance was going to win him comfort and freedom from work for the rest of his days. Every once in a while during the course of the act he would forget his noble ancestry and slump back into his usual weary, worn-out appearance. But on the whole, as Hop said afterwards, he made a much better-looking show horse than anyone had expected; and so far as the audience was concerned, his success surpassed anything Blossom had ever exhibited.

After doing a few tricks, Colonel Pufftupski turned to the people and offered (in remarkably good English) to make the horse do anything they asked. Immediately a little boy in the front row cried out, 'Tell him to come over here and take my hat off.'

The Doctor made a sign or two and Beppo went straight to the boy, lifted the cap from his head, and put it into his hand. Then numberless questions were shouted by the audience, and to every one Beppo gave an answer – sometimes by tapping the floor, sometimes by shaking his head, and sometimes by word of mouth, which the Doctor translated. The people enjoyed it so much that Blossom, watching through a slit outside, thought they'd never be done. And when at last the gallant Pufftupski led his horse out of the ring the audience clapped and cheered and called to him again and again to come back and receive their applause.

The news of the wonderful success of the circus's first performance in Bridgeton, mostly brought about by the marvellous talking horse, quickly spread through the town. And long before the

evening show was due people were lined up outside the big tent, four deep, waiting patiently to
make sure of seats, while the rest of the enclosure
and all the side shows were packed and thronged
so tight that you could hardly move through the
crowds.

Chapter Six
BEPPO THE GREAT

THE money, over which poor Dab-Dab had so worried, was soon replaced in the Dolittle savings box. During the days at Bridgeton the throngs that crowded into the enclosure left so many sixpences at the booth of the two-headed animal from the jungles of Africa that Too-Too prophesied the record of the Ashby week would be easily beaten.

'I estimate, Doctor,' said he, putting his mathematical head on one side and closing his left eye, 'that in six days we should easily make sixteen pounds — and that's not allowing for any extra business on the market day or Saturday.'

'And most of that you can put down to the Doctor's act with Beppo,' said Jip. 'If it wasn't for that act, and the talk it has made, the crowds wouldn't be half as big.'

Finding what a success John Dolittle's performance was making, Blossom came to him after the first showing and begged him to keep it up for the whole of the week that the circus stayed at Bridgeton.

'Well, but look here,' said John Dolittle, 'I've

promised Beppo that he would be pensioned off for
obliging you in your emergency. I don't know how
soon Nino will be able to work again, but I did not
say anything to Beppo about acting all week. I
supposed you would put something else on in our
place as soon as you had time to look around.'

'Good Lord, Doctor!' said Blossom. 'I couldn't find
anything to take the place of your act if I looked
around for a year. There's never been anything
like it since the circus was invented. The news of
it has gone all over the town – and a good ways
outside of it, too. They say folks are coming all the
way from Whittlethorpe to see your act. Listen,
can't you ask Beppo to oblige us? It ain't heavy
work for 'im. Tell 'im we'll give 'im anything 'e
likes – asparagus for breakfast and a featherbed
to sleep in – if 'e only says the word. My outfit,
with the sideshows and all, is taking in pretty
near fifty pounds a day now. Never saw such
business! If this keeps up we shan't 'ave to stay in
the game long before we're all on easy street.'

There was something of contempt in the Doctor's
face as he looked at Blossom and paused a moment
before he answered.

'Oh, yes,' he said rather sadly, 'you're willing
enough to treat your poor old servant well now,
aren't you? – now he is bringing you in money.
For years and years he has worked for you and
never even got his coat brushed in return – just
enough hay and oats to keep him going. Now you'll
give anything in the world. Money! Bah! It's a
curse.'

'Well,' said Blossom, 'I'm helping to make up
for it now, ain't I? It ain't 'eavy work, answering

questions and doin' tricks. You go and talk to 'im,
Doctor. Lord bless me! Don't it sound queer? – me
asking you to go and talk to 'im – and twenty-four
hours ago I didn't know there ever was such a
thing as talking to 'orses!'

'Except with a whip,' said John Dolittle. 'I wish
I could put you in his place and make you work
thirty-five years for Beppo in return for hay and
water and a lot of beating and neglect. All right,
I'll put your request before him and see what he
says. But remember, his decision is to be final. If
he refuses to give one single performance more I
shall hold you to your promise – a comfortable
home for him and a good pasture to graze in for the
rest of his life. And I almost hope he'll say no.'

The Doctor turned on his heel and, leaving the
ringmaster's wagon, set off towards the stables.

'Poor old Beppo!' he murmured. 'His ancestor
carried Julius Caesar in military reviews – heard
the legions cheer the conqueror of the world, who
sat astride his back! Poor old Beppo!'

When he entered the stables he found the wagon
horse gazing out of the window of his stall at the
pleasant fields that lay beyond the circus
enclosure.

'Is that you, John Dolittle?' said he, as the Doctor
opened the door. 'Have you come to take me away?'

'Beppo,' said John Dolittle, putting his hand on
the veteran's gaunt and bony back, 'it seems you
are now a great man – I mean a great horse.'

'How's that, Doctor? I don't understand.'

'You've become famous, Beppo. This is a funny
world. And we humans, I often think, are the fun-
niest animals in it. Mr Blossom has just found out,

after you have been in his service for thirty-five years, how valuable and intelligent you are.'

'In what way valuable?'

'Because you talk, Beppo.'

'But I've always talked.'

'Yes, I know. But Mr Blossom and the world *didn't* know until I proved it to them in the circus ring. You have made a great sensation, Beppo, just on the eve of your retirement. Now, they don't want you to retire. They want you to continue being wonderful – just talking, the way you've always done.'

'It sounds crazy, doesn't it Doctor?'

'Perfectly. But you have suddenly become so valuable to Blossom that he will give you asparagus for breakfast, a valet to brush your coat, and another to curl your mane if you'll only stay and act for him for the rest of the week.'

'Humph! That's what it means to be famous, does it? I'd sooner be turned out into a nice big field.'

'Well, Beppo, you are to suit yourself – at last, after thirty-five years of suiting other people. I've told Blossom I'm going to hold him to his bargain. If you don't want to do it, say so. You shall retire today if you wish.'

'What would you advise me to do, Doctor?'

'There is this about it,' said John Dolittle, 'if you give Blossom what he wants now, we may be able to get you what you want – that is, more exactly what you want – later. You see, he has no farm of his own to put you on; he would have to get a farmer to graze you and take care of you for him. And besides, he will probably be better disposed

'He had handbills given away in the streets'

towards me and some plans I have for the other animals.'

'All right, Doctor,' said Beppo. 'Then that settles it. I'll do it.'

There was no happier man in the world than Alexander Blossom when John Dolittle came and told him that Beppo had consented to act all the week. He at once got handbills printed and had them sent to the neighbouring towns and given away in the streets. These told the public that the world-famous talking horse was to be seen at

Bridgeton for only four remaining days, and that those who did not wish to miss the chance of a lifetime had better hurry up and come to Blossom's Mammoth Circus.

Nothing succeeds like success. It was only necessary to have the news go through the town that people were being turned away, to make twice the number clamour for admission. 'Bridgeton week' came to be spoken of among the showfolk for a long time afterwards as the outstanding period in the circus's whole career.

Chapter Seven
THE PERFECT PASTURE

IN the meantime John Dolittle was making Blossom fulfil the other parts of his bargain. It was not long after the circus had opened at Bridgeton that the elephant sent Jip for the Doctor because he was suffering from an acute attack of rheumatism – brought on by living in an exceedingly damp and dirty stable.

The poor creature was in considerable pain. The Doctor, after examining, prescribed massage. Blossom was sent for and ordered to buy a barrel of a special costly kind of balm. A few weeks before, of course, the ringmaster would have flatly refused to go to such an expense for his animals' comfort. But now, with John Dolittle bringing him in the biggest business that his show had ever seen, he was ready to do almost anything to please him. The balm was sent for right away and then the Doctor demanded six strong men to help him.

Massaging an elephant is no light work. A large audience gathered in the menagerie to watch the six men and the Doctor crawling over the elephant's body, rubbing and pummelling the

'Massaging the elephant'

ointment into his hide till the sweat ran from their foreheads.

Then the Doctor ordered a new stable to be built for the big creature, with a special kind of wooden floor with drainage under it and a lot of other up-to-date features. And, although this work was also expensive, carpenters were brought in and it was completed in three hours. The result was that the elephant got well in a very short time.

The Doctor also drew up rules for the menagerie keeper that improved the condition of all the other animals. And in spite of the fact that the keeper grumbled a good deal about 'running a zoo like a beauty parlour,' Blossom made him understand that he would be discharged immediately if the Doctor's new regulations were not strictly obeyed.

Poor Nino was still pretty sick. He was getting better, but his recovery was dreadfully slow. The Doctor visited him twice a day. But Blossom now realized that the cob's act, which had always been done under his own guidance, could never take the place of the far finer performance of Beppo and the Doctor. Beppo, his age and appearance notwithstanding, was a much cleverer horse than Nino.

Well, the week wore on towards its end. John Dolittle had made arrangements with Blossom that after the last performance on Saturday he and Beppo were to leave and go away to a certain farmer who had agreed to keep the old horse in good grazing for the remainder of his days. He was to have all the oats he wanted and white radishes (a delicacy that Beppo was particularly fond of) twice a week. The Doctor and Beppo were going to inspect this farm, and if they didn't like it, another one to their satisfaction was to be found.

The last performance was over; the big tent was being pulled down, and the Doctor and Beppo were all ready for their departure. The old horse's luggage consisted of a blanket (a new one the Doctor had made Blossom buy as a farewell present), which he wore. The Doctor's luggage was his little black bag and a small bundle, which was also carried on Beppo's back. John Dolittle was standing at the gate, his hand on Beppo's bridle waiting for Matthew, who had run back to the wagon to get some sandwiches, which Dab-Dab was preparing.

Presently he saw Blossom hurrying across the enclosure in a great state of excitement. A little way behind walked a short, very smartly dressed man.

'Listen, Doc,' panted the ringmaster coming up, 'I've just had the biggest offer I ever got in my life. That toff coming along is the proprietor of the Manchester Amphitheatre. He wants my outfit to show in his theatre – one of the biggest in the country – week after next. And 'e specially wants Beppo. What do you think he guarantees us? A hundred pounds a day! And maybe more if—'

'No!' the Doctor interrupted firmly, holding up his hand. 'Beppo may not have many more years to live, but what he has he's going to spend in comfort. Tell that to your proprietor. Beppo retires – today – from the circus business for good.'

And without waiting for his sandwiches, he led the old horse out of the enclosure and hurried down the road.

Beppo and John Dolittle had not gone very far before they were overtaken by Too-Too.

'Doctor,' said the owl, 'I came after you to let you know about the money.'

'Too-Too,' John Dolittle replied, 'at the present moment the subject of money is more than usually distasteful to me. Beppo and I are trying to get away from the very smell of it.'

'But just think what you can *do* with money, Doctor,' said Too-Too.

'Yes, that's the trouble with the beastly stuff. It's the power of it that makes it such a curse.'

'Dab-Dab asked me,' Too-Too went on, 'to come and let you know how much the pushmi-pullyu had made this week at Bridgeton because she thought perhaps you might think of retiring to Puddleby when you heard. I only just got it figured out – deducting Blossom's share and the bills we owe the tradespeople. It was a big piece of arithmetic, I can tell you. My estimate was way off. Instead of sixteen pounds, we made twenty-six pounds, thirteen shillings, and tenpence, clear profit.'

'Humph,' murmured the Doctor. 'It's a large amount, but not enough for us to retire on, Too-Too. Still, it would go quite a long way towards it. Tell Dab-Dab to keep it safe for me and we will talk over the matter when I get back. I am returning tomorrow, you know. Good-bye – and thank you very much for bringing me the news.'

Now, the Doctor had in his pocket the address of the farmer to whom they were going. Imagine his surprise on reaching his destination to find that it was the same farm as the one where his old friend, the plough horse, lived!

There were hearty greetings, a good deal of astonishment, and much joy at the meeting. The old plough horse, beaming through his green spectacles, was introduced to Beppo, and Beppo was introduced to him. It was curious that although the Doctor had known the plough horse for so long he had never heard his name. And it was only on introducing the two old horses to one another that he learned it for the first time. It was Toggle.

'You know,' said the plough horse, 'I am tremendously glad to see you both, but I am a little sorry,

'The old plough horse was introduced to Beppo'

for Beppo's sake, that it was to this farm that
Blossom sent him. The farmer himself is a very
decent fellow, but this pasture I have here leaves
a good deal to be desired.'

'But we don't *have* to stay here,' said the Doctor.
'I told Blossom that if it did not meet with Beppo's
approval he must find another. In what way is this
place unsuitable? Is the grass bad?'

'No,' said Toggle, 'the grass is all right – a little
rank in August if there's much rain, but it's sweet
enough most of the year. But the meadow slopes

the wrong way. You see, this hillside is facing
north-east. It's only in midsummer that you get
any sun. It stays behind the hill the rest of the
year. Then the prevailing wind is a cold north-
easter that blows across the meadow, and there's
little protection from it – except along that
hedge over there and one soon eats up that bit of
grass.'

'Well, tell me,' said the Doctor, turning to Beppo,
'what, for you, would be the ideal, the most attrac-
tive place for an old horses' home?'

'The place I've always dreamed of,' said Beppo,
gazing across the landscape with a wistful look in
his old eyes, 'is like this – part of it is sloping and
part of it is flat. Slopes are such a nice change: the
grass is nearer to your nose, and the flats are
restful to get back to after the slopes. Then it has
trees, big spreading trees with fat trunks – the
kind horses love to stand under and think – after
a hearty meal. It has a copse where herbs and wild
roots grow, the sorts we love to nibble for a change
– especially wild mint, which is soothing to the
stomach when you've eaten too much. It has good
water – not a muddy little pond, but a decent
brook where the water is always sparkling and
clear. In a hollow it has a nice old shelter with a
dry floor and a mossy, tiled roof that doesn't let the
rain in. The pasture varies: some places are firm,
croppy turf; others are deep, luscious, long hay-
grass, with buttercups and fragrant wild flowers
mixed in it. At the top of the hilly part you can get
a view of the sunsets to the westward and the
south. And on the summit there is a good firm post
to scratch your neck on. I love to watch the sun go

down as I scratch my neck of an evening. The whole place is protected with good fences from snappy dogs and worrisome people. It is quiet. It is peaceful. And that, John Dolittle, is the place where I would spend my old age.'

'Humph!' murmured the Doctor when Beppo had ended. 'Your description sounds delightful – almost like the place where I'd wish to spend my own old age – though I suppose I'd want a little more furniture than a scratching post. Toggle, do you know of a pasture such as this that Beppo speaks of?'

'I do, indeed, Doctor,' said Toggle. 'Come with me and I'll show you.'

Then the plough horse led them over the brow of the hill and down the other side a way. Here, facing the sunny southward, they looked over a farm gate into the loveliest meadow you ever saw. It was almost as if some fairy had made old Beppo's wish come true, for it was the retreat he had described in every detail: there was the clump of great elm trees; there was the copse and the sparkling brook; there was the snug shelter in the hollow; and on the summit of the slope, against the red glow of the setting sun, stood the post for Beppo to scratch his neck on.

'This is it, Doctor,' said Beppo quietly. 'This is the spot – just as I had always planned it. No horse could ask for any better place to pass his old age.'

'It's wonderful,' said the Doctor, himself entirely captivated by the beauty of the scene. 'It has character, that meadow. Does this land belong to your farmer, Toggle?'

'They looked over a wide farm gate'

'No,' said the plough horse. 'I've often tried to break in here and graze. And I did get through the hedge once or twice, but the owner always chased me out again. It belongs to a farmer who lives in that little house down there with the red roof.'

'I see,' said the Doctor. 'I wonder how much a piece of ground like that would cost.'

'Not very much, I shouldn't think,' said Toggle. 'Although it is large, the farmer has never raised anything but hay on it.'

'But, Doctor,' said Beppo, 'why buy it? I thought

you said that Blossom was going to pay for my pensioning off.'

'Yes,' said the Doctor. 'But he has only agreed to pay for your board and lodging. I've always had an idea I'd like to start a home for retired cab and wagon horses. And this place is such an ideal one for aged horses that I thought, if I could, I'd buy it. Then we would form The Retired Cab and Wagon Horses' Association and you could keep the place for your own, for good.'

'What a marvellous idea!' cried both horses together.

'But have you got enough money, Doctor?' asked Beppo. 'Jip often told me that you were as poor as a church mouse.'

'That is so — more or less,' the Doctor agreed. 'Money with me has always been a most uncertain thing. But, as you heard Too-Too come and tell me shortly after we had left the circus, I am now some twenty-six pounds to the good. I owe a sailor a lot of money for a boat, but his need is not so urgent as your own — I sent a bird to find out, so I know. I can make some more money later on to pay him with. Of course, twenty-six pounds is not enough to buy a piece of land that big, outright. But perhaps the farmer will let me pay so much down and the rest by instalments every year. If he will, it becomes yours right away and nobody can take it away from you — unless I fail in my payments. Now, you two wait here, and I'll go and see him about it.'

Leaving the two horses by the gate, the Doctor set off across country for the little red-roofed house that Toggle had pointed out.

Chapter Eight
THE RETIRED CAB AND WAGON HORSES' ASSOCIATION

NOW, the farmer who owned the land which the Doctor wished to buy was, at the moment when John Dolittle knocked upon his door, sitting at his parlour table talking to Toggle's farmer. He was sorely in need of twenty pounds to buy seed potatoes with. But Toggle's farmer, with many apologies, had been compelled to refuse him because he himself was very short of money at this time. It was this conversation which the Doctor's call interrupted.

The farmer was very hospitable and invited John Dolittle to come in and sit down at the table with his other guest. Mugs of fragrant cider were brought in by the host's wife. Then the Doctor described the piece of ground that Toggle had shown him and asked if it was for sale. And as it was one which the farmer seldom used he immediately said yes, it was. For how much, the Doctor asked. For one hundred and twenty pounds, the farmer told him.

'Well,' said the Doctor, 'I only have twenty-six pounds at present. Suppose I gave you that down and promised to pay the rest in twenty-pound

'John Dolittle knocked upon his door'

instalments every six months: would you let me have it?'

The farmer, seeing a chance of getting his seed potatoes, was going to agree at once, but the other, Toggle's farmer, broke into the conversation.

'What be you going to use the land for, stranger?' he asked. 'You ain't thinkin' of puttin' up no glue factory, I hope.'

'Oh, no,' said the Doctor. 'I want to make it into a rest farm for old horses – just a grazing ground. Practically nothing will be altered.'

The two farmers thought the stranger must be crazy. But, as he and the plan he proposed seemed harmless enough, they readily gave in.

'By the way,' said the Doctor, still speaking to Toggle's owner, 'you have a friend of mine at your farm, a plough horse: he wears spectacles, which I gave him years ago when he lived in Puddleby.'

'Oh, aye,' said the farmer. 'I know 'un – Toggle. A queer beast, that. 'E wouldn't be parted from them specs for anything. What about 'im?'

'He is too old to work, isn't he?' said the Doctor. 'You let him graze now most of the time, I understand. He wishes to use this same pasture with the horse I have brought today. Will you let him?'

'That I will,' said the farmer. 'But how come you to know all this about my horse?'

'Oh, well,' said the Doctor, looking sort of embarrassed. 'I have ways of my own knowing what horses want. I'm a naturalist.'

'Sounds like you was an *unnaturalist* to me,' said the farmer, winking at his neighbour.

After a little discussion on how the first money would be sent, the bargain was closed and the Doctor was told that now, as long as his part of the arrangement was fulfilled, the land belonged to him.

'Not me,' he said as he rose and bade the farmers farewell. 'The land belongs to the Association. I am turning it over to the horses themselves.'

Having inquired of his host where he could find a carpenter, the Doctor left. And when a half hour later, the two farmers walked across the field together they saw the strange naturalist and the carpenter busily putting up a large signboard in

the middle of the pasture. On it was written in big
letters:

REST FARM

THIS LAND IS THE PROPERTY OF THE RETIRED CAB AND
WAGON HORSES' ASSOCIATION. TRESPASSERS AND VICIOUS
DOGS WILL BE KICKED.

BY ORDER
(Signed, on behalf of the Committee.)
BEPPO, President.
TOGGLE, Vice President.

NOTE – MEMBERSHIP FREE
FOR ADMISSION APPLY AT THE GATE

Well, after seeing the first two members of the
Association enter into possession of their new
quarters, John Dolittle bade Beppo and Toggle
farewell and set off on his return journey.

As he passed down the road he looked back many
times to watch the two old veterans prancing
around their beautiful new home. The sight
warmed his heart and he smiled as he hurried on.

'I'm not sure,' he murmured to himself, 'but I
think that is almost the best job I ever did. Poor
creatures! They are happy at last, growing young
again after a life of hard work. I must establish
some more institutions like that. I've one or two in
mind. The Rat and Mouse Club, for instance. I'd
like to see that started. Of course, I shall get in a
frightful row over this from Dab-Dab when she
finds out that I've spent all the money again. Oh,
well, it's worth it. I'll send some London cab horses
down to join them as soon as I get to the city again.

Humph' – the Doctor paused and looked back – 'There they are – at it still – Beppo rolling down the hill and Toggle splashing through the brook . . . Great heavens! I forgot all about the radishes. Why didn't Beppo remind me?'

He hurried back. On the way he met a lad playing in the road. Questioning him, he found he was the son of the farmer who had sold the land.

'Would you like to earn a shilling a week?' asked the Doctor.

'I'd like to earn a shilling a month,' said the boy. 'I want to save up and buy some skates for next winter. I've got only ninepence so far.'

'Do you know how to grow radishes?'

'Yes,' answered the boy. 'That's easy. They're about the only thing I can grow.'

'Very good,' said John Dolittle. 'Now, you see that meadow where the horses are – and the shelter at the bottom? Well, I've just bought that land from your father. It's to be a home for horses. If you'll plant me a radish bed behind the shelter, the white kind, you know, I'll pay you a shilling a week for keeping it in order. Are you willing?'

'I should say I am, sir!' cried the boy.

'All right. Here's your first shilling – and here's a penny to buy a packet of seed with. I appoint you head gardener to the rest farm. You're now on the payroll of the Retired Cab and Wagon Horses' Association. Make the radish bed fairly big because I may be sending down some more horses later. When the radishes are ripe, you make them up into bunches and hand them out to the members twice a week. And don't forget to plant

' "Would you like to earn a shilling a week?" '

new seed every so often, to keep up the supply. Understand?'

'Yes, sir.'

'Now give me your Christian name,' said the Doctor, 'and I'll send you your wages every week. And if you should have to leave your job – to go away or anything – get your father to write me a letter. He knows how to reach me.'

The boy, pleased as Punch with his good luck, gave the Doctor his name, took his money, and ran off to get a spade and fork and start his new work.

'Well, so that's that,' the Doctor murmured as he

hurried on towards Bridgeton. 'Now, I must try to think out a way to break the news gently to Dab-Dab that our money box is emptied again.'

The rest farm that the Doctor established that day continued to flourish and grow for many years. And another worry was added to the many which harassed Dab-Dab, the careful house-keeper. For not only had the Doctor bound himself to send the farmer twenty pounds every six months, but he further reduced the Dolittle fortunes by buying, every once in a while, some specially old and weary horse that he would meet on the streets. He bought them from cab drivers, from rag-and-bone men, from all sorts of people. Poor Dab-Dab used to be terrified when she saw a Gypsy wagon come in sight on the road. For Gypsies' horses were always particularly thin and scrawny-looking, and it was almost certain that the Doctor would try to buy the poor creatures from men who were much better skilled than he in shrewd bargaining.

All these old waifs and wrecks of horses the Doctor would send down to the rest farm to be made free members of the Association. Beppo's and Toggle's partnership grew into quite a family circle of old cronies – horses from all walks of life. And many were the interesting tales of bygone days told beneath the big trees of an evening or around the post on top of the hill. Here the old fellows would stand in line, waiting to scratch their necks, watching the beauty of the peaceful landscape grow dim in the red glow of the setting sun.

And still the membership list grew longer and

' "What's the use?" cried Too-Too'

longer. The boy who kept the radish garden sent
a letter to the Doctor, saying he had had to enlarge
the bed and needed help. He had a school friend,
he wrote, who was also saving up to buy skates.
Would the Doctor employ him, too?

The Doctor did; and the payroll of the Association advanced to two shillings a week. John
Dolittle paid a visit to the farm after it had been
going for about three months. On consulting with
the committee (five of the oldest veterans), he
found that money was required for repairing

fences and keeping the ditches clear beneath the hedges. Some of the members needed their hoofs trimmed (they didn't bother to wear shoes, of course). So he arranged with the lad he had first appointed as gardener to extend the radish bed considerably, in order that quite a large crop of vegetables could be grown – more than was needed for the members.

The lad had a good head for business and this was done; and two more friends of his were employed for the extra work. Then the money that was made by selling the vegetables was used to form a Fencing and Farriers' Fund, to hire hedgers and ditchers and blacksmiths every so often to keep the fences in repair and to trim the members' hoofs.

Paying the extra boys, of course, took still more from the Dolittle money box – and added still more to the worries of Dab-Dab the housekeeper.

'What's the use?' cried Too-Too one evening when they were discussing accounts. 'What's the use of my doing all this double-entry book-keeping – making my head fairly ache with arithmetic? It doesn't do any good to calculate how much the Doctor has – or to estimate how much he's going to have. No matter what it is, he spends it all!'

PART V

Chapter One
MR BELLAMY OF MANCHESTER

BY getting a lift on the road, John Dolittle reached the circus late that night instead of early the following morning, as he had expected. And the first thing that Matthew Mugg said to him as he entered the wagon was, 'Blossom told me he wanted to see you as soon as you got in. That toff from Manchester is still with him.'

Thereupon the Doctor immediately left his own wagon and set out for that of the ringmaster. Jip asked could he come along, and the Doctor said yes.

The circus was now all packed up ready for departure early tomorrow morning. As John Dolittle approached Blossom's caravan he saw a light in the window. It was very late – after midnight.

Within, he found the ringmaster sitting at the little table with the smartly dressed man whom he had seen earlier in the day.

'Good evening, Doctor,' said the ringmaster. 'This gentleman is Mr Frederick Bellamy, proprietor and manager of the Manchester

Amphitheatre. He has something 'e'd like to say to you.'

The Doctor shook hands with Mr Bellamy, who at once leaned back in his chair, put his thumbs in the armholes of his white waistcoat and began:

'I have delayed my return to Manchester, Doctor Dolittle – in spite of urgent and pressing business – in order to discuss with you an engagement that I had offered to Mr Blossom this afternoon. I witnessed your act with the talking horse and was greatly interested in it. Mr Blossom tells me that he tried to get you to consent to take part in his show's performance in my theatre, but that you refused – took the horse away to put him grazing.'

The Doctor nodded, and Mr Bellamy went on:

'I then supposed that the deal was off, because – I don't mind telling you – without your act I would not be interested in this circus. But Mr Blossom has persuaded me to remain and talk with you myself. He assured me that the intelligence of the performance was not in that particular horse, but in your own unusual powers with animals – that you could give as good a show with any horse. He tells me, though I confess I can hardly believe it, that you can actually communicate with animals in their own language. Is that so?'

'Well,' said the Doctor, looking uncomfortable, 'I'm sorry that Mr Blossom told you this. I don't claim it or talk of it myself because I find that people don't usually believe me. But . . . yes, it is true. With most animals I can converse freely.'

'Indeed,' said Mr Bellamy. 'Most extraordinary! That being the case, we had thought that perhaps you would be willing to do us an act with some

other animal, or animals, in place of the horse that
you have just taken away. My idea is to make it
something more elaborate – to have it form the
bigger, more important part of Mr Blossom's show.
It is something quite new, this gift of yours. And,
properly put on, it ought to make a great sensation. Of course, you understand, it would be well
paid for – very, I might say. Would you consider
it?'

'I haven't any other act worked out at the
moment,' said the Doctor. 'I am somewhat new to
this business. My idea of shows with animals is
that they must always be done with the consent
and willing co-operation of the animals themselves.'

'Oh, quite, quite,' said Mr Bellamy. 'It is very
late now. Suppose you think it over until tomorrow. I cannot catch the coach tonight. And if you
consider it, let me know in the morning, eh?'

When the Dolittle household awoke next morning they found that the wagon was moving. This
was nothing new for them. It only meant that the
circus had got underway very early while they
were still asleep – as it often did in moving from
town to town. It was a part of the life, this, that
Gub-Gub greatly enjoyed – waking in the morning and looking out of the window to see what kind
of new scene lay around their moving home.

Gub-Gub used to boast that this showed he was
a born traveller, that he loved change, like the
Doctor. As a matter of fact, he was really by nature
much more like Dab-Dab, for no one loved regular
habits, especially regular meals, more than he. It
was just that the Gypsy life provided a continuous

HUGH LOFTING

'It was a part of the life Gub-Gub greatly enjoyed'

and safe sort of adventure for him. He liked excitement, but comfortable excitement, without hardship or danger. Matthew Mugg came in while the family was still at breakfast.

'Doctor,' said he, 'that Mr Bellamy is still with the outfit. Said he might as well come along with us, as we was going the same way as him. But, if you ask me, I reckon the real reason is because he's afraid he may lose sight of you. He's just crazy to get you to perform at his theatre – don't care nothin' about the rest of Blossom's show. But he's willin' to pay any amount to get you to give a performance of your own with animals.'

'Well,' said the Doctor, 'it isn't as easy as it sounds, Matthew. My own pets here are anxious to do a play. I wrote a sort of comedy last night after they had gone to bed. But, of course, it will have to be rehearsed. The animals must know their parts properly. You might go forward and tell him that I will let him see it tomorrow, if we are far enough on with it.'

'All right,' said Matthew, and he stepped out of the back of the moving wagon and ran forward to overtake the ringmaster's caravan with his message.

Doctor Dolittle had written plays before for animals – dozens of them. I have told you of his very famous little book called *One-Act Plays for Penguins*. He had also written longer dramas for monkeys and others. But all these had been intended for audiences of animals and were written in animal languages. The penguin plays were performed during the long winter nights, where the birds sit around on the rocks in solemn groups, clapping their flipper-like wings when anything said by the actors strikes them as particularly sensible.

The plays for monkeys were of a much lighter kind. They preferred comedies to the more serious dramas that the penguins liked.

So you see, John Dolittle was quite experienced as a playwright for animals. But the thing needed by Mr Bellamy, which was to be shown to an audience of people, had to be different because people don't understand animal languages. And after much thought the Doctor decided to do away with language altogether. The whole play was to be action. And he called it *The Puddleby Pantomime*.

The rehearsals for the pantomime were greatly enjoyed by everyone except Dab-Dab. The poor housekeeper, who had herself a part to play in it, was continually stopping the performance to row with someone about upsetting the furniture or breaking the teacups or pulling down the curtains.

The pantomime was just like the old-fashioned Harlequinade, a funny musical play about two men who both love and fight for Columbine. Also in the play is a policeman chasing a thief, who has stolen a string of sausages. Toby played the part of Harlequin, Dab-Dab was Columbine, Gub-Gub was Pantaloon, Swizzle was the policeman, and Jip was Pierrot. The dance by Harlequin, Columbine, and Pierrot caused a lot of merriment because whenever the dancers were on the tips of their toes, that was certain to be the time when the wagon would give an extra bad lurch and throw the dancers under the bed.

Swizzle, as the policeman, was always arresting poor Pierrot (Jip) and anybody else he met. For a club he used a cucumber – until he broke it in half over Pantaloon (Gub-Gub), whom he was supposed to chase all round the wagon for stealing the string of sausages. Then the prisoner took the policeman's club away from him and ate it. And the Doctor decided to put that idea into the real show and to use a cucumber in Manchester.

Coming on and off the 'stage' was very difficult because the performers had to go out of the door and stand on the narrow steps while the wagon was still going. Gub-Gub, in his part of the comic Pantaloon, had a hard time. He had to make many entrances and many exits – bounding in and out with the red-hot poker or the string of sausages. And in spite of the Doctor's warning him repeatedly to go out carefully, he always forgot that the wagon was moving, and, making his flying exit, he almost invariably fell out of the wagon, upside down, into the road. Then the rehearsal would have to be stopped while Mr Pantaloon picked himself up and ran after his moving theatre to get on the stage again.

The piece was gone through four or five times during that morning while the circus was travelling on to the next town. And when the train of wagons halted for the night the Doctor sent word to Mr Bellamy that, although the act was still very imperfect and no costumes ready yet, he could come and see if it would do.

Then the pantomime was performed again, this time on the solid ground by the side of the road, before an audience of Mr Bellamy, Blossom, Matthew Mugg and the strong man. On this stage that stood still instead of lurching from side to side, the piece went much better; and, although Pantaloon got a bit mixed up and popped on and off the stage many times too often, the audience clapped loud and long when it was over and declared it one of the most amusing shows they had ever seen. 'Perfectly splendid!' cried Mr Bellamy. 'It's just the thing we want. With a little more rehearsing and proper clothes, that should make a great hit. Nobody can say this act is not enjoyed by the animals that take part in it. Now,

'The pantomime was performed by the side of the road'

I'm going on to Manchester this evening. And after Mr Blossom has played his week in Little Plimpton he'll bring you on to my theatre to open the beginning of the following week, Monday the seventeenth. In the meantime, I'll do some advertising. And I think we can promise you an audience worth playing to.'

Theodosia Mugg was very busy during these days, making the costumes. Fitting suits of clothes to animals is not easy. Gub-Gub gave the most trouble. At the first dress rehearsal he came on with his suit upside down, and his wig back-to-front. He had his hind legs through the sleeves of the coat, wearing them as trousers. His make-up, too, gave a lot of extra work to the stage manager. Mr Pantaloon liked the taste of grease paint and he would keep licking his chops during the performance. So of course the rouge on his cheeks very soon got smeared all round his mouth and made him look as though he had been eating bread and jam.

But Pantaloon's greatest trial was his trousers. At first he fastened his trousers with a belt. But his stomach was so round and smooth that his belt would keep slipping off it. Whenever he ran on to the stage he would lose his trousers on the way and arrive wearing only a coat and a wig. Then Theodosia made a special pair of braces for him to keep his trousers up with, and the Doctor always inspected his dressing himself.

A similar accident happened frequently at the beginning to Dab-Dab. Theodosia had made her a very cunning little ballet skirt of stiff pink net. But the first time she wore it, doing an especially high kick in her dance with Harlequin, she kicked her skirt right over her partner's head. The excitement was added to considerably when Pantaloon, who had just rushed in, picked up the skirt and put it on himself in place of the trousers he had lost in his hurried entrance.

Many times the Doctor was in despair over the costuming part of it. However, Theodosia worked out a lot of very cunning dodges, by means of secret buttons, hooks, elastics and tapes, to hold the clothes and hats and wigs in place. Then by

'He would arrive on the stage wearing only a coat and a wig'

making the actors wear their costumes all day long the Doctor finally got his performers so they could move and run and dance in clothes as easily as they could without them.

Chapter Two
THE POSTER AND THE STATUE

THE day the circus moved to Manchester was a great one for the Dolittle household. None of the animals except Jip had been in a really large city before. On the way there Gub-Gub was constantly at the window of the caravan, watching the road and shouting out over his shoulder to the others when anything new or wonderful came in sight.

Mr Bellamy's show place was a big amusement park, with all sorts of sideshows of its own and a large theatre building in the centre. Prize-fights, wrestling matches, brass-band contests and all manner of entertainments were held in a large open-air place behind the theatre. It was oval in shape and had seats banked up high all around it. This it was that had given it its name, the Amphitheatre because it was like the great open-air theatres of the Romans.

To Mr Bellamy's amusement park the citizens of Manchester came out in thousands when they were in need of recreation – especially Saturday afternoons and in the evenings. At night the whole place was lit up with strings of little lights, and very gay and pretty it looked.

The park was so big that Blossom's Mammoth Circus could fit into one corner of it and not be seen. The ringmaster was greatly impressed.

'Lor' bless me,' he said to the Doctor, 'this is the way to run the show all right – on a grand scale. Bellamy must be rolling in money. Why, the theatre building alone could hold three times as many people as we can fit in our big tent!'

Blossom's circus party, feeling dreadfully small and unimportant in such a large concern, was guided to a place where it could halt and settle down. Shortly after the horses were stabled, the great Mr Bellamy himself turned up. The first thing he inquired for was the Puddleby pantomime troupe.

'As for the rest of your show,' he said to Blossom, 'I'll leave you this corner of the grounds, and you can set up and do what business you can on your own. We get the biggest crowds after five o'clock in the evening and all Saturday afternoon – when we usually run a prize-fight over in the arena. But Doctor Dolittle's company I am going to take care of separately. Of course, I'll pay the money through you, as I told you, and you divide it in whatever way you two arrange. But from now on he and his animals are under my management, you understand, and are not to be interfered with by anybody else. That's what we agreed on, isn't it?'

Then while Blossom and his men got their own sideshows set up, the Dolittle household and its wagon were taken off to another part of the grounds – close to the theatre – and given a space

within a high fence, where they could settle down
in comfort.

Here they found a few other tents and caravans,
the homes of various special performers taking
part in the daily, or rather nightly, show that was
given in the theatre. Dancers they were, tightrope walkers, singers, and what-not.

After the beds were made up and the Dolittle
wagon put in order, the Doctor suggested a walk
through the city. Jip and Gub-Gub at once asked
could they come, and the Doctor consented.
Dab-Dab thought she ought to remain behind
and finish unpacking and get food cooked for
supper.

Then when the Doctor had been over to make
sure that Matthew Mugg had got the pushmi-
pullyu comfortably settled he set out, accompanied by Gub-Gub and Jip, to see the sights of
Manchester.

To reach the city proper they had to walk about
half a mile through districts of ordinary houses
and gardens that surrounded the big town.

Of course, John Dolittle and Jip, having been in
London more than once, knew what a regular city
looked like. But Gub-Gub, when they entered the
thronged streets, teeming with traffic, bordered
by grand shops and buildings, was greatly
impressed.

'What a lot of people!' he murmured, his eyes
nearly popping out of his head. 'And just look at
the cabs! I didn't know there were so many in the
world — following one another down the street
like a parade. And such splendid vegetable shops!
Did you *ever* see such enormous tomatoes! Oh, I

'He set out to see the sights of Manchester'

like this place. It's much bigger than Puddleby, isn't it? And much livelier. Yes, I like this town.'

They came to an open place, a big square, with especially fine stone buildings on all sides of it. Gub-Gub wanted to know all about each of them, and the Doctor had to explain what a bank was, and a corn exchange and a municipal hall, and many more.

'And what's that?' asked Gub-Gub, pointing to the middle of the square.

'That's a statue,' said the Doctor.

It was a very grand monument of a man on horseback. And Gub-Gub asked who he was.

'That's General Slade,' said the Doctor.

'But why do they put a statue up to him?'

'Because he was a famous man,' answered the Doctor. 'He fought in India – against the French.'

They passed out of this square and a little further on entered another, a smaller one, with no statue in it. As they were crossing it Gub-Gub suddenly stopped dead.

'Great heavens, Doctor!' he cried. 'Look!'

At the far side of the square, on a hoarding, was an enormous poster – a picture of a pig dressed as Pantaloon, holding a string of sausages.

'Why, it's *me*, Doctor!' said Gub-Gub, hurrying towards it.

And sure enough, written across the top in large letters was *The Puddleby Pantomime. A Mystery. Come and see the Unique Harlequinade. Bellamy's Amphitheatre. Next Monday.*

The manager had been as good as his word. He had had an artist make pictures of the characters in the Doctor's play and posted them all over the city.

They couldn't get Gub-Gub away from it. The idea of coming into this big town and finding his own pictures on the walls and himself a famous actor already, entirely fascinated him.

'Perhaps they'll put up a statue of me next,' he said – 'like the general. Look, there's room for one here. They haven't got any in this square.'

As they went through the streets they found more pictures of their show – some of Dab-Dab, poised on her toes in a ballet skirt; some of Swizzle, with a policeman's helmet on his head. But whenever they passed one of Pantaloon they had the hardest work dragging Gub-Gub away. He would have sat in front of it all night, if they had let him, admiring himself as a famous actor.

'I really think you ought to speak to the mayor about my statue, Doctor,' said he, as he sauntered homeward with his nose carried high in the air. 'Perhaps they'll want to move the general into a smaller square and put me in the larger one.'

On the morning of Monday, the day when the pantomime was to make its first appearance before the public, there was a dress rehearsal of it and the rest of the show to be given in the theatre. This was what is known as a variety show. There were a number of different acts – dancers, singers, jugglers, and so forth. They came on to the stage in turn and went through their performance, with the orchestra playing the proper music for each one.

At the sides of the stage there were little frames, and at the beginning of each act footmen in livery came out and pushed big cards into them. These cards had the name of the new act on them, and were displayed in this way so that the audience could read what was coming. The Doctor suggested that with *The Puddleby Pantomime* the card changing should be done by animals, instead of footmen. Mr Bellamy thought it was a splendid idea. And while the Doctor was wondering what animals he could get, Too-Too suggested that he be given the job.

'But we need two,' said the Doctor 'You see how

'The footman came out and pushed big cards into them'

the footmen do it — like soldiers. They march out with the cards in their hand — just as though they were drilling, go to each side of the stage — pull the old card out and stick the new one in.'

'That's all right, Doctor,' said Too-Too. 'I can soon get another owl, and we'll make a better pair than those footmen. You wait till I take a hunt around the country outside the city.'

Too-Too flew off, and before half an hour had passed he was back again, with another owl who was the dead image of himself, and the exact size.

Then stools were placed on the corners of the stage, so that the little birds could reach the frames and the owl footmen were drilled in their parts.

Even the musicians in the orchestra, accustomed to seeing wonderful things done on the stage, were astonished when Too-Too and his brother owl appeared from behind the curtains. They were really much smarter at the job than the footmen in velvet. Like two clockwork figures, they hopped on to the stools, changed the cards, bowed to the imaginary audience and retired.

'My!' said the bass fiddler to the trombone player. 'Did you ever see the like? You'd think they'd been working in a variety hall all their lives!'

Then the Doctor, who was himself quite a musician, discussed with the conductor what kind of music should be played while the pantomime was going on.

'I want something lively,' said John Dolittle, 'but very, very soft – pianissimo the whole time.'

'All right,' said the conductor. 'I'll play you the thing we do for the tightrope walkers – sort of tense.'

Then he tapped his desk with his baton to make the orchestra get ready, and played a few opening bars. It was exciting, trembly music, played very, very quietly. It made you think of fairies fluttering across lawns in the moonlight.

'That's splendid,' said the Doctor, as the conductor stopped. 'Now, when Columbine begins to dance I want the minuet from *Don Juan* – because that's the tune she has always practised to. And every time Pantaloon falls down have the percussion give the bass drum a good bang, please.'

Then *The Puddleby Pantomime* was gone through on a real stage, with a real orchestra and real scenery – the last dress rehearsal. Gub-Gub found the glare of the footlights dazzling and confusing. But he and all the actors had, by this time, done the piece so often that they could have played it in their sleep. And the show went with a dash from beginning to end, without a single accident or slip.

When it was over Mr Bellamy said, 'Just one thing more: when the audience is here, your actors will be called out before the curtain. You'll have to show them how to take the call.'

Then the performers were rehearsed in bowing. The five of them trooped on again, hand in hand, bowed to the empty theatre and trooped off.

In the course of their eventful lives the animals of Doctor Dolittle's household had had many exciting times. But I doubt if anything ever happened to them that they remembered longer or spoke of afterwards more often than their first appearance before the public in the famous Puddleby pantomime.

I say famous because it did, in fact, become very famous. Not only was it reported in the newspapers of Manchester as a sensational success, but it was written up in those magazines devoted to stage-craft and theatrical news, as something entirely new to the show business. Lots of acts with animals dressed as people had been done before, of course – some very good. But in all of them the performers never knew just why they

did the things they did or the meaning of most of
their act. Whereas the Doctor, being able to converse with his actors in their own language, had
produced a play which was entirely perfect, down
to the smallest detail. For instance, he had spent
days in showing Toby how to wink one eye, and
still longer in getting Pantaloon to throw back his
head and laugh like a person. Gub-Gub used to
practise it in front of a mirror by the hour. Pigs
have their own way of laughing, of course, which
most people don't know of; and that is just as well
because sometimes they find humans very amusing. But to have animals laughing and frowning
and smiling at the right places in a play – perfectly naturally and exactly the way people would
do it – was something that had never been seen on
the stage before.

Good weather and Mr Bellamy's advertising had
brought a large crowd out to the amusement park
on Monday evening. Long before the show was due
to start the theatre was beginning to fill.

Of the Dolittle troupe, waiting their turn behind
the scene, no one was more anxious than the
Doctor himself. None of his animals, with the
exception of Swizzle, had ever performed before a
real audience before. And it did not follow that
because they had acted all right with only Mr
Bellamy and a few others looking on, they would
be just as good when facing a packed theatre.

As he heard the first few notes of the orchestra
tuning up their instruments the Doctor peeped
through the curtain into the audience. He could
see nothing but faces. There did not seem to be
room to get another in anywhere, but still the

HUGH LOFTING

'Gub-Gub used to practise it by the hour'

people crowded up to the big entrances at the end of the long hall, trying to find standing room in the aisles – or even outside the doorways, where, on tiptoe, they could still get a glimpse of the stage.

'Doctor,' whispered Dab-Dab, who was also peeping, 'this at last ought to make us rich. Blossom said that Mr Bellamy had promised him one hundred pounds a day – and more, if the audiences were larger than a certain number. It would be impossible for it to be bigger than this. You couldn't get a fly into that theatre, it's so packed. What are they stamping and whistling for?'

'That's because the show is late in beginning,' said the Doctor, looking at his watch. 'They're impatient. Oh, look out! Let's get off the stage. They're going to pull the curtain up. See, there's the singing couple in the wings, ready to do the first act. Come on, hurry! Where's Gub-Gub got to? I'm so afraid that wig of his will slip out of place . . . Oh, here he is. Thank goodness, it's all right – and his trousers, too. Now, all of you stay here and keep together. Our show goes on as soon as this act is over. Stop licking your face, Gub-Gub, for heaven's sake! I won't have time to make you up again.'

Chapter Three
FAME, FORTUNE – AND RAIN

STAGE Manager Dolittle's anxiety about his company's behaviour before a real audience turned out to be unnecessary. The lights and the music and the enormous crowd, instead of scaring the animals, had the effect of making them act all the better. The Doctor said afterwards that they had never done as well in rehearsal.

As for the audience, from the moment that the curtain went up they were simply spellbound. At the beginning many people would not believe that the actors were animals. They whispered to one another that it must be a troupe of boys or dwarfs, with masks on their faces. But there could be no disguising the two little owls who had opened the show by marching out like soldiers with the announcement cards. And as the pantomime proceeded even the most unbelieving of the audience could see that no human actors, no matter how well trained and disguised, could move and look like this.

At first Gub-Gub was an easy favourite. His grimaces and antics made the audience rock with laughter. But when Dab-Dab came on, opinion was divided. Her dance with Toby and Jip simply brought down the house, as the saying goes. She captivated everybody. And it was really marvellous, considering how ungainly she usually was in her movements, to see with what grace she did the minuet. The people clapped, stamped the floor, yelled 'Encore!' and just wouldn't let the show go on till she had done her dance a second time.

Then a lady in the front row threw a bunch of violets on to the stage. Dab-Dab had never had flowers thrown at her before and didn't know what to make of it. But Swizzle, an old actor, understood. Springing forward, he picked up the bouquet and handed it with a flourish to Columbine.

'Bow!' whispered the Doctor from the wings in duck language. 'Bow to the audience – to the lady who threw the bouquet!'

And Dab-Dab curtsied like a regular ballerina.

When the curtain came down at the end and the music of the orchestra blared out loud the applause was deafening. The company trooped on hand in hand and bowed again and again. And still the audience called them back. Then the Doctor made them take the calls separately. Gub-Gub did antics and made faces; Swizzle took off his helmet and bowed; Toby sprang into the air with harlequinish agility; Jip struck tragic Pierrot-like attitudes, and Dab-Dab once more brought down the house by pirouetting across the stage on her toes, flipping kisses to the audience with the tips of her wings.

More bouquets were thrown to Columbine and a

HUGH LOFTING

'Dab-Dab curtsied like a regular ballerina'

bunch of carrots to Pantaloon – which he started eating before he left the stage.

Mr Bellamy said he had never seen such enthusiasm in the theatre since he had owned it. And he immediately asked Blossom if he would be willing to renew the engagement for a second week.

When the other acts were over and the audience left the theatre Gub-Gub went out into the hall to look at the stage from the seats. There he found many programmes scattered around the floor. He asked the Doctor what they were. And he was delighted when he was shown his own name printed there as playing the part of Pantaloon.

'Humph!' said he, folding it carefully. 'I must keep this. I think I'll put it in my menu album.'

'Don't you mean your stamp album?' asked the Doctor.

'No,' said Gub-Gub. 'I gave up collecting stamps some time go. I collect menus now. They're much better fun to look at.'

The Dolittle household, now that they were encamped near the theatre, did not see so much of their old friends of the circus. Nevertheless, the Doctor frequently went across the amusement park to see how Matthew and the pushmi-pullyu were getting on. And Hop the clown, Hercules, and the Pintos often visited the theatre to see the pantomime and to make tea at the Dolittle wagon.

The extraordinary success of the Doctor's play continued throughout the week – the crowds growing greater, if anything, with each performance. It became necessary to secure seats a long way in advance if you wanted to see the show, a thing which had only happened once before at the Amphitheatre when a world-famous violinist had played there.

Wealthy gentlemen and elegant ladies called at the Doctor's little wagon almost every evening to congratulate him and to see and pet his marvellous animal actors. Gub-Gub got frightfully conceited and put on no end of temperamental airs, often refusing to see his admirers if they called during the hour he was accustomed to take for his nap.

'Famous artists have to be very careful of themselves,' he said. 'I am only at home to callers between ten and twelve in the morning. You better have that printed in the newspapers, Doctor.'

One lady brought an autograph album for him to sign, and, with the Doctor's help, he put a very clumsy *'G.G.'* in it for her and the picture of a parsnip, which, he said, was his family crest.

Dab-Dab, although she had become just as famous, was much more easily interviewed by visitors. Immediately after each performance she could be seen bustling about her household duties in the wagon, often still wearing her ballet skirt while she made beds or fried potatoes.

'That pig makes me tired,' she said. 'What's the use of our putting on airs? None of us would be famous if it hadn't been for the Doctor. Any animal could do what we do if they had him to teach them. By the way, Doctor,' she added, spreading the tablecloth for supper, 'have you been to see Blossom about the money?'

'No,' said the Doctor. 'Why bother yet? The first week is hardly over. And I understand the pantomime is to run a second one. No, I haven't seen Blossom in – let me see – not in three days.'

'Well, you ought to. You should go and get your share of the money every night.'

'Why? Blossom is a trustworthy man.'

'Is he?' said Dab-Dab, putting the salt cellars on the table. 'Well, I wouldn't trust him further than I could see him. If you take my advice, you'll get your money each night. There must be a lot owing

to you, especially since they put the pantomime on
twice a day instead of only in the evening.'

'Oh, that's all right, Dab-Dab,' said the Doctor.
'Don't worry. Blossom will bring me the money as
soon as he has his accounts staightened out.'

The housekeeper during the next few days frequently asked John Dolittle to see about this
matter, but he never would. And even after the
first week was over and the second nearly so
Blossom had not come forward with the Doctor's
share, nor, indeed, was he often seen by any
member of the Dolittle household. The pushmi-
pullyu had also done well with his sideshow, and,
as the money made by this was quite sufficient for
living expenses, the easy-going Doctor, as usual,
refused to worry.

Towards the end of the second week the fame of
The Puddleby Pantomime had become so great
and so many people had called to interview the
Doctor and his company that it was decided to
invite the public to tea.

Then for a whole morning the good housekeeper
was more than usually busy. Over two hundred
printed cards of invitation had been sent out. Mrs
Mugg was called in to help. A large number of
small tables were set about the wagon: the inside
of the caravan was decorated with flowers; lots of
tea and cakes were prepared and at four o'clock on
Saturday afternoon the gates of the little
enclosure beside the theatre were thrown open to
visitors.

All the animals, some of them dressed in their
pantomime costumes, then acted as hosts and sat
around at the tables, sipping tea with the elegant

ladies and gentlemen who were anxious to meet
them. It was a farewell party, for the next day the
whole of Blossom's circus was to leave. The mayor
of the city came and the mayoress and a number
of newspaper reporters, who made sketches in
their notebooks of Hostess Dab-Dab pouring tea
and Gub-Gub handing round cakes.

The next day, after one of the most successful
visits of its career, the circus packed up and moved
out of Manchester.

The town they went to was a small one, some
twelve miles to the north-east. Rain began to fall
as the wagons arrived at the showground and the
work of setting up was very disagreeable for
everyone. For, besides the wretched, steady driz-
zle, the dirt underfoot soon got worked up into
mud with the constant tramping of feet.

The rain continued the next day and the next.
This, of course, was a terrible thing for the circus
business because nobody came to see the show.

'Well, never mind,' said the Doctor, as his family
sat down to breakfast on the third rainy morning.
'We made plenty of money in Manchester. That
should tide us over a bad spell easily.'

'Yes, but you haven't got that money yet,
remember,' said Dab-Dab, 'though goodness
knows I've told you often enough to ask Blossom
for it.'

'I saw him this morning,' said John Dolittle,
'Just before I came in to breakfast. It's quite all
right. He says it was such a large amount he was
afraid to keep it on him or in his wagon. So he put
it in a bank in Manchester.'

'Well, why didn't he take it out of the bank

HUGH LOFTING

'Gub-Gub handing around cakes'

when he left,' asked Dab-Dab, 'and give you half of it?'

'It was a Sunday,' said the Doctor. 'And, of course, the banks were closed.'

'But what does he mean to do about it, then?' asked the housekeeper. 'He isn't going to leave it there, is he?'

'He's going back today to fetch it. He was just starting off on horseback when I spoke to him. I didn't envy him his ride in the rain.'

Now, running a circus is an expensive thing.

The animals have to be fed, the workmen and performers have to be paid, and there are a whole lot of other expenses for which money must be handed out hourly. So that during these rainy days, when no people came and the enclosure stood wet and empty instead of making money, The Mammoth Circus was losing it every day – every hour, in fact.

Just as the Doctor finished speaking the menagerie keeper, with his coat collar turned up against the rain, poked his head in the door.

'Seen the boss anywhere around?' he asked.

'Mr Blossom has gone into Manchester,' said John Dolittle. 'He expects to be back about two in the afternoon, he told me.'

'Humph!' said the man. 'That's a nuisance.'

'Why?' asked the Doctor. 'Is there anything I can do for you?'

'I want money for rice and hay – for the menagerie,' said the keeper. 'The boss said he'd give me some this morning. The corn dealer's brought the feed. 'E won't leave it unless he gets his money. And my animals need the stuff bad.'

'Oh, I suppose it slipped Mr Blossom's mind,' said the Doctor. 'I'll pay the bill for you and get it from him when he returns. How much is it?'

'Thirty shillings,' said the keeper, 'for two bales of hay and fifty pounds of rice.'

'All right,' said the Doctor. 'Too-Too, give me the money box.'

'There you are! There you are!' Dab-Dab broke in, her feathers all ruffled up with anger. 'Instead of getting the money from Blossom that he owes you, you are paying his bills for him! The animals' feed isn't your concern. What's the use? What's the use? Blossom getting richer and you getting poorer; that's you all over.'

'The animals must be fed,' said the Doctor, taking the money from the box and giving it to the keeper. 'I'll get it back, Dab-Dab. Don't worry!'

The rain grew heavier and heavier all that morning. This was the circus's fourth day in this town. Hardly a penny had been taken in at the gates since the tents had been set up.

The Doctor, ever since his performance with Beppo at Bridgeton, had been looked upon by the showfolk with an almost superstitious respect. Any man, they felt, who could talk the language of animals must know more about them than a mere ringmaster like Blossom. The Doctor had, little by little, made great changes throughout the management of the whole concern – though there still remained a tremendous lot that he wished to alter. Many of the performers had for some time considered him as the most important man in the circus and Blossom as just a figurehead.

The menagerie keeper had hardly left before another man turned up wanting money for some other of the daily expenses of the show. And throughout that morning people kept coming to the Doctor with tales that Blossom had promised them payment at a certain time. The result, of course, was that before long the Dolittle money box (which had been quite well filled by the pushmi-pullyu's exhibition the last two weeks) was empty once more.

Two o'clock in the afternoon came – three o'clock – and still Mr Blossom hadn't returned.

'Oh, he must have been delayed,' said the Doctor
to Dab-Dab, who was getting more anxious and
more angry every minute. 'He'll be here soon. He's
honest. I'm sure of that. Don't worry.'

At half past three Jip, who had been out nosing
around in the rain, suddenly rushed in.

'Doctor!' he cried. 'Come over to Blossom's
wagon. I think there's something wrong.'

'Why, Jip? What's the matter?' said the Doctor,
reaching for his hat.

'Mrs Blossom isn't there,' said Jip. 'At first I
thought the door was locked. But I pushed it, and
it wasn't. There's nobody in it. His trunk is gone
– and nearly everything else, too. Come over and
look. There's something queer about this.'

Chapter Four
MR BLOSSOM'S MYSTERIOUS DISAPPEARANCE

JIP'S words brought a puzzled frown into the Doctor's face. Slowly he put on his hat and followed the dog out into the rain.

On reaching Blossom's wagon he found everything as Jip had described it. There was no one within. Every article of value had been taken away. A few torn papers lay scattered on the floor. In the inner room, Mrs Blossom's private boudoir, the same situation met the Doctor's eyes. The whole place looked as though those who lived there had left in a hurry, to be gone a long time.

While John Dolittle was still gazing confusedly around him someone touched him on the shoulder from behind. It was Matthew Mugg.

'Looks kind of bad, don't it?' he said. 'Blossom didn't have to take his trunk and all to go and get his money out of the bank. If you was to ask me, I've kind of a notion that we ain't goin' to see our good, kind manager no more. Eh?'

'Well, Matthew,' said the Doctor, 'we mustn't jump to conclusions. He said he'd be back. He may have been delayed. As to his trunk and things, they're his own. He has a right to do what he wants with them. It would be wrong to pass any judgments until we have more evidence than that.'

'Humph!' muttered the cat's-meat man. 'O' course, you always did hate to think anybody crooked. Still, I think you can say good-bye to the money you earned in Manchester.'

'We haven't any proof, Matthew,' said the Doctor. 'And listen, if what you suspect is true, it's going to be a very serious matter for all the people in the circus. Please don't say anything of your suspicions for the present, will you? There is no need to get the showfolk excited until we really know. Now, will you please saddle up a horse quietly and go into Manchester for me. See Mr Bellamy and ask him if he knows anything of what has become of Blossom. Get back here and bring me word as soon as you can, will you?'

'All right,' said Matthew, turning to go. 'But I don't think Mr Bellamy'll know any more of where our manager's gone than what you do.'

Jip, after listening to this conversation, slipped away and joined the other animals in the Doctor's own wagon.

'Fellows,' he said, shaking the wet off himself, 'Alexander Blossom has skedaddled.'

'Good heavens!' cried Too-Too. 'With the money?'

'Yes, with the money – drat him!' growled Jip. 'And there was enough coming to the Doctor to keep us in comfort for the rest of our days.'

'I knew it!' groaned Dab-Dab, throwing out her wings in despair. 'I told the Doctor not to trust him. I guessed him to be a fishy customer from the start. Now he's wallowing in luxury while we scrape and pinch to pay the bills he left behind.'

'Oh, what does it matter?' cried Gub-Gub. 'So much the better if he's gone. Now we'll have a real circus – the Dolittle Circus – which the animals have always hoped for. Good riddance to Blossom – the crook! I'm glad he's gone.'

'What you *don't* know,' said Dab-Dab, turning on the pig severely, 'would fill a library. How is the Doctor to run a circus without a penny in his pocket? How is he going to pay wages – ground rent? How is he going to feed the animals and himself? It costs pounds and pounds a day to keep a circus going, you pudding, you! And look at the rain – coming down as though it never meant to stop! And the whole show just standing here and not a soul coming to see it! And the payroll of dozens of men mounting higher every minute. "*Glad* he's gone!" – you sausage!'

After Matthew had gone the Doctor remained within the shelter of Blossom's deserted wagon, thoughtfully watching the rain splatter into the muddy puddles outside. Presently he sat down on an old packing case and lit his pipe. From time to time he took out his watch and looked at it, frowning.

After half an hour had gone by he saw Hercules, dressed in ordinary clothes, approaching across the enclosure. He was running to avoid the rain. Reaching the wagon, he sprang within, and then shook his wet overcoat outside the doorway.

'I hear the boss has skipped,' he said. 'Is it true?'

'I have no idea,' said the Doctor. 'He is late in returning from Manchester. But something may have detained him.'

'Well, I hope he comes soon,' said Hercules. 'He owes me a week's wages. And I need it.'

The strong man sat down, and he and the Doctor fell to chatting about weather and weather signs.

Not many minutes later along came Hop the clown, with his dog, Swizzle. Evil news travels fast. He, too, had heard a rumour that Blossom had deserted the circus. The Doctor tried again to excuse the ringmaster and insisted that he be not suspected till proof was obtained.

Then, rather awkwardly and without much interest, the conversation continued about the weather.

Next, the Pinto brothers, trapeze artists, arrived with mackintoshes thrown over their gaudy tights. They also wanted to know where Blossom was and why they hadn't received the pay that they had been promised would be given them this morning. The Doctor, growing more and more distressed, hoping Blossom would turn up any minute, began to find it hard to keep the talk on any other subject but the mysterious disappearance of the manager.

At last the foreman of the tent riggers joined the circle.

'It looks rummy to me,' he said when he had been told all there was to be told — 'I got three children and a wife to keep. 'Ow are they going to live if I don't get no wages? My missus ain't got enough food in the wagon for another meal.'

'Yes,' said one of the Pinto brothers. 'And we got

HUGH LOFTING

'The Pinto brothers arrived'

a new baby in the family. If Blossom's running off with the money we ought to let the police know.'

'But we have no proof he is running off,' said the Doctor. 'He may arrive any minute.'

'And he may not, Doctor,' Hercules put in. 'If he is a queer one, by the time you get your proof he'll be in China, maybe – where nobody can get at him. It's nearly six now. The Pintos are right. What are we standing around here for, guessing and wondering? At least we ought to send somebody into Manchester to find out what we can.'

'I have sent somebody in,' said the Doctor. 'Matthew Mugg, my assistant, has gone.'

'Humph!' said one of the acrobats. 'So you got kind of suspicious yourself, Doctor, eh? What time did you send him?'

The Doctor looked at his watch again.

'About four hours ago,' said he.

'Time to get there and back,' grunted Hercules. ' 'E couldn't find no trace of 'im, I'll warrant. Boys, it looks to me like we was ditched, all right. . . . Lord! I wish I had 'im here. I'd make Mr Blossom look like the last rose of summer.'

And the strong man's ham-like hands went through the action of twisting the top off something.

''But 'e's left an awful lot of property behind,' said the tent rigger. 'I don't yet understand what made 'im skip at this stage of the game.'

'What 'e left behind – besides unpaid bills,' said Hercules, 'ain't nothing compared with what 'e took with 'im. 'Eaven only knows what 'e got from Bellamy for the Doctor's show – biggest takings this outfit ever saw. And all 'e give us was excuses – kept puttin' off payin' us for some fake reason or other – for three weeks back. I reckon 'e 'ad it in 'is mind to clear out all the time – 'ad it planned as soon as 'e saw a big haul in sight.'

'Well, what are we going to do?' asked Hop.

'Yes, that's the question,' said the Pintos. 'What are we going to do now?'

'We got to find another manager,' said Hercules. 'Someone to take over the outfit and get us out of this hole.'

Chapter Five
THE DOCTOR BECOMES
MANAGER OF THE CIRCUS

IT was curious to see how, as soon as the strong man spoke of a new manager, all the eyes of the little crowd gathered in the wagon turned upon John Dolittle.

'Doctor,' said Hercules, 'it looks to me like you'd got to be the new boss. And if anybody was to ask me, I'll say you'd make a pretty good one. How about it, boys?'

'Aye! Aye!' they all cried. 'The Doc's the man.'

'That being the case,' said Hercules, 'in the name of the staff of the greatest show on earth, I present you, Doctor, with the circus of the late lamented Alexander Blossom. From now on, with us, your word is law.'

'But – good heavens!' the Doctor stammered. 'I don't know anything about circus management, and, besides, I—'

'Oh, yes, you do,' Hercules broke in. 'Wasn't it your act with Beppo that made the big week at Bridgeton? And wasn't it you what got the circus brought to Manchester? Why, bless me, you can talk to the bloomin' animals! We ain't worried. Meself, I've a kind of an idea we'll make more

' "But I don't know anything about circus management!" '

money under you than ever we made – or lost –
under Blossom. You go ahead and manage.'
'Yes,' said Hop. 'That's right, Doctor. Lord only
knows what's going to happen to us if you don't.
We're in the soup – dead broke. And you're the
one to pull us out.'
For a full minute the Doctor did not answer –
just sat, thinking, on his packing case. At last he
looked around at the miserable waiting group and
said:
'Very well. I had not intended going into this

business for long when I started. But I certainly can't get out of it now – not only on your account, but on account of my own animals and my responsibility to them. For I, too, am – er – dead broke. If you want me to manage for you, I'll try it. But I'm going to do it a little differently from Blossom's way. I'm going to run the circus on a co-operative basis – that is, instead of wages, we will all take our share of the money made, after expenses are paid. That means that when business is bad you will get very little – may even have to pay a little; and when business is good you will do well. Also, I claim the right to dismiss anyone from the circus without notice at any moment.'

'That's the idea!' said Hercules. 'That's the way a circus should be run – everybody partners in the business, but one man boss.'

'But listen,' said the Doctor. 'For the beginning it's going to be hard work and very little money. We haven't got a cent in hand, and until the rain stops we shan't make a penny. What's worse, we will probably run into debt for a while – supposing, even, that we can get anybody to give us supplies on credit. Are you willing?'

'You bet we are!' . . . 'We're with you, Doc!' . . . 'Nobody's going to grumble!' . . . 'You're the right boss!' they cried. And immediately the appearance of the whole crowd had changed from miserable gloom to hopeful smiles and enthusiasm.

In the midst of this arrived Matthew Mugg, with Mr Bellamy himself.

'I'm terrible sorry to hear of this,' said Mr Bellamy, addressing the Doctor. 'I gave that scoundrel Blossom two thousand pounds. He has cleared out with the whole lot, it seems – even left tradespeople unpaid in the city. It was their coming to me that first told me of his crookedness; and then your Mr Mugg arrived. I've put the police on Blossom's trail, but I don't think there's the least chance of their catching him. You had better come back to Manchester, and I will give you space at the Amphitheatre park until you have made enough to carry on.'

'Hooray!' yelled Hop. 'And, look, the rain has stopped! Our luck has changed. Hooray for the Dolittle Circus.'

'Pardon me!' said a small, polite voice from the door. 'Is Doctor Dolittle here?'

Everyone turned; and there stood a small man in the entrance. Behind him the sun was now shining brightly.

'I am John Dolittle,' said the Doctor.

'How do you do,' said the little man. 'I have been sent on a special mission by a firm of theatrical producers. I am instructed to make you an offer. They wish you to bring your troupe to London next month – if you have not been already booked.'

'Hah!' cried Hercules. 'What did I tell you, boys? First minute he's manager he gets an offer from Manchester and another from London. Three cheers for the Doctor!'

It was a day of great rejoicing for both the animals and the people of the circus when the Doctor took over the management. As soon as the news got round the enclosure, tent riggers, stableboys, performers – everybody, in fact, who was part of the establishment – came to the Doctor to congratulate him and to say how glad they were to

'Putting up the new sign'

be under his direction. With the stopping of the
rain a general cheerfulness and bustle began. And
the very first thing done was the taking down of
the Blossom's Mammoth Circus sign over the
main entrance and erecting in its place the
Dolittle Circus – a more modest title, but one
which was to become far greater and better known
than Blossom's had ever been.

Mr Bellamy was very kind. Realizing that the
Doctor and everyone had been left practically penniless, he offered to help the new management

with loans of money or in any other way he could. However, John Dolittle was most anxious to avoid getting the circus further into debt than it already was, and all he asked of Mr Bellamy was to visit some of the tradespeople of this town with him and ask them to give him credit, to trust him for a while. Mr Bellamy was, of course, very well known for miles and miles around Manchester. And the local corn dealer, grocer, butcher and the rest were perfectly willing, when he asked them, to give the Doctor provisions and to wait for their money till the circus had made enough to pay its bills.

Chapter Six
MATTHEW MUGG,
ASSISTANT MANAGER

ANOTHER, member of the staff, besides Too-Too the accountant, to be more than usually occupied in the first days of the Dolittle Circus was Dab-Dab, the housekeeper.

'You know,' said she to Too-Too and Jip one night, 'all this looks very nice – and I certainly don't want to be a killjoy – but I wish we had someone else besides the Doctor to take care of the business end of things. He is fine where working out of new animal shows is concerned. As a stage manager no one could be better. But I know what's going to happen: all the other partners, Hercules and Hop and the Pintos and the rest, are going to get rich; and the Doctor is going to stay poor. Why, only last night he was talking about sending the opossum back to Virginia. He wants to climb trees, it seems – in the moonlight – and we haven't got the right kind of trees or moonlight here. I told him the moon in England is just as good as it is in Virginia. But he says it isn't – not green enough. Heaven only knows how much his ticket to America would cost. Yet I'm certain that as soon as the Doctor has the price of it he'll send

him. He spoke of the lion and the leopard, too —
says the big hunting animals should never be
kept in confinement. I do wish we had some other
man as well — somebody with good business
sense — who could keep an eye on the Doctor's
schemes.'

'I quite agree with you,' said Jip. 'But I have
great hopes of Matthew Mugg, myself. He isn't
nearly such a fool as he looks.'

'He's a very kind fellow,' Swizzle put in. 'Almost
every time he meets me or Toby he pulls a bone or
something out of his pocket and gives it to us.'

'Oh, yes,' said Jip. 'That used to be his profession
— cat's-meat man, you know. He has a good heart.
And I think, Dab-Dab, you'll find he has a pretty
good business head, too. It was he who arranged
about the next three towns we're going to. The
Doctor didn't know how to book the circus ahead
or where to go next or anything about touring a
circus around the country. He consulted Matthew.
And Mugg went off at once to the next town and
found out when the fair week was usually held and
arranged for fodder supply and renting a show
ground and everything. And he's just crazy about
the circus business. I've often heard him boasting
to Gypsies and the like along the road that he's
the partner of John Dolittle, M.D. — the famous
showman. He knows how to advertise, too — and
that's important in this game. It was Matthew
who got the Doctor to have those big posters
printed. I hear they're already stuck up in
every street in Tilmouth, our next town. Yes,
I'm quite hopeful about Matthew. He's a good
man.'

The Dolittle Circus was an entirely new kind of circus. Now the Doctor proceeded to bring about the reforms and changes that he had so often wished for in the day of Blossom's management.

Certainly the average circus-going public had never seen anything like his show before. For one thing, John Dolittle insisted on the strictest politeness from all attendants. For another, he would allow no form of misrepresentation, as he called it. Ordinarily, circus folk had often been accustomed to say that their shows were 'the greatest on earth', that their animals were 'the only ones in captivity' – or something similarly extravagant and exaggerated.

This the Doctor would not permit. He said he wanted everything advertised just as it was, in order that the public should not be misled or cheated into paying to see something that they didn't see. To this, at the beginning, Matthew Mugg objected. He said you could never get a good crowd unless you 'played it up big.' But he soon found that the Doctor was right. When the people got to realize that whatever was promised in the Dolittle advertisements would be actually provided, the new circus earned a reputation for honesty that brought people in a way that nothing else would.

Another thing that worried Matthew was the Doctor's insistence on providing tea, free, for the public.

'Why, Doctor,' he said, 'you'll be ruined! You can't serve tea for thousands of people without charging them for it. This ain't a hotel – or a Widows and Orphans Home!'

HUGH LOFTING

'Free packets of peppermints for the children'

'Matthew,' said the Doctor, 'the people who come to visit my show come long distances – with babies to carry. Afternoon tea is a nice custom. I hate to go without it myself. It won't cost so much when we buy the tea and sugar by the hundred-weight. Theodosia can make it.'

So afternoon tea for all visitors became an institution. And shortly after, another one was added: that of free packets of peppermints for the children. And what the Doctor prophesied came true. In one town where the Dolittle Circus crossed paths with another, much bigger show, the Doctor's concern did twice the business that the other one did because the people knew that they'd be given tea and treated honestly and politely.

Chapter Seven
THE DOLITTLE CIRCUS

IT was six weeks before the show was due to appear in London. The first town to be visited on the way there was Tilmouth. And it was here that the Doctor once more got put in prison — but only for one night. This is how it came about:

The animals, as I have said, were, if anything, even more pleased to exchange Blossom for the Doctor as a boss than were the human performers. And one of the first things that John Dolittle did, as soon as a little extra money was made, was to go round and ask all the animals if they had any complaints to make. Of course, there were plenty. To begin with, nearly every creature in the menagerie wanted his den repainted. So the Doctor had all the cages done over, each in the colours that its owner preferred.

Not long after the Doctor had had the menagerie done up, he received another complaint. This, indeed, was one that he had often heard before. The lion and the leopard were weary of confinement. They longed to get out of their narrow cages and stretch their legs in freedom.

'Well, you know,' said John Dolittle, 'myself, I

don't approve of keeping you shut up at all. If I had my way I'd ship you back to Africa and let you go free in the jungle. But the trouble is the money. However, as soon as I get enough together I will attend to it.'

'If we could only get out a few minutes each day,' said the lion, looking wistfully over the Doctor's shoulder towards the rolling hills of the country-side, 'it wouldn't be so bad.'

'No,' said the leopard, 'that would make life bearable. Oh, I'm so sick of the four walls of this wretched box!'

The tone of the leopard's voice was so pathetic and the lion's face so sad the Doctor felt that something just had to be done right away.

'Look here,' he said, 'if I let you out for a run every evening, would you promise me something?'

'Anything,' said the two together.

'Would you come back at the end of half an hour? Honestly?'

'We would.'

'And would you promise solemnly not to eat any people?'

'On our word of honour.'

'All right,' said the Doctor. 'Then every evening after the show is over I'll open your cages and you can run free for half an hour.'

So this, too, like the afternoon tea and the children's peppermints, became a custom of the Dolittle Circus. The menagerie animals were put upon their honour and allowed to run free every evening, provided they came back of their own accord. It worked surprisingly well for quite a while. The show people soon realized that the animals were acting up to their promise and could be trusted not to molest anyone. And even Theodosia got used to the idea of meeting a lion or a leopard roaming through the enclosure after dark on his way back to his den when his evening run was over.

'It is quite proper,' said the Doctor. 'I don't know why I didn't think of it before. They work all day, the same as we do — being on show. They deserve a little freedom and play-time at night.'

Of course, the animals, when they went beyond the circus fence, were careful to keep out of the way of people because they didn't want to scare them — and people didn't interest them anyway. They were, in fact, heartily sick of them, having them gazing and staring in at the cages all day. But one evening when the circus had moved to a new town a rather serious thing happened. Matthew came rushing to the Doctor's wagon about ten o'clock and said, 'Governor, the lion hasn't come back! I went round to lock up just now and found the cage empty. And it's more than an hour since I let him out.'

'Good heavens!' cried the Doctor, jumping up and dashing off towards the menagerie with Matthew at his heels, 'I wonder what's wrong. He certainly wouldn't have run away after giving me his promise. I hope no accident has happened to him.'

On reaching the menagerie the Doctor went to the leopard's cage and asked him if he knew where the lion was.

'I think he must have got lost, Doctor,' said the leopard. 'We started out together and went for a stroll across that moor to the eastward. But it was new country to us. We came to a stream and couldn't get across. He went up stream and I went down, looking for a shallow place where we could get over to the other side. I had no luck. The stream got wider and deeper the further I went along the bank. Then I heard the church clock strike and I realized it was time to be getting back. I expected to find the lion here when I got home. But he wasn't.'

'You didn't meet any people?' the Doctor asked.

'Not a soul,' said the leopard. 'I passed a farm, but I went around it to avoid scaring anyone. He'll find his way back. Don't worry.'

The Doctor stayed up all that night, waiting for the lion to return. He even went out into the country and hunted along the stream that the leopard had spoken of. But no trace of the missing animal could he find.

Morning came and still no lion. And the Doctor was very worried. However, the opening of the circus kept his mind occupied. The people came thronging in and good business claimed everyone's attention.

At teatime, as was his custom, John Dolittle acted as host to his visitors, and Theodosia was kept running back and forth waiting on the many little tables crowded with holiday-makers in their Sunday clothes.

Suddenly, just as the Doctor was passing among the tables to offer a lady a dish of cakes, he spied Mr Lion strolling into the circus through the main gate. At the moment everybody was busy eating and drinking, and the Doctor hoped that the lion, who was quietly making for the menagerie, would reach his den before he was seen by the guests. But, alas! a party, a farmer and his family, coming out of the sideshow, ran right into the lion before he got to the menagerie door. There was a scream from the farmer's wife, who grabbed her children and ran. The farmer threw his walking stick at the lion and also ran. Then for a couple of minutes pandemonium reigned. Women shrieked, tables were overturned, and finally some stupid person in the crowd fired a gun. The poor lion, thoroughly frightened, turned about and ran for his life.

The excitement now partly died down, but the people were far too upset to stay and enjoy the circus any further, and very soon they all went off home and the enclosure was deserted.

So Mr Lion, after his brief reappearance, was again missing; and the Doctor feared that now, terrified at his reception, he would be harder to find than ever.

John Dolittle was arranging search parties to go out and hunt when two policemen came to the circus and put him under arrest. He was charged, they told him, with keeping wild animals at large and endangering the public. Furthermore, the lion, it seemed, had broken into a chicken yard and eaten all the chickens. As the Doctor was marched through the town to the jail the owner of the chickens followed him, calling him names and telling him how much he owed him.

The Doctor spent the night in prison. But in the meantime the lion had taken refuge in the cellar of a bakery, and neither the baker nor anybody else dared go down to him. Everybody in the house was scared to go to bed. Messages were sent to the circus to send someone to take the lion away. But the wily Matthew Mugg, although he knew the lion was easily handled by those who knew him, told the people that the Doctor was the only one who dared go near him, and they better hurry up and let him out of jail if they wanted the lion taken away.

So early the next morning they came and set the Doctor free. Then he went down into the cellar and talked to the lion.

'I'm fearfully sorry, Doctor,' said he, 'but I lost my way out on that moor. I wandered around all over the place. And it wasn't until the next day that I found my own tracks and made my way back to the circus. I tried to slip into the menagerie without being seen. But when that fool started firing a gun I got scared and ran for it.'

'But the chickens?' said the Doctor. 'I thought you promised me not to molest anything when you were out?'

'I promised only not to eat people,' said the lion. 'I had to eat something. I was starved to death after wandering around that moor all night. How much are they charging you for the chickens?'

'One pound, ten shillings, and sixpence,' said the Doctor. 'Eleven at half a crown apiece.'

'It's highway robbery,' said the lion. 'They were the toughest old things I ever tasted. And anyway, I ate only nine.'

'Well, in the future,' said the Doctor, 'I think I had better accompany you on your walks.'

Then he led the lion home. And the terrified townsfolk watched through the cracks of doors

as the dread animal strolled down the street at
John Dolittle's heels as meek and quiet as a
lamb.

And now that the Doctor could give the animals
the kind of consideration he wished, he really
enjoyed the life himself a good deal. And poor
Dab-Dab began to feel that her chance of getting
him away from it, back to his own life at
Puddleby, grew dimmer and more distant every
day.

John Dolittle's chief occupation in his spare time
was, as I have told you, thinking out new and
interesting animal shows. And in doing this he
always kept the children particularly in mind as
an audience, and designed his plays and entertainments more for them than for the grown-ups.
The success of the talking horse and *The Puddleby
Pantomime* showed him that his knowledge of
animal languages could be put to great use here.
The snakes that he had bought from Fatima, for
example, were later trained by him to give a little
show of their own. Instead of a snake-charmer's
tent with a stupid fat woman in it, pretending to
be something that she wasn't, the Dolittle Circus
had a sideshow where the snakes gave their own
performance, entirely unaided by any person. To
the tune of a music box they danced a very
peculiar but graceful sort of dance. It was
something like a mixture between a quadrille and
a game of cat's cradle. On a little stage of their own
they glided about on their tails in time to the
music, bowing to their partners, doing the grand
chain, looping into knots with one another, drilling like soldiers, and doing a hundred fascinating

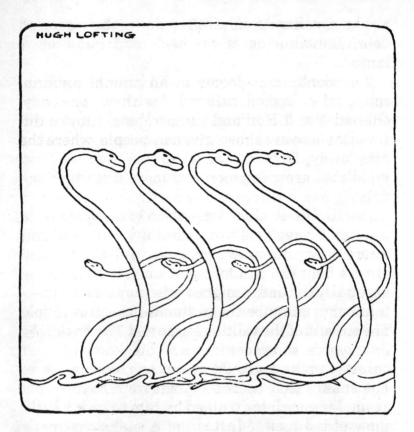

HUGH LOFTING

'The snakes' quadrille'

things that people had never seen snakes do
before.

Indeed, as time went on, the Dolittle Circus's
animal sideshows were almost without exception
run independently by the animals themselves.
There were a great number of them and each one
was descriptive of that particular animal's special
quality. The snakes' entertainment, for instance,
was designed to show off their gracefulness for, in
John Dolittle's opinion, the snake was the most
graceful creature in the world. The elephant, on

the other hand, did feats of strength instead of silly balancing tricks for which he wasn't suited.

'You don't want people in an animal perform-ance,' the Doctor said to Matthew one day. 'Hercules and Hop and the acrobats, they're different. Those are shows given by people, where the human performers are the whole thing. But what's the sense in seeing a stupid man in uniform driving a lion through hoops with a whip? People seem to think that animals have no ideas to express. If they're left to themselves they can give much better shows on their own, once they're told what kind of things amuse a human audience — especially in the funny shows. The animal sense of humour is far superior to the human. But people are too stupid to see the funniness of things that animals do to amuse one another. And in most cases I have to bring them down to our level — to have them make their style of jokes rather — er — crude and broad. Otherwise people mightn't understand them at all.'

And so, you see, the Dolittle Circus was indeed quite different from any other. The Doctor's kind and hospitable treatment of all who came to see his show made it more like a sort of family gather-ing than a strictly business matter.

There were no rules, or hardly any. And if little boys wanted to see 'behind the scenes' or to go into the elephant's stall and pet him, they were per-sonally conducted wherever they wished to go. This alone gave the circus a quality quite in-dividual. And whenever the wagon train moved on its way, the children would follow it for miles

along the road and for weeks after would talk of
nothing but when it would come back again to
visit their town. For children everywhere were
beginning to regard the Dolittle Circus as
something peculiarly their own.

About the Author

HUGH LOFTING was born in Maidenhead, England, in 1886 and was educated at home with his brothers and sister until he was eight. He studied engineering in London and at the Massachusetts Institute of Technology. After his marriage in 1912 he settled in the United States.

During World War One he left his job as a civil engineer, was commissioned a lieutenant in the Irish Guards, and found that writing illustrated letters to his children eased the strain of war. 'There seemed to be very little to write to youngsters from the front; the news was either too horrible or too dull. One thing that kept forcing itself more and more upon my attention was the very considerable part the animals were playing in the war. That was the beginning of an idea: an eccentric country physician with a bent for natural history and a great love of pets . . . '

These letters became *The Story of Doctor Dolittle,* published in 1920. Children all over the world have read this book and the eleven that followed, for they have been translated into almost every language. *The Voyages of Doctor*

Dolittle won the Newbery Medal in 1923. Drawing from the twelve *Doctor Dolittle* volumes, Hugh Lofting's sister-in-law, Olga Fricker, later compiled *Doctor Dolittle: A Treasury.*

Hugh Lofting died in 1947 at his home in Topanga, California.